DEATH ON THE PONT NOIR

1963, France. A farmer reports a truck ramming into a car near Picardie, followed by gunfire. A group of Englishmen are brought in after a bar fight. A tramp's body is discovered in a burnt out truck. All this occurring after multiple attempts on the President's life. Inspector Lucas Rocco knows there's a connection somewhere. Yet despite all clues pointing to the Pont Noir for the next attempt, both Massin and Saint-Cloud reject his suspicions. Left with no other option, Rocco decides to investigate the situation alone, risking censure by his superiors.

DEATH ON THE PONT NOIR

DEATH ON THE PONT NOIR

by

Adrian Magson

Magna Large Print Books
Long Preston, North Yorkshire,
BD23 4ND, England.

British Library Cataloguing in Publication Data.

Magson, Adrian
    Death on the Pont Noir.

    A catalogue record of this book is
    available from the British Library

    ISBN   978-0-7505-3784-1

First published in Great Britain by Allison & Busby in 2012

Copyright © 2012 by Adrian Magson

Cover illustration © Nikki Smith by arrangement with
Arcangel Images

Published in Large Print 2013 by arrangement with
Allison & Busby Limited

Magna Large Print is an imprint of Library Magna Books Ltd.

Printed and bound in Great Britain by
T.J. (International) Ltd., Cornwall, PL28 8RW

*This one's for all those readers who
enjoy Lucas Rocco.
And, of course, for Ann, his biggest fan.*

CHAPTER ONE

December 1963 – Picardie, France

The gleaming black Citroën DS with the curtained rear windows ghosted along the deserted country road at a steady 70 kph, its hydropneumatic suspension making light of the undulating, pitted surface. Inside the car, its two occupants were as shielded from the cold tarmac underneath as they were from the frost-glazed mud of the fields on either side, warmed by the controlled whisper of heated air wafting gently around them.

'Belt up tight,' said the driver. His name was Calloway. 'This could hurt, otherwise.' He checked his double shoulder harness with its quick-release button and, for luck, tapped the padding on the roll cage, an ugly non-factory addition to the otherwise plush, stylish interior.

'Just get on with it,' muttered Tasker, his passenger. 'You talk too bloody much.' But he checked his harness and settled lower in his seat, bracing himself with both hands.

Calloway flicked a glance across the field to his right, to where the stubby shape of a truck was moving away from a strand of pine trees. It accelerated quickly, bouncing along a rough track on heavy-duty tyres, bits of mud and vegetation flicking up in its wake. Olive green in colour, it had the low, front-heavy bulk of a bulldog, made uglier by a large black oblong strapped across the grill.

And it was aiming towards the road in front of them on an intercept path.

'Two hundred yards,' Calloway murmured, watching the truck's progress. He was calculating its trajectory, his foot steady on the accelerator. A quick glance at the road, keeping to the centre line, then back to the truck, the eye movement and speed of the two vehicles bringing them closer together in sharp bursts like the stuttering frames of an old film reel.

'Hundred yards.'

'He's gonna miss.'

'No, he's not. Seventy.' Eyes to the road and back. Surface clear, no other traffic, just as they'd been assured. Something on the grass verge but no time to look now. Concentrate.

'He's bloody shifting a bit, isn't he?'

'Fifty yards.' The truck was suddenly bigger, solid. Brutish.

'Go.'

'Thirty.'

'Go, for God's sake!' Tasker pounded the dashboard in panic as the Renault tore out of the end of the track and loomed all over them, its grill grotesquely dwarfed by a railway sleeper held in place by steel hawsers.

Calloway calmly flicked the wheel and stamped on the accelerator. It was too late for a complete miss, but limiting the damage was as instinctive to him as breathing. The Citroën's rear end drifted sideways on the slippery surface, an elegant shuffle of its aerodynamic lines like a lady performing a two-step. The movement absorbed some of the impact, but the wooden sleeper still slammed into the car just aft of the passenger seat, punching the panel hard against the reinforcing struts welded into the interior. The car spun violently on its axis, jerking both men hard against their harnesses, and the scream of tortured metal and rubber echoed across the cold acres on either side of the road.

'What's he trying to do – *bloody kill us?*' Tasker turned to glare at the truck driver, who was grinning down at them as he slammed the truck into reverse and pulled back several yards along the road.

'Isn't that the general idea?' Calloway coolly spun the wheel and stamped on the accelerator, taking the car back up the road, its rear end sinking under the extra power being transmitted to the wheels.

'Idea! I'll bloody give him an idea,' Tasker raged. 'Let me out! *Now!*'

Calloway stood obediently on the brakes. Stopping the car altogether took a while due to the extra weight of steel reinforcements. But he compensated by spinning the wheel again and bringing the Citroën to a wallowing halt side-on to the truck, now stationary on the grass verge. The sleeper, he noticed, was hanging drunkenly from the front where it had become dislodged by the impact.

Throwing off the harness, Tasker struggled into the rear seats and kicked at the door on the undamaged side, moving with difficulty in the confined space. His breathing whistled harshly through his ex-boxer's smashed nose and his face was flushed with anger.

Before he could clamber out fully, however, two shapes rose up like wraiths from a nearby ditch and ran towards the damaged car. Dressed in camouflage smocks, each man carried two bottles with rags stuffed in the necks. They paused a short distance away, breath puffing white in the cold air, and hurled the bottles against the side of the vehicle. As the glass smashed on impact, the two men stepped closer, drew handguns and opened fire at pointblank range.

Three hundred metres away across the fields, a farmer named Simeon watched from behind his prized horse, a heavy grey percheron, as the sounds of gunshots drifted across on the breeze. He didn't know what was going on, only that strangers were behaving like lunatics for no good reason. *Probably Parisians,* he thought, and spat on the ground. Too much money and time on their hands, mostly. Thought they were God's gift. He recognised a film camera when he saw one, though. It was parked on a tripod by a clump of spindly pine trees, although if it was working, it was doing so all by itself, because there was nobody with it. The truck had barrelled along the narrow track by the trees, passing the camera by no more than a couple of metres before slamming into the Citroën with a loud bang.

Simeon decided it was none of his business. As for the gunshots, he valued his horse too highly to risk it being hit by a stray bullet. He gathered up the lead rein, urging the animal on with a gentle clicking noise. Time to be gone, instinct told him, heading for dead ground where he

14

couldn't be easily seen. Madness like this was best left to its own company. He'd come back later when they'd gone. Or maybe call the local *garde champêtre*, Lamotte. Let him deal with it.

Back on the road, Tasker had finally calmed down and was pulling on a cigarette, the smoke billowing around his head as he watched Calloway inspecting the damaged coachwork.

'Not too serious.' Calloway patted the panel. 'Thanks to the welding. We were lucky, though.' He turned and flicked some fragments of broken bottle to one side with his foot, gesturing at the Renault. 'Any faster and we'd have been toast.'

'It worked, didn't it?' The truck driver called defensively, and jumped down with a grunt from the cab. Jack Fletcher was big across the shoulders and spreading around the midsection, with a face that had seen a few too many hard fights and late nights. Alongside Calloway, he made the former race driver look slim and boyish. He held a match to a roll-up. The loosely packed tobacco caught with a burst of flame, and he sucked hungrily, consuming a third of its length in one drag. His voice had the scratchy quality of a heavy smoker. 'Came at you square on, just like I was told.' He huddled inside his coat, shivering against the cold breeze knifing across the flat terrain. It brought with it a metallic smell of standing water and cold, wet earth.

Tasker nodded grudgingly, his fury gone as suddenly as it had arrived. 'Yeah, it worked. But you bloody near killed us in the process, you ponce. You didn't need to hit us that hard.' He

15

dropped the cigarette on the road and stamped on it, watching the two men in camouflage smocks gathering up the glass debris to throw in the ditch. As he bent to pick up the cigarette butt, he froze in a half crouch. 'Christ,' he whispered. 'Where the hell did *he* spring from?'

'Who?' Fletcher turned, and saw the big man staring beneath the truck.

'Him.' Tasker pointed under the rear wheels. 'What's left of him, anyway.'

Fletcher squatted for a look and uttered an oath. Lying under the rear wheels was a man's body, twisted and torn and covered in grass, grease and dirt. It had been rolled beneath the wheels and dragged, somehow managing to become caught up in the chassis, where it now hung like a collection of bloody rags.

Fletcher stood up, his face grey. He'd seen bodies before, in varying states of disrepair. But this was different. Unexpected. 'What do we do?'

'We get rid, what do you think?' Tasker whistled for the two bottle throwers to come and help, and stood back as they wormed their way beneath the truck. They untangled the dead man's limbs until the body flopped onto the stubby grass.

'He must have been on the verge,' said Calloway, remembering. He glanced at Fletcher. 'Didn't you see him?'

'Of course I bloody didn't.' Fletcher lit another cigarette. 'I was busy at the time, remember? Didn't you clock him?'

'No. I thought I caught something in the background, but I couldn't make out what it was.' He bent and stared at the body. 'Looks like a tramp,

16

poor bastard.' He sniffed the air. 'Smells like one, too. Maybe he died out here in the cold and you were unlucky enough to hit him.'

'Makes no odds what he is or what he did,' Tasker muttered coldly. 'He's dead. Someone might miss him.' He gestured at the truck and said, 'Get him in there and cover him up good. We'll find a place to dispose of him later.'

'Why not in the trees?' said Fletcher. 'Nobody'd look, not out here.'

'We don't know that. We'll take him with us. We've got to torch the truck anyway; we can do both together. Then let's get out of here. I need some breakfast and a strong drink to warm me up.' He turned and scanned the bleak horizon, city eyes oblivious to the farmer and his horse low down against the colourless backdrop, seeing only stretches of cold, featureless fields rolling into the distance with no obvious buildings, few hedges or trees and fewer signs of life. 'Fucking Nora. Who'd want to live out here?'

CHAPTER TWO

The dull pounding in Lucas Rocco's head gradually moved outwards, morphing from a foggy background noise in a sludgy dream to the more identifiable sound of someone hitting his front door with what sounded like a sledgehammer.

He swung out of bed, instinctively snatching up his MAB 38 on the way. If it was the local priest finally come to welcome him into his flock, he'd simply put a few rounds through the wood before going back to sleep. Just in case it was Mme Denis next door, he yanked the door open with the gun behind his back.

'Do you know it's gone ten in the morning?' It was the stocky figure of Claude Lamotte, the local *garde champêtre* for the village of Poissons-les-Marais and the surrounding district. 'You're not on holiday, are you?' He raised heavy eyebrows at the sight of Rocco in his shorts, his muscular chest covered in goosebumps. 'Christ, that's a sight a man could do without.'

Rocco stood aside and beckoned him inside with the gun, squinting at the grey light of a December morning. 'Very funny. What do you want?'

'Coffee and a bite to eat, first,' said Claude. He brushed past and dropped a fresh baguette on the table, then headed for the sink and began filling a saucepan with water. 'Some of us have been up since dawn, you know that?' He put the water on the boil, then turned and looked at the gun as Rocco slumped into a chair. 'You weren't about to end it all, were you? Only I'd hate to interrupt a man in his hour of despair.' He bent and peered closely into Rocco's face. 'You do look like crap, though.'

'You should see it from my side. I was on a stake-out most of the night.' He put down the gun and rubbed his eyes. They felt full of grit and the view was hazy, like looking through muslin.

'Really? Sounds like fun. Any results?'

'No. A no-show. We had information about tobacco smuggling but I think it was a decoy.

18

When I catch up with the so-called informant, I'm going to shoot off his toes one by one.' He looked at the baguette. 'Is that mine?' The baker came round every morning in a battered old 2CV, and if Rocco was out, left it by the door in a plastic box.

'It is. No longer warm, but fresh and too good to waste.' Claude tore off one end and took a bite with great relish. '*Superbe.* Best bit of the loaf. You want the other end?' Before Rocco could answer, he looked around expectantly. 'You got any butter in this place?'

Rocco waved a hand. 'Cupboard, top shelf. Help yourself but please do it quietly.'

'Okay. You want coffee?'

'Why not? Now you've ruined my sleep I might as well get dressed. Excuse me.' He got up and wandered through to the bathroom. By the time he had dressed and come back, Claude had made coffee and smeared thick butter on slices of baguette, and was sprinkling a layer of cocoa powder over his. He sighed in expectation. 'This is the way to start the day.' He took a huge bite and coughed as he inhaled some of the powder, then winked in enjoyment. 'Takes me right back.'

Rocco sat down and picked up a slice of bread, ignoring the cocoa powder. 'You country cretins have some disgusting habits.'

Claude dunked his bread in his coffee. 'That's the trouble with you fancy city-bred cops – you've forgotten how to enjoy yourselves. All croissants and china cups, that's your trouble. This, my friend, is one of life's unique pleasures. You should enjoy it while you can.'

'If I was twelve, I would.' Rocco took a mouthful of coffee and swallowed. At least Claude knew how to make a wake-up drink. He felt his synapses respond to the jolt of caffeine and shook himself. 'To what do I owe this debatable pleasure, anyway? Have you lost your way home?'

'Not quite.' Claude put down his bread and brushed crumbs from his hands. 'I had a call this morning from a farmer who works a couple of fields about six kilometres from here, towards Bray. Name's Simeon. He was calling from a café where he'd gone to take a medicinal drink. Seems he had a nasty shock. He claims he saw a truck ram a car this morning on an open stretch of road out near his fields. Then two men jumped out of a ditch and opened fire on it with handguns.' He picked up his bread and took another bite. 'How about that?'

Rocco stared at him. 'Have you been drinking paraffin?'

'No. I'm serious.' Claude held out a hand. 'See – steady as a rock.' As Rocco made to get up, reaching for his gun, he added pragmatically, 'There's nothing to see. They've all gone – car, truck and men. We'll go out in a while. You want more coffee?'

Rocco sank back onto his chair. As he'd learnt in the past few months since being posted here, there was world time and there was Poissons time. And trying to bring the two together usually gave him a headache.

'Go on, then. I think I'm going to need it.'

'An army truck?' Lucas Rocco tried to imagine what any military vehicle would be doing out here on a deserted road in the middle of open farmland. There was a small barracks in Amiens, but it was used for shipping local army conscripts in and out, and relied almost exclusively on the station for its troop movements.

'Yes. Small and stubby – not one of the big ones. But it was going fast. It smashed right into the car, as clear as day. Deliberately, I swear it.' The farmer, a weather-beaten stick of a man named Simeon, dressed in heavy trousers and large rubber boots, pushed his cap to the back of his head and eyed Rocco with caution, as if awed by the sight of a man just over two metres in height with shoulders to match. Or maybe it was the all-black clothing and shoes; black in these parts was usually the prerogative of the old or the Church. Rocco, however, was clearly no priest.

'And it happened here?'

'That's right.' Sensing a willing if unusual audience, Simeon settled his feet apart and got ready to tell his story all over again. 'Right here.' He pointed at the section of road where they were standing, a little-used stretch of straight and surprisingly wide tarmac recently made redundant by a new section of road built three kilometres away under a local government regeneration scheme. 'I saw it with my own eyes.'

You'd have had trouble seeing it with anyone else's, Rocco wanted to say, still dulled by lack of sleep in spite of Claude's industrial-strength coffee. He forced himself to concentrate. 'Where were you when you saw this crash happen?'

'Out there.' Simeon pointed across the fields, still sugar-iced by the remnants of frost. 'By the

21

old machine-gun site. I was about to hitch the horse up to drag an old stump out of the ground when I heard the noise. See the blackthorn?' He leant towards Rocco as he pointed, bringing with him a waft of sour breath and cheap wine. 'Just to the left. There's a bit of dead ground, so they couldn't see me.'

Rocco nodded. He had to assume that a blackthorn was what he was looking at because it was the only bush in sight. 'But you could see them?'

'Sure. Well, pretty good, anyway. The light wasn't great and my eyesight's not what it was, but it was clear enough.'

Rocco wondered if the day would ever come when he'd get a witness carrying a camera and a total power of recall. 'Tell me what happened.'

'Well, as I already told Lamotte, here, after the truck rammed the car, both vehicles stopped, then two men jumped out from the side of the road and threw things – but I couldn't see what they were. Then they took out guns and started shooting. I got out of here as quick as I could at that point. It was like a war zone ... apart from the camera.'

'Camera?' There had been no mention of a camera in his call to Claude Lamotte. A car being rammed by a truck and guns firing had been the sum total of the story.

Rocco glanced at Claude who looked blank. 'He didn't mention it before.'

'Didn't I? I thought I did. By the trees over there.' Simeon pointed at the only clump of trees around, two hundred metres away. Pines, Rocco noted, sharp and spiky and rigid with cold against the horizon, like a scene from the Eastern

Front. 'The truck came down the track from behind the trees, and that's when I noticed the camera, sitting on a tripod thing. But there was nobody with it. Don't they usually have a man sitting behind it with a megaphone shouting at everyone and wearing riding britches?' He looked at Rocco. 'Don't they?'

Rocco decided to change tack before he lost the will to live. 'Can you describe the men?'

Simeon considered the question, then said, 'No. Not really. At least four, I'd say. Two drivers, two gunmen ... and maybe one other.' He mimed drawing a gun and firing, making a soft *paff-paff* noise, and smiled. 'But from here...? I didn't get any detail.'

'What time was this?'

'Earlier today – about eight. Roughly. I don't have a watch. No need, see. Seasons are more important in my line of work.' He pursed his lips and frowned, as if he'd just surprised himself by saying something profound.

Rocco shook his head and walked away towards the copse. It was shaping up to be another tale of unlikely events unsubstantiated by reality or facts, and likely due to the after-effects of too much *vin de pays* and a bad night's sleep.

Simeon watched him go, then nudged Claude. 'Is he for real? I heard we had a new *flic* in the neighbourhood, but not one like him.'

'Where've you been hiding?' Claude muttered. 'He's been here a while now. And he's good, so you'd better watch yourself.'

'Yeah, well, I've been off sick, haven't I? It's why I'm trying to catch up, pulling out tree roots in this shitty weather instead of leaving it until spring.' He sniffed and lifted his chin towards Rocco. 'Does he always dress like he's going to a funeral?'

'Always. He goes hunting in the marais like that, too, when he has to. Just mind you don't tick him off because when he goes after someone, he doesn't stop. He's ... what do they call it – relentless.'

'That was him?' Simeon's eyes widened. 'I heard about that. A gun battle, so they say. Grenades, too.' He pulled a face then spat on the ground. 'And to think it used to be so peaceful around here.'

CHAPTER THREE

Rocco reached the trees and did a careful examination, quartering the ground in a grid fashion. If anyone had been here, especially with a camera, there would be signs. It was a god-forsaken spot, made worse by the bitter breeze cutting through the branches and whining like a soul in torment. The ground surrounding the trees was mostly covered with clumps of coarse grass, with a carpet of pine needles closer in. He noted other details and dismissed them: scraps of fertiliser bags rotting away beneath a bush; old bottles without labels glinted dully in the shadows; a rusting bucket without a handle; and further back, where the ground was clear, a set of footprints side by side where someone had stood

24

and taken a leak, the story etched in the frosty ground. Size 42 or 43, he guessed, which told him nothing he could use. He finally found a spot by the side of the road where three holes had been pierced in the earth in a triangular spread about a metre across. A tripod, just as Simeon had said. So he hadn't imagined that bit. But was it a camera or something else? The grass around it was trampled flat, but not as much as he would have expected if a cameraman had been working it. So what had been the point?

He flicked some pine needles from the cuffs of his trousers and walked back to join Claude and Simeon, scanning the ground as he went. Then he saw something in the grass verge. He stopped. The stems here had been either crushed or churned up, as if something heavy had rolled across here recently. But it wasn't the grass or the earth that caught his attention.

It was the blood. Lots of it.

He took a rubber glove from his coat pocket and slipped it on, then carefully lifted some of the grass clumps to one side. The earth beneath was dark brown, and in parts, where it had been covered, more of a dark red. He wondered if a wild boar had been shot by a farmer and carted off as a trophy. Or maybe hit by a car. Both were possibilities. But the spread of blood seemed too extensive. And tied in with what Simeon had witnessed, there seemed to be another, less mundane possibility. He stepped back along the verge, his unease growing. More blood, flecks of it scattered across the grass, some on the edge of the tarmac, the bigger flecks with a covering of insects feeding on this rare bounty.

And a human tooth.

Forget the boar, then.

The tooth was worn down, and chipped around the top edges. A molar, by the look of it, stained with blood. Not a young one, either.

There was something else in among the bloody earth. Too uniform to be a stone and too rounded to be a piece of dirt. Rocco plucked the object out of the blood and turned it over.

It was a metal button embossed with a number five. A child's button? His blood ran cold at the implication. But the tooth went against that – it was definitely an adult's.

He scanned the fields, feeling a familiar buzz building in his head: the signal which told him something was beginning; that something bad had happened here. If anyone had been killed or injured in the crash seen by Simeon, then Amiens hospital, less than twenty kilometres away, would soon provide the answer.

Failing that, he would need Rizzotti's help. In the absence of a bigger budget, the on-loan doctor was the only person approaching a scientific presence the local police force had. Although he might not be able to make sense of this with his limited equipment and experience, he would be able to gather evidence to prove whether the blood was animal or human, although the teeth pretty much made that a given.

'Lucas,' Claude Lamotte called. His voice sounded odd. He was standing a couple of metres away, holding in his hand a fragment of curved glass that glinted in the weak sunlight. Then he

26

picked up another fragment and walked over to join Rocco. He was holding the top of a bottle, with a piece of rag stuffed through it. Both pieces of glass were dark green, clearly from the same vessel. 'There's more fragments back there, in the grass,' Claude said. 'Could be what Simeon saw being thrown.'

Rocco wrapped the button in a scrap of paper and put it in his pocket, then took the bottle top with the piece of rag and sniffed. No smell. Yet the rag was wet. He touched it with his finger. Not oily. 'It's water.'

'That's a Molotov cocktail, that is,' said Simeon knowingly, shuffling over to join them and lifting one leg to scratch at his groin. 'Light the rag and chuck the bottle, the car goes up in flames. *Pouf!*' He grinned, revealing a mouthful of discoloured teeth.

Rocco didn't doubt him. The farmer was of an age where he would know; where men and women just like him would have learnt the art of sabotage against an invading foe; where a wine bottle filled with petrol was an easily sourced weapon and all it took to be useful was someone willing to get in close, light the rag and throw it.

'Can you describe the car?' he asked.

Simeon shrugged. 'Fancy. Black. Shiny – like the ones they use in official processions. Citroën, I think. I'm better with horses, of course ... I know about them.'

'A DS?' Claude suggested. 'They're used in processions – especially black ones. And funerals. There are none round here, though. Too expensive, and who wants to drive round looking like a funeral director – or a politician?'

Rocco shook his head as the buzz increased. So what they had was a truck ramming an official-looking car, and two men jumping out of the ditch and throwing pretend petrol bombs and firing guns. It prompted a thought. He turned to where Claude had picked up the glass.

'Any shell cases?'

'No. I thought about that. They must have picked them up ... unless they used revolvers.'

'They weren't real, anyway.'

Rocco and Claude turned and looked at Simeon, who was scrubbing at his groin again like an old dog.

'Say again?' Rocco was trying not to imagine what was going on down there. The man looked as if he and hot water and soap were distant acquaintances.

'Guns. I know guns, too. They weren't firing live rounds. The sound wasn't right. Too flat and dull, like damp fireworks.'

Make that pretend petrol bombs and blank rounds, thought Rocco. He said, 'Did you see where they went afterwards?'

'No. Like I told you, I was on my way back home with the horse. But I could hear them. Sound travels out here, you see; nothing to stop it. Wherever it was they went, they had a sick Renault to take with them. It sounded more like a tractor and kept banging, like there was something broken–'

'Hey!' Claude jumped in. 'You didn't say anything about it being a Renault before.'

'Well, I only just realised, didn't I? There's a builder over towards Fonzet uses one just like it.

Got it cheap off the military, he said.' He nodded. 'Renault. Bet you anything.'

Rocco shook his head. No bet. Camera, men, vehicles, fake petrol bombs and blank bullets, lots of blood and a tooth. On the surface it added up to nothing more improbable than a makeshift film set. He wasn't sure but he had a feeling film-makers were supposed to get a licence for shoot-ing scenes on public roads, even out here. It could soon be checked. And the blood might well turn out to be a simple accident; a stuntman who'd miscalculated and performed his final *cascade*.

Except, where were the film crew and equip-ment?

CHAPTER FOUR

George Tasker sat back and eyed the long mirror above the café bar. It glittered under the lights, and had gold-coloured patterns at each corner, like scrolls. That had to go, he decided; something that big was just asking for it. A well-placed chair would do it – maybe a table if things really got going.

He sipped at a glass of cognac and watched the others getting tanked. He didn't much care for spirits, and would rather have had a pint of Guin-ness. But the excuse for a bar they had chosen didn't stock decent beer and the bartender didn't seem to care one way or another. The food on offer was pretty much limited to bread, boiled eggs and cold meat, which didn't hold a candle to free booze as far as Fletcher and the others were concerned. They'd piled in with venom, eager to try drinks they never would have normally, encouraged by the wad of francs Tasker had slapped on the bar.

He sighed and rubbed the calloused knuckles of his right hand, waiting for the fun to kick off. Instructions were to take root here and let the rest take care of itself ... with a little help from him and the readies supplied for the trip. He didn't know and didn't much care what else was going on, only that he had his part to play. The truck and the dented Citroën had been dumped as instructed, the truck torched along with the body of whoever it was had fallen underneath it, and the car left at a breaker's yard to be 'disappeared'. It seemed a waste to him, chopping a decent set of wheels like that, but arguing tactics wasn't his call. They'd be getting a train out of here, anyway.

He felt something sharp and metallic in his pocket. It was the spare key to the truck; he'd trousered it when they'd first picked up the vehicle, in case Fletcher lost his. The big man was useful in tight corners and for jobs that didn't require much thinking, but there were times when his age began to show and he got careless. Like the way he'd hit the Citroën full pelt, nearly taking Tasker and Calloway out of the game for good. No judgement, that was his problem. Brains scrambled by too many lost fights and too much booze. If he had his way, this would be Fletcher's last job for the Firm before he got relegated to something where he couldn't harm anyone.

He watched as the man chugged back a tall glass of thin, gassy beer, egged on by roars of approval from the others, before slamming the empty down on the bar and laughing like he'd won the Olympics. The bartender said something Fletcher clearly heard but didn't understand. His response was to stick a thick middle finger in the air right in front of the man's face and belch, then watch the Frenchie go red.

Big bloke to upset, that bartender, Tasker noted. Probably handy in a ruckus, too; like any barman worth his job, accustomed to chucking out troublesome drunks. But he wasn't big enough or handy enough for these lads once they got going. He sipped the cognac and waited. Checked his watch. Nearly lunchtime already.

Time for some fun.

Less than three miles away, Olivier Bellin, the owner of the breaker's yard where the Citroën DS had been left, walked round the car studying the damage. It was pretty serious, he noted. Whatever this had skidded into had been solid enough not to give. Still, he'd seen worse over the years; driven some, too, when he'd had to. As bad as it seemed, though, given the right treatment it could be made to look right. As long as nobody looked too close.

He scratched his head. He was in a not un-common dilemma. He'd been paid to take in this car, no questions asked, and get rid of it. He'd done it plenty of times before when a vehicle had to cease to exist. That was 'get rid' as in destroy, chop up, crush, cut and reduce down to the last nut and washer. But Bellin was greedy, always on

31

the lookout to make an easy killing. His view was that since the man paying for the job to be done was a long way from here, and unlikely ever to show his face anywhere near Amiens – and certainly not down this end of town – what was the problem? And this car was just so tasty ... if viewed from the right angle. Suffering the indignity of being reduced to scrap this early in its life would be a sacrilege.

He checked the odometer. The numbers were fairly high but not a killer. The condition of the seats and carpet wasn't bad, either. A wash and brush-up and they'd look like new. The rest of the bodywork was sound, as were the tyres. The way the side had been caved in was a bit serious, there was no denying, and there might be some underlying problems with the structure. But he knew a couple of guys who could take care of that.

He stared up at the sky, juggling the need for some quick cash from a punter wanting a cheap DS to show off to his neighbours, and the likelihood of The Man in Paris ever finding out that his instructions had not been carried out to the letter.

The Man in Paris. Bellin licked his lips nervously. Now there was someone he didn't like to think about. Several guys who'd disobeyed him were rumoured to have disappeared over the years, probably in yards pretty much like this one, come to think of it. And he had no wish to end up the same way.

He turned and caught a glimpse of his reflection in the window of the cabin, which served as his office. He saw himself with one hand on the Citroën's roof like he owned it. It caught him by surprise, standing alongside a picture-perfect DS as if born to it. He smiled.

No doubt about it, it was too good to pass up. He made a decision.

Unfortunately for Olivier Bellin, it was the worst mistake of his life.

CHAPTER FIVE

'Any thoughts?' Rocco rejoined Claude Lamotte and they watched Simeon throw his leg over an ancient moped and wobble away down the road in a cloud of blue smoke.

'Only one: if he makes it home without falling off, it'll be a miracle.' He turned to stare at the clump of pine trees, then the road. 'But this ... it all sounds a bit bizarre to me.'

'Bizarre why?' Rocco valued Claude's opinion; although a countryside policeman based in Poissons, and looked on with faint derision by some on the force, he was a better cop than they knew and had the instincts of a born hunter. He also knew the people around here, which was a big advantage.

'The camera. If it was back there by the trees, it would have been pointing east to catch the action, right?'

'Agreed. So?'

'Right into the morning sun? I doubt it.' When Rocco didn't respond, he puffed out his cheeks and said, 'What – you think I don't know about these things?'

'Not at all. I just wondered how.'

'Because back when I was driving a taxi in Paris, before I put on the uniform–'

'Which, let's be honest,' Rocco pointed out, 'you don't very often.' As if to prove it, Claude was currently dressed in a pair of shabby brown corduroys, lace-up boots and a green hunting jacket. With his heavy build and round face, he looked more like a bandit than an officer of the law.

'I have to blend in, don't I? People won't talk if I look like a cop all the time. Where was I? Oh, yes. There was this regular ride; he used to get me to take him to the Bois de Boulogne, where he made short films that never sold. They call it *cinéma vérité* now. Real life, it's supposed to be, without all the glitzy crap they have in Hollywood. Myself, I quite like the glitzy crap. But he was eccentric, like lots of people in that business. Before his time, but okay – and he always paid his bills, so...' He shrugged. 'He liked to talk about his work while I drove and listened. That's how I know about shooting against the sun.'

'Don't they have filters and lenses for that?'

'Of course.' Claude held out his hand and rubbed his fingers and thumb together. 'But they're expensive. Also, why have the camera there, so close to the track? Once the truck goes by, the shot's ruined. Vibration, see – that's something else he told me about. Kills a good scene like a dead dog.'

'Maybe it's all part of the *vérité*,' Rocco murmured with a wry smile. He changed the subject. 'How's Alix?'

34

Claude scowled. 'Always busy. She's trying to make *commissaire* before I retire, I reckon.' One of Claude's two daughters, Alix had returned to Poissons following a failed marriage, but having joined the police force. Claude had been both shocked and proud at once, and Rocco guessed he was still trying to come to terms with having a daughter in uniform and a looming divorce in the family.

'She has a lot to prove, that's all. It was a tough move, joining the uniforms.'

Claude huffed his cheeks. 'You don't need to tell me that. I still can't believe she did it. Still, I bet you see her more often than I do.' He peered speculatively at Rocco. 'How's she shaping up?'

Rocco squinted back at him. The comment had contained a certain tone, and he thought he knew why. 'Actually, I don't see her that much. Canet assigns her work, not me. But I think she'll be fine. She's got good instincts, like someone else I know.'

Claude looked sheepish. 'Sorry, Lucas. I'm an idiot. It's not my place to worry about her. She's a grown woman. I just...'

'Worry about her?'

'Yes. Pathetic, isn't it, because she'd flay the skin off me if she knew. But what's a man to do in my position?'

'Don't ask me, for a start,' Rocco murmured. 'I'm no expert.'

A police van arrived and the driver hopped out and saluted. 'We've come to mark out the scene, Inspector. Dr Rizzotti is on his way, and there's a message for you from Captain Canet.'

'What about?'

'There's been a big fight in town. A bar's been

35

wrecked and he thinks you might be able to help.'

The *Canard Doré* was more than wrecked. It looked like a tornado had gone through the place after a carpet-bombing. What wasn't broken seemed scarred and ripped beyond repair; half the furniture was on the pavement outside, having taken the plate glass windows and net curtains with it, and the front door was hanging from the hinges. Inside, the drinks-bottle shelves had been swept clean, a coffee machine flattened and the full-length wall mirrors had been hammered into fragments. The cash till was lying upside down in the sink, a scattering of coins and notes on the floor and drainer, and the pinball machine was lying flat on its belly like a beached whale, the glass splintered and the light display gutted. Only the counter, built of solid hardwood, seemed to have survived intact, although the surface was awash with spilt alcohol and embedded with fragments of broken glass. The aroma of beer and spirits was heavy in the air, mixing with a tang of stale sweat and cheap tobacco.

The bar owner, André Mote, was sporting a large bruise over one eye and a bloodied shirt, and sitting in a corner looking murderous. The object of his anger was a group of five men who had been corralled in a corner of the bar by a number of tough *Gardes Mobiles* and a muscular Detective René Desmoulins. With batons drawn, they looked as if they were itching for an excuse to teach the fighters a lesson.

'Why are they still here?' said Rocco to *Sous-Brigadier* Godard, the head of the group.

'It was easier keeping them confined here than trying to transfer them to the station on a charge of fighting, only to have a magistrate let them go. And there are too many civilians around to do it safely.' Godard, a big man with a battle-scarred face, had the scepticism of many policemen, but was good at his job. He was right, too. If this lot were transferred to the street without taking precautions, they'd cause mayhem.

Rocco nodded. 'Good thinking. But this wasn't a fight – it was open warfare. Now they're subdued, get them cuffed and back to the station and lock them up. I'll be along in a while.'

'They're foreign visitors, Lucas. English. Won't there be repercussions if we lock them up?' He rubbed his fingers and thumb together, referring to the recent 'advisory' bulletins circulated to all forces by the Interior Ministry regarding the treatment of visitors from overseas, and how the economy depended on not alienating foreign currency and those with the willingness to spend it.

'Maybe.' Rocco thought the advice applied less to areas like Picardie, and more to the tourist resorts in the south where visitors had money to splash around. 'Just make sure they don't fall down any stairs on the way. It won't do them any harm to taste a bit of French jail comfort for a couple of hours.' He knew that Godard was referring to *Commissaire* Massin, their boss, and his known fear of causing waves which might reach his superiors in Paris. 'And you can leave Massin to me.'

Godard grinned. *'D'accord.* Can I cuff them really tight?'

'After what they've done here, I'd insist on it.'

He waited while Godard organised his men and swiftly got the five Englishmen restrained before they could resist. Four of them made do with mild protests, but one man, who seemed to be their leader, pulled his wrists away and swore at Godard. He stood up, showing an impressive breadth of shoulders and a beaten pug face.

'Piss off, Froggy. Nobody puts them things on me.'

Godard turned and scowled at Rocco. 'What did he say?'

Rocco said, 'I think he called you a frog-eater and an ugly son of an ugly bitch. You going to stand for that?'

'No. I'm not. Can you look away, please?' As soon as Rocco did so, Godard signalled to two of his men and they closed in on either side of the Englishman. Grabbing him by the arms, they slammed him unceremoniously against the wall and cuffed his hands behind him, then turned him around for Godard to plant a heavy knee into his groin. The Englishman gasped and his face lost all its colour.

'And that, Monsieur *Rosbif*,' Godard muttered, 'is how we treat animals like you.' He prodded the man's shoulder. 'And for your information, if you could speak our language, anyway, which you obviously cannot, I don't eat frogs.' He signalled to his men to take the five men away.

'How many of them were involved?' To Rocco it was academic, but it was useful to know for the record how many men Mote had seen causing the damage.

'All of them,' growled Mote. 'All English, all drunk and violent, like pigs. *Animals!*' His eyes glittered with anger and bruised pride. He brushed his face with damaged knuckles. 'Mostly it was the big one. I want them arrested and charged, Inspector. Do you know how many years it has taken me to build this business, me and my wife? *Hein?*' He slapped his chest with the flat of his hand and stared around at his wife for her support. Mme Mote, a mousy-looking woman in a floral apron, nodded dutifully and patted her husband's hand, then dabbed her eyes with a handkerchief. She had a large mole on her chin with a single hair sprouting from it, which Rocco found himself suffering an irrational desire to point out to her.

'Charges will follow,' he assured Mote. 'What started it?'

He listened with detachment as the story unfolded. It was a well-worn route to strife: someone had drunk too much, remarks and gestures had been made, the owner had refused further drinks and a brawl had ensued. It was nothing unusual for the establishment, Desmoulins had earlier confided. The *Canard Doré* wasn't known for its upscale clientele and had been the location of more than a few bar brawls. But this damage was of a greater scale than normal.

'I'll say.' Rocco had seen the results of far worse bar fights than this, especially in Marseilles when visiting naval ships were in and men had been too long at sea on service rations. But for Amiens, it was extreme.

'I'll have someone come round to take statements and assess the damage,' he said finally, when Mote had finished his story. 'You'll have to apply for compensation, but the court will probably make it a condition of their sentence.'

'You mean in return for their release?' Mote didn't sound very surprised. Maybe, thought Rocco, the idea of money to refurbish the bar would be enough to salve his feelings and let the matter drop.

'We'll see what the magistrate says.'

Outside, he found a uniformed officer waiting for him.

'Inspector Rocco? Captain Canet would be pleased if you could return to the station. The five men charged with the assault are all English.'

'I know. So?'

The man shrugged. 'You are the only person with that language, sir. We have to take their statements ... but...' He hesitated.

'But what?'

'They are being difficult, sir. Even with *Sous-Brigadier* Godard's men to help. They seem happy to just sit there laughing at us.'

'The fresh air must have woken them up.' Men in Godard's unit – often mistaken for the national *Compagnies Républicaines de Sécurité* (CRS) – were used when strength in numbers was needed. If even they were having trouble, then the leader of the Englishmen must have stirred his men into making a fuss.

'Two of them are pretty big, sir – possibly ex-boxers. The others are just drunk.'

'I noticed.'

Fifteen minutes later, Rocco was talking to Captain Eric Canet, in charge of the uniformed officers. The captain looked mildly unsettled, as if facing a problem he didn't much relish dealing with.

'We don't need this, Lucas,' he breathed. 'We need to get rid of these louts as soon as possible. The magistrate has agreed to deal with them at a special sitting in the morning. He'll impose a fine and compensation big enough to please the bar owner, after which we can wave them goodbye. But I think you should talk to them; warn them off coming back.' He handed Rocco a filing tray piled with wallets, passports and envelopes containing money and other personal effects.

'If they'll listen.' Rocco looked around. 'Where's Massin?' The *commissaire* had a nose for bad news and was usually quick to stamp on trouble taking place in his precinct. Rocco was surprised he wasn't already out here handing out advice.

'He's been called to a conference in head-quarters. Something about a security review ... or should I say, *another* security review. Perronnet went with him.' *Commissaire* Perronnet was Massin's deputy, and clung to him like a tick. It was the job of a commissaire like Massin to attend numerous meetings which seemed on the surface to have little to do with day-to-day policing, but a lot to do with a visible national readiness after years of doubt. It also gave him the opportunity he craved, which was to consort with the upper levels of the police force and the Interior Ministry in the hopes of gaining a more favourable posting. 'I'd like to get this done before he comes back,'

Canet added dryly, 'then we can all go back to the usual levels of violence and mayhem.'

Rocco nodded. It was a wise move. The less Massin had to complain about, the better all round. 'Right. I'll see them in a minute. But don't let on that I speak English.'

He turned as Desmoulins wandered up, sporting a livid bruise on one cheek.

'What happened to you?'

The detective sniffed in disgust. 'I must be getting slow. The big bastard caught me with a backward head butt as we were getting him in the van.' He waited until Canet was out of earshot, then added, 'But he tripped on the way back out, so we're even. Clumsy fella.'

'Clearly. Also not aware of when he's caused enough trouble.' He had a random thought about the ramming incident involving the truck and the Citroën. 'Three things I need you to check on: put someone on ringing the hospitals here and in a thirty-kilometre radius. Ask if they've taken in any road accident victims, dead or injured.'

'Sure. Anything specific?'

'We're looking for anyone with facial damage, loss of teeth – that kind of thing.'

'Is this from the call earlier this morning?'

'Yes. Something odd is going on, but it could be nothing. Second, get someone to check the garages in the area for a military-style Renault truck and a black Citroën DS brought in showing crash damage. Check the barracks, too, see if they're missing a truck. And third, find out if anyone has applied for a permit to film on public roads in the region.'

'Got it. You going to talk to the English?'

'In a while. Let them stew a bit longer.'

'You want me there?'

Rocco smiled at Desmoulins' readiness to pitch in where trouble loomed. 'Thanks, but Godard and his men are a lot uglier.'

CHAPTER SIX

'Remember, nobody says nothing unless I give the nod.' Tasker glared at each of his companions in turn: Fletcher, the grey-haired and heavily jowled bruiser; the two bottle throwers, Jarvis and Biggs, ex-soldiers in their thirties; and Calloway, tanned, slim and looking out of place in their company. They were gathered around a table bolted to the floor, in a holding cell big enough to take all five men. Most looked hung-over and jittery to varying degrees. 'If any of these monkeys manages to find someone who speaks English,' Tasker continued, '–which I doubt – we came over for some fun, got pissed and it got out of hand. End of story. We all clear?'

They nodded, either too cowed or too tired to argue.

Tasker sat back, satisfied they'd follow instructions. Biggs and Jarvis were green but would go with the flow. Fletcher had done some jail time, so he knew what the score was when it came to being patient. And Tasker had served a couple of terms himself, several years ago, one for involvement in a bank robbery. He'd put it down to experience; it was one of many bank jobs he'd done, but the only one he'd been hauled in for and convicted.

'How long is this going to take?' breathed Calloway, studying his nails. Of them all, he seemed the most calm and untroubled. 'Only I have a date lined up for tomorrow that I'd rather not miss.'

'Tough shit, pretty boy,' Tasker replied nastily. 'You'll have to give it a miss, won't you? Just sit tight until I say so or there might be an accident happening in this cell any moment soon.'

Calloway looked unaffected by the man's air of menace, but shrugged. 'If you say so.'

'I do. Anyone else got anything to say?' Nobody replied. 'Good. Now, they got to let us go soon, so we ain't got long.'

Calloway looked doubtful. 'I wouldn't bet on it.'

'What do you mean?'

'You don't know French cops. They don't play nice when it suits them, and those boys in blue weren't being too gentle, in case you hadn't noticed.'

Tasker shrugged. 'So what? We're still in one piece, aren't we? It's no worse than a dust-up down Brick Lane. You take the bruises and you get the money. They might not let us go today ... but they have to sometime. We sit here until they do, then we go home.' He grinned without humour. 'It's all part of the plan – and you're being paid well for it, so don't screw it up.'

The threat in his voice was a chilling reminder of his authority, and the men said nothing. Out in the corridor, they heard footsteps approaching.

The door was unlocked.

A uniformed officer stepped in and stood in the doorway. Big and ready, he was holding a short baton in both hands. Two others stood just behind him, similarly armed. The lead man pointed at Tasker with the business end of the baton and beckoned.

Tasker folded his arms and sat back. 'You want me, Pierre, you'll have to come in and get me. Only you might have to get used to wearing your little stick through your nose.'

The officer hesitated, unsure of what the Englishman had said. But the body language was clear enough. The three officers made a move to step forward, then a voice murmured behind them and they stepped aside.

Another man entered the room.

Rocco stopped just inside the door and looked around at the five prisoners. They stared back, clearly surprised by his appearance. What they had no doubt expected was a group of heavies coming in in force; what they were seeing was a taller-than-average man, dark-haired and tanned, with broad shoulders, dressed in a good-quality, long, dark coat and trousers and expensive shoes. And seemingly unconcerned by their number in the confined space.

'Well, well. Look what the cat's brought in.' Tasker was the first to speak. 'Fe fi fo fum ... I smell a senior frog-eater.' He kept his eyes on Rocco but his next words were clear enough. 'Shtumm, boys, remember.'

Rocco moved further inside the room. He was

45

holding a handful of British passports. Flicking them open, he studied the contents at length, allowing the silence to build. Then he compared faces with photos, going from one man to the next, staring them in the eye and noting their reactions. When he was finished, he slapped the passports shut and put them away, then studied the state of the men's hands.

The big man, Tasker, was clearly the leader. Every group of individuals had one – even a group of violent drunks. And authority radiated off this man like an electric current. He was forty-five years old, married and listed as a business-man. He had the brutal appearance of a barroom brawler, although his suit looked expensive, if flash, as did the large gold rings on his fingers. Somewhere along the road of his life, someone had flattened his nose, and he had developed layers of old scar tissue over his eyes and was missing half of one eyebrow. He'd probably been a good puncher in his time, thought Rocco, eyeing his big shoulders and bunched knuckles, but with a poor defence. And judging by the fresh cuts and abrasions on his hands, he had been using those knuckles only a short while ago.

The second big man, Fletcher, was older at fifty-one. He had the dull eyes of a follower and a hard-man body going to seed around the edges. His clothes were also flashy, but cheap. He, too, was nursing cuts to his hands. Two younger men named Biggs and Jarvis were working hard at ig-noring Rocco, but failing. They looked fit, like former soldiers or athletes, but beginning to go soft, their fingers yellowed by nicotine and reddened with scratches and cuts. Both were listed as customer managers. And then there was a man named Calloway, occupation professional driver, more French than English by appearance and somehow aloof from his companions. And smarter.

Rocco couldn't think when he'd last seen such a mixed bunch, and decided it would have been back in Paris. They would have been criminals, too, just like this lot, of that he was certain.

'For your information, Mr Tasker,' he said in English, looking at the big man, 'my name is Rocco. Inspector Rocco. That's a strange word, "shtumm". Is it London slang?' He held Tasker's gaze but the man looked too surprised to say anything. 'Is there a particular reason why your friends should remain quiet?'

'Terrific.' The soft murmur came from Calloway, on hearing Rocco's easy grasp of the language.

Tasker glared at him, but said to Rocco, 'Go screw yourself, copper.'

'See, that is what I do not understand,' Rocco replied, and looked at each of the men in turn. He walked up and down, forcing them to follow him with their eyes, each turn taking him closer and closer until he was right in front of them, and they were having to crane their necks to see his face. 'Five ... friends, come to France and have a little fun. They drink too much of our wine and beer – even a bottle or two of cognac, according to the bar owner – and end up drunk. So drunk they completely ruin a bar.' He shrugged. 'It happens, of course. Even here we are not immune to the odd *fracas*. But then the men prove

47

... difficult when taken in for questioning.'

'So?' Tasker stuck his chin out. 'What's your point?'

'My point, Mr Tasker, is why? Most people in your situation would be eager – is that the word, eager? – to get out of here. After all, our jails are not famous for being comfortable.' He shook his head. 'It's a constant source of national shame, but budgets are very limited. However, you men are different. No, for some reason, you make more of this ... episode than it needs. Almost as if you want to stay here. Is it the British military cemeteries which have attracted you to our region? I think not. It can hardly be the local fishing because you do not look like any fishermen I have ever seen. I'm just a little puzzled, that's all. Perhaps we should talk about it.' He studied Tasker's eyes very carefully, looking for something, but failing to find it. It only added to his bafflement. He decided to unsettle him and turned to the three officers, pointing at Calloway. 'Bring that man.' Then he turned and left the cell.

'Hey!' Tasker was on his feet in an instant. 'Come back here, copper! Why aren't you questioning me? Hey – frog!'

But Rocco's footsteps were already fading along the corridor.

Tasker could only watch as the officers lifted Calloway from his seat and took him away.

CHAPTER SEVEN

'One of my colleagues,' Rocco said in a conversational tone when they were all seated in a room upstairs, 'recognised you from Le Mans a few years ago. You were good, he says, but your team let you go after an accident. Is that correct?'

'Something like that.' Calloway shifted in his seat. It was clear even to Rocco from his accent that the former race driver came from a different strata of English society to the other men, and he wondered about the man's apparent fall from grace. He was good-looking in a soft-focus kind of way, like a film star just past his prime. Clean-shaven and tanned, he'd clearly been following the sun. No doubt some women would find him attractive.

'You do not seem at ease with those others, Mr Calloway. Would you care to tell me why you are with them?'

'A couple are friends from way back,' Calloway replied easily. 'I heard they were coming here for a bit of fun and decided to tag along.'

'Fun. In Picardie in December? What kind of fun would that be? You think we have skiing here?'

A wry grin. 'It seemed a good idea at the time.' The comment showed a level of wit and intelligence, highlighting further his difference from the other men.

Rocco flicked a hand sideways. 'You call what

49

you did to that café fun?'

'Yeah, well, maybe it did get out of hand a bit. We're sorry. Your English is pretty good. Where did you learn it?'

'Here and there.' Rocco reached across the table and grasped Calloway's hands. The palms were clean and soft. Driver's hands, unmarked by rough labour ... or glass splinters from a wall mirror. He flipped them over. Not a scratch on the backs, either.

'You didn't take part, did you? In that destruction. Why is that? Were you looking after your hands?'

'I don't know what you mean.' Calloway was beginning to look uncomfortable under the closeness of Rocco's scrutiny. He tugged his hands out of Rocco's grip and thrust them in his pockets.

'Of course you do.' Rocco stood up and grabbed the Englishman by the collar and lifted him off his feet with no great effort. He sniffed. Aftershave, like old leather, but sweeter. Calloway was a man who cared about his appearance, unlike his companions. Something else that set him apart.

'You are not drunk, either.' Another oddity. He released the driver, who flopped back into his seat, his face suddenly pale under the tan.

Calloway tugged his collar down and looked resentful. 'I don't need it, that's why. I only drink to be sociable. The others, though ... they expect it.'

'Do you always do what they want?'

'I like a quiet life.'

'You were not alone.' When Calloway looked puzzled, Rocco explained, 'The leader of your little group of violent drunks: Tasker. He's had a

50

few drinks, but he's a long, long way from being drunk.'

'I don't know how you can tell.'

'His eyes are too clear and his movements too relaxed. Believe me, as a policeman in Paris, I've seen more than enough to be able to read the signs.'

'I'm sure. Look, Inspector, is this going to take long? I know we did a lot of damage, and I'll be happy to pay for my share, but I have to be back in England for work in a couple of days.'

'Your share?' Rocco pulled a sheet of paper towards him. It listed the property of each of the men arrested. 'You have just over thirty pounds sterling on you, your colleagues even less. Except for Mr Tasker, who has rather more. Quite a lot more, in fact.' He looked up. 'How do you propose to pay? I should warn you we don't take cheques.'

'Tasker will cover it.'

Before Rocco could respond, the door opened and Detective Desmoulins appeared.

Rocco beckoned him in.

'I've checked all the hospitals,' Desmoulins said. 'No bodies, serious injuries or records of facial damage since last weekend. And no permits issued for filming. The truck and car search is going to take longer.' He gestured at the Englishman. 'Is he being cooperative?' He flexed his muscular shoulders and rubbed his knuckles with a menacing grin, which made Calloway shrink in his seat.

'No. Not really.' Rocco pursed his lips and sat back. He wasn't going to get much from this man, and the others were clearly too in awe of Tasker to say anything. A waste of time, therefore.

51

He said to the guards, 'Take him to a separate cell and bring Tasker.'

When they brought the big man upstairs, he came without a fight, Rocco noted. He wasn't surprised; he'd seen it before in groups with an obvious hierarchy. Better for the lead man to go voluntarily and try to score a point in front of his men than to be dragged out ignominiously by the heels.

He pointed to the chair. 'Sit.'

Tasker did so, a sly smile lurking at the corner of his mouth. He glanced round at Desmoulins, and gave him a sneer, but pointedly ignored the two members of Godard's squad who had brought him upstairs and were now standing by the door. 'What's up, copper, safety in numbers? Got to go mob-handed?' When there was no answer, he changed tack. 'Calloway give you the old silent treatment, did he? You should learn how to speak nice to people.' His eyes glittered. 'Where is he, by the way?'

Rocco eyed him coldly. The more he saw of this man the less he liked him. Very few people affected him this way – usually the worst of criminals or the most pompous of officials. But there was something about Tasker which went beyond the norm. It was as if he were trying deliberately not to be liked.

And that puzzled him.

He emptied an envelope containing Tasker's personal effects onto the table. A large amount of cash in sterling and francs, a cheap pen, a packet of mints, a contraceptive in a foil packet, a comb, a wallet, a small key with no brand name.

'I said, where's Calloway?' Tasker growled.

'He is in another room, writing a statement.'

'Statement?' Tasker frowned, then sat up suddenly as Rocco picked up the key. 'Hey – that's my stuff!' He reached forward but was brought up short by Desmoulins clamping a hand on one shoulder and slamming him back in his chair.

Rocco signalled for Desmoulins to let him go, then dropped the key back on the table. 'No need to get excited, Mr Tasker. It is merely "stuff", as you call it. What is so special about it – apart from the money? That is a lot to be carrying around with you.'

'That's a crime in this poxy country, is it?' Tasker's eyes glittered and he suddenly relaxed, looking away from Rocco. 'Like having a bit of fun.'

'Of course not.' Rocco dropped a finger on the key. 'What is this for?'

Tasker's face went blank. 'No idea. It's not mine. Probably someone else's crap.'

Rocco changed tack. 'I brought you up here to give you a chance to ... spill the beans, isn't that the expression?'

'About what?'

'About what you are doing here and why you wrecked the bar.'

'We were visiting, that's all. Like you said, seeing the cemeteries, a bit of food, some drink.' He shrugged. 'Yeah, okay, a lot of drink. The boys can get a bit excitable when they get away from the manor. Don't tell me you've never let rip before.'

'Manor?'

'The area where we live.'

Rocco gave a cold smile. 'Somehow I did not

53

think you meant a big house.' He scratched his chin. 'So, you came for a visit and ... it got out of hand. Is that all? Only, I have to say, Mr Tasker, the more I think about this, the more it seems to me to have been almost ... deliberate.'

Tasker shrugged. 'Think what you like. That's all I'm saying.' He scowled. 'What's Calloway making a statement about?'

'What do you think? About your visit. He's being very cooperative.'

There was a knock at the door. One of Godard's men opened it to reveal a *gardienne* – a woman officer – standing outside. She was slim, with short auburn hair and freckles across her nose.

Alix Poulon, Claude Lamotte's daughter.

At a nod from Rocco, she entered and placed a sheet of paper on the table in front of him. It was an estimate given by Madame Mote at the *Canard Doré* of the damage to the bar. Rocco whistled silently. She might have been shocked by the events, but it hadn't prevented her making an itemised and generous assessment of what she felt they were owed. He pushed it to one side and looked up to find Tasker's eyes fastened on Alix with the gleam of a predator.

'So, you got women cops now,' Tasker breathed, his eyes travelling slowly up Alix's body. 'Nice uniform. She fills it out well, too. Perks of the job, eh?' He glanced slyly at Rocco. 'Bet you been there and done that, ain'tcha, Rocco?' He laughed outright, his tongue flicking obscenely across his upper lip. 'I heard Froggie tarts know a few tricks. Never tried one meself. Maybe I should, eh?' He gave Alix a slow grin. 'Maybe I'll come back sometime and we can get together – what do you say?'

Rocco held up a hand. It was enough to stop Desmoulins and the two guards from moving forward. They hadn't understood Tasker's words, but the meaning was obvious, and Alix Poulon was sufficiently highly regarded around the station to engender an instinctive need to protect her.

'Take him downstairs,' Rocco said quietly.

'What a horrible character,' said Alix, once the men had gone. 'What did he say?'

'I think you can guess,' said Rocco. 'Men like him, their vocabulary is about as limited as their imagination.'

He decided he'd had enough. He'd let the magistrate deal with them in the morning and send them home again. There were far more important things for him to deal with than a bunch of drunks, no matter how unpleasant they were.

'Three mysteries in one day,' he said aloud, and picked up the small key. 'A vanishing *cinéma vérité* film crew, a missing body and a bunch of English hard men who don't know when to go home. And,' he added, 'I wonder why Mr Tasker was lying about this little item?'

CHAPTER EIGHT

'All hands on deck,' Desmoulins murmured. 'The bosses have landed.'

Rocco looked up from the case file he was working on to see *Commissaire* Massin striding along the glass-walled corridor running the length of the building, heading for the stairs to his office. Impeccable in his uniform, he was trailing behind him three men in dark suits, well coiffed and austere of face. Two looked neither right nor left, as if homing in on a target. The third man, a more leisurely three paces to the rear, ran a sharp look over the office, finally settling on Rocco and lingering a moment before flicking away. This man was tall and slim, with the athletic build and easy stride of a soldier.

Officials. Ministry men.

Rocco watched them go. No doubt Massin would put in an appearance later, showing off his terrain and his men, anxious to impress his visitors from the big city.

He knew Massin of old. The autocratic, ascetic and by-the-book police *commissaire* had been the same in the army in Indochina, when Rocco had witnessed him having a serious crisis of courage under fire. He hadn't set eyes on the man since escorting him off the battlefield to safety, until fate had intervened several months ago. Rocco had found himself transferred out from Paris on a new policing 'initiative' to spread investigative facilities around the provinces.

From Clichy to Picardie had been quite a change, from gangs to … well, anything, strange crash sites on a country road being the latest. But as Rocco had discovered very quickly, crime here was the same animal as anywhere else. It sometimes came disguised as something different, but crime it remained.

Coinciding with his transfer to the Amiens

region, Massin had turned up in his life once more. The atmosphere had been strained ever since, with Rocco fully expecting to be transferred out again at any moment. That it hadn't happened yet was a minor miracle, and probably due to Massin needing a period of calm and playing a waiting game until Rocco tripped up and gave him the excuse he needed.

Surprisingly, Massin and his three visitors stayed upstairs out of sight, with instructions issued for them not to be disturbed. Deputy *Commissaire* Perronnet did a brief tour instead, checking shift details and ongoing tasks while skilfully avoiding answering any questions about the identity of the three men.

'Bloody strange,' said Desmoulins.

The comings and goings went on for the rest of the day. Massin and his visitors went out for a late lunch, returning at the end of the afternoon when the shifts were changing. They looked sombre in spite of the break, raising speculation among the officers and staff who watched them pass by.

'Something's going on,' one of the desk sergeants professed knowingly. 'The top kepis don't act this secretive unless it's going to be bad news for the troops.'

'We could be in for a pay rise,' Desmoulins countered. 'Of course, I have been known to underestimate our esteemed superiors on numerous occasions before.'

Rocco continued working, using the period of calm to make sure his paperwork was in order. Joining in with the speculation was pointless; it broke down the barriers between the ranks in an entirely damaging way and encouraged rumour. But his cop's nose was beginning to make him uneasy. The men were right; something was going on.

Then the identity of the military-looking man came to him in a flash. He was neither Interior Ministry nor police. Rocco had seen the man once, maybe twice before, but only in passing. Colonel Jean-Philippe Saint-Cloud eschewed any kind of publicity, but was always much closer to the public than many would have believed, moving among them and seen only by those who knew where to look. Never identified by the press or Government, he had one purpose in life and one only: to run a top-class protection squad.

He was, in name at least, the president's chief bodyguard.

The three visitors and Massin were already in when Rocco arrived next morning. The atmosphere in the building was still tense, but Perronnet and Captain Canet were surprisingly calm, which gave Rocco a degree of confidence that nothing serious was about to happen. The brass had a way of channelling news without saying anything, so maybe the general feeling of suspicion had been misplaced.

He checked the overnight list of reports and early calls, and noted one from Claude Lamotte. A local vagrant known as Pantoufle had been reported missing by the priest of a village called Audelet, not far from Poissons and within Claude's patch. The man had a regular circular route around the area, which took in Audelet village church each Friday. That was the day Father Maurice handed out parcels of bread and cheese to the needy. His failure to turn up was sufficiently unusual for the priest to have alerted Claude.

Rocco was about to pass the task back to Claude to deal with, when he happened to glance at the large wall map of the region, idly tracing the usual route taken by Pantoufle from Audelet through Poissons and around the other nearby hamlets until he fetched up again back at Audelet.

The route ran along the same stretch of road where they had found the blood and the tooth.

CHAPTER NINE

'What do you know about this Pantoufle?' Rocco was driving his black Citroën Traction, with Claude in the passenger seat fiddling with the radio. They were on their way to see Father Maurice in Audelet. Rocco had never met the priest, and had asked Claude to come along in case he needed the familiarity of a known face. He had little time for men of any cloth and felt uncomfortable in their presence, as if they were trying to read his soul. It was fanciful rubbish, he knew that, but he preferred not to encourage them.

'He's a *clochard*,' Claude replied. 'A tramp. Always has been, I think – or as long as anyone can remember, anyway. Some say he was wounded in 1918 by a shellburst, and lost his memory. He's been wandering around the district ever since, sleeping in barns and under hedges. It's not his real name, by the way.'

Pantoufle. Slipper. Rocco thought the name oddly appropriate for a tramp, a gentleman of the road. A hobo, as the Americans called them. A hobo in slippers. 'What is his real name?'

'Nobody knows. He popped up in the area about forty years ago, I gather. People asked his name, but he always went blank. I asked him myself once; it was like looking into an empty bottle. Nothing there. After a while, people gave up. Then some wag gave him the name Pantoufle because he always wore slippers, even on the road. Reckoned proper shoes hurt his feet. He must have gone through a few thousand pairs over the years. The name stuck. He's genial enough and harmless, so they leave him alone.'

Rocco wondered if they were chasing a false line of enquiry. All the indications at the crash scene pointed to a serious injury or death. But add in the report of a missing person – a tramp – who frequented the very road where the crash had happened, and it was hard to ignore the possibility that the two might be connected. While he was certain that Massin would want him to concentrate on more serious issues, there was something about the information at the crash scene which had remained with him, as if it were trying to convey a message. The only way to get to the bottom of it was to clarify at least this aspect and prove that this particular person wasn't involved.

'About Alix,' Claude continued after a while, sounding uncomfortable. 'I didn't mean to imply anything before – you know that, right? It's just that ... well, I worry about her. She's not as tough as she makes out.' He clamped his mouth shut and looked out the window at the passing greenery.

'You have every right to worry,' Rocco replied. 'Let's be honest, she's what the Americans would call a hot dame. Of course, we'll make sure you're the first to know when we decide to get together.'

Claude's head snapped round, his mouth open. 'What?'

'Calm down, you idiot. I'm kidding. Anyway, how do I know she won't turn out to look like you in a few years?' He shuddered. 'That doesn't bear thinking about.'

'Bloody cheek!' Claude pretended to be disgruntled. 'She looks like her mother, if you must know – and she was a real beauty. You could do worse than–' He stopped. 'What am I saying? It's just that ... Alix speaks highly of you. Says you're an honourable cop – for a man.' He reached out for the radio. 'It's just that I–'

'I know what you were thinking. Stop worrying.'

Honourable. That wasn't a word Rocco or any other cop heard too often. And he was pretty sure it didn't apply to him. He'd bent the rules occasionally when it suited him, although usually to get closer to securing evidence and a conviction, never to implicate an innocent man. Not very long ago, days after Alix had joined the Amiens district, he'd deliberately disposed of a piece of evidence from a murder case. He'd done it knowing that an investigation would have achieved nothing, unless you called it nothing to track down and prosecute a terrified young mother fighting for her life and

61

the life of her child. A conviction hadn't been likely, anyway, in his view, even if they'd managed to find her.

Fortunately, she'd disappeared like smoke, probably out of the country, and Rocco had thrown away the one bit of evidence likely to have been used against her: the weapon she had used to defend herself.

Although Alix had been close when he'd disposed of the weapon in the canal, it had been too dark for her to have seen. But she had to have known what he'd done. She hadn't spoken about it, then or since. The shared knowledge had bound them together, somehow, loosely knotted but unbreakable. Yet distant.

Audelet turned out to be larger than Poissons, but not by much. A collection of houses, a church, two cafés, a small garage and a crumbling chateau with a sad, neglected air and sheep grazing around the grounds. Rocco counted two cars and a tractor as they entered the village, and two pedestrians. And a horse walking along the road untended, minding its own business. Compared with Poissons, it was almost humming with activity.

He pulled into the inevitable square and parked in front of the church. It was neat and solid, the way of all churches in the region, and grimly austere. Or maybe it was just him.

He and Claude climbed out and walked up the path alongside the church to a small house with flowers around the door. At least that was a good sign.

Father Maurice was waiting for them. He

62

poured coffee into thick brown cups and offered a box of sugar lumps and a metal jug of fresh milk, the kind children carried to the farm to fetch their daily quota, with a handle and a metal lid. After Clichy and its air of sophistication, where milk came from a store in a cold sealed container, it was like stepping back in time. But Rocco was getting used to it, like lots of things around here.

Such as a priest who wasn't wearing a dog collar.

Father Maurice was dressed in baggy corduroys and a heavyweight knitted jumper. He was smoking a dark-brown cigarillo, waving away the smoke with a beefy hand, and looked more fisherman than cleric. In Clichy, Paris, priests wore their uniform like a badge, to give them an identity in a bustling, impatient world. Out here, not everyone conformed to type.

'Pantoufle is a complex character,' the priest said, pushing the filled cups across the table. 'He's war-damaged, like many others, and deserving of our understanding.' He eyed Rocco keenly. 'A man of your age and experience, I imagine you've been there, Inspector? War, I mean.'

Rocco said nothing. His war history was none of this man's business. But he was prepared to let the priest get to the point, as long as it didn't include a spot of God-fearing psychoanalysis along the way.

He made do with a shrug.

'Of course, many men learn to live with it. But Pantoufle?' Father Maurice flicked ash from his cigarillo. 'Whatever happened to him left no visible scars ... and no idea of who he used to be. Or maybe he chose to leave that person behind

63

deliberately. A sad case but not unusual.' He glanced at Rocco beneath bushy eyebrows. 'You have some news about him?'

'That's what I'd like to establish,' Rocco replied easily. They were back on the safe ground of earthly investigations. 'We don't have a body, if that's what you mean. But we do have this.' He reached into his pocket and took out the button he'd found at the crash scene. It was wrapped in a fold of paper. Without showing the priest what it was, he asked, 'Did Pantoufle have a full set of teeth?'

Father Maurice looked surprised by the question, but recovered quickly. 'Um ... yes, he did. Well, nearly a full set. There were a few gaps here and there, now I come to think of it.' He looked at Claude for support. Claude nodded but said nothing. 'Men of his lifestyle don't, always. Hygiene and self-care are not high on their agendas and Pantoufle ... well, he was eccentric and disconnected, I think one might call it. But he was no different in that respect. Why?'

Rocco unwrapped the button and placed it on the table. It lay there, winking in the daylight. He had cleaned off the worst of the blood and mud.

'Goodness.' It was obvious by his expression that Father Maurice recognised the button instantly. He crossed himself with an economic flick of his thumb, an instinctive warding off of evil. 'Where did you get this?'

'You recognise it?'

'Yes, I do. It was one of several on the old man's jacket.' He stared at Rocco. 'I know what you're going to ask, Inspector: why should I recognise a simple button?'

'And I hope you're going to tell me.'

'It's very easy. One of our helpers, a wonderful woman – she used to be a mission worker in Gabon – noticed one day that Pantoufle had lost all the buttons from his jacket. He had a habit of twisting them – a bit like a child does when anxious – until they fell off. Anyway, she came in one Friday, when we were giving out food, and persuaded him to take off his jacket so she could replace the buttons. He wasn't keen to begin with, but she showed him these birthday buttons from a child's coat that was too damaged to give away, and he agreed. She sewed them on using fishing line so he couldn't twist them off.' He stared down at the button and pushed it with the tip of his finger. 'Where did you find it? Could it have fallen off and he's out there wandering–'

'I'm sorry, Father,' Rocco interrupted him. This wasn't a family matter and he saw no point in pretending there was any great chance of finding the missing vagrant alive. Besides, experience told him that most people preferred the truth rather than false hope. 'We found it at the scene of a car crash. There was no sign of a body, but the indications are that he might have been hit by a car or a truck.'

'Indications? Inspector, come on – I used to do work in Africa. I'm not going to faint with shock.'

'There was a lot of blood.'

'I see.' A repeat flick of the hand as Father Maurice crossed himself. 'I'll say a prayer for him this evening.'

'Do whatever you think is best.' Rocco finished

his coffee and scooped up the button. He would have to speak to Simeon again; the man might recall seeing Pantoufle in the area just before the crash. 'Only I don't think prayer's done him a lot of good so far.'

CHAPTER TEN

'Do you think that's it?' said Claude, once they were outside. 'It's just one button.'

'You tell me.' Rocco led the way back to the car. 'What's your instinct?'

Claude puffed and clambered into the passenger seat with a sigh. 'Yes, you're right. He was too much a man of habit to miss some free food.' He stared out of the window towards the church. 'I'd still like to find him, though. It doesn't feel right, him being out there somewhere.'

'Same here.' Rocco started the car. 'I'd also like to find out how he died.'

Claude said, 'You don't like the clergy much, do you?'

'I've never found one I'd care to share a car with, no.'

Claude's eyebrows shot up and down, and he smiled. 'Thanks – I'll take that as a compliment.' He turned on the radio and began spinning the dial.

As they drove out of the village, Rocco was surprised to see Simeon standing by the side of the road, waving them down. His old moped was

66

leaning against a concrete lamp post. Rocco pulled over and stopped.

'Can I help you?'

'Other way round, Inspector,' the old farmer replied. 'It's I who can help you. I've just remembered something else about that business yesterday.'

'Like what?'

'There was someone else out there.'

Rocco felt his spirits plummet. With some witnesses, it was like their memory came in dribbles, each one smaller and more distant than the last. It was as if they couldn't let go, determined to recall every detail until, inevitably, they began to remember things which had never happened.

'Pantoufle, I know. We're trying to find him. We think he's dead.'

'What makes you say that? I know about the blood and stuff. But it wasn't him I saw.'

'Who, then?'

'There was someone in the wood, watching what was going on. A man. But not Pantoufle – I'd know him immediately. I only worked it out this morning; it was bothering me all night. He was standing right at the back of the trees – in shadow. Just watching. But as I was leaving, I heard a motorbike moving away after the crash. Not hurrying, though – like he was being careful not to make too much noise.'

'He might have been with the other men,' said Claude.

'The cameraman,' Rocco agreed, and wondered how he'd missed the signs. Taking a leak, most likely, away from his precious equipment.

Odd lapse in timing, though, with all the action going on out front.

'That's just it, Inspector; he was riding along the track in the opposite direction. I mean, if he was with the others, why go the other way?'

CHAPTER ELEVEN

George Tasker stared out through the window as the Calais train drifted slowly into the channel port, and shifted uncomfortably on the shiny plastic seat. He'd be glad to get off this cattle wagon and hit the ferry bar for a few bevvies. Set himself up for their arrival back in the smoke. That's when the tough questions would start.

'What do you reckon they'll say?' said Calloway, voicing their collective concerns.

Tasker shrugged, feigning indifference, although he didn't feel it. 'Search me. We'll soon find out, won't we?' He gave a nasty smile and looked around at the other men. 'Nothing's changed, right? You let me do the talking. If the bosses ask, we did what we came to do. Any of you talk out of turn, you'll have me to answer to. Got it?'

Privately, he wasn't looking forward to getting back. They'd been told to keep it going for at least two days, hopefully tying up resources as much as they could, creating a logjam for the simple country Frenchies to fight their way out of. He'd have done it, too, if it hadn't been for Calloway getting a sneak phone call out to one of his friends. Bloody nancy boy was too clever for his own good, fooling the guards with that lame story. He was asking for a good smack ... and he'd get one if this all went tits up because of that call.

He was also niggled by the way the French cop, Rocco, had questioned Calloway first. Being overlooked in front of the others was something he wasn't used to, and the more he thought about it the more it got under his skin. He had a name and reputation in London and across the South, and it had been earned the hard way. Having some snooty Frog copper treat him like a nobody just wasn't on. Christ, he got more respect from the Sweeney – the Flying Squad. He was also annoyed at the game Rocco had played. Calloway hadn't been writing a statement at all; he'd been kept in an adjacent room, then put back in with the others while Tasker was being questioned. Unfortunately, Tasker had already given him a rough time before anyone had clued him in.

And there was the truck key. He shifted in his seat; he'd made a mistake there. He should have told Rocco it was his front door key or something. Instead he'd fluffed it and ended up sounding false. Still, what were the chances they'd connect the key to the truck? It was a blank copy with no serial number or brand name, so no way would they trace it back.

He sniffed at the strong smell of stale seawater and engine smoke. At least they were getting off French soil; he didn't like France or the French, and if he never came back, it would be too soon. Except that he was beginning to fantasise about having a quiet talk with Rocco – preferably down a dark alley. Nobody treated him like second best. And that woman copper with the nice arse; now, she was something else. He'd like to get her down a dark alley, too. Only it wouldn't be to do any talking.

'You reckon the big guy was an ordinary copper, George?' Fletcher asked. He hadn't said much since last night, which had surprised nobody. With the face on him, it was clear he was still fighting off the effects of all the booze he'd poured down his gullet in the bar.

'Nah. Just another French bean picker, full of himself because he could speak English.' He wanted to add that it was lucky Rocco had had the other cops there, but he knew it would sound false. Sod 'em. Let them think what they liked.

'He didn't look much like a bumpkin to me,' Calloway murmured. 'Not the way he was dressed. Expensive clothes, good shoes. Quality stuff ... for a bumpkin.' He smiled and stretched his legs, and Tasker very nearly launched himself across the carriage to wipe the grin off his face. He'd have enjoyed shoving his fist down that smarmy throat. But starting a fight here wasn't clever, and anyway, Calloway wasn't without influential friends back in London; friends of people who paid Tasker his wages. No, now they were out, they had to stay out and get home.

'Forget him,' he growled. 'And once we're on the boat, keep your mouths shut. There's too many people about who'll be earwigging what we say. So button it.' He stared at Calloway in particular. 'And you all know who we'll have to deal with if word gets out about what we were doing.'

That put a dampener on the atmosphere, until Fletcher looked up and said, 'I suppose we could always go and join the Richardsons.'

The comment was met by a stunned silence all round. There were certain names that were never mentioned in some quarters, and the Richardsons, who ran a gang south of the river, sat right at the top of the list.

Tasker shook his head. He wasn't smiling, and everyone knew why: it was the thought of what might happen if a certain someone closer to home took the way the operation had gone the wrong way.

'Glad you're feeling so bloody cocky, Fletch,' Tasker breathed finally. 'Just remember, when they ask who cut the operation short by crocking that truck, there's only one name in the frame – and it ain't mine.'

While Tasker and his men were travelling home, Rocco drove back to the scene of the crash thinking about what had happened here, trying to build a series of images in his mind to match the location. Was it simply a bit of wild filming which had gone wrong? Or a bizarre accident? If so, why out here? What the hell were the odds of a truck and a smart car coming to grief together in the middle of nowhere like this?

He walked along the road from the supposed point of impact to the trees. Remembering what Simeon had said about the watcher, he scouted round the back of the small copse and found where someone had arrived on a moped or motorcycle, and had pulled the machine onto its

71

stand, leaving two indentations in the mud behind the trees. It was away from the track, he noted, and far enough to one side to be out of sight from anyone taking a casual glance.

So, the men involved in the crash had had a covert watcher. Interesting.

He walked back to the car. It was the small details of an incident that very often told the full story; the details that were missed at first glance, or were concealed by accident or intent. Among that detail was often some anecdotal fact thrown up by a witness like Simeon, which might have no obvious significance, yet which turned out to be fundamental to an investigation.

And right now, he felt he was missing too much.

CHAPTER TWELVE

'Shut the door, Inspector.' Massin was seated behind his desk, shuffling through a thin batch of papers. He gestured to a chair and continued reading for a moment, then sat back and looked at Rocco. 'You appear to have consigned a group of English visitors to the cells. Would you care to explain why?'

'They got drunk and wrecked a bar.' Rocco wondered where this was going, although he could guess. Massin was having a twitch about the treatment of foreigners. He had no doubt found out about the reasons for the men's detention from Canet, but had clearly chosen to go head-to-head about it.

'Is that all – a bar brawl?'

'By "wrecked", I mean destroyed. They also assaulted the owner and Desmoulins got a head-butt to the face. A magistrate was lined up to deal with them today.'

'Is Desmoulins all right?'

'He'll survive.'

'So why were you involved? I would have thought you had better things to be doing than dealing with drunks on the rampage.'

'I was called in because I speak English. They were being difficult.'

'I see.' Massin flicked at a piece of fluff on his desk and arranged a pencil in line with his blotter. 'Well, I've had the prisoners released and put on a train to Calais.' He held up a hand to stop Rocco's automatic reaction. 'Not my doing, I assure you. I actually agreed with your actions; a spot of time in the cells would have done them good. But...' He shrugged. 'They should be on the boat by now.'

'Orders from the Ministry?' Rocco bit hard down on the words he really wanted to utter. Querying Massin's unwillingness to stand up to the senior drones in the Ministry would not have improved the prickly relationship that existed between them. Besides, he was puzzled by Massin's obvious air of discomfort. Maybe, he thought, it was merely a spot of verbal indigestion at having agreed with his decision to hold the men in the first place.

'In a manner of speaking.' Massin pursed his lips. 'It seems representations were made to the Ministry very early this morning by the British

73

consulate office in Lille, originating from the office of a member of the British Parliament.'

'What?' Rocco had difficulty relating the men he'd seen with any member of the British Government. He was aware that even politicians were rarely the best judges of the company they kept, but picturing any public servant interested in helping out a man like Tasker took a real stretch of the imagination. He wondered instinctively about who had made the phone call to London in the first place.

'How did the British find out?'

'One of the men...' Massin leant forward and checked a note on his blotter. '...named Calloway, indicated that he had chest pains and needed some allergy tablets. The duty officer quite rightly didn't want to take a chance of a foreign prisoner dying in custody, but he couldn't find an appropriate remedy here. Calloway asked permission to call his doctor in London for information.'

So Calloway spoke French – or, at least, enough. It showed he was smart, even devious, and he knew how to talk to people. It was more than could be said of the other thugs.

'Don't tell me: there was no doctor.'

'Probably not. Less than an hour later, the Ministry called and recommended the release of all five men.' He waved a hand. 'It's hard to accept, I know, after what they did. But the Ministry's concern was that we should show willing ... in the interests of international relations, you understand. The men deposited a sum of money to compensate the owner of the *Canard Doré*. He's lucky – it'll allow him to refurbish the dump.' He shuffled the papers on his desk and sat up, smoothly changing the subject. 'However, that is not why I asked you in here.' His expression grew grave.

Great, thought Rocco. *Here it comes.* Remembered hurts coming back to bite him.

But Massin surprised him. 'This is confidential for the time being, but I know you will not discuss this outside. I have just been briefed about what appears to be another attempt on the life of the president, two days ago. Thankfully, it failed, which is a blessing, of course.'

'Another?' How many attempts had there been on de Gaulle over the years? Some said it was already more even than there had been on Adolf Hitler. Unless you counted the efforts of British Bomber Command; that would increase the numbers a fair bit.

Massin sighed. 'Perhaps it would be simpler if you read the summary yourself.' He passed a sheet of paper across to Rocco and stood up, taking a walk around the room.

There wasn't much to it, culled, no doubt from an official release which would be going out sooner or later. What there was did not vary much from some of the other abortive attempts on the life of de Gaulle. One of the fleet of official Government cars had been heading south-east from Paris on the N19 near Guignes, some forty kilometres from the city centre, accompanied by two *Garde Mobile* outriders, when men with automatic weapons had opened fire from a belt of trees at the side of the road. The car had been slowing down for some roadworks – fake, as it had turned out – and the attackers had used the opportunity to hose it down with bullets. A classic ambush technique.

Fortunately, one of the outriders had been thrown from his bike into a culvert and, although wounded, had been able to draw his weapon and give covering fire. After several minutes, the gunmen had abandoned their attempt and driven away in a stolen Simca Ariane, later found abandoned. They had left behind one of their number dead, identified as a renegade former NCO dismissed from the French military some years before.

To Rocco, it was disturbingly familiar. In August 1962, in Le Petit-Clamart, a southwestern suburb of Paris, an attempt had been made on de Gaulle's life by men from the OAS – the *Organisation Armée Secrète* – a group opposed to any idea of Algerian independence and formed by a mix of military and civilians, colonists and students. The man said to be the driving force behind the attempt, Jean-Marie Bastien-Thiry, a former lieutenant colonel and weapons engineer, had since been convicted and executed just months ago, in March. It had become a landmark event, stirring up old hatreds and enmities and polarising further the extremes on all sides.

Rocco put the paper down. Nothing much had changed, then.

'They're still trying.' And pretty desperate, he figured, to use a Simca Ariane as a getaway car. Hardly a powerful vehicle – unless they'd been trying to blend in to the background – it was never going to win any races pursued by vengeful security personnel.

76

'It would seem so.' Massin returned to his seat and steepled his fingers. 'Fortunately, the attackers had been misinformed. The car was not carrying General de Gaulle, but a junior member of cabinet taking important documents out to the president's residence in Colombey-les-deux-Eglises.'

Rocco let a few seconds go by while assessing the implications, during which he could hear a clock ticking on the wall behind him. 'Misinformed?' It was an odd choice of word to use. 'Did they have someone on the inside?'

Massin waved a hand. 'Clearly they knew about *a* car. But not the correct one.'

Rocco let it go. 'It's a long way to take important documents by car.' Colombey was over two hundred kilometres from the centre of Paris. As far as he knew, the president normally flew down by helicopter. Clearly the same courtesy wasn't extended to official documents ... or to members of his staff.

'I agree. But it is not our place to comment on that.'

'What about the passenger?'

'Dead. Although an official vehicle, the car was not armoured. The driver was seriously wounded and not expected to live. It was a salutary lesson that the President's enemies have not given up.'

Rocco said nothing. Another one to add to the lengthening list of assassination attempts on the country's leader. He was ambivalent about many things de Gaulle had achieved, but he didn't discount the man's utter commitment to his country. If it had been him in the hot seat, he'd have given up the job long ago and taken up

77

knitting. Maybe de Gaulle hadn't yet got the message that someone didn't like him – although that wasn't a thought he could share with Massin; the man had a broomstick up his back about anyone in power and lacked the ability to see the occasional absurdities in life.

'Is that anything to do with why the colonel was here?'

Massin threw him a sharp look. 'You know Saint-Cloud?'

'Not personally. But I know what he does for a living.'

Massin looked slightly peeved, as if he had had his thunder stolen. 'The colonel and his colleagues were here on a fact-finding visit. You should not read anything into that. As a region, we are no more important than any other for future itineraries. But it makes good sense to check that all is well here should the president decide to include us in any future tour.'

'Does that mean he's coming or not?' Rocco felt a momentary impatience with Massin's tortuous evasiveness. Either he knew de Gaulle was planning on coming to the region or he wasn't; pretending otherwise was a waste of time.

'I cannot say.' Massin sniffed and stretched his neck against his shirt collar, as if the admission was being wrenched out of him. 'All I can say is, you should be aware that increased security measures in light of this latest attempt will mean everyone will be expected to be in attendance. If we are given the green light, I don't need to tell you that every potential hazard will be investigated in advance.'

'By "hazard", you mean threat.'

'Yes. Colonel Saint-Cloud and his staff are checking a list of known agitators, and this will be circulated to all offices in the region. But I'm sure you know which groups they include.'

Rocco nodded. Take your pick. OAS. Resistance veterans. Military men. Communists. Government conspirators. Police. Students. Algerians. The CIA. The British. The favoured list among conspiracy nuts was endless. Even NATO had taken a crack, so rumour had it, a temper tantrum in response to de Gaulle's decision to withdraw French military facilities from the organisation. Rocco didn't believe that one, if only because it would have required a full council meeting and de Gaulle's signature to assassinate himself. He doubted even *Le Grand Charles* was capable of that level of arrogance.

'What do you want me to do?' He still couldn't figure out why Massin had told him all this. Somehow he doubted this was an occasion for covering his back.

'You may need to assist in preventing anything happening. As you know, Saint-Cloud runs a very small group, albeit very effective in what it does do. But while he is away checking routes and itineraries, he cannot do his main job, which is to oversee closely the protection of the president.' He rearranged the already immaculate pencil. 'It would be a disaster if anything were to happen in this region.'

Rocco nearly laughed at the outrageousness of the build-up. So Massin was covering his back after all. He asked, 'Why me?'

Massin hesitated before answering, a flicker of something approaching doubt on his face. Then he said, 'Because Colonel Saint-Cloud suggested it. He asked for names and selected you. His own team is stretched very thin, so he is having to use whatever facilities he can. Meet him here tomorrow at nine for a briefing.'

'I've never been called a facility before,' Rocco murmured dryly. 'But I'll do what I can.' *Short,* he thought, *of deliberately throwing myself in the way of a bullet, anyway.*

Massin's eyes were hooded when he looked up. 'I'm delighted to hear it. I trust you will not let me down. You hear me?'

Home in Poissons earlier than usual, Rocco called in at the co-op store for some meat for dinner. Mme Drolet, the owner, fluttered her eyelashes and hurried round the end of the counter on high heels to join him, bringing with her a rush of perfume and powder.

'I've got some nice cutlets,' she suggested breathlessly. 'Very filling for a big man like you.'

'Thanks,' he said, wondering if she spoke to Delsaire, the plumber, this way. He'd met Madame Delsaire, who looked the sort to eat thistles for breakfast. 'I'll just take some minced beef.'

'Don't you know how to cook cutlets?' She reached up and patted her hair, which was frozen in some kind of unmoving, shimmering beehive. 'I could pop down and do them for you, if you like.'

'There's no need–'

'It's really no problem. I'm nearly done here. Just give me fifteen minutes to freshen up.'

If she was any fresher, Rocco decided, she'd be as crisp as a newly peeled endive. He pointed at a piece of beef under the glass and said, 'That minced would be fine. Really.'

She gave him a half smile, one eyebrow curving upwards. 'There's no need to be frightened, Inspector ... I was only offering to cook, you know.' She picked up the beef and fed it through the mincer, turning the handle with what seemed unnecessary vigour, and he wondered whether she had eaten any husbands in the past.

At the house he rented down the lane from the village square, he found some eggs in a basket on the front step. Mme Denis, his neighbour, making sure he was well stocked with the basics in life. Some days it was vegetables, others it was fruit. Today eggs.

He glanced through the fence separating their properties and caught a fleeting glimpse of the old lady ducking indoors, and smiled. She habitually wore an apron over a grey dress, and a triangle of headscarf pinned over her head. It was her uniform, her and others of her age; a sign of cleanliness, hard work and a lack of show. She was an independent old bird, and had become fiercely protective of the *flic* living next door. Her defensiveness had even included flinging hot tisane in a man's face when he'd threatened her with a gun, saving Rocco's life in the process.

'You think because I'm old I'm a charity case?' she had once asked him, eyes flashing dangerously behind thick glasses. Rocco had just offered to take her out for a meal in return for all her kindness since he'd arrived in the village. Big mistake. 'You are a welcome guest here, Inspector,' she'd explained primly. 'We look after our guests.'

'In that case,' he'd replied, 'feel free to go out on the town and get drunk and disorderly, and I'll make sure they drop any charges.'

She'd giggled and told him she would hold him to it.

The interior of the house was cold. He lit the fire and fixed dinner, then rang Claude to check if there were any developments from Father Maurice. There were none. Wherever Pantoufle had disappeared to, it was not looking good.

He did a stint at the ancient hand pump out in the garden. It was reluctant to draw water, a sure sign that the cold in the atmosphere was reaching freezing levels once more. He'd already had to set a fire around it to loosen the ice more than once, and would no doubt have to do so again. The laying of pipes in the road outside had been completed and covered over, but there the work had stopped, nobody knew why.

Back indoors, the *fouines* – fruit rats – were skittering back and forth in the loft as if excited by his return. They seemed oblivious to the drop in temperature and intent on playing their nightly games instead of hibernating. Rocco had become used to them, finding their presence oddly comforting. He still wasn't sure who was the guest and who the host here, but so far, the relationship had worked well.

And in his experience, there were far worse rats in the world to deal with.

CHAPTER THIRTEEN

Up close, Rocco thought Colonel Jean-Philippe Saint-Cloud, formerly Lt Colonel of the *1er Régiment Étranger de Parachutistes* – 1st Foreign Parachute Regiment – looked older than his walk or demeanour showed. He had sallow skin, but still possessed the build and apparent vitality of a younger man. His neat moustache and haircut *en brosse* were clear visual clues to his military background, as were the neat double-breasted suit and highly polished shoes, and the tie knot as tight and hard as a nut.

He was waiting for Rocco at the front desk, staring into the middle distance and ignoring the gaggle of overnight miscreants gathered for logging or release, depending on their offences. He turned and led Rocco without greeting through the office, where the daily briefing was being conducted by *Commissaire* Perronnet and Captain Canet. Numerous pairs of eyes swivelled to follow as Rocco and the security chief passed down the corridor, which made Rocco question how discreet his involvement with Saint-Cloud was going to be.

'Sit down, Inspector.' Saint-Cloud led the way into an empty office and closed the door. 'Thank you for being so prompt.' His voice was calm, with the quiet confidence of a man accustomed to his authority. He sat and crossed his legs, his move-

83

ments economic and controlled. He put Rocco in mind of an attack dog he'd once seen in a scrapyard: not the slavering, snarling beast most commonly imagined, but a quiet, almost serene animal with quite possibly the most evil eyes he'd ever seen.

Rocco sat and waited. This was probably one of the most powerful men in the land. But it wasn't through any position in the chain of command, rather his close association with the president. In fact, there was rumoured to be only one man closer, and that was the main physical bodyguard himself, Paul Comiti, a man sworn to protect de Gaulle to the death.

Saint-Cloud, however, was the organiser, the bureaucrat with quiet muscle, always behind the scenes, pulling strings, making arrangements. To him fell the task of keeping the president's visits and sorties as minutely planned and as secure as possible. At the point of contact with the public, however, it was down to Comiti's small team of men to catch the bullet.

So far, they had succeeded in their job against many expectations and attempts.

'You have an impressive record, Rocco,' Saint-Cloud continued. 'Both in the army and the police. You were in Indochina, I believe.'

Rocco nodded. As were the 1st RÉP, he recalled. A tough bunch of men, they had been disbanded in 1961 following service in Algeria. It seemed Lt Colonel Saint-Cloud had moved on to better, if not bigger, things.

'What can I do for you, Colonel?' he asked. He wanted to find out what this man wanted of him, not to relive old war stories.

'I want you to do your duty as a sworn police officer and help protect the president, of course.' Saint-Cloud's eyebrows lifted slightly, as if surprised by Rocco's blunt approach. 'I appreciate this is not your normal work, and I'm sure you have many pressing matters to investigate. But as the man on the ground here, I would like to seek your cooperation in ensuring that those ... forces keen to confront the president with violence are not successful. You've heard about the latest attempt?'

'I have.'

'Badly planned, poorly executed, but a clear warning that we cannot relax our guard while the dangers still exist.' He studied his fingernails. 'I need you to act as our eyes and ears on the matter of security in this area. Other of your colleagues spread around the country are doing the same. It is vital that you unearth anything – any group or individual – threatening the safety of the president, and by inference, France.'

'Don't you have files on these people already?' Rocco was puzzled. As far as he was aware, the names of the main conspirators were well documented and their movements monitored and recorded. Unless Saint-Cloud was holding something back, he wasn't sure what new groups or individuals were out there or where they had emerged from. Many of the existing ones had originated years before, some no doubt now advancing in age and lacking in strength, numbers or organisation. It took energy and commitment to keep anti-government groups active, especially when no certain progress in their aims was being made. Other groups, younger ones, such as students, were more difficult to pin down because they were harder to infiltrate due to their age, or lacked the cohesiveness required to mount an effective attack. But even they eventually became careless, and were generally known to the authorities.

'We have extensive files, of course.' Saint-Cloud tilted his head to one side, reminding Rocco of a teacher many years ago who used a similar tactic to make his students uneasy. 'But these organisations are not static; they gain new members all the time, often bringing with them new grievances and new agendas. Others leave, tempted by new arguments or impatient to pursue a new line of aggression. As such, their public faces change. Our job is to find the more focused activists before they can achieve their objectives.'

'So when is he coming here?'

For a moment the colonel looked as though he were about to respond. Then he shook his head. 'That is not clear. You will, of course, be advised should a date and itinerary be decided.' He brushed an imaginary speck of lint from his knee. 'Be aware that, for now, we believe the main threat to his person comes from disaffected elements of the military who have joined with the OAS and ... others.'

'Others?'

'Mercenaries. Assassins. Men who will do anything for money. This latest attempt seems to be a mix of both. The dead attacker was a former army officer who supported the OAS, and we think at least one of his colleagues may have been Corsican or Sicilian.'

Rocco didn't waste time thinking about it. There were always members of groups who were on the periphery, not quite as involved as the hard core, but headstrong and useful as soldiers. Expendable. To concentrate on them was to miss the main members, the heart of any organisation and usually consisting of no more than a fanatical handful. And that handful rarely, if ever, allowed their soldiers to lead back to them.

'There's one thing that puzzles me about that,' said Rocco, echoing his comment to Massin. 'Why were official documents being transferred in a car?'

Saint-Cloud scowled before replying. 'A grave mistake, in my opinion. I have already raised it with my superiors. It was felt the car would go untouched because the president was known to be at his country retreat and not on the move. Clearly, however, the people mounting the attack didn't share that knowledge. There is, on the other hand,' he continued, seemingly choosing his words with care, 'an element, shall we say, who believe that drawing out attackers might show the direction any future effort will be coming from; that such an assault would reveal their hand.'

'An element?'

'Internal Security.'

Jesus. Rocco was amazed. 'An ordinary government car? No armour-proofing and just two outriders?'

'Correct.' The colonel had his eyes half shut, effectively screening his thoughts.

87

'But that was putting the driver and passenger in harm's way.'

'We have no basis for assuming that.' Saint-Cloud's answer was non-committal, but as good as a yes in Rocco's mind. He wondered at the kind of people employed in the upper echelons of authority, the kind of men who decided these things.

'Who the hell thought of that bright idea?' The words were out before he could stop them. A planned ruse to draw out an attacker was one thing, usually involving backup forces and a calculated degree of safety for those being used as bait – in this case the car and occupants. But an ad hoc affair like this one, if true, was madness.

Saint-Cloud shrugged, the universal sloughing of responsibility for actions sane men did not wish to contemplate. 'Undoubtedly it was a committee decision,' he suggested dryly. 'It usually is.'

'So what do you want me to do?' Rocco sought to bring the discussion back on track. 'I have no information on these groups. I hope you do?'

'Of course. I will make available to you any names we have in this area. It will be a start point. At this stage we merely need to check their movements without alerting them to that fact.'

A lot of footwork, in other words, Rocco thought. He'd need some help if there were many names, preferably someone unknown who could go unnoticed in the area. 'Can I use any resources?'

'You have someone in mind – someone outside this force?' Saint-Cloud was ahead of him.

'I do. But he might not agree.' Caspar, he thought ... if he wasn't too far gone. A former undercover cop who had operated too close to the shadows for too long, Marc Casparon had been placed on permanent sick leave, deemed no longer effective. Rocco had used him since, but it had been a close-run thing and he'd nearly come to grief. He'd check with Michel Santer first. If anyone knew Caspar's present state, his former boss in Clichy would.

'If you can trust this person without revealing too much, go ahead.' Saint-Cloud paused, eyes on Rocco's face. 'There is one other thing.'

'Yes?'

'You have been assigned to work with me, which has been cleared by the Interior Ministry. As such, bearing in mind the, ah ... delicacy of the situation, you are not to discuss these matters with anyone else in this station.'

'You mean apart from *Commissaire* Massin?'

A slow shake of the head. 'I mean anyone.'

CHAPTER FOURTEEN

'So. You lost the car and the truck. You smashed up a bar. Then you got tossed out of the country. All within forty-eight hours. Nice going, George.' The words dripped into the room with a total lack of emotion, and George Tasker felt the skin go cold across his shoulders. The 'nice going' was not a term of praise. Not around this man. 'Nice' wasn't good enough; 'nice' was for jobs half done and therefore unsatisfactory. Especially when delivered in this half-dead tone of voice.

As soon as he and the other men had got back to London, Tasker had been summoned to this upstairs room at the rear of a club called The Old Bourbon, in Stepney, and told to let the others go until they were needed. One of several properties spread across the city, it was more an occasional meeting point than a regular office, and owned – on paper, at least – by a friend of the man sitting in front of him. For that reason alone, Tasker was beginning to wonder if there wasn't a more sinister reason for him being called here.

When displeased with anyone, it was common practice to make their final meeting at a location which couldn't be linked directly back, should anything go wrong.

By 'wrong', read 'dead'.

His throat had gone suddenly dry. He coughed. 'That's right, boss. But we figured since the car was going to be cut up and the truck torched, it was no problem.' He shifted uneasily on the hardback chair, trying to find the words to deflect attention away from what was clearly being seen as a failure on his part.

'Of course they were. Not the point, though, is it? It was meant to go on longer, wasn't it? That was the plan.' The man behind the desk played a slow drum tattoo on his thumbnail with a gold pen, the tap-tap loud and ominous in the quiet room. Heavily inscribed and crowned with a dark-red ruby, a nod of admiration to the man holding it, the pen was rumoured to have been a gift from an admirer named 'Topper' Harris. Harris, the wealthy owner of a string of betting shops across the South East, was now dead and buried after an ostentatious funeral cortège complete with carriage and black horses down the Mile End Road, East London.

It had been Gerald 'Ruby' Ketch who had arranged the hit, just as he'd subsequently arranged the flashy sendoff funeral. But everyone knew that the orders had come from his employers, known only as the Twins. Ketch was a frontman, but wielded considerable power. His was the day-to-day running of the Firm, as the gang was known, but every move was monitored by his bosses, who reigned supreme in their manor but discreetly out of the picture.

Following several close calls with the police, and excessive interest from the Metropolitan Police Flying Squad, they had taken an apparent back seat, leaving Ketch to take over operations. It left him more exposed than them, but he was well paid for the risk and took his job seriously.

And he didn't want to end up in the ground like some others in the past, enemies real or imagined.

The funeral had been no more than a cynical East End stunt, a warning to anyone else who fancied changing sides. Seen allegedly talking to the Richardson gang who operated in South London, the dead man had been scooped up and shot dead with little hesitation. Rivals in crime, the Richardsons operated slots, protection rackets and the large-scale handling of stolen goods. Even being seen on their manor was viewed as a betrayal with only one outcome.

Unfortunately late for the dead man, it had emerged that he was innocent, and had been set up by another gang member. He had died vainly protesting his innocence, closely followed by his accuser, who was now rumoured to be holding up part of a new council car park in Basildon.

'You see, George, we came to an arrangement with certain parties across the water,' Ketch continued. 'That arrangement was for you and the boys to go through a–' He snapped his fingers and looked past Tasker. 'What was it called, Brayne?'

'A scenario.' The answer came from a man sitting near the door.

'That's it. A *scenario.*' Ruby Ketch smiled, pleased with his choice of word, and ran a hand over his Brylcreemed hair. He had similar dark good looks to those of his bosses, slightly spoilt by a broken nose, the result of an opponent's headbutt in the boxing ring. Tasker didn't like to think about what had happened to the other fighter. 'To go through a scenario. But you cut it short, didn't you? You came out early. Now, how am I supposed to explain that to our associates over there, eh? It's embarrassing, is what it is. And I don't like being embarrassed.'

Tasker felt his blood running cold. Ketch wasn't really bothered by what the French thought; he'd be more wary of the Twins and their reaction. They were closer, for one thing – and unpredictable.

'Sorry, boss.' Christ, was this it? He'd never imagined getting himself in this sort of crack. Cock-ups were inevitable every now and then, no matter what precautions you took; timings got screwed, plans went out the window, people didn't do what they were supposed to, someone got lucky. *Fucking Calloway*. He wondered who the poncey driver had phoned from the French cop shop. He'd never thought to ask him, only relieved at the time that they'd got out before the Froggies got really pissed off and threw them all in the Bastille.

History wasn't Tasker's strong point.

As if reading his mind earlier, Ketch said, 'How did Calloway perform? Do the business, did he?'

There was a discreet cough and Tasker glanced at the other man, whose name was Leslie Brayne. A bluff, well-fed individual in an expensive suit, he had sleek grey hair and a silk handkerchief tucked in his top pocket. *Trying to look like the accountant he used to be,* thought Tasker, who knew the man's history. Now he just looked like the crooked numbers man he really was. He was nursing a glass of whisky, his favoured tipple and, as Ketch's trusted advisor, was never far from his side.

Tasker considered dropping Calloway in it, then decided against it. 'He did all right. Good enough wheel man ... for a nancy boy.'

He realised his mistake the moment the words had left his mouth. Ketch went very still, his eyes hooded. Tasker felt sick. It was rumoured that one of the Twins, whom nobody saw much, had once taken against an associate who'd made a joke about homosexuals. The associate had disappeared shortly afterwards. 'Sorry.'

'What do you reckon, Brayne?' Ketch started playing with his pen again. Tap-tap. Tap-tap.

Brayne looked up at the ceiling, then at Tasker, before replying. 'Well, no harm done, was there? They got a result, according to their man. No foul, no penalty.'

'Their man?' Tasker wondered what that meant.

Ketch didn't answer. He dropped the pen onto the blotter and sat back, tugging at the sleeves of his pinstripe suit to reveal cufflinks glittering with stones. Nudged his large tie knot into place.

'Yeah, I suppose.' He leant forward and stared hard at Tasker, his eyes as cold as night. A thin bead of perspiration was showing on his brow. 'Only thing is, I'm not sure what the result was. Are you, Brayne?'

'A try-out, wasn't that what they said? Testing the water.'

'Yeah, but what for?' Ketch was still looking at Tasker. 'What do you reckon, George? What were they really looking for over there?'

'No idea, boss. We did what you said, that's all.' He was puzzled. What the hell was Ketch talking about? How did he know what the point of it all had been? It was a job, that was all he knew. A bloody weird one, but just a job. Set it up, create the crash and away.

'Yeah, so you did.' He sat back. More tapping with the pen. 'Okay. What about Fletcher?'

'What about him?'

'I hear he overdid things. Buggered the truck and bent the car. Could have been messy, getting stranded out there miles from home ... especially if the cops had got involved. Not part of the plan, see, getting caught *with* the vehicles.'

'That's right.' There was nothing more to say. Tasker was damned if he was going to defend the man. He was likely to end up going down with him if he did that, and he didn't owe Fletcher a thing.

'I reckon,' Ketch murmured, 'we might have to

rethink Fletch's terms of employment. Pity, though; he's been with the Firm a long time. Knows a lot of stuff. And he's got friends.'

Tasker waited, not sure if he was expected to make a contribution. If the 'friends' Ketch was referring to were the Twins, he was better off saying nothing. Let the man who was paid the money make the running with that one.

'Yes, boss.'

'You got lucky this time, George,' Ketch murmured softly, and the temperature in the room suddenly seemed a few degrees colder. 'Dead lucky. They had a watcher on you, see. Checking out how you and the boys did.' He smiled without a trace of humour. 'I bet you never saw him, did you?'

A watcher. Christ, where? Tasker had checked out the scenery before and after the crash. There had been nobody within miles, he was certain of it. Yet if Ketch said there was...

'No, boss. Can't say I did.' He felt his ears redden at the admission.

'Damn right, you can't. Good job for you it went well, all I can say. They reckon it was just what they needed; they learnt a lot ... whatever that was. Did you get rid of the wheels? Be a shame if they turned up and the cops got evidence. Did you know they still use the guillotine over there?' His eyes were blank, and Tasker couldn't make out whether he was out of the woods or not. This mad fucker could change at the snap of a finger. 'Chop-chop. No coming back from the big blade, is there? No appeal, no further statements possible.' He grinned suddenly. 'Mind you, no more headaches, either.' Ketch was rumoured to suffer from regular debilitating migraines.

'Yeah. I heard.' His voice was hoarse. Jesus, how long was this going to last?

Then Brayne pitched in with a question. He stood up and moved into Tasker's line of sight and said, 'I hear you had a spot of bother in Amiens nick.'

'Nothing worth talking about.' Tasker fought to keep his voice and temper level. This was taking the piss. What bloody right did this number-cruncher have to ask him questions? Then he realised Ketch was looking at him, waiting for an answer. 'The cops got a bit heavy,' he said grudgingly. 'Pushed us around a bit. Nothing we couldn't handle.'

Ketch looked at Brayne. 'Is that what you heard?'

Brayne nodded, but with a tight smile on his heavy face. 'That's about the strength of it. They questioned Calloway and George, but left the others alone. Calloway made a call, our friend in Westminster did the business, then George handed over a wad of cash as compensation and they were out of there. No charges, no record.' He looked at Tasker. 'I think I got that straight?'

'Yeah. That's about it.' Tasker barely bothered to hide a sneer, but he was worried. How the hell did he come to know so much? He *really* didn't like Brayne; the man was a smooth talker and thought himself above everyone else in the organisation. Tasker knew he had a string of bankrupt businesses behind him and wasn't as clever as he thought he was. But Ketch and the

Twins had decided he was the dog's bollocks and relied on him for financial advice. And that made him untouchable.

For now, anyway.

'Okay, George.' Ketch stood up and flicked his sleeves straight. He wasn't as tall standing as he looked, and Tasker knew he wore lifts in his shoes to compensate. But he was no pushover and had done more than enough to gain a bad reputation. 'Time we were going. You keep yourself handy, you hear? Might need you to go back over there for a repeat performance.' He smiled and adjusted a handkerchief in his sleeve. 'Actually, there's no might about it. It's a cert. You'd better start getting the team ready and practising your French.'

'Sure, boss. When?' Tasker felt his spirits slump. Out of the fire into ... what?

'Not sure, George. Waiting for the word ... or *le mot,* as they say in French. Soon as I know, you'll know. But soon.' He flashed another smile, as false as the rest, and tapped Tasker's chest with the back of his hand. 'Chin up, my son; much more of this international travel and you might develop a taste for the old French cuisine, eh?'

CHAPTER FIFTEEN

'Lucas?' It was late in the afternoon when Desmoulins stuck his head round the door and got Rocco's attention. 'Those crash-damaged vehicles you were asking about?'

Rocco blinked, his thoughts still on Saint-Cloud's briefing and his final words. He wasn't in the habit of telling Massin everything he was doing day to day because it wasn't necessary. But he didn't like being told by an outsider to hold back information about his movements; it went against the grain of all he'd been taught.

'What about them?' He'd forgotten about the Englishmen, and had almost pushed the crash investigation to the back of his mind. If Saint-Cloud wanted his help on security checks for de Gaulle, he would have to hand over some of his caseload for others to handle. Still, his curiosity in unexplained events never entirely vanished, no matter what other priorities came up.

'Nothing's shown up in any local garages, but a Renault truck has been found torched in a quarry near Picquigny. There are remnants of camouflage canvas and green wood on the scene, so it could be the one you're looking for. The locals thought the smoke was a farmer burning dead wood, so they didn't bother checking it out earlier. They only just got round to calling it in when they realised what it was.'

Picquigny. About ten kilometres to the west of Amiens. Rocco stood up. He needed a break and some fresh air. 'Better take a look, then. Get Rizzotti, will you? And tell him to bring his camera. Let's go see what we can find.' He wasn't expecting much, but it was an outstanding matter to be checked out, and it might serve to clear his mind a little.

By the time they arrived, the remains of the truck were cold, with only a thin veil of smoke hanging in the air like a ghost. The carcass had settled onto the axles, and the tyres had burnt down to the rims. The throat-catching aroma of burnt metal and rubber was overlaid with the harsher tang of petrol fumes.

Rocco recognised the model by its stubby size and shape. A Renault Goelette 4x4, a small, brutishly effective workhorse, often used as a military ambulance among other functions. There were a few about in private hands, sold off by the military and used in all manner of capacities. He stood back from the scene while Dr Rizzotti took an initial look around, but could see nothing about the location to tell him why the truck had been torched here. It was parked off the road in an old chalk quarry, just out of sight of passing vehicles, but he could think of lots of other places where it would have probably remained unseen for longer. But why set fire to it? It was screaming to be noticed by someone sooner or later, no matter how uninquisitive the locals might be. Perhaps it had become a liability and the men driving it had been left with no choice but to dump it and leave.

'You think I can tell anything from this?' Dr Rizzotti murmured, gesturing at the remains. 'I'm a doctor, not a mechanic.'

'I'm not asking for an annual service on it,' Rocco replied. 'I need your scientific eye, that's all.' He had initially found Bernard Rizzotti defensive and overcautious in his opinions, but over the ensuing months they had formed a good working relationship. The doctor had found the investigative side of his work rewarding, and responded well to Rocco including him in the procedure whenever possible.

Rizzotti grunted and smiled an acknowledgement. 'Very well. Let me see. As you can see from the remains, the fire was clearly fierce enough to scorch the surrounding vegetation and blacken the chalk face of the diggings. But there is not enough soft material in a truck cab like this to cause that level of heat, so I think perhaps the person who set the fire used petrol to help it along.' He shrugged. 'That would suggest they wanted to obliterate as much as possible of the vehicle and leave nothing for us – you – to work with.'

The fire had certainly done that, eating away at anything consumable on the truck and leaving a shell of thin metal for the cab and hood, and the bare metal structure of the rear bed with the wooden floor and sides almost completely gone.

Desmoulins found a stick and began teasing open the driver's door and poking around inside, while Rocco went round to the front of the cab, where Rizzotti was squatting before a pile of ash on the ground.

'Interesting,' Rizzotti muttered. Under the remains of the vehicle's front wing, he had found a thick section of wood that had not burnt all the way through. The end of the wood showed traces of saw marks and a sticky coating. Rocco bent to touch it. Was it tar ... or black paint?

Rizzotti supplied the answer. 'It looks like a railway sleeper. I bought a couple recently from the rail depot, for my garden. Extremely heavy and durable.' He prodded the end with his pen. 'See? Weathered by age and preservative. The flames ran out of heat before they could consume the wood

100

completely.' He dug gingerly in the pile of ash and lifted something from the powdery remains. It was curved and uniform, the thickness of a little finger, and heavy, about a metre in length.

'Steel cable,' said Rocco. He recognised the spiral shape of the burnt metal. He'd seen plenty in burnt-out trucks in Indochina. The sight triggered flashes of memory he didn't wish to pursue. He shook his head and focused hard on what he was seeing.

Rizzotti pursed his lips, anticipating Rocco's question. 'The sleeper could have been lashed to the front of the truck to act as a counterweight,' he suggested. 'Maybe the truck had a small crane or winch fitted by a previous owner.' He gestured towards the rear of the vehicle. 'It's definitely not there now, though.'

Rocco recalled what Simeon had told them. The truck had rammed the car, coming out of the track at speed. That being the case, a large lump of wood on the front would have acted as an ideal battering ram and added extra weight to the collision.

Desmoulins came round to join them. 'Nothing useful in the cab,' he said. 'Apart from this.' He opened his hand to reveal a thin circular metal disc. Although burnt black, it had clearly withstood the worst of the heat and showed a portrait on one side, and a date.

'It's an English penny.' Rocco took it from him and turned it over. Sure enough, the figure of Britannia showed on one side, with the royal profile just visible on the opposite face.

'War relic?' suggested Desmoulins. It wasn't un-common to find English coins in the fields around here, lost during both wars as soldiers passed through on their way to and from the front ... or back towards Dunkirk in May and June 1940.

'Not unless the war happened within the last two years and nobody told us,' replied Rocco. He held it up for them to see.

The coin was dated 1961.

Ten minutes later, Rizzotti stood up from where he had been examining the rear of the truck. 'Lucas.' He looked shocked, and was pointing at the ground between the truck's rear wheels.

Rocco joined him. All he could see was more ash, some remnants of oil, and a few remnants of unburnt wood beneath the scorched heavy metal of the truck's axle assembly.

Then Rizzotti used a stick to move the ash, gently flicking it to one side. It revealed a grey-white object, stick-like but clearly not wooden.

Rocco felt his gut tighten. He'd seen this kind of thing before. 'Is that what I think it is?'

Rizzotti nodded. 'A thigh bone. At a guess, male, not young, and quite long.' He poked around a little more and uncovered more bones and, to one side, a fragment of cloth which had somehow escaped the worst of the flames. Attached to it was a single metal coat button. 'The fire in the truck bed must have been fierce,' Rizzotti continued. 'They were probably carrying a fuel can or some liquid which acted as an accelerant.'

'Or lots of dry wood.' Rocco stepped round the ruined truck to where a tangle of branches lay in a heap, the sides scorched and blackened, but not burnt through. He squatted and looked closer at the ground beneath the truck. 'Would the truck bed produce this much ash?' From what he could recall, Renault trucks weren't that big, built more for utilitarian use, not style or comfort.

'Possibly not.' Rizzotti had walked back to the car to get his camera, and was setting it up to take pictures. He studied the branches, then looked around at the sides of the quarry walls. The quarry had long been abandoned, allowing a thick spread of bushes and trees to proliferate. Some older trunks showed evidence of having been cut some time ago, no doubt for fence posts, while others had fallen down from the quarry rim of their own accord, no doubt due to wind damage, and lay rotting on the quarry floor. 'I see what you mean,' he concluded. 'This is brushwood and dry tinder.' He pointed at the branches Rocco had noticed. 'It looks like they piled them under and on top of the bed of the truck – perhaps covering this poor unfortunate – then set fire to it. It would have acted like a Viking funeral pyre.' He grimaced and began clicking away with the camera. Then he paused and looked at Rocco, who hadn't answered. 'You okay?'

But Rocco was barely listening. He was staring at the button retrieved from the ashes and reflecting on how often these investigations hinged on chance discoveries. If he hadn't gone to see Father Maurice, he wouldn't have known anything more about the button he'd found on the side of the road, or that it had come from a tramp's jacket. Yet now its twin was staring up at him.

A child's birthday coat button, clearly embossed with the number 5.

CHAPTER SIXTEEN

'We need to find the DS,' said Rocco. He was more convinced than ever that he was now leading a murder hunt. It might have been an accident to begin with, whatever had happened out on that stretch of road. Pantoufle might have wandered into the path of the truck, befuddled perhaps by cold or drink or hunger. But covering up the death and burning the body changed everything.

They were back in the office, putting their thoughts together. Rizzotti was compiling detailed notes on the burnt truck and the body, prior to requesting some scientific confirmation, while Rocco and Desmoulins went over the facts they had amassed so far.

On paper, it didn't amount to much, other than a dead body and an unexplained event involving a truck and a car. But there was something tugging at his instincts that told him this was far deeper than a cover-up of a dead vagrant. Why go to so much trouble? They could have left him lying in the ditch and nobody would have been any the wiser. The road wasn't used much; it could have been days, maybe weeks, before a body might be discovered, especially with snow on the way.

A phone jangled across the other side of the office. A uniformed officer listened for a moment, then held out the receiver to get Rocco's attention. 'Are you looking for a DS? Black, lots of side-impact damage?'

Rocco jumped up and strode across the office, snatching the phone from the man's hand.

'Rocco. You've found a DS?'

The man on the other end was a patrol officer who had stopped by a remote car breaker's yard looking for a spare mirror, and had spotted a clean but badly damaged Citroën DS about to go under the breaker's cutters. 'It's weird,' he said. 'The inside's been fitted out like a race car – loads of reinforcing struts and padding. But it's taken a hell of a bang on one side.' He read out the car registration, which Rocco wrote down for checking later. 'What do you want me to do, Inspector?'

'Stay there and don't let anyone near it,' he ordered. 'If anyone tries, shoot them in the foot.' He dropped the phone back on its cradle and handed the registration number to the uniformed officer. 'Check that, will you? Urgent.' He looked at Desmoulins with a tight grin. 'All good things come to those who wait. Let's go.'

The breaker's yard, a polite misnomer for a scrap metal dump, was located down a single-track lane on the northern outskirts of Amiens. Surrounded by a corrugated tin fence two metres high, with rolled barbed wire pinned along the top, it looked damp, unwelcoming and sinister. Like a hundred such similar sites Rocco had been to during his investigations, it was not intended as a place of beauty. But he also knew that places like this often hid by design a wealth of detail from passing eyes.

He drove through the entrance, a sagging pair

105

of wooden frames covered in corrugated steel and wire, and stopped in the middle of an open, muddy space with a tired-looking office cabin on one side looking out at an expanse of broken cars and car parts arranged in rows. The place was sour and depressing, and he felt instantly unclean. A dog was barking somewhere close by, the noise angry and menacing, and he checked that his MAB 38 was within easy reach. He'd seen the mess some scrapyard dogs could make of a man, and had no desire to find himself on this one's menu.

The yard's owner, Olivier Bellin, was an overweight, rat-faced individual clothed in a grubby vest and trousers and a surly manner. He stared aggressively at Rocco around a yellow cigarette end and lifted his unshaven chin in query. A sharp wind was whistling around the yard, but he seemed not to notice.

'What do you want? And why's this Nazi stopping me and my men going about our lawful work?' He jerked an oily thumb at the patrol officer who was leaning against a DS parked at the front of the yard. Two men in filthy overalls and welder's goggles were sitting on a pair of rotting car seats nearby, smoking. 'You've no right doing this. I'm a respectable businessman.'

'Yes, and next year I'll be pope.' Lucas had heard all about Bellin and his illicit dealings over the years on the way from the station. The man had a lengthy record, had served two prison sentences for assault and robbery, and was suspected of having 'disappeared' at least two cars involved in major bank jobs. All in all, not one of

Amiens' finest citizens.

'Where did the DS come from?' he asked. 'And be careful who you're calling names.'

Bellin shrugged, which made his chest wobble. 'Search me. It had been left outside the gates. Happens all the time ... people treat this place like a rubbish dump.'

Rocco looked around at the muddy yard with its piles of dead cars and other junk. 'I wonder why?' He fixed the man with a hard stare. 'Don't mess with me, Bellin, I'm not in the mood. I'm investigating a possible murder and I think this car was involved.'

'So?' Bellin spat the cigarette out. The soggy mess landed very close to one of Rocco's English brogues. 'Nothing to do with me. I don't know anything about any murder.'

'Well, the car is now in your hands. That lands it on your doorstep – literally. Do you know what conspiracy is?'

Bellin feigned a look of boredom. 'No. Should I?'

'It means an agreement between people to commit a criminal act. One of the most serious is in the murder of a third party. Even after the event.' He waited while Bellin processed what he was hearing. It was a slow grind, rather like watching one of those tumbling-man toys in action. But understanding dawned slowly on the scrap dealer's face.

'So – how does that affect me?'

'It means anyone involved,' Rocco explained carefully, 'anyone – no matter what their role – gets the same sentence as the person who drove the car.' It wasn't entirely correct because of the likelihood of extenuating circumstances, but he wasn't about to tell Bellin. Let the grubby little toad sweat a bit.

'Hey – no! Wait!' Bellin appeared to wake up as the words finally dropped into place like coins in a slot machine. 'That's not right. I told your man, the car was outside when I got here. I don't know who left it there. I can't be held responsible for what happened before it came here, can I?'

'You can,' Desmoulins put in, 'if you don't explain why you're about to cut up an expensive car like that. You'd make a nice sum even if you sold it to one of your grubby criminal *potes* to do up. Give it new paperwork and a bit of paint, and sooner or later some mug will buy it.' He leant closer. 'And don't tell me that hasn't crossed your devious little mind, because I know you better than that.'

Bellin said nothing, but his beady eyes were going runabout, Rocco noticed. Not that he would crumble too easily; men like him would only cave in if they were on the brink of arrest and saw no other way out.

'I think Mr Bellin gets the message,' he said. 'We'll let him think it over.' He walked away and stopped alongside the Citroën.

The uniformed officer gave a nod of recognition. 'I hope this is the one you're looking for.'

Rocco studied the damage to the side of the car. It looked as if a giant fist had hit the car amidships, pushing in both front and rear passenger doors. Had it not been for a network of sturdy metal poles welded together and covered in foam padding to form a protective cage, he guessed the damage would have been more extensive. He tugged a splinter of oily wood from the gap between the doors and sniffed at it. It smelt faintly of tar.

A connection.

'I think it just might be. But we'll soon find out. Well spotted.' He looked around at the oil-sodden ground they were standing on and nodded at Desmoulins, who was peering in the driver's side. 'We need to get this out of here. Can you get it picked up and taken to the station? We can get Rizzotti to have a proper look there.'

'Sure.' Desmoulins looked at the patrol officer. 'Can I use your car radio?'

The two men walked away, leaving Rocco to consider the car and what secrets it might eventually give up. That the vehicle had been left here to quietly disappear, he had no doubt. The same happened in Paris and other cities on a regular basis. Cars used in criminal enterprises were routinely repainted, re-registered or underwent some other transformation, often permanent. And yards like this were nearly always involved. They had the equipment and willingness to do such work ... and their unwelcoming appearance, aided by guard dogs, was usually enough to put off casual snoopers from paying too much attention to what they were doing.

He peered through the splintered glass remaining in the side windows. He could see nothing inside, neither normal travel rubbish nor personal effects, and if there was any kind of crime involved, such as the death of a vagrant, even accidentally, it was probable that it had already been cleaned out. But as he knew well, even the most

109

careful cleaning sometimes failed to remove every-thing.

He rejoined Bellin, who was busy lighting another foul-looking cigarette. The man had to take three tries before it caught, and he avoided looking Rocco in the eye.

'Last opportunity,' Rocco murmured. 'See, I know you're lying. But there's no need for your men to hear. Tell me where the car came from ... or who wants it to disappear. Phone number, name, location – any or all will do. Otherwise I'll put a squad in here this afternoon and they'll go through this rat hole centimetre by centimetre.' He took his diary from his coat pocket. It was leather-bound and slim. 'See this?'

Bellin nodded. 'Yes. So?'

'It's the official log of every car stolen in northern France over the last eight months. Now, what are the odds of me finding one of the plates listed here among all that shit out there?' He nodded at the piles of junk. 'Or do you trust your men implicitly?'

Bellin stared at the diary, then his eyes flicked away. He nodded. 'Okay. But I'm not admitting anything. This guy called me last week, said a car would be dropped off. It'd probably be badly dam-aged, he said, and he'd pay good money for it to be scrapped. I didn't argue, and why would I? The demand for scrap metal isn't that good at the moment. I can barely keep those two men on as it is.'

'My heart bleeds for you. Who was this benevolent person?'

'No idea. On my mother's life!' He was looking

intense and Rocco detected a note of desperation in his voice. Maybe he was telling the truth ... or maybe he was more scared of the man who'd called him than he was of the police.

'All right. Who dropped it off?'

'I told you, it was–'

'Suit yourself.' Rocco began to turn away. 'This yard is closed as of now. Nothing leaves here. Send your men home and give me the keys to your office.'

'Wait!' Bellin looked shocked and grabbed Rocco by the elbow, then let go with a cry of dismay when Rocco instinctively bunched his arm. 'Sorry ... I didn't mean anything.' His voice dropped to a hoarse whisper. 'But you've got to listen to me ... being seen talking to you could get me in the middle of one of those piles.' He nodded at the heaps of chopped-up car parts lying around the yard. Few of them were much bigger than a man's torso.

Rocco waited, his interest kicking into overdrive. If Bellin was this scared, he'd like to meet the person who could inspire this level of dread.

'You'd better hurry, then, hadn't you? Then I can be out of your hair.'

Bellin hesitated, then caved. He said quietly, 'All right. This *mec* – I didn't ask his name – just turned up outside the gate. He said this was the car for cutting, as arranged. That's all. Then he jumped into another car that was waiting and that was the last I saw of him. And before you ask, I didn't take a note of the registration or see the other driver. It wasn't worth my face to look.'

'When was this?'

'Two days ago.'

Rocco considered it for a moment. The time frame was right, at least. But was he telling the whole truth? So, a guy turns up at the yard and dumps a car. Where hadn't he heard that story before? It was probably going on right now in every other city across France, no questions asked, in exchange for hard cash or favours. Some of those favours might include leaving the yard owner's face in one piece, as Bellin was suggesting. He guessed he wasn't going to get much more from this man. Even crooks had their limits when self-preservation was at stake.

'Can you describe him? Young, old, dark, fair, bad breath ... what?'

Bellin gave an elaborate shrug, undoubtedly more for the benefit of his two men than anything, a display of obduracy should anyone have cause to ask later. 'Youngish, early thirties, medium height, dark hair, a bit of a tan. Didn't notice anything else.'

'Like a million other Frenchmen. That's a big help.'

Bellin's eyes narrowed, as if he'd suddenly seen a way out. He dropped his cigarette in the mud and stamped on it. 'Actually, that's the thing. Not like any Frenchman – not in that way, anyway.'

'What do you mean?'

'He spoke French okay ... but not good. And he wasn't dressed like anyone around here.'

'Go on.'

'I think he was a *Rosbif*. An Englishman.'

CHAPTER SEVENTEEN

If there had ever been a street name to the narrow run of ruined buildings on the outskirts of Créteil, in south-east Paris, it no longer existed save on old maps of the *commune* or in the memories of its more senior inhabitants.

Now, and in the dark, it was a place visited by bored kids looking for trouble, the occasional drunk seeking a place to doss down, and the various creatures of the night which had made it their own.

Halfway down the street stood the gutted remains of a butcher's shop. The wooden sign was still there, hanging drunkenly by a single chain, but warped and rendered illegible by the elements. Only its telltale shape of a horse's head remained. The building, though, like its neighbours, was a shell of crumbling brick and rotten plaster-and-lath construction, waiting for progress and the promised redevelopment of the area to erase its existence and replace it with another.

A dark Renault van with battered panelwork and a broken side window was the only vehicle in sight, left skewed at an angle to the kerb in front of the shop. A ripped plastic bench seat was leaning against the driver's door, and a worn car tyre sat on the bonnet, indications to anyone passing that the vehicle had been abandoned to its fate.

A flicker of movement showed a small dog trotting along the pavement, following a zigzag course from scent to scent. It paused to cock its leg against a rear wheel, then sniffed along the van's side before moving on into the night. A cat across the street watched it go, the fur on its back lifting momentarily, then settling as the dog vanished into the shadows.

Lights flickered in the darkness at the top of the street, where it connected with that part of the town which still had life and movement. The flicker grew to a glow, and a car's engine puttered steadily over the silence as a vehicle nosed into the street, the headlights pushing back the dark and revealing the walls and empty windows of a dead zone. The light rushed on, washing quickly over the abandoned Renault and down to the far end, where a row of small garages with corrugated metal roofs stood like orphans, their walls and dilapidated wooden doors covered in graffiti, a tangled mess of emblems, slogans and angry cries for attention which would only ever come in the form of a developer's bulldozer.

The car – a dark Panhard with a crumpled rear wing – slowed alongside the Renault, its occupants checking it out as the dog had before them. The car's tyres crunched through a mess of rubble, a reminder that few vehicles ever passed this way. It was enough to satisfy them; they drove on and did a U-turn at the end and stopped facing back the way they had come.

The headlights were extinguished, returning the street to darkness.

Five minutes ticked by. The engine remained on, a muffled rumble in the dark. Other than that, no lights, no sound.

Finally, the front passenger door opened and a man stepped out. He stood with his head back, like an animal probing the night air. He was tall and athletic, and moved with confidence. Moments later he was followed by two other men, one the driver, who left the engine running and the door open. His companion stepped to one side to keep watch.

The lead man moved to one of the garages and produced a key, opening a large padlock holding the double doors together. The two men disappeared inside the garage, lighting the dark with the yellow glow of a flashlight.

'*Coucou*, Baptiste. Time to go tickle a trout.' A hoarse whisper echoed softly in the dark of the abandoned Renault van, and a foot tapped on the floor. Moments later, a figure rolled out from between the wheels and stood upright on the pavement. Turning, he padded silently along the street, hugging the ratty buildings, unobserved by the watcher at the garage who was taking an artistic leak over a pile of bricks to one side.

Another figure appeared on the far side of the street, surprising even the cat, which vanished without a sound. This one paralleled the first, treading carefully over a route scouted earlier that evening to note any obstacles to be avoided later. Both men were dressed in dark clothing and soft boots, and wore balaclavas pulled down over their faces.

Both were armed with handguns.

The man on watch shook himself and turned, mouth dropping open as he picked up a sound or a sense of something in the atmosphere. But he was too late. The first figure reached out a pair of brawny arms and plucked him off his feet, while the second stepped in and rammed an elbow into his stomach, stifling the warning he was about to utter. Only a soft *whoosh* of expelled air escaped.

But it was enough.

'Franco?' The light inside the garage moved and a voice called out softly, 'You all right?'

'Yeah. Hurry up!' One of the newcomers hissed, and clamped a large hand over the prisoner's mouth, staring into his eyes with a gaze cold enough to freeze the blood.

Then two more men appeared out of the night, taking up positions on either side of the garage entrance. Both carried pistols. A brief exchange of signals, and the first two men hustled silently away back down the street, carrying their prisoner with them.

Seconds passed, then a shrill whistle pierced the night. Suddenly the abandoned Renault burst into life. It charged away from the kerb, shrugging off the bench seat from the door and the tyre on the bonnet, and roared towards the garages, the high-performance whine of the engine giving lie to the poor state of the bodywork. The headlights flared on with shocking intensity, illuminating the garage and the two men who were emerging from the interior.

They froze, their faces registering shock at this sudden eruption of activity and the sight of men with guns standing almost alongside them. With a scream of rubber, the van stopped facing the garage opening. Before they could gather themselves, they heard the rattle of weapons being cocked and a bellowed order from the Renault.

'*Stand still or we shoot!*'

The men obeyed. Lit up like the fourteenth of July and facing automatic weapons, they were too stunned to do anything but stare dumbly around them at a scene which, moments earlier, had been theirs and theirs alone.

'*Alors*. What have we got here, then?' A slim figure in dark clothing stepped into view. Like the other men, his face was covered, but his eyes glittered with grim humour. 'Doing a spot of tidying up, were we? Trying to make the place look nice?' He peered into the garage, where a work-bench against one wall held an array of weapons, the blued steel and wooden stocks clearly visible in the glow from the Renault's lights. 'Oh dear. Now that's a prison sentence, all ready and waiting.' He turned and looked at the lead man. 'You three must have really upset someone, you know that? Shame. You can't rely on anyone to keep a secret these days, can you?' He signalled for his men to check them for weapons and cuff them. 'We don't want any nasty surprises, do we?'

'What did you mean just then?' The lead man seemed perfectly calm, as if accepting that being caught was part of the risk, and therefore to be expected. He spoke well, his voice carrying a natural tone of authority. He turned his back and clasped his hands behind him. 'We upset someone.'

'You were sold out,' replied the slim figure, who seemed to enjoy turning the screw. 'Like chickens at a Saturday market. Never mind; you'll have plenty of time to figure out who by, I'm sure.'

CHAPTER EIGHTEEN

The battered DS looked forlorn in the yard behind the police station the following morning, its black finish whitened under a layer of morning frost. It had been brought in on a trailer and was now lying low on its wheels like a beached whale. One of the front tyres had deflated overnight and its brief stay in Bellin's oily pit of a yard had not done the coachwork many favours, even without the damaged bodywork.

Dr Rizzotti had drawn a chalk line around it, and had forbidden anyone from approaching it, taking his cue from a bulletin from the National Police Science Centre about crime scene protection. He had asked Captain Canet to assign an officer to take notes and help with the inspection, and a young, fresh-faced *gardien* was standing by with a clipboard, huddled inside a heavy coat and puffing vapour into the cold air.

When Rocco arrived, he found Rizzotti sitting behind the wheel. He was motionless, absorbing the atmosphere. Rocco knew all about that; it was vitally important when studying a crime scene, and more could be gained by a few minutes of quiet reflection than charging in and spoiling whatever clues might be available.

Rizzotti checked the seat setting. 'Whoever last drove this wasn't very tall. A bit less than medium height.' He sniffed the air. 'Cigarette smoke –

could be from the men at the scrapyard, of course. But something else, too.' He sniffed again, then looked at the young policeman, who was making notes. 'Do you have a good wine nose, boy?' When the man shrugged, he glanced at Rocco. 'Lucas?'

'Not in this weather and not this early. Why?'

Rizzotti climbed out of the car and shut the door. 'Pity. I can smell something other than the normal car smells. It could be perfume, but I need to be sure before the aroma fades altogether.'

'You think it's important?'

'I don't know. Maybe.' He chewed his lip. 'Women are more sensitive to that kind of thing, in my experience.' He looked to Rocco for help. 'They like nice smells – especially in a man. To a woman, smell is important. Ask any of them.' He shrugged and pulled a face. 'My wife would know but only if it was on my shirt collar.'

'There's the new *gardienne*,' the young uni-formed officer volunteered tentatively. 'Alix – I mean, Officer Poulon.' He blushed. 'Shall I get her?'

Rizzotti nodded. 'Please do.' He waited for the young man to leave, then said softly, 'Sweet. I think he's in love.'

When the officer returned, he had Alix with him. She looked at Rocco and Rizzotti with a frown as if sensing a practical joke. 'Is he serious?' she murmured, nodding at her colleague. 'You actually want me to smell this car?'

'If you would, please,' said Rizzotti. 'I'd like you to get in and tell me what immediately comes to mind. Don't think about it too much, simply use your instincts.'

119

She did as he requested and sat in the driver's seat, closing the door behind her with a soft thump. She inhaled at length, then opened the door and climbed out again.

'Aftershave,' she said without hesitation. 'I assume you know cigarette smoke, plastic and leather, so it must be the other smell you're interested in.'

'Excellent,' said Rizzotti. He sounded impressed. 'Good diagnosis. I don't suppose you could tell us what brand and how expensive it is?' His expression suggested that he was only half joking.

Alix shook her head. 'Not unpleasant – but a bit heavy for my tastes. I don't recognise it, but...'

'But what?'

'The man wearing this is trying to impress.' She looked at Rocco with a faint lift of one eyebrow. 'If you want my opinion, more men should try it. Oh, by the way, that man Saint-Cloud is looking for you.' She turned and walked away, leaving them staring after her.

'See what I mean?' said Rizzotti, grinning as though he'd just solved the origins of the universe. 'I told you. Women.'

'I'll put you in for a medal,' Rocco growled. He wondered what the security chief wanted. If it was to demand what he'd found out about threats to the president, he was going to be unlucky. He ducked his head inside the car and sniffed for himself. It smelt like a railway carriage. Alix was right, though: plastic, leather and smoke and... He sniffed again, drawing in a gentle lungful of air. There *was* something else; something familiar lurking at the edge of his consciousness, soft and

120

fragrant. But where the hell had he come across it before? Was it soap? Damn, that was irritating–

Then it came to him.

Calloway. When he'd grabbed the man during the interrogation, he'd picked up the smell of aftershave. He'd likened it to the aroma of leather at the time. Whatever it was, it had been distinctive and heavy. The kind of smell to hang in the air for a long time afterwards. Then he thought about Calloway the man: thirty-ish, tanned, dark hair, slim build. English. And as a former racing driver, he'd probably spent time on the French circuits. Most likely picked up a working knowledge of French, too – certainly enough to convey a message to someone like Olivier Bellin.

He got out of the car. 'Did you find anything in here?'

'I've only made a cursory check so far. But we've already found something interesting.' Rizzotti indicated to his assistant to pop the boot and they gathered around. Nestling inside was a large cine-camera with a matt-black case. Folded around it were three lengths of metal joined by a small platform with a complicated screw assembly and rubber-lined handle grip.

'I don't know about you,' said Rizzotti, 'but I didn't expect this. A body, maybe, or some weapons ... but not a camera.'

'It's the car we're looking for,' Rocco confirmed. He was studying the ends of the camera tripod legs, which were coated in dried soil, and a scattering of pine needles littering the floor of the boot. 'But why dump an expensive piece of equipment like this?'

121

Rizzotti lifted one side of the casing. It moved with ease. 'Because it's not real,' he explained. 'At least, the casing is, but there's nothing inside. It's a dummy.'

Rocco tested the weight, then tapped the casing. Rizzotti was right: it was empty.

'Damn. But why?'

Rizzotti shrugged. 'Give me an hour or so and we'll turn the car inside out. I'd rather do it alone with young Romeo here, to prevent any further contamination. I'll call you if we find anything.' He looked at the young officer, who was shivering. 'Better put down your clipboard, young man, and be prepared to get dirty as well as cold.'

'What about the truck and the body?' Rocco asked him.

'Ah, that. I've been on to the forensic laboratory in Lille. They're sending a team to collect the remains and do an analysis. It could take some time, though. There's not much to go on and they've got a backlog.'

'Don't worry. Any help they can give is better than none.' There were half a dozen police scientific laboratories throughout the country, the nearest being Lille, but the advance in forensic skills being shared from Britain, the United States and other countries was making their workload increasingly tough; the more they became capable of doing, the more was asked of them.

Rocco left Rizzotti and his helper to their task and went in search of Saint-Cloud.

He found the colonel in one of the upstairs offices in conversation with one of the suited individuals who had been with him and Massin two days before. This man nodded without introduction and walked away.

'Inspector. Did you receive the files?' Saint-Cloud asked.

'What files?' So far Rocco had seen nothing of the information promised by the security chief. Without it he was virtually powerless to even begin investigating any anti-Gaullist groups. It would be like throwing stones into a lake and hoping to hit a fish.

Saint-Cloud, however, seemed surprisingly sanguine. 'They're on their way, I assure you. I just wanted to see where we stood.' He went round behind the desk and picked up a sheet of paper. 'This news has just reached me. Three men were picked up last night in Créteil, in southeast Paris, and a cache of armaments discovered in a garage lock-up they were using. One of the guns shows evidence of recent firing and is thought to have been used in the N19 attack near Guignes.'

Rocco knew the area, but not well. Créteil and Guignes were hardly close neighbours, but near enough. 'Who are they?'

'One is a French national, the other two are one Spanish, one Corsican. What makes this interesting is that all three are former members of the Foreign Legion. So far they are not talking, but one has turned up on our files before. He's affiliated to a pro-OAS group.' He sniffed with distaste. 'None of this is surprising, I suppose, but it's a clear indication that there is more than one group wishing ill of the president.'

'And more than one nationality.'

'Quite. What we have to find out is whether there are any such groups with resources active in the Picardie region or,' he dropped the paper on the desk, 'whether we're in danger of overreacting. May I ask what you are doing at present?'

He seemed to have slipped very easily into using the 'we' all of a sudden, thought Rocco. But he gave him a summary of the ramming incident and the Englishmen destroying the café in Amiens. 'The ramming looks like an illicit film project which may have gone badly wrong. The Englishmen, I'm not sure what that's about. They could be what they claim: a group of men looking for some fun and it got out of hand. It wouldn't be the first time. The English don't react well to drink.'

Saint-Cloud nodded. 'Neither of which seems to border on my concerns, I have to say, although...' He paused and stared at the wall.

'Yes?'

'The use of a black DS seems a little ... odd, though, don't you think? The president uses such a vehicle. It could be what it seems – a film project. I wouldn't like you to go wasting your time chasing shadows, Inspector.'

'It's hardly a shadow,' Rocco pointed out mildly. 'There's a death involved.'

'A tramp? Tramps die all the time. Considering their way of life, I imagine it's an occupational hazard, isn't it?' Saint-Cloud's face was bare of all emotion, but his voice betrayed indifference, and Rocco wondered whether anything beyond the president's safety ever touched him. 'Why is this one so special?'

'He's not. But investigating an unexplained

death is what I do. If I find there's been a crime, I go after the perpetrators.'

Saint-Cloud said nothing. After a moment, he nodded, his eyes clouding over.

CHAPTER NINETEEN

Back downstairs, Rocco rang Michel Santer, his former boss in Clichy. Although a long way from where the attack on the official car had taken place, he was aware of how tight the police community was. Details of the incident would have spread very quickly throughout the force, gathering speed because of the unusual nature of the offence. Among all gossips, cops were high on the list of overachievers, and Santer, like many long-time cops, seemed to act as a filter for much of it.

'Who?' Santer's voice echoed down the line as Rocco's call was transferred. 'Did you say Rocco? Never heard of him. Is he the new community dog catcher?'

'Very droll,' said Rocco. 'You were a sad loss to the music hall.'

'Oh, *that* Rocco! The one who only ever calls me when he's in trouble and owes me at least several long lunches.' A dry chuckle followed. 'How are you, you bloody *paysan?*'

Rocco ignored the friendly insult. 'Not in any trouble. At least, I don't think so.'

'Really? That doesn't sound right. What's up?'

'The attack on the N19 a few days ago.'

125

'What about it?' Santer sounded immediately cautious, and Rocco heard a grunt as the captain stood up and closed his office door with a bang. The signal would be clear to everyone outside: don't disturb.

'That's what I'd like to know. I've had the official line but that's all. Anything you can tell me?'

'Like what? You think I have the security departments in my back pocket? They don't tell us anything, you know that. Anyone would think we were the enemy, the way they behave.'

'But you hear stuff.' The attack had taken place on the opposite side of the city, well beyond the Clichy boundaries. Due to the target, it would have received an immediate security clampdown to avoid any details getting out other than those officially sanctioned for broadcast via news channels. But for the police fraternity, Paris was a small world and Rocco knew how bad news travelled faster than good. It was the unofficial grapevine of which even official orders couldn't dam the flow completely.

'You haven't got one of those recorder things going, have you?'

'Spare me. What do you know?'

'A little. We had a security guy through here a few days ago, dropping the odd bit of news. His cousin works here in the back office, so he was strutting his stuff and trying to impress the new kids. I was surprised he didn't insist on taking out his gun and letting off a few rounds. Anyway, beyond juicing it up slightly, he pretty much stuck to the official bulletin.'

'That's it?' Rocco felt a sense of disappointment. He had hoped for something more, although he wasn't sure what.

'That's it.' Santer's voice dropped suddenly. 'Unless you count a second gunman being spirited away.'

'Say again?' The report had mentioned one body, a former NCO who must have joined the OAS for reasons best known to himself, no doubt hatred of de Gaulle being one of them.

'There were two left behind, not one. The security guy reckons the other was taken away on orders from on high before the press got to him.'

Something Saint-Cloud hadn't known or had kept to himself? 'Did he say why?'

'No. Possibly because the second man had a face they didn't want identified.'

He was probably right, Rocco thought. After the Bastien-Thiry incident, there was a genuine fear among the authorities of another highly placed or high-born individual being revealed to be a member of a terrorist organisation. Too many examples like that and people might begin to wonder about their own stance. Even in a republic, where the old ways of deference were supposed to be long gone, it was a subtle method of influencing popular thought in favour of the Government line.

'Any idea what happened to him?'

'None. A quiet family funeral in the country, I imagine. Why?'

'No reason. Just curious.'

'Yeah, right. Now that makes me curious, too. What's going on, Lucas? You got your nose into something you shouldn't?'

Rocco debated how far to go with Santer. They

were friends and former colleagues, and for that reason he didn't want to involve him in any way that would compromise him. But neither did he want to insult Santer by being coy. And he trusted the captain more than anyone he could think of, with the exception, perhaps, of Claude Lamotte.

'Saint-Cloud. You know him?'

'Saint-Cloud?' Santer's voice went even lower. 'Would that be the *Colonel* Saint-Cloud who runs the–'

'That's him.'

'Christ. Of course, I know *of* him. How the hell do you?'

Rocco explained in brief what Saint-Cloud had asked him to do. 'He has others doing the same thing – a sort of territorial eyes and ears on the lookout for groups likely to consider an attack.'

'You mean other investigators?'

'That's what he said.'

'*Pfff.*' A noise indicating disbelief came down the line. 'Why would he need to do that? They've got the entire security directorate to do that stuff – why get ordinary cops involved? No offence, mind.'

Santer had a point, but it wouldn't be the first time a security agency had stepped outside its normal parameters of operation to get what it wanted. In any case, the Directorate of Territorial Surveillance (DST) was part of the National Police, and responsible for domestic intelligence. As such, it could demand whatever assistance it liked. Quite where Saint-Cloud came in the scheme of things Rocco wasn't sure, but as he had demonstrated in Amiens, he clearly had the

128

power to walk in anywhere he pleased.

'Oh – hang on.' Santer wasn't finished. 'There was something else. I made a note. Yes, they found the car, as the briefing said.'

'A Simca Ariane. I know.'

'What they didn't say was that it wasn't as clean as the bad guys thought it was. They found a packet of cigarettes beneath one of the seats. An English make, with filters. Could be nothing, of course, but pretty unusual all the same.'

Rocco knew what he was getting at. People were moving around much more than they ever did, in the search for jobs, a better life, more opportunity. And criminals were no different. The world was smaller than it used to be, and those with money had access to things such as cigarettes that wouldn't have been quite so easy just a few years ago. But still. English cigarettes in a car used for an attack on the Establishment? It was a little odd. French criminals, if anything, were inclined towards the more popular American brands, especially those seen in the latest Hollywood films. It carried a special cachet, being seen to smoke an imported brand; made the user somehow more appealing, even if only in his own imagination.

'Do they know who might have been using them?' Find the smoker and check his movements; it was the logical step towards tracing the person's history and contacts.

'He didn't say. If they know, they're not including us in the briefing notes. Maybe one of them had been hiding out in England. It happens.' He hesitated, then added carefully, 'You know you should watch your back, Lucas. These people ...

they're not to be trusted, you know what I'm saying?'

'I know.' Santer was warning him about Saint-Cloud. The security establishment as a group had their own agendas, and Saint-Cloud was no different. He had enormous responsibilities for the French head of state's safety, and that meant that he would use any means he could to do his job. And if that included using a cop like Rocco in the line of duty, and not looking back if things went sour, he wouldn't hesitate. 'Did you hear anything over the wires from last night, about the South East?' It might be too early for word of the police raid on the garage to have reached Santer's ears, but it was worth a try.

'Like what? This is a big city, you know, with lights and the *Métro* and everything.' His voice was a sarcastic drawl. 'We even have cars and trucks and trains and buildings which almost reach the sky.'

'Créteil, you cretin. A raid on a garage. Three men taken in.'

'No. I haven't heard that. But I'll ask around.'

'Thanks. There's one more thing. Is Caspar still around?'

A heavy silence. For a brief moment Rocco thought Santer had gone. Then the captain said, 'He's around. Why?' He sounded cagey, and Rocco knew why.

'I might have some light work for him, if he's up to it.' Marc Casparon, better known as Caspar, was a burnt-out cop who'd worked too long undercover and had had to be quietly retired. Rocco had recently used him to penetrate an

Algerian gang, and it had nearly got him killed. But he knew Caspar was desperate to get back into the job; it was all he knew how to do. Rocco's problem might be getting past Santer, who was fiercely protective of the man.

'What sort of work?'

'Some legwork among the OAS groups and their affiliates. Who their contacts might be out this way. Is he well?'

'Actually, he's fine.' Santer surprised him. 'He's been doing jobs for a security company in St Denis. It seems to be working for him. You know he has limits, though, right? He pushes himself too far.'

In other words, don't put Caspar in direct danger.

'I understand.'

'Fine. You got his number?'

'Yes.'

'Right.' An urgent voice sounded in the background and Santer said, 'Listen I've got to go. I'll call if I hear anything else about ... you know. Remember what I said, Lucas: watch yourself. And start saving for that big lunch you owe me.'

The phone went dead.

Rocco dialled Caspar's number. It rang six times before the familiar voice answered. Caspar sounded alert, much more so than when Rocco had last seen him a few weeks ago. Then, he had been through a grinder and very nearly lost his life. Fortunately, he was made of tough stuff and had escaped with a slight flesh wound and a beating from a group of Algerian gangsters.

'It's Rocco,' he said. 'I need some help. It's police work but private billing. Are you available?'

He could almost hear the smile as Caspar's voice came down the line. 'You bet. Where and when?'

CHAPTER TWENTY

Rocco drove back out to the scrapyard. Caspar was on his way and would be here in the morning. He'd offered to go to Paris to brief him on his own ground, but Caspar had suggested the trip out and the change of scenery would help get the kinks of the city out of his system.

For now Rocco needed to lean on Bellin. It was too bad if the fat man was scared of being seen talking to the police; he should learn to mix with a nicer brand of people.

But he was out of luck. The yard was locked tight, two heavy chains holding the gates together. He banged on the corrugated sheets and immediately heard a dog barking followed by the skitter of paws as the animal raced up and down along the inside of the fence. It sounded big and mean and desperate to bite someone. Had Bellin panicked and decided to go home and keep his head down, or was his departure more long-term? He'd have to try again later.

He drove back to the station and sought out Dr Rizzotti in his office across the yard. He had completed his inspection of the car and was writing a full report with the help of the notes

132

dictated to the young officer.

'Interesting vehicle,' said Rizzotti, putting down his pen and stretching. 'If you like puzzles. Long or short version?'

'Short. I can read your report later.'

'All right. Very short, then. A Citroën DS, less than one year old, done a high number of kilometres for its age but with a registration not its own. The plates are home-made. Ten to one there's another car driving around somewhere with the same plates, only genuine. God knows where this one came from.'

Rocco nodded. 'So, a criminal enterprise. Anything else?'

'Not really. The addition of the framework inside is unusual, as are the seat harnesses. I've only ever seen those on rally cars before ... oh, and a stunt team who did a display here in Amiens last year. They wore them. Other than that, the car was clean save for the camera in the back, which I still can't explain. It's an old model, twenty years at least, as far as I can determine, probably lifted from an old studio junk heap. But who would drive around with an empty camera casing in the boot of their car?'

'Someone who wanted people to think he was making a film?'

'To impress the ladies?' He pursed his lips. 'It's possible, I suppose.'

'Was that all?'

Rizzotti smiled, the expression of a man who had a surprise in store. 'Actually, no. We found this under the carpet.' He pushed an envelope across his desk.

Rocco opened it. Inside was a butt end, smoked halfway down and flattened. A filter tip, with some printing on the white paper. *Wills.*

'English make,' said Rizzotti. 'I'm not sure which specific brand – the company of Wills make several. We could always send it to them for verifying if you wish. As you can see, it looks reasonably fresh – the paper hasn't been stained by damp or dirt.'

Yet another reference to England. First the English drunks in the *Canard Doré*, then the cigarette packet in the car used for the attack on the N19, followed by the English penny in the burnt-out truck. Now this. Add the smell of an Englishman's aftershave in the Citroën as well, which, although a flimsy link and all but impossible to prove, seemed very conclusive. Or was he jumping to too many conclusions in the hopes of a rapid resolution?

'Thanks, Doc.' He was turning to leave when he noticed a small key lying on Rizzotti's desk. It was discoloured along the toothed edge and blackened on the inside of the hole where it would be held on a ring. 'What's that?'

'It's the key to the burnt truck. I was hoping to have it traced but there's no serial number. It looks like a cheap copy. You can get them made up almost anywhere for a few francs. Why?'

Rocco felt in his pocket and took out the key Tasker had been staring at, but had denied knowing anything about. He dropped it alongside the one on Rizzotti's desk.

They were an exact match.

He walked round to a nearby bar frequented by cops, his mind on what he could do with this latest information. The key tied Tasker to the Renault truck, he was convinced. But even if they got him back, he would simply deny knowing anything about the key and claim it had been left lying around in the station by someone else and became mixed with his personal possessions. A clever lawyer would have it thrown out in an instant.

He took a table in the corner, nodding at a few familiar faces at the bar. Cops going off duty taking a drink, cops going on duty hitting the coffee to stay awake throughout their shift. The same scene would be replicated in every town across the country. He saw Alix at a table on the far side of the room. She was sitting with the young officer who'd been helping Rizzotti with his examination of the DS. She smiled faintly and nodded, then excused herself and stood up. She crossed the room and stopped at his table.

'So, Inspector,' she said, 'have you solved the puzzle of the fragrance yet?'

'Not yet. But I will. Thank you for your help, by the way. You were correct – it was aftershave.'

'But you don't know whose?'

'Actually, I do.'

Her eyebrows lifted. 'So it's true what they say about you. You are some kind of wizard when it comes to finding clues. I must remember never to do anything wrong with you around.' Her eyes remained innocent, and Rocco felt he'd missed something. Or maybe not.

'I'm not a Canadian Mountie,' he said. 'I don't always get my man.' He looked past her to where the young officer whom Rizzotti had referred to as Romeo was throwing dark looks his way. 'Is he trying to convey some sort of message?'

Alix clearly didn't need to turn and see who he was talking about. 'He's young,' she said, which, coming from her made it sound like a capital offence. 'He thinks because I said yes to coffee, it means something else. I'm not sure how to break the bad news to him that I'm not interested.'

'I do. Introduce him to your father.'

She laughed aloud, a burst of spontaneity that seemed to go well with the freckles on her nose. 'That's a low blow. A good idea, though.' She turned and went back to the table, leaving Rocco to conclude that if Romeo persisted in his pursuit of Alix, Claude Lamotte was probably going to get a phone call soon asking him to bring his shotgun.

His coffee arrived and he went back to thinking about his immediate problems. He still couldn't make out what the crash was all about. It patently wasn't a real film set, as evidenced by the fake camera. So what was it? A stunt of some kind? The presence of seat harnesses clearly indicated that the driver and passenger had expected to be involved in some kind of dangerous manoeuvre, but how and why was open to speculation.

Then there was the increasing likelihood that the group of English drunks were involved. Certainly Calloway was. If he had driven the DS, what about the other men? Had one of them – Tasker, perhaps – been driving the Renault truck, with the others playing the gunmen who had attacked the car after the ramming?

It was the DS which puzzled him most. Nobody trashes a car like that without good cause. A rehearsal for a film, maybe, but with a fake camera, this was clearly no film.

Which left one thing.

It had been a rehearsal for something else.

CHAPTER TWENTY-ONE

Unable to sleep for the thoughts whirling around in his head, Rocco got up early, put a saucepan of water on a low heat, then dressed quickly in a tracksuit and went for a run. It was still dark outside, but he was able to follow the lane out from the village easily enough, his usual training route when he was in the mood.

The air was bitingly cold and deathly still, and he'd even got the jump on the village cockerels, usually so vocal and quick to wake everyone. Other than the brief stomping of a few cows startled by his passing, and one or two early birds ignoring the mad human to start the day with their singing, he was alone. No traffic, either, as usual. Perfect.

He covered a kilometre at a brisk rate, then turned and jogged back. In spite of the temperature, he'd built up a sweat and his lungs were aching as they took in the chilled air. As a training run it was nothing like enough, but better than nothing.

Back indoors, he bathed, drank his coffee, then headed for the car. He wanted to get to the office

137

before the main shift came on and the atmosphere got blown to hell by noise, confusion and the daily briefing, which he tried to miss anyway. He also wanted to take a good look at the wall map and have a think.

The map in the main office was big enough to include even small details of the countryside up to thirty kilometres out from Amiens, including tracks, streams, old WWI and WWII ammunition sites, trenches and other topographical details natural and man-made. The only items not marked were the many filled-in shell craters left over from the war, their locations circular white scars on the land and still visible if one knew where to look.

Rocco focused on the roads.

He grabbed a chair and sat down with a fresh coffee, staring up at the map and following the network of major roads likely to be used during a visit, linking Amiens with the safest routes in and out, and the quickest route to and from Paris. He discounted the main national roads, where ambush points were aplenty simply by being accessible from both sides. Saint-Cloud and his men would have the most obvious choke points covered, using the local police to flood the area and discourage anyone from considering any possible assault. Instead, he looked for some kind of pattern elsewhere, something that would jump off the wall and smack him between the eyes.

But nothing did.

He made more coffee, brutally strong this time, with lots of sugar, and tried to stop thinking like a policeman. He had to get into the mind of the attackers, of the men who wanted de Gaulle out of the picture for ever. He had to picture how, rather than preventing a killing, he would execute one. He had to go against the grain.

To think like an assassin.

He shuffled close to the map on the chair and sat back, eyeing the uneven web of roads. He automatically discounted anywhere close to villages or towns, anywhere where security forces would be certain to close down the area, flooding all possible means of escape with men and guns. That way lay certain failure.

So, somewhere remote, then.

He thought about where de Gaulle would be likely to go if he came here. And come here he would, he was certain of that. There could only be a limited number of places the president would consider worthwhile visiting out here, from strategically important industrial sites to places of national interest. And each one of those would have to be a point of maximum political impact. The president would want it, the advisors would suggest it – and the public would expect it.

Something out there must ring a bell.

He thought back to previous attacks. The only common denominators seemed to be de Gaulle on one side and his enemies on the other. And although the use of cars, guns and explosives was common, as were roadside attacks, none of them presented a pattern. All the attacks were clearly planned, but the methodology was almost random in nature, perpetrated by different groups with different training, skills and reasoning. Except that they all aimed at what usually turned out to be an official car.

An official car.

Like they use in processions.

A Citroën DS.

He skidded the chair closer, his heart tripping faster as the possibilities began building in his mind. He was looking at the section of the map which included the road where Simeon had witnessed the ramming incident, and thinking about rehearsals. The road was nowhere special ... not even on a regular through-route and little used even by locals. But that surely made it ideal for a practice run; something you didn't want anyone to see, where timing and distance had to be specific.

A truck with a battering ram on the front. Thinking of assaults on a car, that detail alone was very unusual: someone had decided that whatever they were going to do, guns alone would not work. So, if it was a rehearsal, all he had to do was figure out where the real event was to take place. Presumably somewhere similar in layout.

Twenty minutes later, he was about to give up when his eyes landed on a straight section of road in the middle of open countryside, several kilometres from any visible habitation. The ground looked level, there were few trees or other natural cover, unless what looked like a smudge mark was a small copse.

Something about it made his gut clench.

He checked the scale of the map. The smudge lay approximately two hundred metres from the road. Almost adjacent to it on the map, the road was flanked by two broad lines and chevrons indicating a cutting. Or was it an embankment? God, he should know this – he'd studied enough maps in his time, reading them like a book to determine fighting terrain, gradients, dead ground, approach routes and exits. He rubbed his face. He'd had too much coffee and too little sleep. He felt a burst of impatience and went to the legend panel in one corner, showing the scale and markings. Chevrons – that was it. It meant the road passed over a bridge with a gully beneath.

Back to the map.

The layout was similar enough to where the ramming had happened, but he could see no reason why anyone, least of all the president, would need to travel along it. It was in the middle of nowhere, for God's sake. Just a boring, straight, little-used piece of tarmac lost in a patchwork of fields made famous only by history.

He bent closer. Faint lettering showed against the bridge.

Pont Noir. Black bridge.

He turned and checked the office. A uniformed officer was working quietly across the far side. He was a long-service member named Berthier, consigned to desk duties. If anyone knew the area, he would.

'What's the Pont Noir?' Rocco asked him.

The man looked blank for a moment, his concentration broken. Then, 'Ah, Pont Noir. You've never been there?'

'No.'

'It's like ... a war relic – a site.'

'A memorial?'

'Not yet – but it's going to be. It's a deep gully, some say formed centuries ago. They uncovered a number of military remains there a couple of

141

years ago, then a lot more just recently. French, mostly, but British, Indians and Australians, too. Like the League of Nations. They think it could have been a field hospital from the First World War, dug into the gully as protective cover. A team of university archaeologists are out there on and off, along with British and Australian volunteers. They've been trying to get it excavated and declared a national monument. It's not the sort of place to take your girlfriend, though.'

'Why?'

The man hesitated, wary of causing offence. 'It's ... creepy. Always chilly, even in summer. It's like there's no life to the place ... like the warmth has been sucked out of it.' He shrugged, embarrassed. 'Sorry, but you'd have to go there to see what I mean.'

'Who would know most about it?'

'There's a British War Graves Commission office in Arras – they've been monitoring and running the excavations. But the local historical society would be involved, too, and the national monuments office in Paris.'

War graves. Rocco remembered John Cooke, the British gardener who worked in the area. He'd met him on his first day in Poissons, when he'd found a dead woman in the British military cemetery just outside the village. The man had been helpful and calm in the face of what had been a daunting discovery.

He checked his watch. Just after eight. Where the hell had time gone? He looked up the number of the Arras office and dialled, and immediately got through to a superintendent named

142

Blake, who spoke fluent French.

'The site was uncovered not long ago after a landfall,' the man told him. 'A number of remains were found, and it was initially thought to have been a roadside burial site, maybe near a field hospital, which they hadn't had time to signpost during a battle. That happened quite a lot, and sites easily got lost. At first it seemed to be mainly British and Australians, then a researcher in London found a reference written on a battlefield map, so they began digging a bit wider. What they discovered was a whole network of graves up to a hundred and fifty strong.'

'So it's a cemetery,' said Rocco.

'Not quite, Inspector. Partly because of the location in the gully, and the difficulty of accessing it for visitors and the likelihood of further subsidence, we're in the process of moving the remains to a site nearby, clear of the road. But there are ... sensitivities about the area.'

'In what way?'

'Some want the road and bridge closed permanently as a mark of respect to the dead. It's actually not used much and they say it would be easy to use alternative routes. But plans have been put forward by the Australian and British Governments, countries which have the majority of dead on the site, for a memorial to be erected nearby, and for the road to be kept open as a sign of unity and determination.'

'What's the likely outcome?'

'Oh, I have no doubt their proposal will go ahead. We've already marked out a potential site with access for visitors. And approval has already come from the highest level, in fact.'

'Meaning?'

'The president himself.' His voice dropped. 'In fact – and this is top secret, you understand – he's expressed a wish to make a private visit when he's next in the area, as a sign of respect. As a military man himself, he likes the idea of a memorial. All we need to know now is when that will be.'

CHAPTER TWENTY-TWO

Rocco thanked Blake and put the phone down. He turned back to the map. His head was buzzing and he suddenly wanted a drink. Unwise, under the circumstances, and not a good idea generally, although it would certainly dull the enormity of the idea forming in his mind. But that was the last thing he wanted to do.

A war memorial in the making, in the middle of nowhere, with de Gaulle's full approval and an expressed desire to visit the site without public ceremony or the customary press entourage. Suddenly Saint-Cloud's briefing and what Massin had told him about the attack on the official car was assuming a whole different slant.

If Blake knew, why hadn't Saint-Cloud mentioned it? Or was Blake merely playing up the possibility to highlight the presence of the burial site?

As he stared at the map, he felt the hairs move on the back of his neck. It wasn't just the road or where it led to that mattered. It was something else. Faintly drawn, as if the draftsman had been unsure about whether it existed or not, a thin line met the road at right angles.

It was a track, coming out of the fields immediately adjacent to the bridge. A single track, probably unsurfaced, and meeting the road immediately opposite a point where the gully was at its deepest.

He grabbed a sheet of white paper and a pencil from a desk nearby and slapped it over the map where the ramming had occurred. Drawing quick lines on the paper, he sketched a rough outline of the track and the road, adding a circle to show the conifers where the camera had been stationed and where Simeon's mysterious watcher had been standing.

Then he slid the paper across and placed it over the area of the Pont Noir, where the road crossed the bridge ... and a track came out of nowhere at right angles. The only thing missing was the clump of pine trees.

Other than that, it was almost identical.

Rocco felt his heart pounding. There were times – not often, but rewardingly common enough – when idle thoughts, coupled with facts and suspicions, turned to absolute certainty. And right now was one of those times.

He picked up the telephone. It was time to call Saint-Cloud. If anyone could confirm the exact itinerary and timing for the president to visit the Pont Noir, it would be his security chief.

Then he put down the receiver.

He couldn't think why, but instinct made him decide against talking to Saint-Cloud just yet. He

145

stared instead at the map, and his overlay of the road and track.

If he understood the map details and the descriptions correctly, the road ran across the bridge, which spanned a drop into a deep gully. Beyond the bridge lay open fields, a smoothly rolling expanse of Somme countryside, no doubt dotted with the trademark white blemishes of former shell-holes and trenches so common in the area. No other roads, no houses or farm buildings. Anyone driving along it had a clear run to the main road three kilometres away. If they made it that far, they were away and free.

He shivered. *He was thinking like an assassin.*

His eyes were drawn back to the bridge. To the track.

He was looking at a kill zone.

CHAPTER TWENTY-THREE

By the time Rocco arrived at the Pont Noir, it was raining hard, cold, stinging needles that numbed the skin and blurred the landscape, moving across the fields in a malevolent cloud, drenching everything in their path. He shrugged it off; bad weather had never bothered him much, not once he'd got an idea firing up and needing answers. And this one was beginning to call loud and clear.

He walked to the centre of the structure. Other than the patter of the rain, it was deathly quiet here, and considerably colder than in town, as if the weather wanted to punish the rolling fields for being there. But there was something else, too: it was, as Berthier had said in his apologetically poetic manner, as if history itself had laid its ghostly hand on the area, draining the land of any warmth. Then a bird sang; a single trill, but distant and faint, as if it didn't wish to come close to disturb this place with its cheerful song. Maybe it was protesting at the rain. Or maybe it had forgotten to leave for warmer climes.

The bridge's parapet consisted of thick wire hawsers linking a series of metal posts each two metres apart. Rocco peered over the wires to the gully below. It was a long way down. He shuffled forward until his toes protruded over the iron lip along the edge and used his rain-spotted toecaps as gun sights, focusing on the ground. He wondered what had caused this enormous gash in the earth. It was overgrown in places, nature having reclaimed it over the years, with an array of rabbit holes in the side of the bank between scrubby bushes holding the soil together. There were clear signs of man-made digging, too, with strips of tape between small white posts marking where measurements had been made.

He shivered and continued walking, his footsteps brisk on the tarmac. The surface of the road was good, solid and smooth, untroubled by the passage of too many heavy trucks. He stepped off the far end of the bridge and walked a hundred metres or so to where something white fluttered on a post adjacent to the road. It stood out because it was so out of place amid these fields. He found an oblong patch of mud the size of a

147

rugby pitch marked out by pegs and white tape. Inside the oblong were more lines and squares, similar to the kind of markings used by builders.

It was the planned memorial site.

Rocco stared across the fields, scanning the area back to the bridge. The landscape lay muffled and still beneath the blanket of cold rain, fields normally full of sugar beet and wheat now empty and soaked, uninviting. A male hare moved against the background in the middle of a field, slow and cautious like an old man testing his limbs, rather than the fleet-footed creature that it could be, and one or two birds circled further away, seeking thermals to carry them higher.

Other than that, nothing.

He tried to picture this place as it had been nearly half a century ago, churned by war and man, an open charnel house, muddy, cold and desolate and dotted with humanity, some alive, most not. Even with his experience of war, he found it difficult; the war here had been like no other. He thought instead of the symbolism involved: of the president coming here to give a nod of his head to a stone representing what had gone before, so that others might feel a sense of recognition, of remembrance. Not that Rocco objected to that; he just wondered what the men themselves would have thought had they been given a voice, their symbolism being shifted without consultation. Ignored in the campaign for a war, ignored in the planning of a battle, pounded beyond recognition during its execution and shunted around for convenience afterwards like pieces of furniture.

He turned and walked back to the bridge. A

148

few metres beyond it lay the mouth of the track he'd seen on the map, coming out at right angles from the fields. It looked little used, although flat and compacted and very straight. There were no ruts that he could see, just a few faint imprints of horses' hooves. Carthorses were still the norm around here, ponderous and powerful beasts, a world away yet from what was common elsewhere. Tractors were coming in, but financial help was expensive. For those rich in time but with little money, the old ways still prevailed.

A sad-looking wooden structure sat alongside the track a hundred and fifty metres away. Too big to be a shed, but too small for a barn, it was black and forlorn and looked as if a strong wind might send it tumbling across the fields at any moment like an empty cardboard box. Topped by a rusting corrugated-metal roof, it looked forgotten and forlorn, like the track itself, with only a line of pigeons sitting on the apex to give it any semblance of current use. Life and progress had passed by very closely over the years, with the road and the bridge, brushing against it. Yet the shed had remained as it had always been, ignored and desolate, a monument to a time long gone.

He walked up the track, the mud sucking at the soles of his shoes, and wondered how far the track ran. The map hadn't been detailed enough for that, and it would take some local knowledge to find out for sure. But someone would know.

He bent and examined the ground. Tyre marks, puddled with muddy water, showed where a vehicle had pulled in and stopped. Clear treads, sharply outlined. Not tractor tyres, nor cartwheels, which would have been worn smooth. Something newer. Heavy. And footprints where the driver had climbed out. Not a farmer's boots, with their heavy, wavy-line patterns and worn-down heels, but flat soles, smooth, with sharply defined edges like his own.

City shoes.

He approached the shed. The pigeons watched him come, then took off in a rush, scattering into the sky in a burst of flapping wings, leaving behind a stained roof and a few drifting feathers. The dilapidated structure they'd been perched on looked even worse up close, a miracle of dogged survival in decayed wood and corrugated sheeting, the slats of the walls curled at the ends and shot through with knot holes that had long lost their hard centres.

He peered through one of the holes. What limited light there was filtering through showed a floor covered by browned, dry grass and nettles to waist height, throttling a set of rusted harrows. Stacks of rotting wooden crates piled haphazardly to the ceiling, remnants of a long-forgotten harvest, took up the remainder of the space. One of the wall slats moved as he touched it, and dropped like a guillotine, narrowly missing his fingers. He decided to leave well alone before the whole place fell on him. Desmoulins would have a field day if he had to come and dig him out from under a fallen barn. He checked the near end of the structure, which had two large doors held together by a huge padlock. It was rusted with age, the keyhole jammed with years of dirt.

A car engine broke into the silence, followed by

the hiss of tyres on wet tarmac. He turned as a beaten-up grey van clattered by on the road, the driver an old man in workman's blues and a peaked cap giving a jaunty salute through the flapping quarter-light.

Rocco watched as it disappeared into the distance, taking the rain with it and leaving behind nothing but the drip-drip and gurgle of water running off the fields and into a storm gully.

It was the only vehicle to have passed by since he'd arrived.

He walked back down the track and heard the beat of wings as the pigeons returned, reclaiming their places on the shed roof. He crossed the road and stopped at the top of the bank on the far side, where stout white poles standing at knee height were the only indication of the road's edge and the drop beneath. He looked down, his feet close to the lip. It wasn't quite so far down at this point as it was in the centre of the bridge, but still dizzying enough.

At the bottom was a gleam of water; a natural pond formed by nature, its surface as forbidding as black glass, the edges an indistinct mass of weeds and reeds.

He tried not to think about what would happen to any car plunging down right here, or the occupants trapped inside.

CHAPTER TWENTY-FOUR

Bellin's scrapyard after the rain looked even more miserable than before. The gates looked shoddy and sad, dripping wet, and the surrounding fence was as unwelcoming as a mausoleum.

Rocco stopped his car just short of the entrance and climbed out.

The DS was somehow at the heart of this whole thing, he was certain of it. As Desmoulins had said, nobody orders the scrapping of an expensive piece of machinery like the DS merely because of a dent in one side – not even extravagant film-makers with their investors' cash to spare.

The gates were unchained.

He slipped through without touching the corrugated cladding, and instantly felt the sour grave-yard atmosphere closing around him, the piles of dead cars and torn metal like jagged, rusting monuments to man's wasteful extravagance.

He remembered the dog barking last time. There was none of that now; no signs of occupation, no banging or grinding of machinery. But guard dogs didn't always signal in advance that they were coming. They just arrived and began chewing bits out of intruders.

He took out the MAB 38 and checked the magazine.

'Bellin?' There was no echo; his voice simply vanished, soaked up by the years of dirt and oil and scrap metal.

An ancient ship's bell was hanging from a post near the cabin door. He rattled the rope and set off a deep clanging noise which seemed to reverberate through the piles of metal like a mad symphony, flushing a clutch of small birds into the air.

But no human reaction.

He checked the cabin, which was unlocked. It was cramped and squalid, doubling as an office and shop, every available centimetre packed with rescued mirrors, lamps, steering wheels, hubcaps and other unnameable car parts from hundreds of different vehicles. A man's coat was draped across a chair, the cloth once good but now worn and shiny and ragged around the hem. A mug of chocolate stood on a small desk, a thin tail of steam curling into the air.

He checked the phone. Still working.

Back outside, he stood listening. He thought he'd heard something. Or maybe it had been the breeze sighing through the twisted towers of metal, setting up a mournful whining sound like souls in torment. If Bellin was here, he was keeping very quiet or was already buried under a pile of his own scrap.

Unless the dog had eaten him.

He walked through the yard, stepping carefully over patches of oil and shimmering multicoloured patches of spilt fuel. Shards of discarded metal sprouted like bright, spiky weeds amid a carpet of windscreen fragments, the whole scene resembling a madman's sordid, glistening patchwork.

He rounded a pile of battered door panels at the very rear of the yard. Bellin was sitting alongside a wrecked tractor sprouting weeds from its wheels, its location and condition a sign of just how old the place was. He was sucking nervously on a roll-up twisted like a stick of pasta and stained by oily fingers. He appeared indifferent to Rocco's arrival, but there was no mistaking the pallor of a man terrified out of his mind.

Rocco said, 'You're a hard man to find.' He glanced round at the walls of metal. It was like a bunker of junk. Except that there was only the one way out.

Bellin eyed the gun. 'What the hell do you want?' he whispered. He dropped the remains of the cigarette on the ground between his feet. It joined several others already laying there, some dug into the earth by his heel.

'I'd like another chat. Is the dog around?'

A shake of the head. 'They're gone.'

'Gone? Who?'

'Jacques and Bruno – who do you think? The two you saw before.' He scrabbled in his shirt pocket and pulled out a flat tin. Prising the lid off with a filthy, curled thumbnail, he extracted another roll-up. He snapped the lid shut and put the tin away, then took out a lighter and fired up the cigarette, dragging in a lungful of smoke. 'That's your doing; you drove them away.'

'Maybe they got a better offer. What about the dog?' He was becoming unnerved by the silence in the yard. All this metal and no noise; it didn't feel right.

'Fuck the dog.' Bellin hawked noisily and spat on the ground. 'You've killed me, you know that?'

'How do you work that out?' Rocco tested the

front wing of a truck and sat down. He had his back to the nearest metal pile, kept the gun in his hand. If the dog came hunting, he'd have two, maybe three seconds to stop it.

'You and your questions, coming here in your big black car and nosing around like God Almighty. It's not right.' Bellin didn't appear to have heard him, but was rambling along on automatic, the bitter, resentful words spilling out as if released from captivity. 'You might as well have put up a sign with a bloody great arrow pointing at me.' He sucked at the cigarette but it had gone out. He crumpled the dead smoke in thick fingers and dropped the shredded remnants on the ground. Spat a mouthful of phlegm after it.

'You're not making much sense.'

'Word. Word got out that you'd come round asking about the DS. Doesn't take any time at all for that to spread.'

'Word got out to whom?'

'I should've burnt that bloody thing the moment it arrived here – and the driver with it. Poured petrol on it and watched it melt.' He dug a heel into the soft ground, grinding some of the butt ends deeper into the mud with studied viciousness. 'I should've known it'd come to no good.'

'If you help me,' said Rocco, 'I can help you.'

Bellin's eyes threw back the futility of that promise. 'You think? You have a safe place where they can't get at me? A big dark hole where even the light doesn't shine?' He sighed. 'I'd be dead inside two days.'

'If that's the case, and you're that important to them – whoever they are – you should consider

155

my offer.'

'Important?' Bellin didn't even lift his head. 'I'm not important.'

'So why would they come after you so quickly?' He knew the answer perfectly well, but it was better to keep Bellin talking.

The scrap dealer gave a tired smile. 'You know why, Rocco. You've been round the block; I've heard things about you, so don't pretend to be the thick-eared country cop. You know how things work.'

He was right. Rocco knew all too well. Whoever Bellin worked for, if they thought he was doing anything more than being seen by the police about a suspicious car, they would come after him. No other reason existed. It was enough that he was seen talking to them out in the open. But if he agreed to go in, it would be seen as the ultimate betrayal, and that would merit an example to be set and a message to others.

Rocco opened his mouth to say more, then closed it again. He'd come across many others like Bellin; recognised them for what they were. Coarsened and brutalised by a life of petty crime and used by others more powerful than them, they strutted through life like winners in their own small world, but underneath it all were in constant fear of retribution from those same people whom they feared or had offended in some way. What Bellin lacked right now, here, today, was the imagination to survive, to tear himself away and flee. He was trapped by his own surroundings, unable to visualise an alternative, like a steer in a slaughter yard awaiting its fate.

CHAPTER TWENTY-FIVE

He left Bellin to his self-imposed misery and drove back to the station. He would come back once the man had taken a while to think over his options. He was almost there, living the threat that was hanging over him, real or imagined; all it would need was a nudge and he'd crumble.

It was nearly lunchtime and quiet. He found Colonel Saint-Cloud in his temporary office studying a sheaf of papers.

'I think I've found a possible attack site,' Rocco told him.

Saint-Cloud gave a slight lift of an eyebrow. He was clearly sceptical but the statement seemed to take him by surprise. 'How could you do that? You don't even know the proposed route or timing.'

'I know the president has expressed a desire to visit a local monument. I also know it will be a private visit, so no entourage, no press and minimum security presence other than his normal bodyguards. And I know how the attack will be carried out. What I don't know for sure is when, or by whom.'

The wall clock ticked loudly several times before the colonel said, 'How could you even know about such a place or the president's interest in it?' His face looked tight, and his voice carried a hint of disbelief. 'Who told you?'

'I learnt about it earlier this morning. It doesn't

matter who told me.' Rocco didn't want Blake to get into trouble, although he couldn't think why Blake would have told him about it unless it was already known in certain quarters.

'I think it matters very much. I would like the name, please, Rocco.'

Rocco shook his head. 'If the information is out there already, Colonel, and I heard about it, then it's too late to matter. The person who told me is not a threat, I promise you. But ignoring it is.'

More ticks of the clock, then, 'Very well. You had better show me.'

Rocco led him downstairs to the wall map, and asked Berthier to clear the office and make sure nobody entered. When the door was closed, he explained in brief what he believed would happen, based on having seen the location and the entrance and exit roads, and its uncanny similarity to the site of the ramming. He used his rough-drawn sketch to back this up, then stood back and let Saint-Cloud think it over. What he didn't mention was Calloway and his colleagues; while all the clues pointed towards their involvement somehow, he still wasn't sure how a group of Englishmen could be tied in with an assassination attempt on the French head of state. That part still made no sense. Besides, there were other reasons why he didn't want to set that particular hare running just yet.

The colonel seemed unimpressed. 'I can see why you would consider this, Inspector. But the president has given no indications to me that he intends going to this Pont Noir, wherever it is. It may well have some historic and social importance to France and other countries, but he has far more important places to visit. In fact, I can show you one where my own experience tells me he is far more vulnerable ... and where I have good reason to believe he'll go very soon.' He gave a thin smile. 'I do have experience of these matters. Ensuring the safety of the President of the Republic is not as straightforward as catching criminals, I assure you.'

Rocco couldn't understand why Saint-Cloud was being so dismissive. But he was remembering Santer's warning about watching his back, and his vulnerability should anything go wrong. He'd been assigned to Saint-Cloud to help with the security review, and that was what he was doing. But he was determined not to be fobbed off because of the security chief's superiority over a police detective. 'I think you need to see this place for yourself.'

Saint-Cloud looked almost affronted at having his decision questioned. He took a deep breath and said coldly, 'Are you absolutely certain, Inspector Rocco, that you have not allowed yourself to be influenced by some ... disconnected but inexplicable events involving a car and a truck, driven by people you have not yet found? I can see why you would draw the conclusions you have, but this all seems ... circumstantial, and frankly, nothing more than cinematic in scope.'

'Maybe. But it won't harm to look, will it? And,' he added dryly, 'your expertise will soon prove it one way or another.'

It was a challenge Saint-Cloud couldn't ignore, nor could he dismiss the suggestion of an eyeball inspection. 'Very well,' he said stiffly. 'How long will it take? Only I have a meeting in one hour. I'll take my own car.'

'Depends how fast you drive,' said Rocco. He headed for the door and the rear car park. 'Follow me and I'll show you.' A strong grain of rebellion resisted the courtesy of offering the colonel a lift. Besides, he had a feeling the man would only sneer at Rocco's Traction and deem it unworthy of a proper policeman.

As he turned along the corridor leading to the back door, leaving Saint-Cloud to get his car keys, he saw Caspar walking towards him, a relaxed grin on his face. They shook hands and Rocco led the former undercover cop outside.

'Good to see you again,' he said quickly, unlocking his car. 'Thanks for coming.'

Caspar looked in good trim, although still gaunt, but less strained than he had previously, less haunted. 'My pleasure. I needed a change of scenery, anyway. And it gave me an excuse to sit on a train and do nothing for a while.'

'Good idea. Santer says you're working.'

'Yes. Some regular jobs doing security and a bit of low-level surveillance. Nothing too big yet. But getting there.' He smiled almost shyly, his demeanour a complete transformation from when Rocco had last seen him. But then, he had been beaten and shot, which tends to make even the strong wilt a little. 'But this is good.'

'You still want to get back in?' Caspar had been suspended on health grounds after the strain of working undercover had become too great. But he'd been desperate to regain his badge ever since, convinced he could still make a contribution.

'Actually, I'm no longer so sure about that.'

'Really? What's changed?'

'The work. The stuff I do now, it's got its moments, but there's no longer the same pressure. There's some risk, but I can handle it.' He shrugged. 'And I'm not kidding myself anymore, you know? I was too near the edge for too long. Problem was, I couldn't see it.' He grinned suddenly. 'Anyway, I've got a girlfriend now. Christ, I'm almost respectable!'

Moments later, Saint-Cloud came out and climbed in his car. If he noticed Caspar, he gave no indication. Rocco led the way out to the Pont Noir, filling in Caspar on the way, including Bellin's part in the car's planned disappearance.

'I'll put the word out,' Caspar said. 'See what the gossips are saying.'

'It was just a car – a tool for a job. But I think Bellin was being paid by someone big to get rid of it; someone he's terrified of.'

'Someone around here?'

Rocco shook his head. 'Someone in Paris.' The capital was full of scary people; people who'd only have to glance at a man like Bellin to throw him into a funk.

Caspar puffed his cheeks. 'Christ, that narrows it down a bit. But not much.' He nodded through the windscreen. 'He looks familiar. Not your boss, is he?'

'Have you heard of Colonel Saint-Cloud?'

'What, Big Charles's bodyguard?' Caspar looked impressed. 'That's him? What's he doing here – and why you?'

'I was about to explain that. You'll be working on his payroll, although I don't expect you to like him for it.'

'Great. And as long as I don't have to throw myself in front of a bullet for him.'

'I had the same thought.' He explained where they were going, and Saint-Cloud's resistance to the idea of an attack site or the method involved.

Caspar caught on fast. He'd been around senior officers and officials enough to know that one always had to be on one's guard. 'Right. So it's eyes and ears to the ground, keep my head down and my mouth shut.'

'Exactly. Find out anything you can about the attack at Guignes ... and whether it's possible they or another group could be planning a follow-up here. They might be crazy enough to try again just because nobody expects it.'

'Or someone will try to top it.' Caspar stared out of the window. 'Wouldn't take much, topping failure with a successful hit.'

'Or that.'

'So he's definitely coming?' Caspar meant de Gaulle.

'Saint-Cloud seems to think so, but he's not giving anything away.' He told him what Blake had said about the private visit.

'I'll see what I can find out. I know a few OAS guys with long memories, but they've gone quiet since independence. I doubt they're still active, although they might know people who are. What exactly do you want me to do?'

'Dig around, see if you can get a line on any groups with contacts out this way. So far I've got nothing because Saint-Cloud's given me nothing. But I don't want to be handed my head on a plate for not trying, and missing something obvious ... something you might be able to dig out instead. Santer will fill you in on the N19 attack, but that ended so badly, I wouldn't rate them as being ready for another go.'

'Sounds like it was costly, losing two men for a carload of paperwork.'

Rocco agreed. It still puzzled him that the attackers, which had included a former soldier, had stumbled so badly. Getting imprecise information on a target's timing or route was always a risk plotters had to juggle with. But getting it so badly wrong had been disastrous on an epic scale. It prompted a thought.

'You might get Santer to find out the name of the motorcycle escort who fought back. See if you can speak to him.'

'Why – you think there's something there?'

'Well, he's wasted riding a bike, for a start. If that's his real job.'

Caspar's eyes went wide as he considered the implications. 'Damn, you've got a devious mind, Rocco.' He nodded. 'I'll see what I can find.'

Rocco pulled in to the side of the road opposite the track, just short of the bridge. He and Caspar climbed out as Saint-Cloud parked in front and walked back to join them.

'Who is this?' he queried, as if noticing Caspar for the first time. He shrugged on a warm coat, the skin on his face pinched and white, and Rocco wondered how often he ever got out of the

163

office on field trips.

He made introductions, but Saint-Cloud seemed barely interested. 'Fine,' he said, when Rocco told him Caspar was on the strength and would be looking into the Paris end of things. 'Whatever you think is necessary. Clear payment with my office.' He glanced at Caspar. 'Just make sure you find me some names, you understand? We'll drop the hammer on them. We need to stop this thing before it goes too far.' He glanced around at the bridge and fields. 'Is this it? This is your suggested attack zone?' He shook his head. 'Rocco, you disappoint me.'

Rocco bit his tongue. Losing his temper with Saint-Cloud would serve no purpose. He indicated the point where the road passed the mouth of the track. 'I believe they'll leave some kind of obstruction here to slow down the president's car... work signs, something like that. But instead of using guns, they'll come down the track past that shed, using a truck to drive the official car off the road here and over the edge.' The shed's pigeons, he noted, were looking at the three men with wary interest. No doubt they had learnt at an early stage that anything that flew was fair game for the end of a long gun.

Rocco led the other two to the brink of the gully and pointed down. The drop drew a faint oath from Saint-Cloud. 'Once down there, there's no coming back. They could do whatever they choose to finish the job. There'll be nobody to stop them.'

Saint-Cloud looked sceptical. 'Oh, you mean wine bottles filled with petrol? Like you said that farmer saw the film crew using? The idiot was deluded. Who throws petrol bombs anymore?'

Caspar frowned, unfazed by Saint-Cloud's rank or position. 'I saw Molotovs being used during a protest in Saint Denis a couple of months back. Pretty effective they were. Set a couple of cop cars on fire, broke up the CRS ranks, too, for a while.' He looked down the slope and murmured, 'If I was going to make sure nobody got out of a car alive, down there is where I'd do it.' He shivered. 'Nasty way to go.'

'Well, thank you for that expert analysis,' Saint-Cloud muttered. 'Believe me, these disaffected groups prefer streets for their cowardly attacks, not open fields. Busy roads, traffic, people – and escape routes for when they run out of courage or ammunition. Out here, they'd be exposed ... vulnerable and frightened.' He turned and walked away across the bridge, stiff-legged and impatient.

'What an arse,' Caspar murmured. 'On past experience, he's right ... but that's just being blinkered. Makes you wonder how de Gaulle survived this long with him in charge.'

'Because when it came down to it, others were providing the real protection,' said Rocco. He felt surprisingly calm in the face of Saint-Cloud's scepticism. He had a feeling he wasn't going to win this one, not here and now. But that meant he'd simply have to prove he was right.

Saint-Cloud came back across the bridge, shaking his head. 'No – I don't buy it. The president is unlikely to come this way, and even if he wanted to, there's no way we could let him come to such an isolated spot without full protection. Once any attackers saw that we were prepared, with no way out, they'd call it off.'

'And go underground,' Rocco pointed out.

'Maybe. Maybe not. But I have a better idea of where they might plan an attack. And it fits with what we know of their methods. Come on.' He walked back to his car, leaving the other two to follow.

Saint-Cloud drove fast and efficiently, showing that he was not entirely without skills outside the office. They soon arrived on the outskirts of Arras, on a wide crossroads dotted with a handful of houses, a café and a depot supplying *Camping Gaz*. Saint-Cloud had parked on a piece of waste ground next to the café, and walked over to join them as Rocco pulled up.

'See this?' He gestured at the four roads in turn. 'This crossroads is my concern. There is a possibility that the president will come here, to open a new library dedicated to the fallen of the two world wars.' He pointed east, along a straight stretch of road. 'He will have to come along this route, which is the quickest approach from the capital. Any other route takes him through too much traffic and narrow streets. But it makes this spot an ideal choke point for an attack.'

Rocco couldn't disagree. It was ideal. Multiple routes in, escape routes out and enough nearby streets and dwellings to cause confusion and for attackers to get lost in. Anyone wishing to fire on the presidential car would be able to cause an obstruction anywhere here and simply hose down the vehicle as it went by. The technique had almost worked in Le Petit-Clamart last August, avoided only by the chauffeur's driving skill.

But this wasn't Le Petit-Clamart.

He wasn't convinced. 'So is he coming here, then?'

'That is not for public consumption.' Saint-Cloud seemed pleased, as if Rocco's lack of dissent signalled a victory. 'But we must be prepared. Should he decide to do so, I will arrange blanket coverage of the area.' He gave a humourless smile, looking beyond them. 'Anyone trying anything will suffer the same fate as the previous ones.'

By the time Rocco dropped Caspar off at the railway station, the light was fading. He went to his office to check for messages and found Berthier waiting for him with a note in his hand. He was scratching his head.

'A man named Bellin rang for you. Sounded drunk or mad. Said something about his dog, and how he's been marked.' He shrugged. 'I don't know what that means, but he wasn't making much sense. Is that Bellin at the scrapyard?'

Rocco dialled the number on the piece of paper. 'Yes. You know him?'

'Unfortunately. He's one of the lower orders around here.'

The phone rang ten times before Bellin picked up. He sounded stressed, his words pouring out in a mad jumble once he recognised Rocco's voice. 'You've got to help me – they've killed Oscar!' His breathing was hoarse, as if he'd run a marathon and was at the end of his reserves.

'Who the hell is Oscar? And who killed him?'

'I don't know ... some men – a man... They

167

don't have the guts to come out into the open. You've got to come – *please!'*

Then the phone went dead.

CHAPTER TWENTY-SIX

Rocco dropped the phone and called across to Berthier. 'Where's Desmoulins?'

'Out on a job. He's due back at any time. Can I help?' He looked excited at the prospect of going out on a call, but Rocco had to disappoint him. This could be a fuss about nothing, Bellin's imagination overcoming rational thought. The dog might simply have run off, as he would have in its place. But if it hadn't, he couldn't place a man on desk work in the line of fire.

'Get him to follow me to Bellin's yard.'

He drove as fast as traffic would allow, wondering if this was a panic over nothing, or whether this might finally produce results. A name was all he needed, then he could make some progress. Soon he was bumping down the lane to Bellin's yard, pulling to a stop clear of the entrance.

He took out his gun and slipped through the gates as he'd done before. The light was fading, throwing the junkyard into something resembling a horror movie scene of jagged edges and shadows. There were no lights on in the cabin and no sign of Bellin. He strode across the yard, slipping on the mud, and peered through the doorway. Empty.

The telephone handset was lying on the floor.

Rocco turned and looked back at the telegraph pole outside the gates, which had once fed the phone line in a loop overhead to the cabin.

The wire had been cut.

He debated the wisdom of going further into the yard alone in search of Bellin. If anything happened, he'd be an easy target. On the other hand, Bellin had asked for his help.

He walked along the first open row, sticking close to the line of junked vehicle bodies, checking every few steps as he came across a gap. He stopped, listening for sounds of voices or movement, but there was nothing. The breeze was just sufficient through the metal piles to throw out a sound all of its own, deadening any other noises and creating a background hum which served to confuse the ears.

Then he heard a clink of metal. It had come from the area where he'd last seen Bellin, sitting morosely at the back of the yard, smoking endless cigarettes. He hoped the scrap dealer was resisting the urge this time; if anyone was here looking for him, all he had to do was follow the smoke.

Rocco loosened his coat buttons and shrugged his shoulders, eyeing the ground in front of him. This was best done at speed, staying on the move. Anyone tracking movements around the yard would be as hampered as he was by the poor light and the shadows, and if they meant business, they would have little chance to pin him down.

He jogged down the row and turned right, holding the gun two-handed, the safety off. The light here was even worse, with giant shapes

169

looming up on either side to create confusion. A truck body lay on its axles, the windows and engine gone and the rear end missing. A battered Simca stood on its nose against a pile of other car bodies, like a child's parking lot at bedtime. Other vehicles were unrecognisable, merging one with another in the gloom.

He rounded the corner where he had last seen Bellin. He was sitting exactly where he had been before.

'Where the fuck have you been?' the man hissed. He jumped up and threw a glance past Rocco's shoulder. He looked terrified and was shaking visibly, thrusting his hands into the pockets of his filthy overalls to hide his nerves.

Rocco urged him back into the recess and made him sit down by the simple process of pushing him by his shoulders until his legs gave way. In Bellin's present state, anyone out there would hear him and be able to pinpoint his location in seconds.

'Tell me what happened,' he said softly. 'Keep your voice down and breathe, and we might get you out of here in one piece.' He turned so that he could keep an eye on the open area towards the back fence. If anyone came looking for Bellin, he wouldn't get much warning, but at least his own presence here might put them off long enough to take evasive action. To emphasise his intentions, he made a play of checking his weapon, which caused Bellin's eyes to widen.

'I got a call,' Bellin muttered, rubbing his face with podgy hands. 'A mate in Paris said I was in deep shit.' His breathing came fast and shallow and his eyes were darting everywhere. 'Told me to run or I'd regret it.'

'Do you trust him?'

'Yes. Well, pretty much. What's that got—'

Rocco clamped a hand over Bellin's mouth as his voice began to rise, cutting him off. 'I've known some people all my life,' he explained. 'But I wouldn't trust them further than I could throw one of these cars.'

Bellin struggled free of Rocco's grip and said softly, 'All right. Maybe he's got an angle – I don't know. But it makes no difference now, does it? Where the hell would I go?'

As he spoke, he heard a dull metallic clank. It had come from beyond the piles of junk at the front of the yard. Someone had pushed against one of the gates, disturbing the corrugated sheeting.

Bellin reacted as if he'd been scalded. He jumped up and stared around as if demons were about to emerge from the scrap metal.

Rocco grabbed his shoulder. 'Are you expecting company?'

'It's them.' Bellin's voice was soft but high-pitched, childlike in fear. His face crumpled and he looked at Rocco as if he were about to burst into tears. 'You've got to stop them.'

'I can't,' said Rocco, 'if you don't tell me who they are.' He checked the gun again, a last-second-before-action subconscious habit. Full magazine. Then he looked around at their position. He'd been in worse spots when attacked before, but he couldn't recall when. Indochina without a doubt. Only the ones coming here were unlikely to be communist *Viet Minh*. But neither was he accompanied by trained and battle-hardened troops. He looked at the fence in front of them. It was nearly three metres high and clad in bashed metal. No handholds and no pile of scrap close enough to get a leg-up. 'How strong is that?'

'Forget it.' Bellin bit the words off, resentful and angry. 'I built it so the locals wouldn't steal everything I had. I can't climb that.'

'You should have thought of that, shouldn't you? So tell me, who is it likely to be, out there?'

Bellin swallowed and ducked his head. 'Them. The ones who arranged the car thing. They've come to settle up.'

'They must have a name?'

Another noise, and Rocco turned towards the front. As he did so, a small shape soared high into the air. It seemed to hang for a moment against the dark grey sky, then fell and bounced with a series of tinny clatters as it penetrated the scrap piles.

Someone had thrown a hubcap.

Another one flew into the air, this one on a lower trajectory. It hit the jib of a crane and dropped harmlessly to the ground. Then another and another, each one aimed at different corners of the yard.

Whoever was throwing them, Rocco decided coolly, had a good arm.

A smaller shape came looping towards them. It tumbled through the air and landed with a crash on a door panel and bounced away, shedding splintered glass like broken fragments of silver.

Scare tactics, Rocco recognised. He glanced at

Bellin, who was now a quivering wreck, eyes wide open and waiting for the next one. The tactics were working.

'Names,' said Rocco. 'Quickly.'

'I can't.' Bellin was trembling. A patch of damp had appeared on the front of his trousers and was spreading fast down his legs, but he seemed not to have noticed. 'What are we going to do?'

'We have to get out of here.' Rocco figured Bellin must have a way of slipping away if an angry 'customer' came calling. To men like Bellin, in his line of business, a back door was as instinctive as breathing. 'Where's your escape route?'

'Blocked.' Bellin waved a hand towards the left-hand end of the yard. 'They left a warning. The dog. Gutted it and left it for me to find.'

'Oscar?'

A quick nod. 'Yes.'

Rocco breathed out. *Now he tells me,* he thought savagely. And whoever was able to handle a big guard dog had to know what they were doing. Somehow he couldn't picture Bellin with a poodle.

With perfect and grisly timing, another object came soaring over the nearest pile of junk. It bounced, this time with a dull thud, off the car wing Rocco had been sitting on moments earlier. Ricocheting off a door panel, it rolled to stop at Bellin's feet.

It was a dog's head. Not a poodle's, either. Oscar had been a big, ugly Rottweiler.

It was too much for Bellin. The fat man turned with a yelp and ran, surprisingly fast on his feet, out of the protective haven they were in, career-

173

ing off a car body and nearly falling, but managing to stay upright, his trouser legs flapping around his ankles like flags.

'*Wait!*' Rocco hissed. But it was too late. Bellin was gone.

Rocco chased after him. It was a lunatic thing to do, he decided, but there was no other way to handle it. At least he might be able to catch whoever was out there. If not, they were both dead.

He found himself in another gap between two rows of scrap. There was plenty of cover if he was quick enough, but that counted just as much for the other man as well. He hunkered down for a moment, breathing easily and listening for sounds of Bellin's progress. Trying to tune in to the atmosphere. He couldn't hear anything, so he stood up and continued, carefully stepping away from shapes of metal rubbish lying in his path.

As he came level with a row between piles of family saloons heaped one on the other, he saw Bellin disappearing into a virtual tunnel to one side, his fat body burrowing like a rat. He followed him in and saw a flash of movement up ahead. The idiot was digging himself deeper into the metal mountain, no doubt hoping the man or men after him would give up. Or that Rocco would act as a handy decoy.

The thought was accompanied by a car window dissolving right next to him. Rocco dived into the open body of a truck cab, bouncing off the bench seat and disturbing a mound of broken windscreen glass and scraps of metal. He waited, lying on his back, the gun pointing at the source of the shot.

174

Then he realised: there had been no sound. The gunman was using a silenced weapon.

He slid on through the cab and out the other side, dropping to the ground and waiting.

Whoever was out there, he thought, was being extra careful not to make any sound. Whoever was out there had done this before.

He breathed out, straining his ears. It was just another kind of jungle, he told himself. Only not soft and hot and fragrant like the last one he'd been in. This one was hard and unforgiving, cold and full of sharp edges. But still a jungle.

Then a dense shadow rose from a patch of gloom about ten metres away. A man, squat and heavy across the shoulders, wearing a short jacket. Something glinted in his hand. A gun with a long barrel. He was looking along the row, not moving.

Rocco held his breath. One sudden movement and the gunman would see him. But the man seemed fixated on a spot further down. When Rocco looked, turning his head with infinite care, he saw a familiar shape coming along the row towards him.

It was Bellin, and he was heading straight towards the gunman.

The gunman moved, sinking to his heels, waiting. He evidently thought there was a risk that Bellin was armed, and was going to take him as he stepped by. The movement put him behind the cover of a car bonnet, where the chances of hitting him from Rocco's position were virtually nil.

Rocco reached behind him and felt around until his hand fastened on a hubcap lying on the ground. Time to play the man at his own game.

He pulled his arm back and flicked the hubcap into the sky. It sailed in a smooth trajectory, catching the air for a moment before starting to fall. The gunman must have caught the sound of Rocco's movement or seen a flash from the hubcap out of the corner of his eye. He spun round, pointing first at Rocco's position, then spinning again as the hubcap landed with a deep boom on a car roof just behind him. Two flashes of vivid light lit him up as he fired, each shot no more than a ragged cough.

Bellin, now just a few paces away, stopped and turned with a yelp, then ran. The gunman, moving smoothly, fired twice more after him, then jumped to his feet.

Rocco whistled. The gunman spun towards him with a grunt of surprise, and almost without aiming, fired twice. The first shot fanned Rocco's face, the second went harmlessly away to one side.

Rocco fired twice, and saw his second shot hit the man in his free arm. He staggered and grunted, then recovered, turned and ran. Seconds later Rocco thought he heard a grunt, followed by a noise like a slap. Then silence.

Then a car started up outside the yard and moved away up the track at speed.

It left behind a heavy silence.

Rocco ran towards the gates. As he rounded the final corner, a flicker of movement came from inside a wrecked truck cab. He swung towards it, levelling his gun, his finger tightening on the trigger. Then he breathed out and relaxed: a strip of fabric caught on the breeze. False alarm.

When he got to the cabin, he stopped.

Bellin was lying face down near the door. His blood was soaking the ground, adding to the oil and other fluids in the soil.

Rocco turned him over onto his back.

He'd been shot in the chest and head, running towards the cabin.

Rocco let out a long breath. A second gunman had been waiting.

By the time Rocco had found a phone at a nearby shop and called for backup and for Rizzotti to come out, he was feeling sticky with humidity and depressed by Bellin's senseless death. Whatever the man had done, he hadn't deserved that. But then, gangland-style killings rarely had much to do with sense and only sometimes carried a hint of the rational.

He met Desmoulins at the gates and got him to seal off and make a detailed search of the cabin. He didn't expect to find anything, but maybe Bellin had been more cautious than he'd given him credit for.

He returned to the station, where he filled out a report. It made grim reading, not least because he felt he'd failed, as the only policeman on the spot and one who'd not made an arrest. He made a notation about having wounded the gunman, suggesting that hospitals in the Paris region be made aware that they report to Amiens any patient being treated for a gunshot wound to the arm.

CHAPTER TWENTY-SEVEN

'I need to go to England. To Scotland Yard.'

Rocco was in early next morning, and went straight to Massin's office. After another fitful night's sleep listening to the *fouines* play, and going over and over in his mind the events at the scrapyard, he had decided on a course of action; but it needed Massin's cooperation, something he couldn't entirely guarantee.

Massin looked up from the papers he was studying, and sat back, eyeing Rocco with a dour expression. 'Do you, indeed? Does it have anything to do with your current caseload?'

'Actually, yes. Partly.'

There was a flicker of interest. 'Go on.'

Rocco explained about the burnt-out truck with the body in the back, and the Citroën DS found in Bellin's scrapyard, followed by Bellin's execution. 'I believe there may be a link between those vehicles and the Englishmen who wrecked the *Canard Doré*.' He began to explain about the car and Bellin's description of the driver, but Massin held up a hand to stop him. He picked up a sheet of paper from his in tray.

'I have Dr Rizzotti's report. It's very detailed. A fake camera, an English cigarette under the mat. But why these men? You have no proof that they were involved in the fake ramming incident. And you still have no proof that it actually happened,

178

beyond some farmer's early morning ramblings.'

'There's the blood at the scene and we have a dead body. Two dead bodies,' he amended, 'if we count Bellin.'

'The first burnt beyond recognition. I doubt even the miracles of modern science will prove who it was.'

'Possibly not. But I think the dead man – a tramp named Pantoufle – happened to be at or near the scene. It was on his usual route and it never varied, winter, summer or spring. I don't know if he died by accident or was killed deliberately. Either way, they burnt his body to conceal his death and prevent recognition.'

'Buttons. Is that the sum total of your clues?' Massin made it sound as if Rocco were grasping at straws.

'Yes.'

'It's not much, is it? And you still can't tie the Englishmen to the truck or the DS. Not definitely.'

'No. Not yet.' Rocco fought to keep a hold on his impatience. He felt he was fighting a losing battle, but refused to give way to Massin's open scepticism. He doubted the *commissaire* had ever followed a clue in his life; had never felt the thrill of a case building out of virtually nothing nor ever felt the clarion call of a chase. 'They were in the Amiens area at the same time,' he pointed out. 'Five men with no valid explanation for being here. And I recognised the smell of Calloway's aftershave from the damaged DS. It wasn't easy to forget.'

'You noticed a man's cologne?'

'In a place where the customary fragrance is

179

sump oil and burnt metal, it stood out.' He wasn't prepared to let it go. 'They set fire to a dead man's body and tried to hide the evidence; normal people don't do that.'

'Is that your argument?' Massin threw a hand in the air. 'You think these men, who trashed a local bar, are some kind of criminal group who also killed a tramp while pretending to make a film? *If* it's the same men – and I say that with great emphasis – they appear to have some influence in the British Parliament, for God's sake. Enough to get them set free!'

'Exactly my point.' Rocco kept his face straight. 'How many ordinary people have that privilege? I don't. Do you? Calloway,' he added quickly as Massin's face clouded dangerously, 'has a different background to the others. It was he who made the phone call that secured their release. But he was still part of the group. I'd like to speak to the British police to find out more about him. I believe they were here for a specific reason.'

'What reason?' Massin tapped the report from Rizzotti. 'How does any of this give you such an impression? Give me even a hint of why I should listen further, Inspector, because right now you are not making much sense. A bunch of English drunks on the rampage, that is *all* you have.'

'I think it might have something to do with the attack Saint-Cloud is investigating.'

It was out before he could stop it, but it was too late to backtrack.

'Ah, yes. Colonel Saint-Cloud and his security review.' The words came out tinged with resentment. It was clear that he did not like Rocco being assigned to the security chief, but was powerless to stop it. Rocco wondered how long he'd been sitting here grinding his teeth over it.

He considered for a moment what Saint-Cloud had said about keeping this assignment quiet. The man had great powers, and in effect, Rocco was now following orders approved by the Interior Ministry. Even so, there were some lines you didn't cross. Being forced by another official to conceal details from his superior officer was one. And while he himself didn't always tell Massin everything he was working on, this was very different.

He took a deep breath, choosing his words with care. 'I believe these Englishmen and the reasons for the local security review are somehow connected.'

A brief silence. 'How?'

'The ramming, the use of a black, official-looking DS ... and the real possibility of a visit to the area by the president.' He mentioned his talk with Blake at the War Graves Commission office. 'It all coincides. I think the ramming witnessed by the farmer, Simeon, may have been a practice run.' He then told him about finding the Pont Noir on the map, and its uncanny similarity to the ramming site. He concluded with the visit with Saint-Cloud to the bridge and the security chief's complete scepticism. 'That aside, I think killing Bellin was closing a door. He knew too much, so he had to go. Someone higher up the chain decided he was a liability. We can't get anything out of Bellin anymore, but we might be able to get something out of the man who delivered the car: Calloway.'

181

Massin said nothing, his face carefully blank. A car revved up outside, and a burst of laughter drifted up from the street. It highlighted to Rocco how everything had receded while he was in this room, as if the outside world had been shut out. Finally Massin sat forward. 'You have to admit, Rocco, that this is all one hell of a leap of the imagination, even for you. You could be wrong.'

'I hope I am,' Rocco replied calmly, adding, 'but dare we take that risk? The location is remote, it fits exactly with where the ramming took place, and if de Gaulle fulfils his expressed wish to make an unpublicised visit to this location, he'll be out in the open with only his immediate guards to protect him.'

'They've never failed him yet.'

'There's always a first time. And the last attempt resulted in one dead and one seriously wounded. In terms of an attack to kill the car's occupants, that would be classified as a success.'

Massin took in a deep breath, his nose pinched. He lifted his chin to ease his collar, and said, 'Have you told Colonel Saint-Cloud all of this?'

'Not everything.'

'Really? What a surprise. I suppose I should feel comforted that you keep him underinformed as well. What did you leave out?'

'The English connection.'

'Why?'

'Because I want to be certain of my facts. If there's a proven foreign element to this, it's very different to anything else that's gone before. Any hint of British involvement will not be kept quiet for long, and if it is a planned attack, the organisers will go underground. Next time we might not get to hear about it until it's too late.'

'But you could still be wrong. This could all be … circumstantial and coincidental.'

'I agree. But I need a couple of days to check it out. Nobody need know that … apart from you.'

Massin looked sceptical. 'Why am I not reassured by your consideration?' He tapped his fingers on the desk, then said, 'Leave it with me for a few minutes. You have presented me with an awkward situation, Rocco. I need to consider my decision carefully. Don't leave the building.'

Rocco was surprised, then puzzled. At least Massin hadn't thrown him out and put him on traffic duties. But why the delay? Then, as he turned to open the door, he saw Massin reaching for the telephone, and knew what was going to happen: he was going to phone the Interior Ministry. It was his way out of a tricky situation.

Fifteen minutes later, the desk sergeant put his head round the door of the main office and said, 'Lucas? The chief wants to see you.' He dropped his lower lip in sympathy and disappeared.

Rocco walked upstairs and into Massin's office. He found the officer staring out of the window. A plain white envelope lay on the desk in front of him.

He wondered how this was going to play out. If ever he had given Massin a reason to get rid of him, short of claiming to see flying saucers over Amiens, an attack of paranoid insanity about foreign involvement in an attack on the president pretty much had the edge on anything else he could think of.

Finally Massin said gravely, 'I'm not convinced by your arguments, Inspector Rocco.'

'Why not?'

'With immediate effect, I'm placing you on sick leave. I believe you are suffering from stress after your recent immersion in the canal, and you need some time off.'

Rocco was stunned. 'What the hell are you talking about?' The incident Massin was referring to had happened just a few weeks before. Rocco had been locked in a canal barge which had been sunk deliberately in the hopes that it would cover up the murder of an illegal immigrant and the illicit employment of others by a local factory with government contracts. It was as close as Rocco had ever come to a watery grave, and he still didn't like to think about it.

Massin stood up and held up a hand to stop Rocco speaking. 'In fact, I suggest you take yourself away for a couple of days to recuperate.' He sniffed and gave a hint of a smile. 'London might be a useful destination.'

Rocco almost didn't hear that; he was about to tell Massin what he could do with his sick leave. But he stopped. 'London?'

'Yes. I hear the air there is quite bracing at this time of year. Especially along the Embankment.' Massin picked up the envelope and held it out to Rocco. 'Here is your letter of authority. It will permit you to talk with a man I met on a seminar in Paris last year. His name is Detective Chief Inspector David Nialls of their Flying Squad. He is expecting you at New Scotland Yard.' His mouth

184

gave a twitch, almost suggesting that he possessed a sense of humour. 'Get well soon, Inspector. I hope when you return, you have a much clearer understanding of your duties. I suggest you leave immediately and without broadcasting your plans.'

CHAPTER TWENTY-EIGHT

Rocco came out of a bustling Victoria station and threaded his way through the streets to the River Thames. It was late afternoon and already dark, the air cold and dry. There had been delays on the line from Dover, but he'd relished the chance to sit and contemplate the emptiness of the opposite seat, or the faux cheerfulness of a poster advertising the delights of a coastal resort called Margate. Such moments were rare enough.

Exchanging the gritty tang of locomotive smoke for the sour odour of street traffic was not much of a trade, no more than the metallic taste of river water in the air; but it was London, and he relished the sights and sounds so different from Paris – or, more dramatically, Poissons-les-Marais. He'd been here once before, with Emilie, shortly after his promotion to inspector in Clichy. It had been a rare break from the pressures of work and ambition and a desire to do something positive. On one level it had been a success: Emilie had loved it, sensing perhaps that her husband's life wasn't entirely dominated by the call of his job. But the time had gone by all too quickly and their relationship had not survived much beyond his return to the office – the late nights, early mornings and especially the days away, working undercover, when she didn't know if he would come back in one piece or in a box, victim of taking a step too far into the dark.

The sight of the Thames brought a tug of regret like a pain in his chest, and he stood for a moment taking in the scenery: the occasional flash of white from the crosscurrents, the passing river craft with their dim pilot lights and unnamed cargoes, and the rush of water in the gloom below. They had done this together many times, he recalled, enjoying the ebb and flow of the water when pavements became too crowded, traffic too noisy or the pull of museums and art galleries faded. Too late now for regrets; Emilie was gone and living another life. He wasn't even sure where. He'd allowed too much outside their married life to dictate the pattern of living successfully in it, and had paid the price.

He followed the embankment to the north, passing the elegant seat of the British Government on the way and turning onto the approach to Westminster Bridge, then taking a sharp left to the imposing Gothic brick-and-concrete structure that was New Scotland Yard, the headquarters of the Metropolitan Police.

'Inspector Rocco?' The sergeant on the desk swivelled the signing-in book and studied his name, then asked him to wait. 'Very good, sir. If you would hang on a bit, I'll ask Chief Inspector Nialls to come down.'

Five minutes later, a tall, slim man in an immaculate grey suit appeared and shook his hand. He had greying hair and a slim moustache, and looked tired; the kind of tired that seeps into the bones. Rocco had seen it before in senior cops on his side of the water. 'Inspector Rocco. David Nialls. I act as liaison with your DGPN. I've been expecting you.'

Rocco showed him the signed letter of authority and waited while the policeman read it. The fact that DCI Nialls had contact with the *Direction Générale de la Police Nationale,* which came second only to the Interior Ministry, was in itself no guarantee of cooperation. The correct protocol would have been to go through channels; but channels were something Rocco had little time for. Massin's last-minute letter was a bonus he hadn't counted on, however. All he had to do now was hope it carried some weight.

It took a moment to realise that Nialls had been reading the letter without great difficulty. The detective looked up and gave a sheepish smile. 'I speak some French, but it's not that brilliant. Do you mind if we speak English?'

'Of course not.'

'Good. François Massin said you could do with some information. I'm not sure how much I can help you, Inspector Rocco, but if you come with me, I'll force you to drink some of our appalling tea and see what we can accomplish.' He led Rocco through a side door and up a flight of narrow stairs, stopping to speak to a young woman in an apron on the way. Then he turned into a small office and shut the door. 'The tea will be along in

187

a moment. Sit down and fire away.'

They sat and Rocco explained about the ramming incident, and the wrecking of the bar by the drunken gang. Nialls seemed little more than politely interested at first, and only reacted at the point where Rocco mentioned George Tasker. Then he sat forward with a frown.

'Tasker? Can you describe him?'

Rocco did so.

They were interrupted by the appearance of the young woman bearing a tray of tea and some biscuits, but Nialls barely allowed her out of the door before continuing. 'I wondered where the bloody man had disappeared to. He dropped off the scene for a few days, and we wondered whether he'd become a building block.' At Rocco's blank look, he explained, 'Got buried under an office block somewhere, victim of revenge for past misdeeds. Obviously he didn't. Still, there's always hope.'

'You know him, then?'

Nialls nodded and sipped his tea. 'Sadly, I do. He's a nasty bit of work suspected of involvement in at least two gangland killings and numerous bank jobs. He's employed by a man named Gerald 'Ruby' Ketch, who's the frontman for an extensive East London gang. They've been around for a few years now, gradually building up their power base. Just recently, Ketch's bosses have been staying in the background pulling strings, but we know they're responsible for pretty much every nasty crime in the book.'

'You do not have enough to convict them?'

'Sadly, no.' He rubbed his face. 'We've been trying, but they have some very competent lawyers and rule by fear. Witnesses have a habit of developing amnesia ... or disappearing altogether. My building block reference was not entirely in jest.' He stared out of the window. 'But what the hell were they doing in France?'

'If my suspicions are correct,' said Rocco, 'pretending to make a film.' He gave him the men's names and described the crash scene witnessed by Simeon, and the state of the Citroën with its interior reinforcements. 'But along the way they appear to have killed a man. It could be an accident, but we will probably never know for sure.'

'What does your instinct tell you?'

'That they were doing something else – but not making films.'

'Like what? They're not exactly known for working outside London and the South East. Our criminal gangs tend to have territories like everyone else.'

Rocco debated how much to tell this man. He didn't know Nialls from a stick of celery, but he couldn't walk away without gaining something from this visit. If his instincts were correct, there was too much riding on getting it wrong. Yet if he suggested that Tasker and his men were somehow involved with an attempted assassination of the French head of state, Nialls might feel compelled to take the matter higher, running the risk of word getting out and driving the plotters underground.

'I think there is a chance that these men, Tasker and his colleagues,' he said carefully, 'may be involved in something much bigger than their usual operations.'

'Like what?' Then Nialls' eyes widened. 'Good

God, you don't mean an attempt on–'

'Perhaps. But not directly.' There. It was out now and too late to take back. Nialls was clearly no fool. He'd instantly run his mind over all the various possibilities that he could think of, and had settled unerringly on the correct one.

'Have you discussed this with your superiors?'

'Some of it. But they are sceptical.'

'Why? I mean, don't misunderstand me, but there have been plenty of attempts on your man already, so it'll hardly come as much of a shock to anyone if someone has another go ... especially on the heels of the Kennedy assassination.' The recent death of the American president was still headline news everywhere, and had caused many world leaders to review their security precautions.

'They have already tried.' Rocco told him about the latest attack on the N19 to the south-east of Paris, and how it had failed, allegedly because of bad information supplied to the gang. Even had de Gaulle been in the car, it might not have carried the same magnitude outside France as the killing of the US president John Kennedy in Dallas, Texas.

Nialls picked up on the failure of information. 'You don't think it was simply a mistake on the attackers' part?'

'I am not sure. So far, the information these groups have worked on has always been correct. The failures have come because of poor organis-ation, good defensive tactics by the bodyguards ... or simply bad luck. Whichever group is in-volved, they do not seem to have much difficulty finding out what the president's movements are.'

Nialls lifted an eyebrow. 'Someone on the inside?'

'Possibly. But I never said that.' Rocco knew all too well that it was next to impossible to keep everything secret. Word leaked out and there was always someone ready to trade on it.

'Maybe this lot were more amateurish than the others.'

'Maybe.'

'But you don't think so.'

He was sharp, Rocco decided. His policeman's nose had picked up on Rocco's hesitation and he had drawn his own conclusions.

'I have been working with a representative of the presidential security team, but I want to be sure of my facts before I go any further.'

'Very wise, although waiting might be risky, don't you think, if there's a plot afoot?'

'Possibly. But we have time. That is all I can say.'

Nialls shrugged. 'Fair enough. What do you want from me?'

Rocco was surprised. 'You will help?'

'As much as I can, yes. It depends what you need, though.' Nialls smiled and explained, 'I'm on my way out of here, due for retirement in a few weeks. It means I have a certain amount of leeway; nobody expects me to begin any new investigations or to be running around like a spring chicken. But you'll have to be quick.'

'Why?'

'There's talk of the complete file on Ketch and his people being handed over to another team.' He gave a wry smile. 'I can't say I'm too sorry, but I'd like to think I can do something useful before I go.'

'Such as solving your train robbery?' Britain's biggest ever cash robbery had been carried out three months previously on a train transporting used banknotes due for incineration. So far they had come nowhere near finding out who had organised it.

Nialls grinned. 'It would be a good one to go out on, wouldn't it? But no, I don't think I'll get that one.'

'Can you tell me anything about Tasker and his people? Calloway in particular – I am sure he has an important role in this. Who they know, who their contacts are in France.'

'That last bit's easy enough, especially with Tasker. He doesn't have any contacts outside London. George Tasker's a thug – a muscleman with enough brains to make him dangerous but with limited horizons. He's like a sergeant in the military; he does what he's told, passes on instructions, and chivvies the troops to do their bit.' He lifted a hand in apology. 'Sorry – "chivvies" means to encourage. Keep forgetting myself.'

'I understood. But thank you for the explanation.'

'Your English is impressive. How come?'

'Thank you,' said Rocco. 'My mother insisted. She felt the world was becoming smaller and it would be an advantage. I was also with United Nations forces in Korea in 1952 for a while, attached to a British unit. I had to learn quickly.'

'That would account for it. Wish I could claim the same with my French.' He got back to the subject under discussion. 'Anyway, Ketch is the man you should be looking at. He's the operational head of the gang. If anyone's in the know about what they were up to over in your neck of the woods, it'll be him. He's a very clever man.'

'You admire him?'

'No. I don't. But I don't underestimate him. Ketch is a broad thinker. He's suspected of having put together a number of clever jobs over the years, every one of them successful and with a big return on their investment.' A dry smile. 'Makes him sound like the boss of ICI, doesn't it? But it's what he's good at: the planning ... and what we've come to recognise recently as smoke and mirrors.'

'I'm sorry...?'

'He takes the widest possible view of staging a job. He doesn't simply look at the direct details, like most of his kind, focusing on the place to hit, how to get in, the men to use, that kind of thing. He uses distraction techniques. The first we'll hear is a welter of rumours, usually spreading from drinking haunts around his manor, some conflicting with others until we don't know what's going on. Then the rumour becomes solid, and a mail van gets jumped. Then another, somewhere else. While we're involved with those two, his men are busy running another – usually bigger job somewhere else. It's a strategy we believe he borrowed from reading about the desert campaigns in North Africa.'

'Hit and run, you mean?' Rocco was familiar with the term; French forces had also used the tactics, relying on feeding out false information about possible attacks, then staging a surprise assault elsewhere.

'Exactly. It's only recently become recognisable, and we're still playing catch-up. If you can get there first, I'd take my hat off to you.'

'But?' Rocco sensed a problem.

'You'll never get close to him. Ketch is paranoid about cops and snitches – informers. He uses Tasker to organise jobs and be the blunt instrument, and has a financial planner and crooked accountant named Brayne to help with his deep thinking. Between them they're a very clever team. He compartmentalises, in other words.'

Rocco shook his head at the term. He thought he could guess, but guesses were no good at this point.

'He keeps everything separate. You know in intelligence structures, they keep cells and cut-outs? If one goes down, they don't compromise the others? Well, it's similar to that. Most of the men he uses never even meet him. Tasker's the recruitment sergeant.'

Rocco understood. It was a tried-and-tested system, also used by some Corsican gangs to reduce risks in case of penetration by undercover police.

Nialls glanced at his watch. 'I won't be able to get you an introduction to Ketch, but I know where he can be found most evenings. At least you'll get a sighting of the man.'

'That would help. And Simon Calloway? A former racing driver, according to a colleague of mine.'

'Really? The name's certainly familiar, but I'll have to check. Some gang members work on a shifting pattern – brought in for special tasks, then let go. He could be one of those.' He picked

194

up the phone and dialled an internal number, then spoke briefly, giving Calloway's name. He put the phone down and said, 'Our intelligence unit. They keep a log of all known names. If he's done time, or been picked up on suspicion of involvement in anything, they'll know. It'll keep until tomorrow. Shall we go look at some of our criminal brethren at play?'

As they walked back downstairs, they stepped aside to allow two men coming up to pass on the narrow stairway. It took Rocco a moment to realise that he recognised the man leading the way. By the time they were face to face, there was no way of feigning ignorance.

'Rocco?' The lead man was short and stocky, clean-shaven and smartly dressed. His tone was imperious and questioning, the singular word tinged with dislike. The last time Rocco had seen Jules Broissard, he was attached to the DST – the *Directorate of Territorial Surveillance* – the French internal security agency. They had clashed over a territorial dispute in Clichy. Rocco had arrested a known explosives specialist whom Broissard had wanted to remain free pending investigations into the man's involvement in anti-government threats and arms supplies. The clear intimation had been that it would be in Rocco's career interests to give way. Broissard had lost the argument, and had clearly not forgiven or forgotten him.

'Broissard.'

'What are you doing here?' Broissard stared hard at Rocco, then at Nialls, as if they were at the centre of some kind of conspiracy. 'And on whose authority?'

CHAPTER TWENTY-NINE

Rocco wondered if he would get away with tossing this little Napoleon down the stairs. Broissard was strutting and ambitious, dismissive of anyone outside his own department, especially of policemen. Fond of hinting at friends with influence, in reality, his authority was limited.

'I really can't discuss that,' he said, and introduced David Nialls. 'What about you?' he added, twisting the knife to show how much he cared for the man's position.

Broissard almost shook with indignation. 'We are here on matters of state security,' he muttered. In other words, nothing to do with you. He belatedly remembered the man with him and introduced him with a casual flick of the hand. 'Henri Portier, a colleague.' Then he ducked away and moved on up the stairs before they could ask any further questions.

'Not a friend, I take it?' said Nialls with a grin.

'No. Not a friend,' said Rocco. He was trying to remember something, a fleeting image prodding at his memory. They were halfway along Whitehall before it finally came to him.

Henri Portier, Broissard's silent colleague. He'd seen him before, too – and recently. He was one of the two suited visitors who had accompanied Colonel Saint-Cloud to the Amiens police station just a few days ago.

The Allendale Club in Mayfair was sleek, smart and busy, with a scattering of expensive suits and early-evening cocktail dresses among the clientele. David Nialls nodded at the doorman, a pug-faced man in a dinner jacket and bow tie, who stood aside to allow them in.

The interior was glossy and richly decorated, with a long curved bar at one side of the main room and tables set for dinner beyond a gold-coloured balustrade at the rear. A three-piece band was playing soft jazz in one corner. Opposite the bar was a row of small booths with bench seats for four and a small table.

Nialls bellied up to the bar and ordered two glasses of whisky, and they carried their drinks over to one of the booths and sat down. Nialls took off his coat and sipped his drink.

'You might as well make yourself comfortable, Lucas,' he said. 'It'll be a while before anyone interesting gets here. Until then we can watch how the other half plays. Are you hungry, by the way?'

It was a reminder to Rocco that he had not eaten since this morning. Nothing on the train or boat had been of interest, and he'd been too busy thinking of this meeting to bother.

'Not yet. Are you recommending this place?'

Nialls grunted. 'A bit rich for my wallet, I'm afraid. But I know a good place near Piccadilly where we can get a decent steak.' He took another small sip. 'We'll wait to see if Ketch turns up and then go eat.'

It was soon very clear to Rocco that the main room, bar and restaurant were not the prime attractions to the Allendale Club, as pleasant as they no doubt were. A door at the rear, which Rocco had missed at first because it was covered by the same wallpaper as the walls on either side, opened discreetly every now and then, and clients would slip through accompanied by a member of the security staff. Most were men of apparent substance above the age of forty, he noted, although there were one or two female companions, notable for their youth, the willingness of their laughter and the casual displays of jewellery. Nialls did not seem particularly interested, but was watching the front entrance, taking occasional sips from his glass.

'It is a casino?' Rocco asked.

'Of course.' Nialls didn't turn to reply. He was intent on watching a group of men who had just entered from the street and were handing over their coats to a young woman attendant.

It was a good place to clean money and make a nice profit in the process, Rocco figured. Mayfair was a wealthy area and the club well placed to draw in those with money to burn. And special clients were allowed access by appointment only, which no doubt gave a measure of their net worth. He'd seen it before in other cities.

He turned to follow Nialls' line of sight. Two of the newcomers were in their fifties, dressed in smart suits and smoking fat cigars. They were accompanied by a slim man in an ordinary business suit and carrying a hat with a brim. He looked relaxed, and it was clear that he was the focus of attention of the two men, who were already hustling him to the bar and calling for drinks. The bartender responded with speed, nodding smartly as he took the order.

'Is one of them Ketch?' said Rocco. He could almost feel Nialls quivering with interest.

'I'm afraid not.' Nialls sat back in his seat and buried his nose in his glass as the three men walked by under the guidance of the maitre d', who was hustling ahead of them like a mother hen, clicking his fingers to gain the attention of a waiter. 'The one on the right,' he continued, 'is Godfrey Harding. He runs a chain of betting shops. The one on the left is known as Turkish John. He has a number of massage parlours and so-called beauty salons across the South East, all centres for prostitution. Both men are about as trustworthy and honest as a two-pound note.' He watched the three men with an air of disgust, adding sadly, 'The man in the plain suit is a detective inspector based at West End Central Station in Savile Row.'

A table was ready and waiting, and a waiter in attendance to take their orders as the men sat down. It was clear that the police detective was being given special treatment.

'Is that normal?' Rocco wasn't sure of the norm here, but in France, policemen and criminals mixed strictly at their own risk, and rarely for any good.

Nialls pulled a face. 'Not normal, no. There's a belief among some older coppers that mixing with the main players keeps them in line ... allows us to gain intelligence on their activities.'

'You don't believe that.'

'No, and I never did. The only guarantee is that

199

we learn only what they want us to learn, and we end up looking bad in the eyes of the public when a case falls apart because of a conflict of interests. But some habits die hard.'

Rocco could only agree with him. Either the man was working, or he was here for some other reason. It seemed Nialls wasn't sure which. 'Are these two men friends of Ketch?'

Nialls nodded. 'Friends, associates – as thick as thieves, to coin an appropriate phrase. Harding has friends in high places, including the Government and the City, and Turkish John has lots of cash money from his businesses. The two go hand in hand. Whatever they're talking about, you can be sure that Ketch has a hand in there somewhere.' He drained his glass and stood up. 'But I don't think we'll see him here this evening; he'll probably steer clear while those three are in. They like to give each other breathing room when they're cooking up a new relationship.' He picked up his coat. 'No doubt the DI will call it working, but cosying up to men like that is never a good thing. Shall we eat?'

As they walked out, a burst of raucous laughter sounded from the restaurant, and Rocco turned to look. A fourth person had joined the three men at their table, and was shaking hands all round. It was clear they were all acquainted. As the waiter stepped away to give them room, the newcomer looked up, giving Rocco a clear view of his profile. He was tall, slim and tanned, with immaculate grey hair and wearing an expensive grey suit, every bit a successful corporate lawyer or businessman.

But Rocco knew better, and felt a cold stab of

recognition. He had known the man for years; had even arrested him once in connection with a bank robbery near Clignancourt, in northern Paris, during which a cashier had died. That time he had walked free, thanks to a clever legal counsel.

His name was Patrice Delarue, and he was one of the French capital's most dangerous criminals.

As they left the club, they passed a mirror set into the wall above the bar. It was a two-way observation point, where an eye could be kept open for important visitors so that they could be assigned a waiter or a girl, depending on their status, or potential troublemakers could be pinpointed and watched before any problems occurred. What neither of the men could see, behind the glass watching with disbelief as the tall Frenchman made his way through the crowd, was George Tasker.

Seconds later, he was reaching for the phone.

CHAPTER THIRTY

'Well, George, it looks like we've got ourselves a problem.'

'Ruby' Ketch was sitting behind the desk of the GoGo Club in Gerard Street, Soho. It was a strictly members-only strip joint, with a few gambling tables for those whose preferred excitement came from naked cards and dice rather than girls. Dressed in a new chalk-stripe suit and pink shirt, he almost glowed with the appearance of good humour and health. But his eyes betrayed his real mood.

George Tasker was on a visitor's chair across from him, while Brayne, the business advisor, was lounging on a couch against one wall, beneath a lurid oil painting of a naked woman wearing a carnation in her hair and a hollow smile.

'Nothing I can't deal with, boss,' Tasker grated. 'Just give me the nod.' He rubbed his knuckles reflectively and smiled. He'd phoned Ketch from the Allendale less than thirty minutes ago, and had been told to get round to the GoGo immediately. The club downstairs was busy, with the thump of music hitting you in the face the moment you walked through the front door. But up here, the atmosphere was dulled to a faint rumble by extensive soundproofing and heavy flock wallpaper. 'He's just a nosey cop, that's all.'

Ketch stared across the desk at him. 'I know. But he's not just any old cop, is he? He's foreign. And that puts a different light on it. We've got to be careful. We don't want this coming back to bite us.' He glanced at Brayne. 'What d'you reckon?'

'I agree.' The advisor pursed his lips and stared at the ceiling. 'The last thing we need is any kind of diplomatic incident. That would ruin everything we've built up.' He dropped his gaze and looked at Ketch, adding, 'Are still building up, in fact. We could, of course, pay him to go away, forget what he saw.'

Tasker snorted. 'No chance.' The words came out before he could stop them.

'Say again?' Ketch lifted his heavy eyebrows.

'You know something about this Inspector Clouseau that we don't?'

Tasker prevented a scowl just in time. It was rumoured that Ketch had somehow obtained a pre-release copy of a new film starring Peter Sellers, called The Pink Panther. It was about a French detective named Clouseau, and Ketch had invited a few select cronies to a private viewing, including the Twins. That it painted the French police in a bumbling light made no difference; any police pratfalls were good for a laugh among the criminal elite, no matter what their nationality.

'No, boss. I just don't think he'd be up for it, that's all.' He had no reason for thinking that, other than instinct born of experience. He'd been around policemen long enough and close enough to be able to judge whether they could be bought or not. Some could, some couldn't. And something told him Rocco wasn't for sale.

'Everyone's up for it,' Brayne muttered sourly, jealous of having his ideas countered by a man like Tasker. 'There's not a cop going who doesn't have a price. All we have to do is find the number that turns them on. And the French are no different. Anyway, we've got the budget, we might as well give it a try.'

'Budget?' Ketch echoed. 'What's that mean?'

Brayne leant forward at his most earnest, ignoring Tasker's scowl of disapproval and dropping smoothly into business mode. 'We've got a new bank account in Paris, to cater for any ... contingencies such as this. I set it up a couple of months ago after you expressed an interest in operating on the Continent. It was just in case we needed access to French francs.' He sat back. 'It's in the name of a shell company, so we could pay him off using cash from that account, no comeback guaranteed.'

Ketch looked impressed. 'Bloody Nora, Brayne, you never cease to amaze me.' His eyes switched to Tasker. 'Hear that, George? Now that's what I call initiative. A bank account in Paris. Not bad for a bunch of East End boys, eh?' He smoothed his hair back and nodded slowly, almost purring. 'I like it. We'll pay this Rocco twerp in his own currency to go away. Think you can handle that?'

Tasker shifted uneasily. Paying 'bungs' to people to look the other way was part of the business, and he was often the bagman. They did it all the time, paying off local officials, businesses, individuals – even cops. Especially the cops they needed to 'dissuade' from taking too close an interest in Ketch's business arrangements. But that was here in London. He knew the ground and the people, the dangers and the risks he could take. France was a whole different game of skittles.

'There's a quicker way, boss,' he breathed, throwing a sly glance at the accountant. 'Cheaper, too – and permanent.'

'Really? What's that, then?' Ketch caught the look and smiled, as if he couldn't guess what was on Tasker's mind. He enjoyed a little conflict between his employees; it kept them all on their toes, stopped them becoming complacent.

'A bullet.' Tasker mimed a two-fingered gun and pointed it at his temple, making a soft *poof* sound with his lips. 'Quick, neat and no need to mess with no Frog money.'

Ketch appeared to consider the idea, tilting his

head from side to side with a touch of drama. Then he said, 'No, I don't think so. It has ... what's the word, Brayne?'

'Merit,' Brayne muttered, and somehow made the word sound banal.

'Merit – that's right. It has merit. But not this time. Not with him having seen our French guest chatting with Harding and Turkish John. There'd be too many repercussions if he suffered an accident right after coming to London, especially as Nialls was with him. I reckon there's a certain ... elegance in paying off this nosey French cop through one of their own banks.' He smiled. 'After all, it's what the Common Market's supposed to be all about, isn't it, making trade easier?'

'Even though we're not in it,' Brayne put in dryly.

'As you say, Brayne, as you say; even though Charlie de Gaulle's playing silly buggers and keeping us out. After all we've done for him, too. But let's not be bitter. We'll pay the man, this Rocco fella. Buy him off. Get yourself over there toot sweet, George. Brayne will arrange access to the readies as soon as you hit Amiens. Isn't that right?'

The accountant nodded. 'No problem.'

'Good. We'll call it Plan A. Oh, and I hope you like flying.'

'Eh?'

Ketch grinned with a touch of malice. 'Little treat for you, George. There's a small airfield at Thurrock, and a pilot who owes the boys a few favours. He'll drop you near Amiens and bring you back.'

'Thurrock?' The idea of flying had caught

205

Tasker unprepared. As hard as he was, he preferred to keep his feet on the ground and wheels
in contact with the earth. But trying to get out of
it would make him appear weak.

'That's right. Head out towards Tilbury and
turn right; you can't miss it. You'll be over and
back before you know it.'

'Do I have to?' Tasker couldn't believe he'd had
the balls to say it. He recovered quickly and said,
'I mean, he might not go for it.' More than anything, the idea of trying to pay off a man like
Rocco filled him with alarm. Paying off people he
didn't like or trust, knowing what their weak
points were and how to exploit their greed, was
part of the game. Most times he actually enjoyed
seeing them squirm before they grabbed the bait
like greedy carp. But this idea was a bad one. He
could feel it in his gut.

Ketch looked at him in surprise and the office
went quiet. Switching the pen in his hand, he held
it like a gun and pointed the barrel at Tasker's face.

'Then, George, *mon ami*,' he said, eyes glittering,
'you switch to Plan B. You fly back over there and
you shoot the interfering French copper dead!'

CHAPTER THIRTY-ONE

By noon the following day, Rocco was on the
Dover train with a firm promise from David Nialls
to keep him informed of the movements of Simon
Calloway and George Tasker. He was studying the

summary file on Calloway provided by Nialls' colleagues. It didn't tell him much of any great relevance: aged thirty-four, the son of a chemist, he was educated at a minor public school – which Rocco knew meant a private establishment – and had gone off the rails at an early age by 'borrowing' cars and running with a group of undesirables. Avoiding a prison sentence by the narrowest of margins and his father's influence, he had found himself using his driving skills with an up-and-coming racing team based in Surrey, to the south of London. He had won a place as a standby driver, until a first-team driver had fallen ill a few days before an appearance at Le Mans. Calloway had stepped in and finished fifth – a more than respectable result for a newcomer, and one that had ensured him a regular place on the team. But whatever was bad in Calloway's make-up had soon made its way to the fore, and after an 'incident' at 150 mph, which had resulted in another driver being seriously burnt, he had been dropped.

The rest of the file gave little information that was current, and Rocco felt a sense of disappointment. No mention of running with Tasker or Ketch, no involvement in politics or anti-Gaullist movements, no recorded views on social injustice abroad which might have been a clincher to this latest business. Then he sat up, his heart thudding. He was looking at a brief sentence describing Calloway's current listed occupation: he worked as a film stunt driver and as a member of a travelling stunt display team.

He put the document away, trying not to jump too quickly to the logical conclusion. Better to let the idea ferment for a while in his mind. But once there, it wouldn't go away. Who was better to use in a crash scene than a trained stunt driver? Even so, was that enough to assume that Calloway would be involved in a potential 'hit' on the president? And was there a connection between Calloway's occupation and the presence in London of Patrice Delarue? He couldn't see it, but neither could he ignore it.

He flicked at the lapel of his new coat. It was dark, as were the trousers, jacket and new brogues. He had taken the opportunity, reminded by Nialls' mention of Savile Row, the location of West End Central Police Station and a number of upmarket tailors, to replenish the parts of his wardrobe that had been spoilt by his immersion in the canal. He'd always had a preference for English clothes, and this had been an opportunity to indulge himself.

It was late by the time he got back to Amiens, but lights were still burning in the upstairs offices used by Saint-Cloud and Massin. He decided to brief Massin first, and told him what he had found out about Calloway's current occupation as a stunt driver.

Massin listened carefully, then said, 'So you think this Calloway will drive the truck which will be used to force the president's car off the road?'

'Well, he's certainly an expert at setting up these things. It would require timing and accuracy – something stuntmen live by.'

'Have you informed Saint-Cloud?'

'Not yet.' He considered his words carefully. 'To be honest, I'm not sure there's much to tell

208

that he would believe.'

'You might be right. But you should brief him, anyway.' Massin stood up and took a turn around the office. 'The fact that you bumped into Broissard and Portier, though – that's a puzzle, although it could be nothing. They both have broad duties to do with the security of the state, and that includes by its nature the president. They could have been in London for any number of reasons. But I'm glad you mentioned it. I'll amend your "sick" note accordingly. In case anyone should ask questions.'

'Thank you.' Rocco was still puzzled by Massin's change of attitude. Here he was being helpful on a grand scale, a total contrast to their early days. 'What about Delarue's presence in London?'

'All I can do is alert the Ministry. We can only speculate about why he was there. I'm sure the criminal intelligence section will be interested to hear about it ... unless they already know, of course.'

Rocco left Massin to it and walked along to the office Saint-Cloud was using. Unsurprisingly, the security chief was less welcoming, having already heard of Rocco's 'sick leave' and his visit to London.

'Was there really a need for such subterfuge, Inspector?' he asked coolly. 'We are, after all, working for the same side.'

'I needed to check out a few facts first.'

'I see. Did you discover anything?' Saint-Cloud sat back and examined his fingernails in a manner that indicated he was about to hear nothing of great importance.

'I've got a location,' said Rocco, 'as I told you already. Now I think I know who the driver will be.'

'Really?' Saint-Cloud looked unimpressed. 'Who?'

Rocco told him and placed Calloway's summary file on the desk, reminding him that the driver had previously been in the Amiens area in company with a gangster named Tasker, who worked for a well-known London gang boss named Gerald Ketch.

'A stunt driver?' Saint-Cloud exclaimed. 'Why on earth would such a man risk his life for this kind of venture? It makes no sense. He's not even French, for the love of God!'

'Nor were some of the previous attackers,' Rocco pointed out. 'The men in the garage at Créteil, for example, were Spanish and Corsican.' He knew he was on weak ground here. He still hadn't figured out what would make Calloway do such a thing, unless the man loved the idea of extreme danger to such an extent that he actually harboured a death wish. But not acting on it carried too much risk. 'I also saw Patrice Delarue in a London restaurant used by criminals. He was with two men who are very close to Ketch.'

'Patrice who?'

Rocco reminded himself that Saint-Cloud was not necessarily familiar with the current big names of the Paris underworld. 'He's a gang boss based in Paris.'

'Did you witness all these people together?'

'No. But they are known by the Metropolitan Police to have close connections.' He felt himself losing ground, and added, 'There's something else. I need more information about the attackers at Guignes.'

'Why?' Saint-Cloud's voice was flat, unpromising. He pushed the summary file to one side with a flick of his hand. 'How can that help now?'

'Because there may be a link. We do the same with crimes bearing similar hallmarks; one bank robbery may have similarities with another because one man might be connected with both teams. Criminals share and trade information and expertise all the time. If one group can't handle a job, they'll trade it on to someone who can. The planning of a bank job or a jewel raid will carry certain recognisable facets – a signature. If the job is a success, sooner or later that signature will occur again.'

'But we are not talking about a bank raid, are we?'

'I know. This is far more serious. All I need is the file on the attack. If it proves unhelpful, well, we've lost nothing.'

'What do you expect the file to tell you that I cannot here and now?'

'The names of the men involved. Where they came from, who else they knew; connections, affiliations, everything about them.'

'But we know of only one man who was killed. Another was thought to have been wounded, but he got away.'

Rocco took a deep breath. 'What about the police escort?'

'What about them? They did their duty, that is all you need to know.'

'They might have seen something that could help; something they didn't recall at the time.'

But Saint-Cloud was already shaking his head. 'No, Inspector, this really will not help.' He stood up and walked over to the door. 'I think you have just wasted two days chasing shadows. Frankly, I had expected better of you.'

Rocco resisted the hand that was trying to propel him towards the door. He sensed that he now had nothing to lose. 'Why were Jules Broissard and Henri Portier at New Scotland Yard? Were they investigating an English link, too?'

Saint-Cloud gave him an almost sympathetic look, shaking his head. 'Inspector, that is an impertinence. What members of the security services do is no concern of yours.' He drew in a deep breath. 'In fact, you may consider yourself no longer assigned to this project. I will bring in another officer capable of being more detached and less ... shall we say, fanciful about what constitutes a real threat to the safety of the president. I will advise *Commissaire* Massin accordingly. Good day to you.'

By the time Rocco was back home in Poissons, he had climbed down off his furious high at Saint-Cloud's decision, realising that there was little he could do about it. The man had the power to do whatever he pleased, and if that meant ignoring warnings about a threat to the president's life, that was up to him. But he was determined not to let the matter rest. For now, though, he had other things to attend to.

He walked round to Mme Denis next door, to

thank her for taking in his mail and bread.

'My pleasure, Lucas,' she murmured. 'Would you care for some tea?'

He shook his head. 'That's very kind, but I need sleep more.' He placed a paper bag on the table and explained about having had to go to London at a moment's notice. 'I tried to steal one from Buckingham Palace, but there were too many guards. I hope this is a good substitute.'

The old lady opened the bag with ill-concealed eagerness and took out a folded square of linen. Throwing Rocco a mock scowl, she opened the square with a small sigh of delight, shaking out the colours into the room like a magician performing a conjuring trick. It was a table square, an intricate design of yellows and golds and subtle blues, and she gazed at it with her mouth forming an oval.

'Mon Dieu, que c'est beau,' she whispered, and looked at him. 'How did you know?'

'I'm a cop,' he said dryly. 'It's my job.'

She flapped a gently admonishing hand against his arm and turned, pulling the existing coated cotton tablecloth off the table and spreading the new one in its place with a practised flick of her hands. She smoothed it down, then stood back and admired it. 'Now that,' she said decisively, 'merits a coffee morning tomorrow, let me tell you. Let the other old biddies try and top that!' She shrugged and smiled. 'I know – a touch of vanity. But every now and then, it's good for the soul.'

But when she turned back, Rocco had already slipped out, pulling the door closed behind him.

'Ah, the wanderer returns.' Claude answered his door in an open shirt, with a smell of cooking wafting around him and a towel thrown across one shoulder. 'I heard you'd gone sick, but I figured that was a ruse. Care to come in and share with your closest colleague or are you sworn to secrecy on pain of the big chop?' He drew a hand across his throat and made a hissing sound.

Rocco handed Claude a duty-free bag. 'Sworn to secrecy but a glass might loosen my tongue.'

'*Aiee, yi yi.*' Claude opened the bag and extracted a bottle of single malt whisky. He looked at Rocco with raised eyebrows. 'You haven't turned bank robber, have you? I mean, I don't mind if you have, but just so I know.' He called over his shoulder, 'Alix – quick, three glasses before I wake up from this dream and this excellent whisky goes *pouf* and disappears!'

Rocco was surprised when Alix stepped into view, holding a serving spoon. 'Sorry,' he apologised. 'I didn't know you had company. I won't stop–'

'Ah, *non!*' Claude grabbed his arm. 'You don't come bearing gifts and depart like a thief into the night, my friend. You must stay for dinner, at least. We have enough, don't we, Alix?'

'Luckily, yes.' Alix gave Rocco a wry smile. 'How did you know I liked whisky?'

'Umm ... I didn't.' It was a moment before Rocco realised she was teasing. He allowed himself to be dragged inside, deciding that sleep would have to wait.

'So,' said Claude, pouring generous measures, his voice dropping conspiratorially as Alix moved away to the kitchen, 'how is Madame Drolet?' He grinned and raised his glass, winking meaningfully. *'Sante, mon vieux.'*

'What do you mean?' Rocco drank, pretending ignorance. No doubt the village rumour mill had been grinding away, making, as his mother used to say, a cake out of a brioche.

'Well, word is she's been circling you like an elegant black widow spider, waiting to strike.' He fluttered his eyebrows. 'Are you feeling frightened?'

'She's harmless.'

'No, she's not. Take my word, if you're not careful, she'll drag you behind the counter one dark evening, roll you up in her web and *paff!* – Mme Denis will be needing a new neighbour.'

'Who needs a new neighbour?' Alix came to join them and relieved her father of his glass and took a small sip. 'Are you two ready to eat?'

CHAPTER THIRTY-TWO

The station the following day was unusually quiet, with a seemingly lower number than usual of miscreants with ill-gotten goods and drunks with sore heads. There was no sign of Saint-Cloud and Massin was in a meeting. Rocco was relieved; it had been a late night and he'd drunk more than he'd intended. But it had been pleasant, too, spending time with Claude and Alix, a welcome diversion from work.

He got to his desk and found a note waiting for him. Inspector David Nialls had called with urgent information. He picked up the phone and dialled the number in London.

'Ah, Lucas,' Nialls greeted him. The British policeman sounded sombre. 'I've got some news. George Tasker was seen getting on a plane yesterday morning at a small airfield outside London. One of our officers was there helping a local customs and excise officer and recognised him. Sorry it's late, but the news only just reached me. I'm not sure if it means anything, but I thought I should mention it.'

'Was Calloway with him?'

'No. He's currently on set at Pinewood Studios, strapped into a car. There was another passenger with Tasker, but our man didn't get a clear sighting of him. As for your chap Delarue, he's already checked out of his hotel. Seems he got a phone call late last night and decided to leave earlier than intended. Your doing, I suspect.'

'I doubt it; I'm pretty certain he didn't see me. But someone might have warned him. Do you know where Tasker was heading?'

'Not for certain. The pilot logged it as a training flight, but since Tasker wouldn't know a joystick from a jelly bean, I would guess he was certainly a passenger and heading your way. Just watch your back – he's a dangerous man.'

Rocco put the phone down. Tasker wasn't the only dangerous man around. Men like Delarue were a threat on a far bigger scale. And if he and some known British gangsters were cosying up, as Nialls had called it, it was going to be bad news for somebody.

He spent the remainder of the day passing on the information about Delarue to Santer and other colleagues with a keen interest in the city's gang activities. Massin might tell his bosses in the Interior Ministry, but on-the-ground information of the kind he'd seen was infinitely fresher and more useful than days-old bulletins. Next he tried Caspar's number, but there was no answer. He then drove out to the site of the ramming, then on to the Pont Noir, clarifying in his own mind the similarities between the two locations. He was off the assignment with Saint-Cloud, but that didn't mean he was off the job. More than ever he was convinced that he was right about the connection between the two. Proving it, however, was a different matter. Beyond a vague theory and a hand-drawn sketch linking them, he hadn't got any firm evidence to back it up. Somehow he had to come up with something tangible – and soon.

It was late in the afternoon and just beginning to get dark when Rocco arrived back in Poissons. He called in at the co-op for some supplies, carefully not responding to Mme Drolet's fluttering eyelashes and coy smiles in light of Claude's gleeful warning, then headed home.

A Peugeot with a rental sticker in the rear window was parked outside his house. Its headlights were on, throwing a theatrical glow along the road, and two men were standing by the driver's door.

One was pencil-thin and dark-haired, dressed in

a crumpled coat. He was watching the lane, and turned as Rocco drove by. It wasn't a face Rocco recognised. A news reporter, possibly, looking for some inside information. His presence in Poissons was no longer a secret, if it ever had been, and the search for up-to-the-minute news meant that reporters were no longer prepared to address all their questions through official channels in Amiens.

The second man was in shadow, and more difficult to see. Then he moved and straightened.

It was the bullish figure of George Tasker.

CHAPTER THIRTY-THREE

Rocco stopped a car's length further on and got out. His MAB 38 was in his coat pocket but he left it there. If these men had wished him harm, they would have waited to catch him unawares, preferably somewhere more remote. And they wouldn't have wanted the area stage-lit like this.

Tasker smirked as he recognised Rocco, and stepped away from the vehicle, placing himself half in shadow. But his hands were in plain sight. He was dressed in a sharp suit with a loud tie, and looked heavy and solid and unstoppable.

'Well, look who's come home at last,' he said, cocking his head to one side. 'You know, you're a hard man to find, Rocco. The locals clammed up when I asked where you lived. Well, I say I asked them ... it was actually Bones here who did the talking on account of he's clever like that and I don't like even thinking about your shitty language. What's all the secrecy about, then? You a bit shy?'

'What do you want, Mr Tasker?' said Rocco. 'I am busy.'

'Hey – is that any way to welcome a man to your manor?' Tasker threw his hands wide, the picture of innocence. 'I mean, you come to mine and I'll make you welcome.' He grinned nastily. 'Very welcome indeed – eh, Bones?'

The man known as Bones shrugged but said nothing. He climbed back in the car and started the engine. Speaking was clearly not his job. Rocco kept his eyes flicking between the two men. He didn't see Bones as a threat; he was probably a driver and interpreter. If Tasker was here to do something physical, he'd want to take care of it himself. But there were still two of them and one of him. What concerned him was that they had gone to the trouble of finding out where he lived. There had to be a reason for that.

'Get to the point.'

Tasker sneered. 'Fair enough. I've got something for you. It's in my jacket, so don't you go shooting me, will you?' He reached very carefully into his inside pocket and took out a white envelope. He stepped forward into the glare of the headlights, turning to glance at the house and gesturing with the envelope. 'Nice place, by the way. Yours, is it?'

Rocco ignored him.

'Never mind. See, thing is, little birdies have been telling us that you've been looking into things which don't concern you. You even went

219

and spoke to DI Nialls in New Scotland Yard.'
He lifted his eyebrows, waiting for a reaction
from Rocco. 'Yeah, you were spotted, don't
worry. We've got spies everywhere. Especially in
the Allendale. I thought it was a bit outside your
jurisdiction, you being French and all. But there
you were, large as life. What was that about?'

'What. Do. You. Want?'

Tasker scowled in mock hurt. 'Aw, come on –
don't be like that.' He pointed the envelope at
Rocco and said, 'We could've planted you first
chance we got, you know that? Followed you
back to that fleapit hotel you stayed in near
Victoria and you'd have been found the next
morning with your throat cut. Or we could have
dropped you in the river with some weights tied
round your ankles.' He paused, dropping the
smile. 'I'd have paid good money to see that, you
kicking against the current. But the boss said he
didn't want no "international incident".'

'Which boss is that?' said Rocco. 'Ruby Ketch?'

A flicker touched Tasker's eyes. 'Yeah, you have
been busy, haven't you? A right little French bea-
ver. Well, fat lot of good it'll do you ... if you're
dead.' He lifted the envelope and slapped it hard
against Rocco's chest. 'But you're lucky – for now.
The boss said to give you this. A little goodwill
gesture, he called it. Personally, I'd rather give you
a bullet.'

He let the envelope go, forcing Rocco to catch it
by reflex before it fell to the ground. It felt heavy,
pliable, a good two-centimetres thick. Paper.

'There's a good boy.' The words were uttered
softly, and Tasker's grin was sly. 'Now, you stay

220

away from our business, Rocco, me boy, and we'll forget you ever existed.'

Rocco tossed the envelope back at him. 'Trying to bribe a policeman in France is a serious offence,' he said. 'Tell Mr Ketch that I do not play those games.'

Tasker's smile was still in place. He slipped the envelope back into his jacket and shrugged. 'I told the boss it was a no-go, but he insisted. He likes to be nice, see, to avoid nastiness.' He pointed a finger at Rocco and mimed pulling a trigger. 'But I don't.'

He turned and walked to the passenger side and got in. Bones was already behind the wheel and closing his door.

Seconds later, they were gone, leaving a whiff of exhaust fumes in the air, and the uncomfortable feeling in Rocco's mind that something bad had just taken place.

CHAPTER THIRTY-FOUR

Caspar nudged open the door of the *Bar Relais* and felt the welcoming brush of warmth against his face. After the cold of the streets outside, his skin began to tingle in response. He walked up to the bar, nodding at one or two faces around the room.

He was on familiar ground here in the 10th arrondissement, not far from the Gare de l'Est. But it didn't mean he felt relaxed. Just a few streets away was the Arab quarter of Belleville, a place he wasn't keen on seeing again anytime soon. Not so long ago he'd run foul of a man named Farek, an Algerian gangster who had been hell-bent on tracking down and killing his runaway wife ... and, as it happened, Lucas Rocco. They had all three been lucky to escape with their lives, especially Caspar, and ever since he had made a point of keeping a careful eye out for hostile forces. The main man might have gone, shot dead on his own brother's instructions it was rumoured, but memories here were long.

'Caspar – you dog!' A tall man with a hooked nose turned and grinned, seeing his reflection in the mirror, and said, 'I thought you were dead. You want a drink?'

'Yeah, thanks, Babon. Ricard, please.' Maurice Babonneau was a former policeman turned co-owner of the café, and spent more time on the customers' side of the bar than behind it, stoking up friendships, trading gossip and generally making sure he could jump on any trouble before it got too heavy. The regular clientele was a mixed brew of North Africans, Asians and Chinese, with a steady flow of cops and ex-soldiers trawling the street network for information or work, depending on their needs. Most were genial neighbours, but occasionally, old enemies ran into each other by chance.

'You working?' Babon's voice dropped. He knew of Caspar's suspension from the force, and was one of the few who were aware of Caspar's former undercover role.

'Here and there. This and that. You know how

222

it is. Is Tatar in?'

'Not yet. Soon will be, though. You need a booth?' The bar had a few private booths in a back room, originally used years ago for assignations between men with money and women without. They were now a favoured meeting place for discreet business of a very different kind.

'Please.'

Babon nodded. 'Okay. Go through to number three. I'll send him in.'

Caspar took his drink and went through a rear door and into a booth made of plywood and leather, with enough room for four people at a crush. The walls had been lined many times over the years, and short of someone standing right outside the curtained entrance with their ear bent round the frame, conversations were guaranteed private.

He sipped his drink and worked on settling his nerves. He hadn't done this for a while, ducking into bars to tap contacts for information. Not people like Tatar, anyway. The sort of security work he did now was more corporate in nature, and free of the kind of threat he'd become used to ... or was it addicted to? He still wasn't sure.

Tatar was a man with a chequered history, most of it washed with the grim spray of illegality. Born and brought up in a Berber family in North Africa, he had joined the OAS almost out of boredom, but also as a way of escaping what he saw as the dying way of life of his forebears. He wanted to get to France, where he saw opportunity. Possessed of a sharp brain, he worked his way up, gathering a pot of money to trade with.

It was the way things were done; you got a pot together as a sign of goodwill and intention. A deal here, a deal there, and soon you were in on the best deals and latest news where credit, if you were trusted, was readily available. From there, the sky was your limit. He had soon begun to set up deals smuggling gold and other valued items across the Med into France, and was now one of the top deal-makers in the city.

He also knew more people than anyone Caspar could think of, with a contacts list like the PTT directory.

The curtain swished back and a large man with a generous belly slipped onto the bench seat across from Caspar. Tatar was dressed in a smart suit and expensive silk shirt and tie. He was in his forties but looked older, a physical attribute he always claimed gave him *gravitas* and was the reason for his success. People didn't trust Young Turks, he reckoned; they liked to deal with men of substance.

'Christ, you've gone over to the dark side,' said Caspar, eyeing the man's clothes, and held out a hand. 'They'll soon have your name down for a private seat at the Bourse.' The last time he'd seen Tatar, the man had been wearing the casual clothes of his part-Berber, part-French way of life, easily mixing with both sides. He'd clearly gone up in the world, a fact he confirmed.

'Been there, done it,' he grinned, and sipped his brandy. 'I've been lucky. Don't worry, Marc; I'm all respectable and glad of the change. As is my wife.' He eyed Caspar with genuine friendship, although neither man could recall how it had formed, only that they had never been enemies. 'What can I do for you?'

Caspar hunched over his drink. 'The attack at Guignes, on the N19.' He'd left a message for Tatar giving the nature of his query. It was the way the Berber did business. 'Anything you can tell me?'

Tatar winced in disgust. *'Quelle horreur!* Like Oran and Tunis in the old days. Bullets flying like mosquitoes. What did you want to know?'

'Who was involved?'

Tatar shook his head. 'Bunch of amateurs, from what I hear. Didn't even get their facts right.' He sniffed. 'They won't be doing it again for a long while, that's for sure.'

Caspar bit his lip. He'd been counting on Tatar to come up with the goods. 'Pity. Never mind.'

'I didn't say I knew nothing.' Tatar gave a slow smile, the look of a man proud to be the bearer of news. 'I've got a brother who works in the Medici Hospital near Versailles.'

'Never heard of it.'

'You wouldn't. It's a small place for the rehabilitation and treatment of special patients. It's not the sort of place to get much publicity.'

Caspar forgot his drink. 'What sort of special patients?'

'Military. The kind they can't put in open wards.'

'Go on.'

'They had two wounded brought in the night of the attack and one dead. One of the wounded was a motorcycle cop, the other a civilian. No papers on him, so probably just a gun hand. He was taken away the same night, only lightly wounded, apparently. But I had my brother get hold of the file on the cop, just out of interest.' He took a sip of his drink. 'And guess what? Turns out he's no ordinary traffic cop.' He slid a folded sheet of paper across the table. 'It's all in there. You didn't get that from me, okay?'

'Of course. It's hot?'

'It's very hot. So hot I don't want to carry it with me any longer than I have to.'

'Tell your brother I owe him.'

'Forget it. He owes me far more. It's about time he paid something back.' He drained his drink and slapped Caspar on the shoulder, his expression suddenly serious. 'You want my opinion, that whole business was a set-up.'

'How do you mean?'

'Simple. The idiots thought they were staging an ambush; but it was them who ended up being whacked. Now, ask yourself who could have arranged such a thing – and why?'

CHAPTER THIRTY-FIVE

'Inspector Rocco?' Massin appeared in the door to the main office. Behind him was *Commissaire* Perronnet and further along the corridor, Colonel Saint-Cloud, watching closely. 'My office, please.'

He turned and walked away, followed by the other two officers, leaving Rocco with a feeling of unease in the pit of his stomach. The mood wasn't helped by the knowledge that this little scene had been played out in front of several colleagues, including Alix and Desmoulins.

He walked up to Massin's office and stepped inside. The three men were waiting for him. Massin pointed to a large brown envelope lying on the edge of his desk. It was addressed to Massin in big black letters, but with no stamps. Hand delivered.

He knew it wasn't going to be good news, and he was right.

'Perhaps, Inspector,' Massin began coolly, 'you would like to comment on the contents of this envelope? It was delivered less than thirty minutes ago.' He remained standing and stared at Rocco with a fixed expression. Saint-Cloud and Perronnet said nothing, but their presence was ominous.

Rocco tipped up the envelope, and out slid a number of photographs, cascading across the polished surface of the desk. They were black and white, fairly grainy but large enough to leave no doubt in anyone's mind what the subject matter was. They had been shot, he noted, at dusk, and in the glare of a car's headlights.

They showed Rocco facing the hulking figure of George Tasker. In the background was Rocco's Citroën Traction, the number plate clear to see. The shots were progressive, a series of images which were as condemning a display of wrongdoing as any Rocco had ever seen. The first showed Tasker taking a white envelope from his pocket; the second showed him holding it out to Rocco; the third showed Rocco holding it against his chest. To the uninitiated, he appeared to be putting it inside his coat.

There was no shot of Rocco throwing the

envelope back at Tasker. Nor of the English gangster putting it back in his pocket.

'It's a set-up,' said Rocco, the words sounding uncomfortably lame, even to him. How often had he heard those same words from others? But he knew what had happened. The man Bones had taken the shots from inside the car while Tasker had manoeuvred Rocco into position. With Rocco's full attention on Tasker as the 'handover' was made, the engine noise'd effectively drowned out any sound of a camera shutter operating.

Saint-Cloud made a noise and looked away in an open display of contempt. Perronnet looked embarrassed, staring down at his shoes. Only Massin showed no expression.

'Who is the man?'

'His name is George Tasker. He's a criminal from London. He and a man he called Bones were waiting outside my house last night.'

'Tasker?' Perronnet looked up. 'Wasn't he one of the Englishmen who smashed up the *Canard Doré?*'

'The same. He works for a London gang boss named Ketch.'

'How do you know this?' Saint-Cloud was enjoying this. Rocco could see it in his eyes and the set of his chin.

'Because I've just been to London, as you know. The Metropolitan Police confirmed the connection between Tasker and Ketch. I also believe Ketch has close links with Patrice Delarue.'

'Perhaps,' said Saint-Cloud softly, cocking his head to one side, 'you could explain who he is?'

'I told you already: he's a known bank robber

and gang boss in Paris.'

The security chief looked blank. It was a convincing performance of someone being presented with information for the very first time. 'Huh. Never mind... You have seen this Ketch and Delarue together? Was Tasker there, too?'

You know he wasn't because I told you, you bastard, Rocco wanted to say. But he held it in. Losing his temper with a man like Saint-Cloud would get him nowhere. He felt suddenly powerless to stop this interview going downhill; whatever he said now was going to sound lame and unconvincing.

'Do you still have the envelope?' said Massin. His voice was bleak and he looked shaken, as if his feet had been kicked out from under him.

'No. I threw it straight back.'

The silence from all three men was brutal. They didn't believe him. He cursed under his breath; what a dumb move that had been. He should have kept it and handed it in immediately.

'I gave it back because they were trying to bribe me,' he insisted. 'I should have seen it coming but I didn't.'

'Bribe you to do what?' asked Perronnet.

'To drop my investigation into the activities of George Tasker and his colleagues.' He stared hard at Saint-Cloud. 'I believe they are complicit in a potential assassination attempt on the president when he comes to the region to visit the burial site at a place called Pont Noir. I've already made my suspicions clear. I even showed Colonel Saint-Cloud the location.'

'He showed me some godforsaken spot, that's true,' replied Saint-Cloud, biting off the words with contempt, 'in the middle of nowhere. There is no planned visit there and Rocco has fabricated this entire "plan" out of nothing. I must confess I was partly convinced by the outside possibility at first because that is my job: investigating and nullifying any threat to the president. But the more Inspector Rocco talked, the less convinced I became. In the end, I was forced to end his assignment to the local security review.'

'What?' Massin looked surprised.

Saint-Cloud turned to him with an apologetic lift of his hands. 'I'm sorry, François – truly I am. I was reluctant to tell you of this development, especially in view of your confidence in your man's abilities. But having such wild speculation attached to the assignment was, frankly, damaging. And now,' he added silkily, sliding in another thrust of the dagger, 'there is this matter of corruption...'

'There is no proof of that,' said Massin sharply. But he didn't sound convinced, and stared down at the photos with a sickened expression. He also could not have failed to pick up the deliberate hint of accusation in the words 'your man', uttered by Saint-Cloud – a damaging piece of word association that would no doubt be repeated higher up the chain of command, adding question marks against his own name.

'If you say so.' Saint-Cloud's voice was silkily soft, insinuating. 'Although one wonders whether there is, perhaps, a connection here.'

'What do you mean?' Even Perronnet, usually self-effacing, was startled enough to make a comment.

'I mean, gentlemen, that experience shows that whenever there is an assassination attempt on a head of state, there is often a ... distraction event not far away.' He flapped a vague hand, the expert bestowing on lesser mortals the benefit of his knowledge. 'It is nothing new, but highly effective.'

'What kind of distraction?' Massin looked puzzled.

Saint-Cloud shrugged expansively. 'Anything. Roadworks causing chaos, a fire, a crash of some kind ... anything to tie up the emergency services and divert the attention of the security cordon. Even,' he stared pointedly at Rocco, 'a fabricated *possibility* of a threat from alleged outsiders conceived to absorb a great deal of our time and resources. Is that not the possibility you discussed with Chief Inspector Nialls in London? Trying to implicate a harmless gang of drunks in some kind of malevolent plot?'

Rocco felt a chill slide across his back. *Broissard. Or Portier.* It had to be. There'd have been no reason for Nialls to conceal the subject of his meeting with Rocco from senior men like them.

'Well?'

'We talked about the possibility, yes. And these men are far from harmless–'

'See?' Saint-Cloud made a guttural noise of disbelief. 'He admits it.' He shook his head. 'It is fanciful rubbish and I have heard enough. I will be bringing in another man to help me instead. Someone we can all trust to focus on getting to these criminals before they can act. And I do not mean chasing bar-room brawlers from London.'

'Bring in somebody who believes your version

231

of horseshit, you mean?' Rocco said softly. 'I wish them well; they'll need it.'

'That's enough!' Massin stepped forward and held out his hand. This time there was none of the playacting used when he had placed Rocco on 'sick leave'. 'I need your weapon and your card, Inspector. You are suspended pending further investigations of this matter. You will remain at home until needed.' His eyes flickered momentarily past Rocco's shoulder and Rocco turned his head at the sound of movement.

Sous-Brigadier Godard and two of his men were standing outside the open door. Godard looked deeply uncomfortable.

'What the hell are they here for?' Rocco demanded, and looked at Massin for support.

But the senior officer could not meet his eye. 'Your weapon and card, please, Inspector,' he said.

Rocco took out his gun. But instead of handing it to Massin, he ejected the magazine and placed it and the weapon side by side on the desk. Then he dropped his police card alongside them and walked out of the office.

The walk down the stairs and through the main office accompanied by Godard and his men was probably the most humiliating of Rocco's life. All talk subsided from a feverish high, no doubt speculating on what was going on upstairs, and dwindled to nothing as he walked by. Telephones went unanswered and all movement ceased, save for faces turning towards him and following his progress.

The news had already spread, disseminated by

232

that peculiar method experienced only in close office environments. Rocco wondered whether a sly whisper here and there from Saint-Cloud had helped it along the way.

Then Detective René Desmoulins stood up and stepped in front of him, his weightlifter's bulk blocking the way. One of Godard's men put out a hand to warn him off, but Desmoulins sneered at him and the man backed off. Alix hovered in the background, her face pale.

'This is shit, Lucas,' Desmoulins said quietly. 'Tell them.'

'I tried,' said Rocco. 'They prefer to believe photos.' He patted Desmoulins on the arm and shook his outstretched hand. 'This isn't over, don't worry.'

As he walked out to his car, he was holding a folded slip of paper Desmoulins had pressed unseen into his palm.

CHAPTER THIRTY-SIX

The phone hauled Rocco out of a fractious sleep. He felt cold and stiff, his head a jumble of confused thoughts.

It was Michel Santer. 'Lucas? Can you talk?'

'Sure. Go ahead.' He rolled over to check the time. It was late afternoon. Or early, depending on one's line of work. If one had a line of work. The scene at the office seemed like a ghastly dream from which he hadn't yet awoken.

233

'You okay?' Santer didn't have to say anything; he'd heard the news of Rocco's suspension. It would be all over the police network by now, talked over and rehashed over coffee breaks and passed along as shifts changed. Most wouldn't believe it; cops being accused of taking bribes was commonplace and usually a derailing exercise, at worst a clumsy form of revenge by a resentful con or his colleagues. But some would take delight in hearing that an investigator had been taken down, even if the accusation hadn't yet been proven.

'I'm catching up on sleep. Other than that, and wanting to shoot someone, which I can't do because they took my gun, I'm fine.'

'Was this because of your trip to London?'

'It didn't help.' He levered himself up and went through to the kitchen trailing the telephone cord after him. Clamping the receiver under one cheek, he put some water on to boil and scooped coffee grounds into a percolator.

'I bet Delarue has something to do with this,' Santer muttered, 'directly or indirectly. He must be getting ambitious.' Santer, like most officers in the capital, was well acquainted with Patrice Delarue's activities over many years, and prayed for the day when the man could be brought down. 'Is it true what they're saying – there are photos?'

'Yes. It was a set-up, but I should have known better – I walked right into it.'

'It's easy to do, everyone knows that. So how do we get you out of it?'

'You don't.' The last thing Rocco wanted was any of his friends putting their careers on the line for him. This thing had to be played out, and

234

until it was, he was effectively on his own. Anyone coming near would be tainted by the accusation against him, and he didn't want that to happen. 'Stay clear of me and don't make waves. I'm not done yet, even if I have to go to London and ram Tasker's teeth down his throat.'

Bones, he thought. *He might be a weak link.* Almost certainly English, by his clothes, since he doubted Tasker would find it easy working with a Frenchman on setting up incriminating photos of a cop being handed an envelope. He'd call Nialls later on. He might recognise the man's name.

'So what can we do?'

Rocco sat down at the table and rubbed his face. That was the question: what could they do? Faced with such clear and unequivocal evidence of an officer taking an envelope, and with Saint-Cloud working away in the background with his sly digs and vaguely worded throwaway lines, Rocco himself would have come to the same conclusions as Massin. Until proven otherwise.

There was only one thing to do.

'We prove I'm right about the proposed attack,' he said.

'But you're suspended. What can you do?'

'I'm suspended, I'm not chained to the wall.'

Santer said, 'Well, that sounds more like the old Rocco I used to know. Thank God for that. For a moment there I thought I was going to have to come down and kick your arse.'

'Not yet, you won't.'

'Good. Actually, I've got some information that might cheer you up. It's about the attack on the car in Guignes. You still want to hear it?'

'More than ever.' Rocco stood up and poured boiling water into the top of a percolator and snapped the lid shut. Even the smell was making him feel more awake.

'The man I told you about, with the cousin in the office here?'

'Yes?'

'He came by a while ago, on his way to a raid on a suspected OAS cell. He said the body spirited away from the N19 scene wasn't a body. The man was wounded but still breathing. Someone identified him and let the word out. His name's Christophe Lamy. He's a former captain in the 1st Foreign Parachute Regiment. He left the regiment along with several others before they got pushed and charged with anti-government agitation over Algeria.'

A military officer with strong opinions and possible sympathy for the OAS. It wasn't news, but it was hardly the kind of information the authorities would want broadcast. Disaffected and potentially violent individuals with no ties to the establishment were easily dismissed as malcontents. But former soldiers – especially former officers from elite regiments – were bad press for a government trying to push a line of propaganda based on national unity.

He sat upright, the clutches of sleep falling away. Colonel François Saint-Cloud. He'd also been a member of the 1st REP. Was there a connection, other than that they liked to throw themselves out of perfectly safe airplanes for a living? He wasn't sure. But it was too close to be ignored, too much of a coincidence to disregard

– especially with his limited number of choices.

Santer hadn't finished. 'There's more. I had a call from Caspar. His contact couldn't get the name of the motorcycle escort who fought off the attack, but he knew the hospital where he was taken. It's a specialist military unit near Versailles. Caspar got close and did some digging. He's still trawling for information at the moment, but he asked me to let you know what he's found so far.'

'Go on.' Rocco sipped the coffee. Strong enough to float a horse; he probably wouldn't asleep for a week after this.

'The escort's name was Jean-Paul Leville. And guess what – he's no normal escort.'

'Don't tell me – another specialist.'

'Damn. How did you know?'

'I didn't. But it seemed unusual for a motorcycle cop to survive coming off his bike enough to fight back and disable two attackers. What is he?'

'A former marine commando. Served with an elite unit in the Horn of Africa, trained men at Lorient, the commando training school, and even ran specialist courses for the Legion on escape and evasion techniques and close-quarter fighting. There are gaps in his résumé of several months at a time, but we can both guess what they were.'

'Covert missions.' It had to be. The alternative was prison. But men with prison records wouldn't get anywhere near becoming a motor-cycle cop, let alone serving as an official security guard. Leville was a government gunman.

'Exactly. Falling off a bike at speed and getting up again would be pretty simple for a guy like him, don't you think?'

'Yes. So what's he doing riding a bike for the official fleet?'

'God knows. Certainly not for the excitement or the fresh air.'

There was only one reason Rocco could think of: someone had known the car was going to be hit and had brought in a specialist. If that were the case, the attackers couldn't have known their plan was exposed, and would have been in ignorance about who they were up against. If they had known, as reckless as some of the extreme groups were, they would have thought twice about launching the attack.

Unless they had been told something completely different.

'Where is this supersoldier now?'

'Disappeared. Caspar said the hospital's now under a shutdown order. He got all this from a contact who got a peek at Leville's medical record.'

'They had it to hand just like that?'

'Seems so. He had light abrasions and a wrenched shoulder. Pretty standard stuff for a para, I'd have thought. They discharged him at his own request and he was gone.' He sighed loudly. 'Listen, Lucas, this isn't over; I'll call you back the moment I get anything. I've got to go.'

'Thanks, Michel.' Rocco put the phone down.

The whole thing smelt wrong. Medical records didn't simply turn up like that at the drop of a hat, not even with improved filing systems. But they might if the person they applied to was expected to suffer injuries and need urgent treatment. The president, for example, was one; soldiers on

238

dangerous missions were others; and specialists on high-risk covert assignments in-country.

The attackers had been set up to fail.

As he thought it over, his eyes settled on a crumpled slip of paper on the table. It was the note Desmoulins had handed him in the station. He hadn't even looked at it yet, too weighed down with what had taken place back at the station. He picked it up and read it. Then read it again. It was in Rizzotti's handwriting, and helpfully concise.

Tell Lucas the DS battery carried a supply sticker from Ets. Lilas Moteurs – a garage in St Gervais.

Rocco felt as if an electric charge had gone through him. St Gervais. If it was the same St Gervais he knew, it was an eastern suburb of Paris and within spitting distance of Delarue's stamping grounds around the 10th and 19th arrondissements.

He grabbed the phone and dialled Santer. When his friend answered, he read him the contents of the note. It was a remote possibility, but what were the chances of a car battery from a garage in eastern Paris ending up out here? Was that why the people behind the killing of Bellin had been so keen on seeing the car destroyed – to eliminate any possibility of a link back to them?

'Anything's possible,' Santer said reasonably. 'But a damn sight better than anything else we've got. I'll get Caspar to go in there. That way we don't have any jurisdictional problems. In the meantime I'll get someone looking into who owns this place. I'll call you as soon as I have anything.'

CHAPTER THIRTY-SEVEN

Tasker was back at the Old Bourbon, in Stepney. Ketch was behind the desk as usual, with Brayne sitting in like a watchful Buddha, saying little but absorbing every word.

'We've had word from our friends across the Channel,' Ketch announced grandly, studying the end of a fat cigar and blowing gently on the burning tip. 'Your pal Inspector Rocco has been suspended pending investigation for corruption. How about that? They don't hang about, do they? One whiff and those Frenchies bring down the chopper.'

Tasker smiled. It was the best bit of news he'd heard all day. 'Pity it doesn't work that quick with our own lot,' he muttered. He was surprised by the speed of events; he'd expected a couple of days at least before anything happened.

'If only. It seems someone dropped off some very tasty pictures showing him accepting a packet of readies. Good work, George. You done well. There'll be a pressie for Bones, too. Nice snaps, they were. Classy.'

Tasker glowed. It was nice earning some praise after the last lash-up. It also made up for the nightmare of a flight that Ketch had put him through. The tiny plane had creaked and rattled all the way over and back, with the pilot acting like a Battle of Britain ace until Tasker had threatened to break a few of his fingers. 'Yeah, well ... he walked right into it, the mug.'

'Thing is, will it stick? They're not stupid; they'll know it's a bit iffy, done out in the open like that. Still, short notice, it was the best we could do.'

'It might slow Rocco down and put a dent in his career prospects,' Brayne ventured. 'The smell lingers. Trust is very difficult to keep under those circumstances.'

Ketch nodded and settled back in his chair. 'You're right there, Brayne. Still, that's done and dusted. On to other things, eh?' He looked at Tasker. 'Our French friends want us to run another "scenario" like the last one. Different place this time, but similar tactics.'

'Again?' Tasker couldn't help it; he needed another trip to France like a dose of the clap. And what were the French playing at?

'Yes. Again. And why?' Ketch lifted his eyebrows, daring Tasker to argue. 'Because we're being paid to do it, that's why. It's a business contract, pure and simple. The only difference is, as well as this scenario,' he lifted his hands and mimed speech marks, 'you'll be doubling up.'

'I don't follow.'

'We've been doing a bit of research on the side, George.' He glanced at Brayne. 'What was the term you used, Brayne?'

'Expanding our area of operations,' the accountant said softly.

'That's it. Expanding our area of operations. And one way of doing that is to look further afield, to somewhere where the bleedin' Sweeney don't have any influence.' He checked the end of

241

his cigar and explained, 'There's a little bank in a small town called Béthune, just across the water, about an hour from Calais. As close as that, it hardly counts as in France, does it? Anyway, word is, this bank is just waiting to be knocked over, and sits on the outskirts of the town. No traffic snarl-ups, good getaway routes to the Channel ... and who'd ever think of a bunch of London boys knocking over a bank over there, eh?'

'What's the risk?' said Tasker. It was something he *was* allowed to say. Risk was something they all shared. For risk, read cops.

'Now that's the beauty of it, see. The cops'll all be looking the other way. Guaranteed.' He grinned knowingly. 'We'll get a friendly local to drop a couple of rumours about jobs planned elsewhere.' He threw his arms out. 'The elegance of this job is bleedin' amazing.'

'What's so special about this place?' Tasker didn't get it. A bank was a bank. Some offered more promise than others, some more risk. Elegance didn't come into it. 'And why now?'

'I'm glad you asked, George. This particular branch is right next to a new industrial zone. They get regular drops of cash for the local factory workers, nicely packed in metal cases ... and it's ours for the taking. In, out and away, neat as ninepence. You won't even need any gear. Just good timing, a show of strength and a fast car. A real old-style blagging. What d'you reckon?'

Tasker thought it sounded too good to be true. No bank in the world just sat there waiting to be knocked over. 'Won't the Frenchies object, us moving in on their turf?'

'The Frenchies, as you insist on calling them, George, are helping us do it. They've scouted it out, they're supplying plans of the inside – everything we need bar them doing it for us.'

'Why don't they do it themselves?'

'Search me. Personally, I think it's a thank you for our help with these scenarios. Never look a gift horse, George, that's what me old mum used to say.' He tapped ash off his cigar. 'Now, are you up for it or not?'

'Two jobs on the same day.' Tasker thought about the men available, men he could trust. 'That's pushing it.'

Ketch showed his teeth. 'Not only on the same day, George. Simultaneously.'

'Eh? How?'

'Division of labour, that's how.' He waved a hand, clearly enjoying the situation. 'It doesn't need more than Fletcher to drive the truck. He's more than capable of buggering up a car with a truck all by himself, as we know.' He gave a malevolent smile. 'And this time, it's for real, not play-acting.'

Tasker suddenly saw where this was going. He felt a shiver of excitement. Christ, this wasn't just messing about; it had all been for a reason. He felt annoyed that he hadn't been told before, but said nothing. 'Who's the target – anyone I know?'

It was a question too far; he saw that instantly. Ketch's face shut down like a fridge door slamming. 'Not your worry, George. While Fletch's doing his bit, you and the boys, with Calloway as wheelman doing what he does best, will be relieving the *Crédit Agricole* – that's the name of this bank – of a nice amount of folding francs.' He pulled on his cigar, watching the grey smoke curling into the air. 'Think you can do that?'

Tasker looked offended. He'd earned his stripes doing bank jobs. His first was aged twenty, with a team in Chelmsford, using a sawn-off and lots of attitude to hide his gut-churning fear from the more experienced men with him. Since then, there had been plenty more, often with him holding the reins. In fact, he prided himself on having become something of an expert over the years, even though he'd copped a couple of prison terms here and there, although never for anything serious like carrying firearms. As soon as he'd been able to, he'd left that to others.

He'd never robbed a French bank before. How hard could it be?

He said, 'No problem, boss.' Be nice to get back to the old game.' He hadn't done one for at least a year. He wouldn't want to get out of practice.

'That's the spirit, George. Good man.' Ketch smiled and blew out a perfect smoke ring. 'And you don't even have to worry about sourcing replacement vehicles. It's all being laid on by our friends over there. Any questions?'

Tasker thought about how the last job had gone down. 'Only about the truck. If this is for real, wouldn't it be better to use a bigger model? More punch that way.' *And Fletcher, the mad fucker, would love it*, he thought nastily. Like a giant kid in a toyshop, looking for something to break.

Ketch shook his head. 'No. It has to be the same model as last time. Personally, I agree with you, bigger would be better. But it's their money,

244

so their call. They said the driver would see why when he gets there. The Renault was reliable enough, wasn't it? Tough little motor, as I hear it.'

'I suppose.' Tasker thought about how hard the small truck had hit them. Anything bigger would have run right over the top.

Ketch's eyes glittered. 'That's that, then. You'd better get going. By train and boat this time, I'm afraid. We need to keep the flights for special occasions.'

Tasker stood up, an electric feeling building in his veins. It was always like this before a job. Now he knew what it was, and what was required, he was itching to go. And by train and boat suited him fine.

'Before you do...' Ketch stood up and came round his desk. 'You asked why now. Our French pals tell me the weather's closing in and there could be a lot of snow on the way. It's changed the agenda over there, that's all. Still, no worries, eh? A job's a job. Tell Fletcher all he needs to do is what he did last time: wind up the spring, wait for the target and hit it square on. As for you, you do your bit and don't you worry about him. He'll be busy.'

Tasker felt uneasy. No matter what Ketch was saying, this was nothing like last time. Last time hadn't been for real.

'He'll be on his own, then.' Jesus, that was cold. Fletcher out in the middle of nowhere ... he'd never make it back. Other than his usual delivery routes, the big idiot barely knew his way around the south-east of England, let alone some foreign patch of mud.

245

Ketch's next words put a cap on the subject with chilling finality.

'Casualties of war, George. Casualties of war.'

CHAPTER THIRTY-EIGHT

Waiting for Santer to call back was going to be agony, and Rocco knew he'd be climbing the walls before that happened. He decided to fight fire with fire. He picked up the telephone and called Inspector Nialls in London.

'Hello, Lucas.' Nialls sounded wary. 'Sounds as if you're having problems.'

The British art of understatement, Rocco figured. He wondered how Nialls had heard.

'I hope,' he said, 'you do not believe everything you hear.'

'I don't. Especially when I heard so quickly. Your friend Broissard called me about an hour ago. He suggested in a roundabout manner that it might be better if I ignored any further approaches from you.' He paused. 'Sorry, Lucas, I shouldn't have told them about our chat, but I figured you were all working in the same neighbourhood.'

'Forget it,' said Rocco. 'I thought the same. Can I still ask for your help?'

'Of course. I'm retiring, so I don't care.' He chuckled lightly down the phone. 'It's a refreshing change after all these years of jumping through hoops and doing the right thing; a bit like being out of school, if I can recall that far back. How did it happen? Broissard wouldn't say; merely suggested you'd been compromised by contacts with a criminal organisation.'

Compromised, not accused. Broissard had been clever, he thought, no doubt acting on instructions from Saint-Cloud. The very mention of being compromised would make many police colleagues back away fast from the officer concerned, and would be enough to sink most careers without further question. 'It was George Tasker and a man called Bones.' He described what had happened and heard Nialls making explosive noises at the other end.

'And they believed that load of old cobblers? Sorry, that means–'

'I know what it means. And the answer is yes, they believed it.'

'Christ Almighty, Tasker being involved would be enough for most coppers this side of the water to smell a rat, he's done it so often. It rather explains where he was flying off to, though, doesn't it? I suppose there are similar small airfields near you where he could have landed?'

'A few,' Rocco agreed. There were often small planes buzzing around the skies in the area, and he had a good idea where the most active club airfield was situated. He made a note to get Desmoulins onto it.

'The other man was Bones, you say?' Nialls continued. 'That sounds disturbingly familiar. Did you get a first name?'

'No. We were not introduced. But he takes a good photograph.' Rocco described the man and heard the sound of a low whistle at the other end.

'I thought so. There's only one man I know who fits that description. Let me double-check, will you? I've a colleague here who knows Tasker's circle of festering little mates better than I do. Won't be a second.' The phone went down with a clunk and Rocco heard a mumble of voices in the background, followed by laughter. Seconds later Nialls was back.

'Well, that was easy. Fortunately, Tasker's no Einstein; he used one of his own friends. My colleague confirms that it was a photographer named Patrick Daniel Skelton, known as "Bones". That's a play on words, although I suspect you know that.'

'I do.'

'Right. Skelton lurks at the lower edges of his profession, providing so-called evidence for divorce scams set up by a couple of private detectives. When he's not doing that, he freelances for one of the nastier news rags and does photographic work for magazines in Soho. He has several minor convictions for handling pornography. I've had the dubious task of talking to him myself on a couple of occasions. I felt like having a bath after each one.'

'And he is a friend of Tasker?'

'Yes, although probably more supplier than friend.'

'What does that mean?'

'I gather George Tasker has a rather brutal approach to getting women. Skelton gets them coming to him all the time, hoping for "film" work. One feeds the other.'

Rocco recalled Tasker's expression when he'd

seen Alix at the station. The air of sexual menace in his eyes had been blatant, and what Nialls had said came as no surprise.

'Can you find out if this Skelton was out of the country at the same time as Tasker?'

'I'll see what I can do. Anything else?'

'What exactly does Fletcher do?'

'You mean when he's not throwing his weight around for Ketch or Tasker? He's a doorman – a bouncer. But when he's not bullying drunks, he drives haulage trucks. Most of it's involved with shifting illegal goods, but we haven't been able to catch him at it yet.'

Rocco thanked him and put down the phone. So, another driver.

A *truck* driver.

A truck ramming a car. He pictured the scene, and thought about the two men involved. Fletcher the giant fist, the battering ram; Calloway the expert, the artist. Which one would be more useful for an attack on the president? A getaway driver with the skill to out-distance any police pursuit must be high up there. In most of the previous attacks, putting distance between themselves and the vengeful authorities had proved the most difficult thing for the gunmen to accomplish. In most cases, anyone who had escaped had done so through a knowledge of the area, of being able to slip away through narrow backstreets and hide among the local population. Or by sheer unadulterated good fortune. Because sometimes luck favoured the ungodly, too.

But if Rocco's suspicions were correct, what use would a racing driver be on a deserted road in the middle of nowhere? With none of the usual security, public or press on hand, why would they need speed to escape afterwards? If the planned visit to the Pont Noir was going to be private, even the normal publicity machine would be unaware of the president's presence. Any ensuing getaway would therefore be almost surreally casual in its execution.

Which meant Calloway wouldn't be required. Not there, at any rate.

Because Fletcher would be the instrument of assault. Fletcher would be the giant fist driving a very blunt instrument. Everything hinged on him.

He'd been looking at the wrong man.

CHAPTER THIRTY-NINE

The Lilas Garage in St Gervais was a hive of activity when Caspar arrived and parked across the street. It was just after seven in the evening. Set amid a row of small houses down a cul-de-sac, the place had an air of neat respectability, with a freshly painted frontage and a large roller door keeping the noise in and, he suspected, unwanted visitors out.

He'd driven out from the city as soon as he'd got the call from Santer, keen to help in any way that he could with Rocco's dilemma, the need to go trawling for OAS leads forgotten. If the DS wrecked near Amiens had come from this garage, and it was tied in with an assassination plot against the president, then he was ready to do whatever it took to prove the link. Not that he felt overly bothered by a threat to de Gaulle. But helping out Rocco, who had given him a chance when nobody else had, was very high on his list of priorities. If that also helped preserve *Le Grand Charles* for another day ... well, you couldn't have everything.

A tour of local bars, playing the part of a cautious motorist seeking a reputable garage to supply and service a decent car, had thrown up the names of one or two local businesses. Oddly, few had mentioned *Ets. Lilas Moteurs,* and those who had had been reluctant to give glowing endorsements, with one or two clamming up when he'd pressed them for details. Caspar's nose for the faintly dubious, along with a friendly call to a one-time colleague in the area, had soon verified that the garage was not quite what it seemed. They did not encourage walk-in customers, and had no visible used-car lot. They appeared, however, to process a good number of vehicles, although few, if any, buyers were ever seen on the premises.

Caspar watched the place and waited. He'd picked up a hint from his one-time colleague that the owner was actually only a manager, but it was going to be difficult to prove who owned the place without going through a lengthy process of accessing business records with the local town hall. That was something Santer'd be able to do legitimately. In the meantime, Caspar preferred to see if he could shake something up the old-fashioned way.

A heavyset man in blue overalls appeared from a Judas gate in the roller door, stepping to one side and lighting up a cigarette. Behind him as

251

the door opened and closed came the bright flutter of a welding torch and the clatter of metal hitting a concrete floor.

Caspar climbed out of his car and wandered across the street, lighting up a cigarette and holding it with the glowing end cupped in his hand. He nodded at the mechanic, who grunted in return, but eyed Caspar warily.

'A guy said this might be a good place to pick up a decent car,' he said casually, and named one of the bars where the garage had been mentioned. 'I think his name was Marco.'

'Is that right?' The man studied him carefully. 'I don't know any Marco.'

'Well, maybe I got it wrong. But you do sell cars, right? For cash?'

'Now and then.' The man indicated with his chin Caspar's car, a dark-blue Peugeot. 'But it looks like you've already got one.'

'It belongs to my brother. He lent it to me but he needs it back.' He dropped the cigarette and stamped on it. 'Still, if you're not interested.'

'Depends how much you want to spend,' said the man. 'We do good work – we're not cheap. And it would have to be cash.'

'Sure. Are you the owner? Only I like to deal with the boss.'

'Are you saying you don't trust me?' The man looked prickly, his eyes narrowing. His voice had dropped to a low growl.

'I'm not suggesting that. I just like to know who I'm dealing with, that's all – especially if I'm going to spend a decent amount of money.'

'Then I'm the boss, yes. You dealing or not?'

The man was lying. Caspar didn't know who he was, but he wasn't the main man – he could feel it. 'Okay. Have you got any models I can see?'

'Not here.' The mechanic flicked his cigarette away and turned to go inside. 'Meet me in thirty minutes ... I need to finish up here first.'

'Sure. Where?'

'Back to the main road, go right and take the third on the right. There's a lock-up down there where we keep our cars. Bring cash. You do have cash, don't you?'

'Of course.' Caspar held out his hand. 'I'm Michel.'

The man ignored the hand. 'Good for you. See you in thirty.'

Caspar drove out of the street and followed the directions to the lock-up. It was as the man had said. The building was fairly new, a brick-built, metal-clad unit of the type springing up everywhere, and big enough, he estimated, to house about a dozen vehicles. It was in darkness, with no cars outside and no signs of life. He parked along the road and walked back to the front door, and peered through the glass. All he could see was an office containing two desks and a scattering of paperwork. He checked he wasn't being watched and walked around the back, where he found a large roller door opening out to a hardstanding. The area was unlit, sunk in heavy shadows. There were no cars here, either. He stepped up close to the roller shutter, where an oval window was set in one of the metal sections. He rubbed away a film of grime and put his face against the glass. It took a few moments for his eyes to adjust to the poor light.

The lock-up was empty.

He stepped back from the roller door and kept moving, walking away from the building until he was standing in the shadow of some trees fifty metres away, off-site. His skin was prickling and he felt his pulse quickening. He'd been in this situation many times before, and had learnt to follow his instincts; and right now, his instincts were telling him to get out – fast.

But he waited.

Ten minutes later, a car appeared and turned in at the front of the building.

The man was early.

Then he saw movement inside the vehicle. At least three occupants, all big. He stood absolutely still. The glow of the headlights wasn't strong enough to reach back here, but he didn't want to take any chances. This was their turf, not his, and they'd soon pick up on anything unusual.

He heard the car doors opening and closing. A murmur of voices, then footsteps. One man appeared, walking away up the road, passing briefly beneath a street light. He was wearing a leather jacket and boots, broad-shouldered and with a shaved head. Checking out the parked cars, Caspar decided.

Then two more men came round the side of the building and checked the rear yard. They were dressed in work clothing and heavy boots, and moved in concert without talking, as if they had done this before.

Caspar heard an oath when they found the area empty, and watched as the men walked back to the front and stood chatting. The first man came back, and as he met his colleagues, he shook his arm and a length of metal pipe slid out of his sleeve.

The three men laughed and got back in the car and drove away.

Caspar found a bar and used the phone at the back. He called Santer at home. 'It's a chop shop,' he reported, using an Americanism. 'And they're very jumpy. Word locally is, they don't do any normal trade, just specialised stuff.'

'Did you talk to anyone inside?'

'Briefly. Their idea of customer relations is a bit unusual. I arranged a buying meet, and three of them came armed with iron bars.'

'Ouch. You okay?'

'Yes. I had a feeling about them and stayed out of the way. I'm pretty sure I wasn't made – I just think they're on high alert. I couldn't even get a name. You'll have to go through the paperwork.'

'I can do that. Thanks, Marc. You'd better put your head down and stay out of trouble.'

'I can follow up one of the OAS leads I've got.'

'Okay. But watch your back.'

CHAPTER FORTY

'I didn't realise today was a national police holiday.' Mme Denis was waiting in the dark outside Rocco's gate when he returned from a punishing five kilometres run along the Danvillers road. A sharp night chill had settled across the countryside – not ideal weather for running, but he'd used the exercise on the deserted road to vent some of the impatience and frustration from his system, and to free up his mind for what lay ahead. He was well aware that if he didn't manage to clear himself of suspicion very quickly, he'd face a rough time indeed and be out of a job at the very least. And that was without the looming possibility that there was a credible threat to the president's life, no matter what Colonel Saint-Cloud believed.

He opened the gate and led his neighbour into the house, his skin tingling at the sudden warmth. The road surface had been a shimmering patchwork of early ice crystals, promising a heavier than normal morning frost, and the grass on the verges was already showing stiff and pale. But the run had managed to make him feel energised once more. He considered how much he could tell his neighbour, and what the likelihood was that she would find out soon enough what had happened to him.

'I've been suspended,' he told her, putting some water on to boil. 'Accused of taking a bribe.'

There, it was out. But he couldn't think of handling it any other way. Mme Denis had welcomed him to Poissons and helped ease him into the village community as much as Claude Lamotte had done, albeit in her own way, and she was no fool; she knew today was no holiday for the police or anyone else.

'Hah!' She barked at him and nudged him to one side. She took the lid off his percolator, inspecting the filter before upending it and banging it onto a sheet of newspaper and dropping the contents into his rubbish bin. She rubbed her fingers on her apron. 'I knew they were up to no good.' She rinsed off the filter and replaced it, then filled it with fresh ground coffee from a tin in the cupboard.

Rocco watched her with amusement. 'I'm glad you know your way around my kitchen. Who are you talking about?'

'Those men who came to see you. Why do strangers think they can sit outside a house in a place like this with the engine running and not be noticed?' She placed two cups and saucers on the table. 'I saw him, the big one. He tried your front door, then went and stood out in the road with the other one. He looked like a weasel.' She looked at Rocco with piercing eyes. 'Not friends of yours, I hope. They looked like trouble. Foreigners. You shouldn't be drinking coffee this late at night – it's bad for the digestion.'

Rocco said, wondering if he wasn't hoping for too much, 'What did you see?'

'I saw the big one hand you an envelope. Is that what this is all about? He was giving you money? Damn stupid of you to take it, if you ask me. No wonder someone thinks you're a bad one.' She pursed her lips and poured water onto the coffee, then placed the percolator on the stove, where it began to bubble with a regular, gloopy sound.

Rocco felt his spirits sag. He could've done with the support of this woman more than most. But if asked, all she would be able to say was that she saw him take an envelope from a stranger. It wasn't going to make for the most convincing defence.

'Still,' she continued, dropping two sugar lumps into his cup, 'you did the right thing by throwing it back at him, although,' she prodded him in the chest, 'I was hoping you were going to knock his head off – but you didn't.'

'You saw me give it back?' He felt a weight lift off his chest. It was no guarantee, bearing in mind that she was his neighbour and friend. But it offered a slim chance that his story might now be believed.

'Of course I did.' She looked up at him and nudged him with her elbow, eyes twinkling. 'What good are nosey neighbours if they never see anything?'

Rocco smiled down at her. 'Thank you.'

'Now, don't go getting all emotional,' she told him. 'You're not out of the mud yet. Who do I speak to?'

Massin. It had to be. '*Commissaire* Massin is my immediate boss,' he said. 'He might pass you on to someone higher – maybe in another station. But he's a start.'

'How do you get on with this Massin? Is he a good boss?'

He shrugged. He wasn't about to go into their shared history, but she might as well know that they were not exactly best *copains*. 'We manage – but that's about all.'

'That's good.' She nodded approvingly. 'Because if *he* believes you, you're in with a chance.' She walked to the door. 'I'll call him from the phone in the café tomorrow first thing and put him right. And don't worry – I'll make sure all the gossip-mongers are out of the room when I do it.'

Half an hour later, there was a knock at the door.

It was Claude Lamotte, carrying a shoebox under one arm.

'Sorry it's late,' he announced, although he didn't look it. He was puffing against the cold. 'Are you in to visitors?' He sniffed. 'Ah, coffee. Lovely. I could do with a cup, thank you.' He brushed past Rocco and dropped the box on the table, then helped himself to a cup and looked into it as if searching for gold.

Rocco took the hint. He lifted a bottle of cognac from the cupboard and handed it over. Claude grinned and added a liberal dose to his cup. He took a sip and looked at Rocco, eyes suddenly serious.

'You all right?'

'I've felt better,' said Rocco. The police grapevine worked, even out here. Or maybe Alix had filled her father in on his news.

Claude cleared his throat and pushed the shoebox across the table. 'That might help.'

Rocco lifted the lid. From the weight, he knew instantly what was inside, even before he smelt the familiar soft tang of oil.

Claude said nothing, merely studied the ceiling, rocking back and forth on his heels and slurping his coffee.

Rocco dropped the lid to one side. Wrapped in cloth in the bottom of the box lay a Walther P38. It had a walnut grip and included several loose rounds of ammunition.

'It's not right,' Claude said quickly, when Rocco looked up at him, 'a cop without a gun. Where the

259

hell do they think this is – England?' He looked flushed and blew out his cheeks with indignation. 'Never heard anything so outrageous.'

Rocco took the pistol out of the box and checked the mechanism. It was in perfect working order and lightly oiled, the metal parts sliding together with immaculate precision. It had been well cared for over the years.

'I suppose it's no good me asking where you got this,' he said.

'I found it in a field.' Claude stared innocently back at him without blinking, then shrugged expansively, daring him to suggest different. 'It's criminal what people leave lying around.'

By 'people', Rocco figured it had been a member of the German military. He wondered if that was all he'd lost. He put the gun down. 'Thank you.'

Claude looked pleased. 'Hey, don't thank me – it was Alix's idea.' His eyebrows lifted and he looked decidedly proud. 'Bloody kids ... no respect for regulations. Still, what can you do, huh?'

The phone rang. Rocco leant across and picked it up. It was Santer.

'Right, two things,' the captain said without preamble. 'The Lilas garage in St Gervais is a chop shop. They don't like casual callers; Caspar went in as a buyer and nearly got himself tenderised with iron bars.'

'Is he all right?'

'He's fine. His radar was working and he ducked out. I told him to stay away, and he's going after some OAS group he's got word on. After that, I did some digging. The garage is owned by a woman called Debussy ... who is the wife of the manager. He in turn happens to be a nephew of ... Patrice Delarue.' He gave a bark of disgust. 'The nerve of these people – they don't even bother trying to hide what they're doing! An intern could have found this in minutes.'

'Delarue's just keeping it in the family,' said Rocco. 'But he keeps his hands clean and the Debussy woman can always claim her husband was working without her knowledge. Nice people. Can we use it?'

'Well, it's enough to allow us in there to look at their paperwork, given a helpful judge to sign it off. If we can trace a receipt for the DS battery, it proves a link. We'll probably find it hard to make that stick, but it'll disrupt his organisation for a while until we get something better.'

'Good work, Michel. I've a feeling a lunch is in order.' It was a step nearer, and one that the Paris police would jump on. They had been after Delarue for far too long to let go easily of a chance to bring him down.

'At last,' Santer breathed, and laughed. 'Food. The man's talking my language. I can't wait.'

'You've earned it. What was the other thing?'

'You recall the paratrooper, Captain Lamy, wounded in the N19 attack?'

'Yes.'

'It seems he's just been found and questioned by the DST, our esteemed internal security organisation. He caught a secondary infection and had to be taken to hospital. He's currently spilling his guts and claims he took part in the attack to help his brother. You now have to ask

261

me who his brother is.'

'I have no idea but you're clearly about to tell me.' He could sense Santer was enjoying this moment of triumph.

'Actually, his name doesn't really matter. Suffice to say he's a gambler and general black sheep of the Lamy crop. Not a good gambler, because he owes a small fortune to a private casino owned by none other than Patrice Delarue. Captain Lamy claims Delarue told him if he didn't help out, his delinquent brother would end his days in the Seine tied to a large piece of concrete. Personally, I think Lamy had to have been a sympathiser, anyway, so the decision wasn't too hard for him to make. It just needed something like his brother's skin to justify why he'd go along with it.'

'That proves Lamy's involved with Delarue. But is he tied in to any anti-Gaullist groups?'

'I can't prove that. But I did find out one little snippet.'

'Which is?'

'Six months ago, Captain Lamy applied to join the presidential security department run by your new best friend, Colonel Saint-Cloud.'

'What?'

'Yes. And in spite of his record of discontent, his name was placed on a reserve list. Given a few weeks and he could have been on the inside.'

CHAPTER FORTY-ONE

Wheels within wheels, thought Rocco, wondering at such audacity – or was it stupidity? – between brother officers. It was always the same: one hand shook another and favours got passed along. But this was a favour like no other. What the hell was Saint-Cloud thinking? Couldn't he see the danger to his own position? Or had he got a blind spot when it came to fellow officers?

He shook his head. It was too much to speculate about. He'd have to come back to it. 'Delarue,' he said. 'I didn't know he was politically active.'

'Me neither. But he's a crook, so what's the difference? The DST reckons he's trying to spread his power base overseas and is playing at middleman for various contracts. The OAS and Corsican gangs are just a couple of the groups he's getting into bed with, and they're prepared to pay good money for the right expertise. Delarue is playing at being a broker.'

'You can add the British to that list. A gangster named Ketch in London, and his associates. If the DST wants chapter and verse, they can contact Detective Inspector David Nialls at Scotland Yard. But don't give the information to Jules Broissard. Find someone else.'

'If you say so.' There was hesitation in Santer's voice. 'Lucas, have you told anyone else about all this?'

'I've tried. They don't believe in the criminal connection.'

'Jesus, you have to push harder; you're leaving yourself open, otherwise.'

'I will, I promise. But right now what I need is something concrete.'

'Good. You haven't said why I shouldn't tell Broissard.'

'I think he's too close to this, and we're hardly friends. I can't prove it, but I don't want to take any chances that he'll just sit on the information until it's too late.'

'Good enough for me. I'll find a way round him.'

Rocco put down the phone and found Claude looking at him with a serious expression.

'Sounds like this is getting heavy, Lucas.'

'It is. I just don't know how heavy.'

The phone rang again and he scooped it up. Probably Massin or the Ministry, summoning him to a disciplinary interview. The Foreign Legion was suddenly looking like an attractive proposition ... if they took mature recruits with police experience.

But it wasn't Massin or the Ministry. It was David Nialls.

'Something's going on, Lucas,' the CID man said crisply. 'Just had word that Tasker, Fletcher and Calloway've just got on a late boat for Calais.'

Like a snowball, Rocco thought. This business was rolling downhill, gathering speed and volume.

'There's not much I can do without some hard facts to pass on,' he said.

Nialls sighed sympathetically. 'Yes, I know. All I

can tell you is, two other men have gone to ground, possibly on the same trip. They're known associates, used mainly as heavies. Their names are Biggs and Jarvis. Ring any bells?'

The two others involved in the wrecking of the *Canard Doré*. Rocco felt a trickle of excitement running through his veins. There was no way these five men would be coming back for another bout of fun and drinking; it just wasn't feasible. It had to be something else.

Nialls confirmed it.

'Look for the distraction, Lucas. It's how they operate.'

'I would if I could figure out what it might be.'

'Well, I'm not sure if this will help, but there's one thing to bear in mind about Tasker: putting aside everything else he does now, he's a born-and-raised bank robber. And he's got two drivers with him. Would that be distraction enough?'

CHAPTER FORTY-TWO

DCI David Nialls sat deep in thought for some time after putting the phone down. The conversation with Rocco had been a disturbing one with some personal echoes; he himself had been accused of taking bribes once, a long time ago. As a young detective trying to make his way up the career ladder, he had run foul of a bookie he'd hauled in for demanding money with menaces. The man had retaliated by claiming Nialls had only arrested him because the cash offer he'd made hadn't been big enough. The accusation had been flawed, and Nialls had assumed that nobody had taken it seriously. But he'd soon discovered that even a light brush with mud has a habit of sticking. It had taken him a couple of years to shake off the allegations completely.

Now Rocco would be going through the same thing and he knew what that felt like. He checked his watch and picked up the phone. There was only one thing for it.

Direct action.

He made a call to an acquaintance in the French embassy, followed by an internal call. Then he walked north to Dean Street, in Soho. He stopped outside a plain wooden door sandwiched between a Chinese restaurant and a strip club. A speaker pad with three buttons was fixed to the side. In the background was the usual volley of touts tasked to entice punters into the various establishments in the area, overlaid by arguments and bursts of laughter from passers-by and residents.

A squat man with the shoulders of a wrestler was standing outside the plain door. He nodded as Nialls approached.

'Hello, Mr Nialls. He's upstairs.'

Nialls smiled. 'You can drop the title, Tom,' he said. 'I'm almost a civilian now. And this job is off the books.'

'Suits me, boss. Just point the way.'

Sergeant Tom McLean had worked the Soho area for many years, and knew his way around its streets, clubs and watering holes like few others. He'd an instinct for trouble and had worked with

Nialls several times before. The two held each other in mutual respect. Nialls had caught him just as he was on his way home, and had asked for a small favour. The sergeant had agreed without question.

'Skelton has helped drop a friend of mine in hot water with some sneaky photos – a false bribery allegation. I'd like to lean on him and make him squeak. There might be some opposition.'

'Sounds like his usual style. He doesn't normally have any minders, but it depends who he's working for. We going straight in?'

'I think so. Hard and fast and don't give him time to think.'

The sergeant stepped up to the door and put the flat of his hand against all three speaker buttons. 'Stay behind me until we get in.' He leant on the buttons until the door clicked, then pushed it back and ran lightly up a flight of grubby stairs littered with cardboard boxes. Nialls was right behind him. They came to a landing with two doors. A Chinese woman in a patterned overall and slippers stood outside one door, scowling at the two men. The other door was open, the flat inside empty. McLean continued on past and up another flight of stairs to a smaller landing with a single door. He waited for Nialls to reach the top step and catch his breath.

Nialls leant against the wall and signalled for McLean to continue. He would have liked to kick it in himself, but it would be a waste of talent.

'Go ahead,' he told him.

The door was flimsy and gave in without a struggle, crashing back against the inside wall and showering the floor with flakes of paint. Both men stepped inside and found themselves in a single room furnished with a couch, a small desk overflowing with camera equipment and spools of film, a wardrobe, a plain screen and an enormous bowl of flowers. Behind the flowers was a buxom, naked woman in her forties, scrambling to hide herself. Sets of angled lights with coloured lenses gave her body a curiously marbled effect.

There was no sign of 'Bones' Skelton, but he was clearly not far away.

'Where is he?' breathed Nialls.

The woman pointed at the backdrop screen. Behind it was a door with a red light overhead. 'It's a developing room.' She remembered that her hand was supposed to be covering her modesty and snatched it back, blushing crimson.

'Get him out, Tom,' Nialls told McLean, and waited while the sergeant stepped behind the screen and opened the door. There was a strangled shout, then he dragged out the skinny frame of Patrick Daniel Skelton. He was dressed in a shirt and trousers, and his feet were bare.

'Sorry, Bones,' Nialls greeted him blandly. He sniffed at the sudden smell of chemicals in the air and studied the photographer's feet. 'Did we interrupt something seedy?'

'It's nothing like that,' Skelton protested. 'I always work barefoot. It helps my artistic creativeness.'

'God help us: a porno snapper with pretensions. And the lady – she's your muse, I suppose.'

'You what?'

'You heard.'

'She's a client. Straight up. She wants some photos for her husband.' He stared imploringly at the woman who was struggling to conceal her ampleness inside a silk robe. 'Go on, tell him.'

The woman nodded. 'That's right. It's our wedding anniversary and I wanted to surprise him with some nice ... photos.'

You'll certainly do that, thought Nialls. But who was he to criticise?

'No law against it, is there?' the woman muttered.

Nialls relaxed. He wasn't interested in her. Skelton was enough to be going on with. 'No, madam, there isn't.' His face softened. 'And your husband is a lucky man. But I'm afraid you'll have to reschedule. I need to borrow Mr Skelton and it might take some time.'

They waited while the woman hustled behind the screen and got dressed. As soon as she had gone, Nialls turned on the photographer. 'Get your socks on – we're going out.'

'Why? I haven't done anything!'

'You've done plenty, you unpleasant little oik. We're going to the French embassy.'

Skelton looked alarmed. 'Why would I want to go there?'

'Because you're going to make a verbal and written statement about your recent trip across the Channel.' He held up a hand to silence the inevitable protest. 'And don't bother denying it – we've got witnesses who saw you take off from Thurrock airfield in Essex. The pilot's already made a full statement.' Neither detail was true, but Nialls said it with absolute conviction and a steady, cold gaze.

He turned to the desk and extracted a British passport from beneath the edge of a pile of papers. 'And look what I've found.'

Skelton swallowed. 'What if I don't want to go?'

'Then I'll have Sergeant McLean here tuck your rancid body under his arm and carry you. I'll also arrange for a quiet word to be dropped in certain clubs around here that you've been most helpful with our investigations with names, dates and times. What's it to be?'

'You can't do that!' Skelton yelped. 'Jesus – they'll kill me!'

'You don't deny it, then?'

Skelton said nothing, but looked as if he were about to bolt for the door.

Nialls nodded at McLean. 'Pick him up, Sergeant.'

'Wait! No need for that ... I'm coming.' Skelton bent and picked up a pair of socks and began to struggle into them. 'What have I got to do to get you lot off my back?'

Nialls felt a rush of relief. None of this was legal or proper, and if it ever got out, he'd find himself having to answer some awkward questions from his superiors. But right now he didn't care. He'd had enough of stepping around people like Skelton all his working life just because they could rustle up a clever lawyer when it suited them. He was helping a fellow police officer in trouble, and the simple fact was, he hadn't enjoyed himself so much in years.

'Just tell the truth, Bones, for once in your scummy existence. I know that's a difficult concept for you, but believe me, the alternative is not

270

one you want to contemplate.'

'Alternative?' Skelton paused in tying his shoes' laces.

'Tasker and his bosses hearing on the grapevine that you've been helping our enquiries.'

'How would they? I'm not going to say any-thing.'

'You might not,' McLean muttered tightly, 'but I wouldn't bet on me not letting it slip before the night's out. I fancy a bit of a pub crawl.'

'That's blackmail!'

'No, it's not,' said Nialls. 'It's a public service.' He glanced at the cameras on the desk. It was an impressive collection and clearly top of the range. 'Before I forget, bring one of those with you.'

'Eh? Why?'

'You'll find out.'

Twenty minutes later, they were inside the French embassy and being ushered into a side room by a security guard. Moments later, an offi-cial appeared and greeted Nialls with a warm handshake.

'David. How nice to see you again. Can I offer you some tea?'

'No thanks, Dominique. It's late enough and I don't want to keep you.' He introduced Sgt Mc-Lean and the two men shook hands.

'Very well. You wished someone to make a statement, I believe?'

Nialls nodded at Skelton. 'This ... gentleman wants to confirm his part in attempting to bribe a French police officer in a village called Pois-sons-le-Marais, near Amiens. He took the photos of the inspector being set up.'

271

Dominique, a third secretary and a liaison officer between the British and French police, whom Nialls had already briefed in his phone call, gestured at the table in the centre of the room, which held a recorder and a notepad. He switched on the recorder and stared at Skelton with a show of disapproval. 'I have spoken to colleagues since your phone call, and the suspension is not yet official, pending investigations. The photographs are quite clear, I understand, although taken at night. They show an officer apparently taking an envelope from a second man. But if this gentleman has something to say on the matter, his ... cooperation would be appreciated.'

'Damn right,' Nialls muttered. 'Taken at night, eh? Not easy to do, I'd have thought ... although you're used to snapping away in the dark, aren't you? Care to enlighten us amateurs, Bones?'

The photographer looked as if he were going to argue. Then his ego got the better of him. 'It's easy enough, if you know what you're doing.'

'And I bet you do. Go on, then: blind us with science.'

'Does 800 ASA mean anything?' At Nialls' blank look, he sniggered. 'Didn't think so. It's a new fast film, just out. Dead simple. Got him in the headlights.' He simulated the clicking of a camera and winked, enjoying his own cleverness.

Nialls wanted to hit him, but smiled instead. The rest would be easy. Once someone like Bones began talking, he'd be hard to stop. He glanced at Dominique. 'You have developing facilities here?'

'Of course. Our security manager can deal with that and have the prints ready for you very

272

quickly. We have a courier going across the Channel first thing in the morning. They should be in Amiens very early.'

'Prints?' Skelton looked from one man to the other. 'What prints?'

'Of you and your statement,' said Nialls. He smiled coolly, although he doubted Skelton would appreciate the irony of the situation. 'You're going to be famous, Bones. I think this is the first time anyone's photographed a statement and sent it to another country with a snap of the guilty party. How about that?'

Skelton scowled, clearly torn between incriminating himself further and being any kind of front runner in the photography world. 'This isn't right. I should call my lawyer.'

'If you think he can protect you, go ahead.' Skelton didn't sound convinced, and was probably weighing up the odds of going along with this against the probability of what would happen if word got out that he'd talked to the police. To speed the photographer's thinking, Nialls leant close and said softly, 'But if you do, I'll have to let you go immediately, won't I? Then you're on your own. And it's cold and dark out there, Skelton. Very dark.'

Skelton blinked rapidly. 'I've got no choice, have I?'

'Put like that – no, you bloody don't. Now start talking, chapter and verse.'

Three hundred and fifty kilometres away, in a smoke-filled bar near Belleville in the north-east of Paris, Marc Casparon was having second

273

thoughts about the wisdom of what he was doing.

He'd found his way here on the recommendation of a contact from his days on the force. He'd ordered a light beer to clear his head while waiting for a man named Susman, who claimed to have an inside link with a hard-core student group calling themselves Red Machine. Opposed to almost anything de Gaulle proposed or did, they were more than a bunch of activist malcontents, having shown themselves capable of violence in street marches, rapidly escalating to organised raids on opposition groups. Now they were rumoured to have picked up some financial backing. It was a worrying development. Rebellious students with no cash soon ran out of everything but hot air; those same students with access to funds were a whole different ball game.

He sipped his beer and reflected on how much time he had spent over the years waiting in late-night bars like this for contacts like Susman to show up. Too many, whatever it was – and not always with anything worth trading. It probably added up to a lot of wasted hours. But that was the life he'd chosen and at least Susman had always proven reliable. Well, fairly reliable. The man had a marijuana habit and sometimes behaved as if he had demons after him. He shook off the thoughts. At least now he was here by choice. It made him wonder how Lucas Rocco was holding up. The news of the investigator's suspension had travelled quickly, but few believed it; every cop worth his salt got accusations flung at him at least once in his career. It was part of the job and didn't mean there was any truth to it. And nothing he'd heard led him to believe Rocco was corrupt. Some cops were and he could call their names to mind. But not Rocco; he'd stake his life on it.

He saw movement at the door, and a face appeared, eyes scanning the room through the glass. Chubby, white, moustache, lank hair. Not a face he recognised. Hard eyes, though, like flints. Another man crowded behind him, almost a carbon copy, but bigger. Their eyes met.

Caspar's survival instincts kicked in. He glanced at the clock above the bar. Susman was thirty minutes overdue. Where the hell had time gone? He'd been daydreaming. He sipped his beer like a man with time to kill, but the training he'd gone through was already kicking in, along with all the hints and tricks he'd picked up over the years of operating undercover. You never, *never* waited longer than ten minutes for a meet, no matter what. When the agreed time plus ten went by, you got out fast and reassessed the situation. Contacts lived for the small cash payments you handed out and the power that trading secret information gave them. If they were late, it was because they weren't coming. Simple as that.

This wasn't good. He'd pushed someone too hard, asked one too many questions; touched a nerve at the wrong moment.

It was time to go.

He left his beer on the bar and wandered towards the back, pausing to watch a game of *baby-foot* in one corner. The two contestants were drunk, spinning the players enthusiastically with no hope of hitting anything. He clapped one of them on the shoulder and shouted encourage-

275

ment, then stepped casually through the rear door and hurried along a narrow corridor.

As he did so, he heard a volley of voices near the street door, and someone shouted an objection. Then there was the sound of a fist smacking something fleshy.

As he exited the back door into a yard and ran past the entrance to the *pissoirs,* he was surprised to see Susman standing in the shadows, beckoning to him.

'Where the hell were you?' he said, and dragged Susman along with him. The man was overweight and soft-looking, dressed in a white shirt and dark trousers from his job as a waiter at a restaurant frequented by members of several street gangs, where he picked up most of his leads. 'We'd better move; there's trouble coming.'

'I know, I heard,' said Susman. He pointed off down the street. 'This way – I don't fancy getting my face rearranged if they see us together.'

When they were three streets away, Susman stopped in a building site between two apartment blocks and stood with his hands on his knees, breathing heavily. 'This is far enough; I'd better get back there or they'll know something's up. I go there most nights, so...'

'Who are those men?'

'Nothing. A couple of bully boys.'

'They didn't look like nothing.'

'I know them from way back. I was talking to them earlier and touching them up about a group they run with. They suddenly got really touchy – and I mean paranoid. Something's in the wind.'

'Yeah, but what?' Caspar felt a shiver of excitement. This was what all those wasted hours had been about: the kick of getting some information before anyone else did and building it into something he could feed back down the line.

'I'm not sure. It's heavy, that's all I can tell you.'

'Heavy. That doesn't help. Heavy as in … a hit?'

Susman ducked his head, then scrambled for a cigarette, eyeing the street behind them. He lit it and blew out a plume of smoke. 'I think so.'

'Think so? Think or know? Come on, there's money on this.'

'Yes. It's a hit.'

'On the big man?' He didn't want to mention the president by name, even out here.

'Who else? He's the nation's favourite bullseye at the moment, isn't he?'

'Tell me something I don't know. Come on, man. I need names.'

'I don't have any, honest. Things are getting difficult … people have shut down since the last failures. It's like … there's been a run of bad luck and they're scared it's contagious.'

Caspar swore quietly. 'Bad luck. Christ, anyone would think it was a game of *boules*. You must have a feeling, though, right? Which groups are likely to be up for a try right now?'

'That's just it – I don't know. Not even a hint. Not with the groups. All I can tell you is, it's not political.'

'Right. There's going to be a hit on the big man and it's not political. It's *all* political, for God's sake!'

Susman took a deep breath and flicked his cigarette into the gutter, clapped his hands together

277

and stuffed them under his arms. 'No. Not this time.'

'What?' The statement had been too definite to ignore. Caspar grabbed Susman's shoulder. 'What do you mean?'

'The sort of people I've been hearing about ... the ones behind the hit: they're gangsters.'

CHAPTER FORTY-THREE

A new day brought a flurry of snow to Poissons, powered by a cutting wind which rattled the trees and curled around the house with a soft whining sound. Rocco went for a short run anyway to get his blood moving and his brain in gear.

He kept going over what Nialls had said on the phone. The idea of an English gang's involvement in hitting a French bank as a distraction exercise hadn't been at the forefront of his mind. But that had now taken on a greater significance. Tasker was known by the London police to have experience at robbing banks; he had two drivers with him, one of them expert in high-speed cars; and with the possible inclusion of Patrice Delarue into the mix – also with a history of high-profile bank robberies – it seemed to point inexorably in one direction. And what other possibilities were there? In a largely rural and unpopulated area, anything less simply wouldn't pull in the police attention that Tasker and his men would be aiming for.

Robbing a bank, however, couldn't fail to

attract maximum attention.

He returned home after fifteen minutes of increasing cold and worked through the mundane routine of cleaning the house, setting a fire round the pump to draw water – even checking the car's oil level, all activities designed to help pass time. As soon as it hit eight o'clock, he picked up the phone and dialled the number for the War Graves Commission office in Arras. It was early but he'd a feeling the superintendent wouldn't be far away.

A woman answered and identified herself as Jean Blake. The superintendent's wife.

'Mrs Blake,' said Rocco, and introduced himself. 'My apologies for ringing so early, but I was wondering if your husband was in?'

'I'm afraid not, Inspector. You just missed him.'

'Already?'

'Yes. He's been invited to the town hall – to a reception.' Her voice carried a hint of quiet pride, he thought, held carefully in check, and he felt a buzz of energy go through him.

Today. It was today.

'I see. I just wanted to check his timings and movements.'

'I can't help you exactly, although I do know he's been advised that the ... event will take place in private at ten, followed by a reception at the town hall and a signature ceremony for the monument to be given the go-ahead. It's all very hush-hush, of course.'

'Of course. I won't say anything.' Rocco swore silently. *At ten this morning?* It meant that any diversion or distraction event would take place earlier ... and just in time to attract the maximum

279

amount of attention. He made his apologies and disconnected, then immediately dialled Desmoulins' home number. The detective was the only one he could trust.

'There's going to be a bank robbery,' he told him, the moment Desmoulins answered. 'This morning some time before ten. I don't know where, but somewhere in this region. You'll only get a call when it's in progress. The gang will be the same men who trashed the *Canard Doré*. They'll probably head back towards the coast immediately afterwards, so as soon as you hear about it, get cars positioned along the main routes to Calais and Boulogne.'

'A bank job? Is that what this has all been about – money?'

'No. That's the point. They're using it as a diversion.' He told Desmoulins about the Pont Noir and de Gaulle's proposed secret visit. 'They'll time the bank job to pull in police resources and tie up lines of communication, leaving the way clear for the hit to go ahead.'

'Christ – we'd better get the troops out. Does Saint-Cloud know about this?'

'Probably more than he lets on. Do you know where he is?'

'He wasn't around much yesterday, but he doesn't exactly take me into his confidence. Do you want me to find him?'

'No. Don't bother. I'll deal with it. You look into the bank end. You might start looking for one with a larger than average cash movement going on today.'

'That's easy enough,' said Desmoulins. 'The

main banks in Amiens, Lille and Arras all have cash movements today for paying local factory workers. And Béthune.'

'How do you know that?'

'It's a regular thing; after a couple of jobs two years ago, we had requests from the banks to have patrol cars keep an eye out for when the deliveries are made.'

'And do they?' Two years for any kind of standing instruction to be maintained rigorously was a long time, and any lack of activity could soon make officers less than attentive in their duties.

'Depends if there's anything else going on and if patrols can be spared. I wouldn't want to bet on it, though.'

'Why Béthune?' Unlike the others, it was a small town about sixty kilometres away, between Arras and Lille. Rocco had only been once, but it had been a fleeting visit and had given him no feel for the place.

'It was set up to service the Bridgestone tyre factory, among others. The *Crédit Agricole*. It's right next to the industrial zone on the outskirts of town.'

'That's got to be it.' Suddenly Rocco knew deep down that this was where it was going to happen. English gangsters wouldn't want to fight their way through busy traffic in a foreign town, especially if they were planning a quick getaway. That automatically knocked Amiens, Lille and Arras out of the equation. But a bank on the outskirts of a small town, loaded with wages money and on the way to the coast? It was a sitting target.

He let Desmoulins get on with his job and

281

disconnected, then called Claude and told him to get ready.

'You're not going into the office?' said Claude.

'I can't. I'm suspended, remember? If I show my face there I'm likely to be arrested.' And even if he managed to get Massin to believe him and a show of force turned up at the bridge, the attackers would simply call it off and go underground. And that would end his chances of proving he'd been right all along.

'So let me get this right,' said Claude slowly. 'You're going to let an attack on you-know-who go ahead … to prove you haven't been blowing smoke.'

'That's right.'

'Mother of God, that's risky, Lucas.'

'It's the only way.'

Claude grunted. 'Well, in that case, I'll see you in ten.'

Rocco shrugged into his coat and picked up the Walther P38 Claude had left behind. He tested the mechanism out of habit and loaded the shells, then slipped the gun in his coat pocket. If he had to use it and there was any fallout, so be it.

His phone rang. It was Santer.

'Caspar says a criminal gang's involved. It's not political.'

'A gang is mixed up in it,' Rocco confirmed, 'but it's definitely political. Tell Caspar thanks. I owe him.'

'Not as much as you owe me, you big lug. Oh, and another thing: I checked that Créteil thing you mentioned. Three men picked up at a lock-up? The security boys got a tip-off and sent in a special unit. Turns out they were planning a hit on the president, down near his place in Colombey.'

'A tip-off.'

'Yes. They think it was a rival group getting rid of the competition. Either way, Saint-Cloud should be happy, because that's another threat off the list. Maybe he can relax a bit.'

'No,' said Rocco. 'I don't think so. It's the exact opposite. That's what everyone was meant to think.' Another distraction move, only this time closer to home.

'What's going on? I can hear that tone in your voice.'

'I've got to go – it's started.'

'Hellfire. Anything I can do?'

'Stroke a rabbit's foot for me.'

'Take it easy, you hear? Don't get yourself killed. And call me.'

Rocco put down the phone and walked out to the car.

CHAPTER FORTY-FOUR

Things began to go wrong the moment George Tasker and his men stepped through the door of the bank.

It was nine-fifteen, with snow in the air dusting the roads and pavements outside. The kind of day you were better off staying at home if you had any sense and nothing more important to do. The kind of day, he reflected, not to be relying on having to drive anywhere fast.

But some days you had no choice.

Leaving Calloway at the wheel of the black DS outside the entrance and facing towards the crossroads ready for a fast getaway, he'd led Biggs and Jarvis, each tooled up with old service revolvers, through the front door. Without pausing, he'd fired a shot from the sawn-off provided by their French contact into the ceiling, bringing down a portion of the tiling and stopping everyone dead in their tracks. Short of shooting someone, it was the single most effective method he'd come across of getting everybody's full and undivided attention.

With the security van gone only minutes ago, Tasker had expected – indeed had been told – to find three handy metal boxes of cash waiting to be picked up. What he saw was one small box, and three men in suits staring at him and his fellow gang members as if they were creatures from outer space.

He plucked a piece of ceiling plaster from his jacket and flicked it away, then stepped over to the centre of the floor. Biggs and Jarvis stayed to cover the door and watch for anyone foolhardy enough to try anything heroic. Pointing his gun at an older man with grizzled grey hair and a hangdog expression, Tasker shouted, *'Where's the money, you French git?'* He fired another shot over the man's head, breaking and reloading the gun in seconds, his hands a blur. It was a make of weapon he'd never seen before, stripped bare and filed clean, but it worked well enough and that was all he needed.

It galvanised the man into action. He muttered something at one of his colleagues, who walked over to a large metal door set in the rear wall. He swung the door back a fraction, revealing a glimpse over the counter of a small room lined with shelves.

'Tasty,' said Jarvis, and made to leap the counter.

'Wait.' Tasker stopped him. It was all too easy. Something about this set-up wasn't right. Forget the fact that it was French; a bank was a bank was a bank. But this one didn't feel good. The manager showing them the bank vault so readily was also odd; it stank of a distraction.

He looked around. No customers. Maybe it was too early in the day – and he hadn't thought to ask about opening times. And most banks he'd ever seen had at least a couple of women workers. But not here.

Then he saw a coat stand in one corner. It held two coats, one red and the other a dull mauve colour, a man's mackintosh and a couple of colourful scarves. Women's stuff.

He pointed at the manager who was glaring at him. 'You. Come here.' He stabbed at a spot in front of him, making sure the man was looking down the twin snouts of the sawn-off.

The man complied. It was only when he was standing before him that Tasker realised something else was missing: that tangible element he was so accustomed to on a bank job, the inevitable reaction of a worker ant being faced by a man with a gun who was not afraid to use it.

Fear.

Something made him lift onto his toes so he

285

could see over the counter into the safe room. A woman was lying on the floor, eyes bulging over a gag around her face, her legs wrapped in rope. Nice legs, too. He could just see a man's shoulder next to her, and beyond that, another stocking-covered leg and a woman's shoe.

'Tasker!' It was Jarvis, shouting a warning.

Tasker turned back to the man in front of him, saw him flicking back his suit jacket and reaching inside. Saw the butt of a revolver stuffed down his waistband.

'It's a set-up!' he shouted. He pulled the trigger, realising in the instant that he did so that this was no police trap. The man in front of him, in spite of being armed, was too old for this kind of job in the name of the state. Too old and, up close, not smart or quick enough. The shot was deafening in the enclosed space, and caught the man in the centre of his chest, hurling him backwards across the floor. At the same moment Biggs began firing at the other two, who had dived for cover behind the counter, drawing weapons of their own.

The small room reverberated to the sounds of gunshots, and for a fleeting second, Tasker felt his blood stir at the noise, the smell of gunpowder and the pounding of conflict. Then survival kicked in and brought him back to reality. This was a dead end; they'd been fooled, suckered into colliding with someone else's job. It was a total lash-up. He fired at the two men behind the counter, seeing one man's hand dissolve under the hail of shot. There was a scream, then the other man stood up and blazed away like a maniac. A yelp came from alongside Tasker and Jarvis was flipped onto his

286

back, his face a bloody mess. Dead.

'Out!' Tasker shouted at Biggs, and stooped to pick up Jarvis's revolver. This was beyond going wrong; it couldn't get any worse. If they stayed here they were dead meat. Running was their only option. He could already hear the first sounds of a siren ... or was it his imagination? Surely the local cops couldn't have got themselves together already.

He felt a shiver go through him, and the first tremors of panic in his legs.

Until that moment, George Tasker had always been lucky. He'd found himself in situations before where things had not run in his favour due to surprise, superior firepower or better tactics by the opposition. You couldn't get it right every time. But he'd always coped and brazened it out; stood up and blasted his way through. But this was different; it was like some kind of horror film unfolding. In the space of two minutes or less, he was a man down and facing gunmen who were on home soil and mad enough to fight back like crazies. And the police sirens were real – and getting louder.

The last brought a disturbing realisation.

They had been sold out.

While Tasker and his men were finding themselves on the brink of disaster, Jack Fletcher was a very happy man. He was sitting alone in the cab of a small Renault truck identical to the previous one he'd driven, with no Tasker watching over him and no smart-Alec Calloway making snide remarks about his driving. And he was doing a job solo. It didn't get much better than this.

287

He was humming as he followed on the heels of a white Peugeot as it negotiated a series of narrow, snow-dusted country lanes, working the pedals of the Renault with care to avoid the truck going into a terminal skid on the slippery surface. Weighed down by the addition of a railway sleeper across the front bumper, covered by a piece of tarpaulin to avoid raising suspicions, the steering was jittery but manageable. But Fletcher wasn't bothered; he'd driven in far more challenging weather and in worse vehicles than this, and even though he was in a left-hooker, he was beginning to get a feel for the way the vehicle handled. All he had to do was follow the Frenchman in front of him, a sour-looking grump in his fifties who had nodded once on introduction, then gestured for Fletcher to stick to his tail before driving off.

Tasker and the others had stood and watched him go, and he'd waved cheerfully and called out, 'Bump into you later, boys!'

He'd enjoyed knowing that they could have no idea of just how prophetic his words were going to be.

CHAPTER FORTY-FIVE

Moments after Tasker and Biggs had thrown themselves back in the DS, Calloway was revving the car and hurtling away from the bank, the engine screaming in protest. Tasker let him get on with it and reloaded the sawn-off, leaning out of the window to fire two parting shots at the front door of the bank to keep the third man's head down. Then he sat back and swore repeatedly. He'd be glad to see the back of this shit town and shit country, and get back home to where he felt able to breathe.

'What,' said Calloway quietly, 'the fuck happened back there?' It was the first time Tasker had ever heard him swear. 'And where's the cash – and Jarvis?'

'There ain't no cash and Jarvis is dead. We were sold a pup.' Tasker was breathing hard, the rush of adrenalin making his nerve ends jangle. He was trying to work out what had just happened, how such a simple job had gone belly up. 'There wasn't the money we were told about, and another mob was already there.'

'Mob?'

'Firm ... crew ... you know what I bloody mean. Frenchies.'

'How?'

'Because we were sent on a sucker job. Somebody's going to pay dearly for this if it's the last bloody thing I ever do!' He dug in his pocket and took out two more cartridges, and sniffed at them as if they were a source of comfort.

Calloway seemed happy with that. 'Fair enough. So, where are we headed – back to Calais?'

'Not yet.' Tasker had been toying with an idea for some time. It had taken root days ago, but had grown fast over the past few hours, fermenting in his mind and now tugging so urgently at his consciousness that he couldn't let it go. 'Soon, though.'

Rocco was the cause of all this. Had been from the very beginning, ever since he'd walked into that cell, revealing that he spoke English and even understood cockney slang, treating Tasker like a nobody, a gofer, and questioning Calloway first. That was right out of order.

He breathed deeply, his blood pressure rising the more he thought about it. Even dropping the suspicion of corruption on the big French cop hadn't given Tasker the satisfaction he'd expected, not long-term. He knew his thinking was irrational, that he was on foreign soil and way out of his depth. But he didn't care.

Because right now he had nothing to go back to. It was over. Ketch had seen to that. Ketch and his smooth-talking, number-crunching weasel, Brayne. They'd talked him and the others into a dead-end job – he didn't need a degree in accountancy to know it, either. Not now. There were only so many ways the game could be played, and after years of using the distraction thing for their purposes, Tasker knew and recognised when he himself had become the distraction. It was the way things were. But he didn't have to like it.

Before anything else, though, he had a score to settle over here. After that, well, he'd get back to the Smoke and make a couple of visits. He stroked the shortened barrels of the shotgun. He'd have to lose this one, but he'd soon get another just like it or better. No sweat.

Then they'd learn what it meant to have crossed George Tasker.

'So where to?'

Tasker leant forward and picked up a road map

of the area, found the place he wanted and stabbed it with a thick finger. It was back towards Amiens, but off to the east. 'Here.'

Calloway glanced across, nodded and began looking for a turn to get them off the main road and double back. 'Poissons-les-Marais? What's there, then?'

'Not what,' said Tasker, rolling the two shotgun cartridges between his fingers. 'More like who.'

CHAPTER FORTY-SIX

Rocco was staring through a veil of tangled, bare branches at the bridge, half a kilometre away, and wondering what the hell he was doing here. He and Claude had found a spot where they could just see the bridge and the road leading over it, but where they were hidden from view by a clump of bushes. It wasn't great but it was the best they could do at short notice.

He shivered and took a turn back and forth, trying to work some warmth back into his feet and lower legs. The air was bitingly cold and, just for the moment, clear, the earlier snow having turned by degrees to a miserable, grey sleet before dying out. But there was more on the way. The clouds looming overhead were heavy, grey and dough-like, waiting to dump their contents on the land below, and he wondered if a change in the weather might interrupt any attack plans. If there were any.

'Where does that track lead?' he said, stepping

291

back alongside the passenger window. 'The map doesn't say.'

'Nowhere. It's just a track through the fields.' Claude held up a hand, giving it some thought. 'Actually, that's not strictly true. If they drive carefully, they *could* reach a road at the other end – but that's ten kilometres over rough ground. And after this weather?' He pulled a face. 'Unlikely. Hardly a quick getaway.'

'So they'd be trapped.' Rocco tensed as a dark shape approached the bridge, wobbling slightly on the road, bouncing on soft suspension. It was a dark-blue saloon with something strapped on the roof. A cupboard or a box – it was difficult to tell from here. The car trundled across the bridge and continued on down the road towards them, passing the proposed site of the new war monument and rattling past them without stopping.

'Unless things went right and nobody saw them.' Claude pursed his lips and eyed the car out of sight. 'If they were cool-headed enough and had the right vehicle, I suppose they could do it.' He grinned. 'Unlikely now, though, huh? With us here.'

Rocco lifted a pair of binoculars off the back seat, focusing on the track beyond the shed. Nothing. No waiting truck, no motorbikes – another favoured form of transport for an attack – and no men. Just the shed, run-down and ready to fall over.

'There aren't many of those left,' Claude told him, following his line of sight. 'I'm amazed it's lasted this long.'

'It was locked tight by rust when I saw it, and

full of farm rubbish. I thought it might be something they'd use, but I was wrong.' Yet he felt sure he'd got the location right. The circumstances, the pointers, the confluence of the ramming idea, de Gaulle's visit and the similarities of the sites ... it had all been so clear. So obvious.

He swung the glasses back to the shed and stared hard, the rubber eyepieces pressed into his skin. It looked the same as it had the other day, so what was he worried about? The roof still stained with bird droppings, the wooden walls peppered with holes and the planking warped by the elements, the whole thing surrounded by a hovering grey mist, like a scene from a ghost film. Yet something was tugging at his mind, gently insistent. Something ... different. What the hell was it? Or was he just desperate for something to show up that would prove he'd been right about this?

'It's an old cart shed,' Claude continued chattily, showing his mastery of all things rural. 'They were just big enough to take a hay cart. Take it in one end, unhitch the horse, fold up the shafts and close the door, take the horse out the other. Saved trying to reverse it in. The logic was impeccable.'

Rocco took his eyes off the road. Tried to follow through what Claude had said. 'What are you saying?' Then it hit him. 'That shed has a back door?' He hadn't looked. It hadn't occurred to him.

'Yes. Same as the front. In one end, out the other. Why?'

Then Rocco realised what had been bothering him.

The pigeons on the roof. There were none. Why was that? And that mist around the base of the

structure: it was moving, billowing gently outwards. Yet there was none anywhere else.

And it was growing.

As he opened his mouth to speak, to voice what
he was seeing, the shed moved. It trembled, then
seemed to shake itself like a living beast, and
lifted, before exploding in a great shower of wood
fragments and smoke, the latter billowing out in
a great cloud to join the mist around the base.

Not mist. *Exhaust smoke.*

'My God! Lucas!' Claude grabbed his arm and
pointed beyond the shed to the road leading to the
bridge. Another car had appeared in the distance.
Only this one was shiny and sleek, and rode the
tarmac with undoubted elegance, at sharp odds
with the sleety brown of the surrounding fields
and the grubby snow clouds gathered overhead.

A gleaming black Citroën DS.

CHAPTER FORTY-SEVEN

Jack Fletcher stared hard at a point in the front
left corner of the shed, his foot poised on the
accelerator, keeping the engine of the Renault at
a smooth pitch. He'd judged the distances
carefully with the help of the man who'd brought
him here. He had spoken passable English, and
between them they had worked out at what point
Fletcher had to hit the gas in order to hit the car
broadside on. From the three test runs he'd
made, he knew precisely what the timing was and

how fast the truck had to be going. And that was Fletcher's speciality. There would be no messing this time, no holding back, even just a little. He'd had his orders. This one was for real.

He felt his heart tripping fast, reverberating through his chest even above the roar of the truck engine in the confined space of the shed. For the first time in years, he felt proud of what he was about to do. 'Ruby' Ketch, passing on orders from a higher authority, had selected him for this job, and him alone. No George bloody Tasker sticking his oar in this time, telling him how he'd screwed up and gone in too heavy. This time, Tasker was going to see *and* feel what heavy was all about. And Calloway. They wouldn't know what had hit them.

He laughed out loud at the absurd beauty of it. Because they bloody would know, of course they would; in the few seconds it would take them to suss it out, by which time it would be too late, they'd go mental as the realisation of what Ketch had planned for them actually sank in.

'We got a big job for you, Jack.' Ketch had said two days ago. He'd treated Fletcher to a few drinks before telling him what he'd wanted. 'Seems we've got a couple of bleedin' twicers in the camp.'

'What?' Fletcher wasn't sure he'd heard right. Twicers. Cheats. Traitors. 'Who?'

Ketch had told him, lighting up a big cigar while Fletcher absorbed the information.

Tasker and Calloway? He could hardly believe it. On the other hand, he'd never liked Tasker, and Calloway was too smooth for his own bleedin' good. Smarmy young git. He found he'd been ready to believe anything of them.

'We need someone we can rely on, Jack, to sort this out,' Ketch had continued, flicking away the match. 'Someone with the balls to do it right.' He'd looked Fletcher in the eye from close up, the smell of the cigar mixing with cologne and filling Fletcher's nose. 'We need 'em to go away, Jack. Gone for good – know what I mean?'

He'd accompanied the words by taking out his trademark pen and writing a number on a paper napkin. It was a big number, so big it had almost made Fletcher's eyes water. And preceded by a pound sign. It was more than Fletcher had earned in years, and he swore the number sat there looking up at him with a devilish grin on its face, calling out to him to pick it up.

Ketch had leant closer, a reassuring hand on Fletcher's shoulder. 'Money like this, you could retire, Jack.'

'Eh?' That had come as a surprise. But not an unwelcome one.

'Call it your signing-off fee, eh? Bloody good sign-off, too. You'd be in clover. And the job you'd be doing, you'd be a legend.' The final four, words were said in a hushed whisper, and Jack Fletcher felt his chest would explode.

He'd picked up the napkin and thought, a job like this, I'd do it for bloody nothing.

Now, watching through the gap he'd made between the planks in the wall, he waited for the black Citroën to appear. They'd be driving at a steady pace, he'd been assured, unsuspecting because Tasker and Calloway had been told the crash would take place a good mile further down the road, on a bend. They'd probably be gassing, telling themselves how clever they were to be cheating on Ketch and the rest, and wouldn't even give the shed a passing glance. To them, it would be a shitty structure in the middle of a vast brown rolling sea of muddy fields.

He looked at his wing mirrors out of habit, before remembering that he'd ripped them off before driving into the shed. They'd have only got in the way, and he wasn't going to use them in any case. And he sure as buggery wasn't going to hand the truck back to anyone, not once he'd finished with it. The drum of petrol in the back would see to that. One match and *woof* – all gone, just like the last one.

He checked his watch. Another five minutes. He was ahead of himself. And nervy. He needed to calm down. He left the motor running and jumped out, squeezing through the narrow gap between the truck and the side of the shed. He shuffled to the back of the truck where he'd made a hole in the rear doors to let out the exhaust smoke. He sparked up a last cigarette, feeling the cold bite of a draught fanning the air around him. That was better. He could do this, no sweat.

He checked the time again. He wasn't sure why it was so critical; Tasker had never been punctual for anything. Still, best follow orders. He tossed the cigarette aside and made his way back to the cab.

A flash of movement showed in the spyhole between the boards, and he revved the engine, his heart going with it. Christ, they were early. No, wait. It was a dark-blue saloon with a cupboard strapped on the top, bobbing about like a jelly. Christ, he'd be pulled over for that back in England, daft bugger. He breathed out in short sharp bursts, willing his heart rate to return to normal.

He coughed, eyes fixed on the road through the gap. His throat was hurting and a veil of smoke drifted in through the open side window. Exhaust fumes were building up inside the shed. He swore but didn't dare take his eyes off the road. He'd been revving the engine too much and it wasn't being carried away sufficiently at the back. He should have thrown out all the wooden crates instead of cramming them alongside the truck. Trouble was, a local might have noticed and come to investigate.

Two minutes seemed to drag by achingly slowly. Then another car appeared. Black, shiny, a pale flash of blinds at the windows.

A Citroën DS.

Fletcher hit the accelerator hard, relieved he'd kept the engine warmed and ready to fly. He coughed again, his throat raw now, as the stubby little truck leapt forward like a terrier going after a rabbit. It hit the front doors with a mighty crash, the railway sleeper strapped to the front ripping through the rotten wood like paper and showering the cab and bonnet with years of accumulated dust and debris, cobwebs and bird shit. The rush of daylight flooding the cab made him blink after the gloom. The truck bounced as it hit the track, and shook off a cascade of planks tumbling around the roof. As it hit clear air, it seemed to gather speed as if revelling in the cold, clear atmosphere like a bull let out to grass.

And Jack Fletcher, fired by the excitement of it all, screamed unintelligible words at the top of his lungs, pounding the steering wheel with his fist, eyes streaming with tears but fixed on the target vehicle, now about two hundred yards away and approaching the end of the track and the bridge without a care in the world.

The instructions had been clear as day. No messing. *No hesitation. Do it.*

So intense was he on the target, so high with excitement, that Fletcher failed to notice the billowing rage of smoke trailing behind him; failed to see the flames started by the cigarette landing in the old dried grass beginning to consume the rear of the truck ... and creeping towards the drum of petrol lashed in the back.

'Broadside on, Jack, as hard as you can. Push the bastard twicers right over the edge.'

He was going to be a legend.

CHAPTER FORTY-EIGHT

Rocco and Claude had a clear view of what happened next. A stubby Renault truck emerged from the inferno of the shed like a horse out of a starting gate. But this horse was hell-bent on death and left destruction in its wake. Without bothering to open the doors, the driver had simply burst through the rotten wood as if they didn't exist. The impact against the padlocked hasp had been enough to send a shock wave rippling throughout the flimsy structure, tearing away the walls and supports and lifting the corrugated roof. Then everything had crashed downwards. But not before the truck was tearing itself clear of the debris and accelerating along the track, its engine screaming in protest and the rear end trailing a gushing swirl of smoke and flames.

'It's the same as before,' said Rocco. The same model truck, the same railway sleeper strapped across the front, the same target.

Only this time the target was real.

They jumped in the car and took off, accelerating hard. It was a fruitless task and Rocco knew they'd never make it. What could they hope to do – stop the official car carrying the president and his bodyguards? The DS would leave them standing. He debated shooting at the truck in an attempt to put Fletcher off his aim, but he knew that was futile, too. The distance was too great and the Englishman would be too focused on his target to even notice. What was more likely was that the bodyguards in the DS would see Rocco and Claude as the attackers and turn their automatic weapons on them instead.

He flashed his lights, hoping the guards would notice and at least look at the area around them. The angle of the Renault's approach was such that it was in a blind spot, and might not be seen until it was too late.

The DS continued its run, cruising smoothly along the tarmac. Rocco even fancied he saw the oval of a face looking through the rear-side window. De Gaulle, perhaps, getting his first view of a site of past death and destruction, unaware that if the truck now bearing down on him did its job, he would be joining all the departed souls in the ground below.

At the last moment, as the DS began to draw level with the mouth of the track, something must have caught the attention of the guards. The noise of the shed being destroyed carrying above the car engine, maybe the swirl of smoke trailing after the burning truck catching the eye or simply a body-guard's instinct kicking in and warning of an impending attack. There was movement inside as the occupants turned to stare at the side where the attacker was coming from.

'Get out of there!' Claude shouted. 'Move it, you idiot!'

As if responding to his call, the DS seemed to sink on its suspension as the driver put on a surge of power, and began to pull away at speed. But they were already a fraction of a second too late. The truck blasted out of the track and across the road, mud churning up from its heavy tyres, the driver's face close to the windscreen, his mouth open in a snarl. Was he even aware of the flames creeping across the back of his vehicle? Did he care?

The railway sleeper seemed almost about to miss its target ... to have all been for nothing. Then it brushed against the rear of the car. It was a near miss, but enough, flicking the heavily armoured DS sideways with near disdain.

The car driver corrected and accelerated again, fighting the wheel. For just a second one of his rear tyres slid out over the bank, spinning in thin air, and Rocco and Claude swore in unison, expecting the worst. But the car's extra weight was its saving grace. With a waggle of its tail, it settled and took off across the bridge trailing a damaged rear wing and bumper.

The truck, still under full power and carried by its own mass, was unable to stop in time. It soared out over the edge, dragging earth, grass, white marker posts and fiery smoke with it, the engine howling as if in a frustrated rage all of its own.

Then it dropped out of sight.

The DS flew towards Rocco's car without stopping, the driver and guard in the front staring hard and clearly expecting another attack. Rocco stamped on the brakes and pulled over to let them pass, holding up his empty hands and bracing himself for a hail of defensive gunfire. But the guards knew their job and held off shooting.

As the car disappeared, Rocco drove across the bridge and stopped. Then he and Claude jumped out and looked over the edge of the drop, standing by the ripped scar where the DS driver had nearly come to grief and where the Renault driver had plunged to his death.

Far below, the truck was just visible, its nose buried in the ice-covered pond and surrounded by a vast cloud of steam and smoke. It held for a moment, and Rocco thought it had gone in as far as it could. Then with a groan, it began to sink further. As it did so, the water around it rippled violently, lighting up with a vivid flash, and a wave of heat came up the bank towards them. Then the remains of the truck sank from sight.

There was no sign of the driver.

CHAPTER FORTY-NINE

'Not far off now,' said Calloway, who had been watching signposts. He had a flair for navigating which Tasker lacked, and had only needed to glance at the map once more to know where he was on the twisting and narrow country roads leading towards the village of Poissons-les-Marais.

Little had been said since they had changed course, although Biggs had kept up a regular muttering about going the wrong way and wasting valuable time. Tasker had said nothing in reply, too absorbed in staring out of the window at the unfolding panorama of brown fields rolling by.

They had met virtually no traffic save for the occasional van or tractor and one or two cyclists, the latter hunched over their handlebars, faces pinched and grey against the cold air. The route Calloway had chosen had kept them clear of villages, passing only one or two ramshackle farms, and a café with a giant Pernod advert painted on the side wall.

'How far?' The words seemed to stir Tasker from his thoughts. He lifted the sawn-off and took out the two spent cartridges, replacing them with the fresh ones. He snapped it shut.

From behind him came a click of metal as Biggs also checked his gun.

'About two miles.'

'This is a waste of time,' the former soldier muttered, slapping a hand on the back of the seat for emphasis. 'What the hell are we doing out here? We'd be in Calais by now if we'd kept going north.'

'We're here because I said so,' Tasker growled. 'It's part of the job, that's all.'

'Yeah – and a proper bleedin' lash-up that was. My mate's dead, thanks for asking, and we're stuck in the middle of bleedin' nowhere. My mother could've organised things better than this. Friggin' amateurs.' He clicked the cylinder back into place and turned to watch the road behind them.

There was silence for a while as they rumbled gently along a stretch of uneven tarmac. Then a vehicle appeared coming the other way.

A police car.

Tasker said calmly, 'Keep going. Don't even eyeball them, you hear?'

The two cars passed each other, and the three Englishmen caught a glimpse of two men in uniform, eyeing the DS with interest.

Tasker turned and looked back. The police car was slowing with a flash of its brake lights. They were turning back. 'Put your foot down,' he said quietly. 'Get us a good lead.'

Calloway nodded and the car leapt forward. They drove in silence for a mile, each alone in their thoughts. Then Tasker said, 'Stop the car.'

Calloway glanced at him. 'You what? They'll be on us in a minute.'

'I said, stop the bloody car. Now!' To emphasise his point, Tasker dropped the stock of the sawn-off into the crook of his elbow so that the barrels were nudging Calloway's ribcage.

Calloway did as he was told, applying the brakes firmly but smoothly. Any sudden movement right now would cost him his life. He coasted to a halt. They were near an expanse of woodland, the trees spiky and rimed with frost. A gathering of crows circled around the uppermost branches, disturbed by the car's arrival, while below them, some cows in a field looked up, breathing out clouds of vapour at this sudden intrusion.

Tasker said without looking round, 'Biggs. Get round to the back and rip off the number plate. Somebody will have reported it and we need to keep 'em guessing.'

Biggs eyed the gun in Tasker's hands, then shrugged and climbed out.

'Right, go,' said Tasker quietly, and lifted the barrels of the sawn-off. 'Nice and quick, now.'

Calloway had no choice. He nodded and stamped on the accelerator. The car fishtailed slightly on the greasy surface, then they were away, leaving Biggs standing at the side of the road, his mouth open in shock.

'What was that for?' said Calloway.

'Because he annoyed me. And he called us amateurs.' He sniffed and lowered the gun to the floor between his knees. 'And he'll slow down that cop car. Now get me close to this bloody village before they catch up with us.'

CHAPTER FIFTY

It didn't take long for the cavalcade of patrol cars, emergency crews, support vehicles and other interested parties to arrive, summoned by the bodyguards in the DS.

Rocco and Claude waited on the bridge, immune to the cold, hands in plain sight as the first cars skidded to a stop and officers jumped out, guns drawn; it would have been too disturbingly ironic to have had a zealous patrol cop, anxious to make a name for himself, start blazing away without asking questions as soon as he saw two men at the site of an attack on the president.

Some looked surprised to see Rocco, men who had heard about his suspension. They either avoided his gaze or muttered between themselves about what he was doing here. Most nodded with familiarity or called a greeting, and went to investigate the crash site.

Among the vehicles were two blue vans with Godard and his *Gardes Mobiles*, who quickly put up roadblocks to keep unwanted gawkers at bay and isolate the scene from the press. A car carrying *Commissaire* Perronnet, Captain Canet and Dr Rizzotti arrived and parked on the far side of the bridge. Both officers nodded at Rocco without comment before walking by and studying the scene of the truck's descent into the pond.

Rizzotti stopped alongside Rocco and Claude,

and took one look over the edge before shaking his head. He eyed Rocco for a moment, then gave him a covert wink before suggesting loudly that someone call a rescue truck with heavy lifting gear.

Then *Commissaire* Massin appeared.

The senior officer uncurled himself from the rear of Perronnet's car with an air of reluctance. He viewed the area for a moment, adjusting his cap with care, then walked along the road onto the bridge, his shoes clicking with parade ground precision. He nodded at Rocco and Claude, then went to view the scene for himself, before returning accompanied by Canet and Perronnet.

As he did so, Detective Desmoulins arrived in a patrol car and jogged across the bridge. He was grinning widely.

'You were right all along, Lucas,' he said loudly, while still several metres away. His words carried clearly in the thin air, drawing the attention of the uniformed officers and support crews securing the scene. All conversation ceased. 'They hit the *Crédit Agricole* in Béthune; four Englishmen in a DS, armed with shotguns and pistols. Three went in and one stayed with the car.' He stopped in front of Rocco and looked around, enjoying the audience. 'Unfortunately, someone else had the same idea. They ran slap bang into another crew and there was a gunfight. I just heard it over the radio. Sounds like it was a rerun of the Valentine's Day Massacre.'

Massin was the first to speak. 'What are you talking about?' He clearly hadn't heard the news.

'The English gang who smashed up the café? Lucas said they were here to do a job, and he was

307

right; they came back to rob the bank in Béthune. Three got away but one was killed. One of the second gang was killed and one wounded. I'd already warned the Béthune office as Lucas suggested, but they were a bit reluctant to believe me, especially...' he paused, then added innocently, 'as they'd heard about his suspension.'

Massin said nothing for a moment, the skin around his eyes going tight. Then he said, 'What else? Was anything stolen?'

'No. That was the joke. There was a last-minute change to the schedule. The bank said the main bulk of money was delivered a day early at the request of the tyre factory. Something about shutting the lines down for a maintenance check, so they paid the workers yesterday instead.'

'Who were the other crew?' Rocco asked.

'One of the local cops reckons the dead man is an old gang soldier from St Denis in Paris who'd retired years ago. The wounded guy and the third one they caught right outside were amateurs. A bunch of nobodies.'

'I see.' Massin looked bemused. 'Where are the Englishmen now?'

'Last seen heading north – probably back to Calais and the white cliffs of Dover. I alerted the Calais division and they're putting out patrols to stop them.' He looked at Rocco and gestured towards the truck below them. 'Sounds like the distraction you described, while all this was going on.'

Rocco nodded, his eyes on Massin. The next step was up to him.

The *commissaire* looked uncomfortable and lifted his chin, then turned and spoke directly to

Rocco. 'I have had ... representations from an eyewitness who confirms that you were handed an envelope by a man answering the description of the Englishman, Tasker.' He glanced around as if making sure everyone was listening, although not a sound could be heard. 'She confirmed that you handed the envelope back with ... "a degree of force", was how she described it.'

Mme Denis, thought Rocco. *You beauty*.

'I have also received documentation via our embassy in London, supporting the fact that you refused on the spot to take the money.'

'Documentation?' Rocco couldn't believe it.

'A copy of a statement made by the accomplice of the man Tasker – the same one who took the photographs – witnessed by a third secretary of our embassy and two members of the Metropolitan Police, one of them Detective Chief Inspector Nialls, who I can vouch for personally.'

Rocco blinked at that. It was quite a thing to say, for Massin.

'I consider it sufficient to back up your claim that it was an attempted entrapment, Inspector, and have already issued directions for your suspension to be lifted. And I apologise for the ... regrettable accusations made against you. I'm sure you understand, however, that I had to follow certain ... procedures.' He coughed. 'I believe you, too, unwittingly, became part of the distraction.'

'Thank you,' he said.

Massin nodded and reached down to his side. For the first time Rocco realised he was wearing a sidearm. Massin unclipped it and held it out. 'I'm sorry – I did not bring your weapon. You

309

might need this.'

It was as good as he was going to get, Rocco figured. And better than he'd expected. He tapped his coat pocket, where he'd put the Walther. 'Thanks. But I'm good to go.' He found his respect for Massin rising a spectral level or two; the senior officer could have hidden behind the procedural veil of further investigations into the affair, but had clearly decided to come out in the open – and in front of these other officers.

Someone clapped him on the back and he heard a volley of congratulations.

Then a stocky figure eased through the crowd, holding up a slim wallet for Massin to see. He had impressively broad shoulders and the face of a fighter, although dressed in a smart suit and tie. He spoke directly to Massin.

'Are you in charge here?'

'I am,' Massin confirmed, and looked at the man's ID. His face registered surprise. 'How can I help you?'

The man pointed at Rocco and Claude. 'You and these two – a word, please?' He turned and walked away a few metres, distancing himself from the crowd of policemen and leaving the other three to follow.

'This is my authority,' the newcomer said, when they were standing alongside him. He showed Rocco and Claude his card. 'It trumps anything you're likely to see here today.' He glanced at Massin with a grim smile. 'I mean no offence, *Commissaire*, I promise you – but this is vitally important.'

'Of course. I understand.' Massin turned to Rocco and Claude. 'This gentleman is one of the president's protection team.'

'Damn,' Claude muttered. 'You were in the front of the car!'

'And you were in the Traction coming towards the bridge. Your names?'

Rocco said, 'I'm Rocco, he's Lamotte. Out of Amiens.'

'Really. Are you undercover?' The bodyguard seemed fascinated by the contrast between Claude and Rocco, one in corduroys and boots, the other in dark, tailored clothing and black brogues.

'That's right,' Massin interjected. 'These officers are under my command. Is the president safe?'

'Perfectly, thank you. All I want to say is, what happened here today stops here.' He glanced at the crowd of policemen, who were now going about their duties. 'No reports, no press interviews, nothing. The president would prefer that another ... incident following on so soon after the last one would not be in the best interests of the state or the people.'

'What about the truck?' Rocco asked, nodding towards the crash site, although he knew it was academic; if the president requested a press blackout, that's what he would get.

The man lifted his shoulders. 'It was an accident. A drunk who took the corner too fast.'

'Corner?' Claude looked up and down the straight road. 'Which one?'

The man smiled with a touch of genuine humour. 'Well, who knows what a drunk sees? You'll think of something. *Commissaire?*' He glanced meaningfully towards the other policemen.

Massin got the message and walked away to

311

spread the word.

The bodyguard turned to go, and Rocco said, 'I'm surprised Colonel Saint-Cloud isn't here to deliver that message himself.'

The bodyguard frowned. 'Saint-Cloud? Why would he?'

'He's in charge of your unit.'

'Not anymore.' The man gave Rocco a hard stare. 'The colonel retired on ... health grounds three weeks ago. It's not been officially announced yet, but he's no longer responsible for this or any other unit.' His face showed no emotion, but the phrasing carried all the meaning Rocco needed.

With that, the bodyguard turned and walked away to the black Citroën DS waiting across the bridge.

Moments later, a uniformed officer hurried across and addressed Rocco.

'A man with a gun has been spotted by a patrol on a back road near Poissons,' he told him. 'They think he was dropped off by a DS with two others on board. The DS disappeared but the patrol stayed near the man's last location.'

'What sort of gun?' The last thing Rocco needed was to waste time hunting a farmer chasing rabbits. He was still trying to digest the bombshell delivered by the bodyguard, and figuring out what to do about it.

'A handgun,' the officer replied.

Rocco pushed the Saint-Cloud business to one side. The colonel would keep for now. He said to Claude, 'Get Desmoulins, Godard and some of his men. The fewer targets the better until we

312

find out what this is.' He had no doubts that it was Tasker and his remaining companions, but flooding the area with uniforms would only create pandemonium, during which the robbers might manage to slip away.

And, in any case, this was personal.

The journey took fifteen minutes, with Rocco driving as fast as he dared over the slippery roads and Claude and Desmoulins riding shotgun. Godard was following in a van with three of his men. The sleet had returned and was beginning to turn softer, falling more slowly but with the relentless regularity that'd soon turn to snow. Rocco studied the sky and thought about advantages: it wasn't yet heavy enough to settle, but it might help them by showing traces of footsteps around the location where the gunman had been seen.

He saw a patrol car parked at the side of the road not far from a wood and stopped behind it. Godard pulled up in front. The two patrol officers climbed out to greet them, stamping their feet.

'He was running toward the trees when we saw him,' said one, and pointed a thumb over a fence at the wood. 'We thought it best to wait for backup. He didn't look as if he wanted to stop and chat.'

'Wise choice,' said Rocco. 'Where did the car go?'

The man jerked his chin up the road. 'Towards Poissons. There are no other turns off this road unless they go straight past.'

'They won't,' Rocco said. He glanced at the wood. 'How thick is it in there?' He knew the trees and copses in the area varied greatly, some thinned by woodcutters and farmers for logs, others left to nature. If anyone'd know, Claude would.

'In there? Heavy going. The owner won't let anyone near it. You thinking of going in?'

Rocco nodded. Whoever was in there wasn't going to come out willingly, he was certain of that. But he was damned if he was going to sit out here and wait for the man to get bored or freeze to death. And, neither could he send in men who had no experience of this kind of thing.

He also needed the names of who was behind this business.

He took out the Walther and said to Claude, 'Bring your shotgun. You others, stay here.' He saw one of Godard's men carrying a rifle. 'He any good with that?'

Godard smiled. 'Best in the unit.'

'If our man comes out, go for a leg wound. If he fights...' He left the rest unsaid. If the man came out, it was likely that he'd have scored one, if not two hits already, and he and Claude would be unable to help.

He ducked beneath the fence and set off across the field with Claude close behind, following the faint tracks left by the fleeing man. Flecks of snow soon began settling on their coat shoulders and in their eyebrows, and the air had gone very quiet. A few cows over by the wood stomped away as they approached.

'You think he'll be in there?' Claude said softly. 'It's a bit obvious.'

'It's the only cover for several kilometres. He'll take what he can get.'

Rocco stopped twenty metres short of the first line of trees and listened. All he could hear was a faint hum of wind, and in the background, a chatter of radio from the police vehicles. That would be good, he thought; hearing it would cut into the man's confidence even more than being stranded out here alone. The knowledge that he was effectively cut off would be demoralising.

'You ready?'

Claude nodded and lifted his shotgun.

At a nod from Rocco, they stepped apart to reduce the targets and walked forward into the trees.

CHAPTER FIFTY-ONE

It was like stepping into a different world, immediately more sombre in spite of the lack of leaves on the trees. The outside sounds faded as the branches overhead seemed to close in on the two men, shutting out the snow-heavy sky and leaving only the chatter of the police radio to remind them of the outside world. The trunks here were jammed close together, never thinned by man, each new growth pushing against the next, reaching skywards and searching for every bit of space. Dead trees lay withered and rotting or, where there hadn't been space to fall, hung limply like drunks off their neighbours.

Claude stopped and sniffed the air, eyes flicking over what he could see, then hunkered down, gesturing to Rocco to do the same.

The minutes slipped by, neither man speaking. Rocco was breathing easily enough, but he'd felt his heart rate increase the moment they had stopped moving. Movement was good, to a city-bred cop. It kept you awake, showed you and everyone else that you were busy and active, allowed you to check you didn't have someone coming up behind you. But as he'd learnt long ago, movement could be a killer in the wrong place. The kill could come from under your feet, rigged to pierce your flesh with needles of bamboo; it could come from overhead, a swish of noise triggered by a careless kick against a carefully laid peg; it could come out of the undergrowth, so thick you couldn't see through it to the danger lurking just a couple of metres away.

He said, 'What are we doing?' Claude was the expert here, the woodsman, and he was content to let him lead the way. But Rocco liked to know what was going on.

'We're waiting.' The reply was low, just above a whisper.

'For what?'

Claude pointed at some trees deeper into the wood, where a few small birds were twittering softly and flitting from branch to branch. 'When they stop, we'll know.'

They waited some more.

'You okay?' Claude queried, and Rocco realised he was grinding his teeth. He relaxed his jaw and nodded. He wasn't, quite, but he was getting there. Another few years of creeping through the woods with this man and he'd be as good as new.

Claude seemed to know what he was thinking.

He leant close and said softly, 'I knew a man once who did what you did. Went through the same thing, but in another war. Couldn't stand the trees. Reckoned they were whispering to him like we are now, calling him names. Actually, he was just scared shitless, but couldn't admit it.'

Rocco said nothing.

'Anyway, in the end, he got over it by facing his demons. Went native instead of hiding in a car in city streets all day.'

Claude was talking about himself.

'I'm like that man, you mean?'

Claude shook his head. 'You're nothing like him. Even in here, if I had you on my tail, I'd be running as fast as I could and I wouldn't stop. I know you don't like it in here, and why should you? But you use it; you don't let it beat you. You're always looking, even when you can't see anything.' He stared at Rocco, holding his gaze. 'But others ... like this man we're looking for, he's a rat in a tunnel. He only reacts to what he can see. Sooner or later, you'd catch him before he caught you.'

'Is this leading anywhere?'

Claude smiled. 'Shit, don't ask me. I'm just talking to calm my own nerves.' He stopped and looked round.

The birds had gone silent. Everywhere.

Only the branches whispered overhead, like an army of crickets. Anyone watching right now, Rocco thought, would have the advantage over a newcomer stepping into the trees from the outside. He slowly turned his head behind them, to the light. It was clear.

He heard a grunting noise, followed by a snap of

a twig somewhere not far away. The sound triggered an unwelcome memory flash from years ago: heavy vegetation underfoot, stifling humidity, no sky to speak of and a wall of green in every direction. Unlike here where there was only brown and black, apart from the top ends of the branches. Then, there had been danger all around and a sense of utter futility facing an enemy they couldn't see until it was too late. He waited, feeling his shoulders stiffen involuntarily; told himself to ignore it and worked hard at not squeezing his eyes shut.

Alongside him, Claude was staring into the dense trees over the barrels of his shotgun, an over-under model, the stock shiny with use and lovingly cared for, darkly functional. A tool of his trade.

Rocco took in the scenery afresh, breathing to relax. All around them was light and shadow and fresh air, and bare, wintry branches and slim trunks clustered tightly together like passengers on the *Métro*. High above, through a latticework of branches, was a glimpse of darkening grey sky.

'Nice weapon,' he whispered. 'You think we need that?'

'Damn right.' Claude puffed out his cheeks. 'It's a Darne. Best gun ever. I bought it from a farmer who'd given up killing stuff. But this isn't for any man; there are wild boar in this area.' He looked at Rocco's blank expression and said, 'You do know about boars, don't you?'

'Of course. You didn't think to mention them before we came in here?' He'd heard the stories; normally placid if left alone and keen to avoid humans, in protection of their young, wild boars were ferocious, especially the sows.

'Would it have made a difference?'

'I suppose not. Are they as bad as they say?'

'If cornered, yes.' Claude chewed on his lip. 'If threatened, they'll kill. Man, beast ... they'll even wreck a car if they feel like it. A herd over by Bapaume opened up a Panhard like a tin can once.' He indicated the base of a nearby tree where the earth'd been ripped and churned over, the surrounding area peppered with small hoof marks. 'These tracks are fresh. The animals roam, but these don't look old. I reckon they're not far away.'

'How big are they?' Rocco couldn't recall seeing a boar close up, but felt uneasy at Claude's obvious concern.

'It's not size you need to worry about. It's weight and speed. You get hit low by a hundred-plus kilos of pissed-off pig, and you'll go down, I promise. Then they'll gore you with their tusks.' He shook his head. 'It won't be nice.'

Rocco took a firmer hold of his gun. *Come on, piggy,* he thought. *As if I haven't got enough problems to be going on with, I'm going face to face with an enraged pork sausage on legs.*

'If they do come,' Claude continued, 'go for the nearest tree. Don't stop to shoot; they're too fast for a pistol shot, and once they're stirred up, they're not easy to stop, even with this thing.' He raised the shotgun. 'Believe me.'

'What will *you* be doing?'

'Me? I'll be up the tree ahead of you.'

He straightened slowly, then stepped past Rocco

319

and led the way deeper into the wood, pausing regularly to peer beneath the thick tangles of branches and other fallen vegetation where the boars' low height would provide good cover.

Rocco followed, watching his friend's back.

They had covered maybe thirty metres when Claude stopped and held out a warning hand. Slowly, very slowly, he sank to the ground and signalled for Rocco to do the same.

As they did so, an eruption of screaming came from ahead of them not twenty metres away, and a dark shape shot out from under a thicket followed by several other smaller shapes.

'A mother and young,' Claude hissed in warning.

And he and Rocco were right in their path.

Rocco felt his gut contract. They had nowhere to go but up, but there was no time. He swore and fired twice into the ground in front of where he thought the boars were. Instead of coming on, the boar turned and went back on its tracks, the young following like little boats on a string.

Suddenly the thicket moved and two shots rang out. One of the young boars flipped over and lay still. Instantly the mother squealed and charged, barrelling through the undergrowth like a vengeful rocket.

This time the scream they heard came from a man.

Claude fired two shots into the air, quickly reloading while Rocco covered him, then fired twice more.

In the silence that followed, they heard the squeals of the boars diminishing towards the far side of the wood, then a groan close by. It was followed by a crackling noise as someone made their way through the trees across their front, but too far away to see clearly.

'He's heading towards the road,' said Claude. 'Come on – we can cut him off.' He showed Rocco the way and both men ran towards the light.

CHAPTER FIFTY-TWO

'Put the gun down.' Rocco's voice didn't need to be loud; sound travelled well in this cold, thin air. But it carried authority.

He and Claude had burst out of the trees and run across the field in time to see the fugitive coming at an angle towards them. If he saw them or the other men waiting by the road, he made no move to change direction, but staggered on, slipping and sliding on the icy ground. He was dragging one leg badly, his breathing laboured and hoarse.

The man looked beaten and hopelessly unsteady on his feet, like a prizefighter at the end of a long, brutal bout. His shoes were clogged with mud and bits of vegetation and the cloth around his injured leg was badly torn, the flesh beneath showing bright red. His shoulders were dusted with snow and muddy, and his face was pinched and near blue with cold.

Biggs, thought Rocco. The other one had been Jarvis.

Then the runner seemed to realise where he was. He stopped, breathing heavily, and glanced back as if he thought the boar might still be after him. When he looked round, he shook his head with something approaching despair and looked at Rocco.

'No way,' he muttered, and coughed. 'Too late, anyway.' He clutched his stomach and spat on the ground. The spittle was bright red.

Claude said, 'She hurt him.'

The end of the man's gun barrel was wavering slightly. Rocco wasn't sure, but he didn't think enlisted men in the British army used pistols. Most had rifles, a few used machine guns. This one was carrying a revolver, probably army issue. He was holding the gun low, like a cowboy in a western.

Rocco stepped sideways, keeping on the move. No point in giving the man a standing target, even a lucky one. He said, 'Put it down and lie on the ground, Mr Biggs. We will not harm you.'

The man's face twisted in surprise on hearing his own name. He looked around wildly, instinctively seeking a way out. When he realised there was none, he said, 'Piss off, copper.' And pulled the trigger.

The shot zipped by Rocco's right leg, hitting the ground three metres behind him.

'I'll kill you with the next one!'

Rocco moved sideways, but kept his distance. Out of the corner of his eye, he saw Claude and, beyond him, a group comprising Desmoulins and Godard and his men. The man with a rifle was standing off to one side, the gun into his shoulder, waiting for a signal.

'Last warning,' Rocco said quietly, just enough for the man to hear. 'You do not want to do this. The man back there will not miss.'

The second round came closer, the sound of the shot making a tearing noise as it went past his head. The gunman pulled the trigger again, but this time there was just a click. Frantically he scrabbled in his jacket pocket and produced a fistful of shells, shards of gold light flashing as some tumbled to the ground from frozen fingers. Grunting with pain and emotion, Biggs began tugging out the empties and feeding fresh ones into the cylinder. Then his face twisted in pain and he grabbed his injured thigh.

He peeled back the torn cloth. Blood was running down his leg and across his shoe, forming a puddle on the ground, bright red against the thin covering of snow.

Rocco didn't bother asking who was behind this. He knew Biggs wasn't going to give up. The man was operating on instincts alone, a form of bravado that'd carry him until he could go no further. He'd seen it before in Indochina and elsewhere, where men on battlefields with nothing else to give surrendered to the last-ditch ethos drummed into them in endless exercises and training.

It was just a pity that it was being misused here.

He turned and walked towards the man. He couldn't let this go on. He waited until the gun came up again, then planted his feet and lifted the Walther, the walnut grip warm and comfortable in his hand.

He fired once.

The shot took Biggs in the left shoulder, lifting

the fabric of his jacket. He staggered and looked at Rocco in shock. But he wasn't finished yet. He swore softly and lifted the pistol again, finger tightening on the trigger. Before Rocco could shoot again, another shot sounded, this time from the rifleman on the road, and Biggs was hit in the chest, flipping him onto his back.

In the silence that followed, a whistle came from the road, carrying eerily across the cold field. Rocco looked round. Desmoulins was making the sign of a telephone call and pointing at Godard's blue van.

Rocco picked up the dead man's revolver and walked towards the road, his shoes heavy with mud, and wondered if he was going to have to buy new ones. This job was getting far too heavy on clothing.

'Sorry, Inspector,' said the driver of the van, as if he'd interrupted something. He was half inside the vehicle. 'A black DS driven by an Englishman named Calloway has been stopped coming out of Poissons.'

'Anyone else inside?' But Rocco already knew the answer to that one.

'No. Calloway said the man named Tasker is in the village.' He frowned and added, 'He said Tasker has gone crazy and is going to kill you.'

CHAPTER FIFTY-THREE

'But why come here?' said Desmoulins. He was driving Rocco's car with the inspector in the passenger seat. Godard and his men were following close behind. They were heading towards Poissons, leaving the two patrolmen to look after Biggs's body. 'He could have been away and clear by now, heading for the ferries.'

'Away, maybe,' Rocco replied, reloading his gun. 'But not clear. Tasker's been used and cut adrift by his own people, and I suspect he knows it. He's got nothing to lose.'

It didn't take much putting together, not once Desmoulins had got the story from the Béthune police. They had interviewed the French gunmen left inside the bank, and the wounded man had been eager to talk. They had been recruited to do the one job, each a solo operator under the command of an older armoured-car specialist, originally from Corsica. He was now dead, shot by the big Englishman, Tasker. They had never met their recruiters, all discussions having been carried out by telephone and through 'contacts'. But investigators were already working on that angle. Rocco, however, had a good idea who was behind the recruitment.

Patrice Delarue.

It all fitted together, an oddly shaped jigsaw of disparate events. The original ramming had been a practice run, using Calloway's skills to avoid maximum damage while giving the important man in the scheme, Fletcher, as near a real scenario as he could get without him knowing. Fletcher the giant fist: the real attacker. The other men had been bit players in a theatrical drama, added to provide a fog to prevent anyone seeing the real picture.

Distraction, too, had been the purpose of the other events, to draw away security and police attention from what was being planned: the smashing of the *Canard Doré,* the openly argumentative front put up by Tasker and his men, all the while knowing they would not be held for long; the burning of the truck, the disappearance – albeit mismanaged – of the damaged Citroën DS. And finally the bank job, skewed deliberately towards failure and using expendable men from two gangs to divert police attention from what was really going to happen.

And that was the real event; the genuine piece of *théâtre.*

It was so simple, Rocco realised, once you peered under the surface. Almost military in terms of ruse and planning, coldly expensive in terms of men – but they were unimportant, anyway, gun fodder to be used and forgotten. What was important was achieving their aims of toppling the president while out from the cover of crowds and the usual security cordon.

And that was where he had a real problem: knowing who was behind the attempted attack. It could be any one of several groups spread across France and Europe, into North Africa. But it was suddenly very clear that Saint-Cloud was in there right at the thick of it. Pretending to still be working for the presidential security unit, while all the time he was ... what? Sick? Deluded? Plotting? He wondered at the sheer size of the bluff the man had pulled off to arrive here, establish himself – dragging Portier and even Broissard along with him, although Rocco had no doubts they were fooled, too – all without revealing that he was no longer employed to protect the president. But then, had anyone thought for a moment to check his credentials? He himself hadn't, nor had Massin. Who, after all, thinks to check the bona fides of one of the most important men in the country?

'Alix is in Poissons,' said Claude from the back seat. He was holding his shotgun across his knees, broken, the cartridges in his hand. He sounded distracted, as if talking to himself. 'She had a day's leave to take in lieu of a late shift. She's been working too hard. I told her to stay at home and relax. She won't, of course. She'll be out and about in the village doing stuff to keep herself occupied.' He stopped talking and stared out of the window, his words hanging in the air between them.

Rocco took out the revolver he'd taken from Biggs. It held two shells. 'Do they know what weapons Tasker was using?'

'A shotgun with sawn-off barrels,' said Desmoulins. 'Nasty brute of a weapon – like the man himself. He's probably got a handgun, too.'

'What do we do if he's in the village, Lucas?' said Claude. He didn't have to explain himself; Tasker was a city gangster, accustomed to the proximity of streets and houses and people. He'd be in his element among buildings, even in a

327

small village like Poissons, with ample protection and hiding places. And he'd be ruthless and desperate enough to use whatever and whomever he could, and to hell with the consequences.

'If he's in there,' said Rocco, 'we'll get him out. Don't worry about it.' He closed the cylinder of the revolver with a soft click, and hoped the other two couldn't hear the uncertainty in his voice.

Because with men like Tasker, at the end of his rope and with nothing to lose, there were no certainties.

They drove into Poissons slowly, watching the buildings for movement, for signs of an impending ambush. If Tasker was a strategist, he'd wait for them to get in among the houses, then take them out one by one. But all the while he'd be waiting for Rocco to show.

A police car was parked across the street, empty, and a group of men was at the door of the village café. Among them Rocco saw M. Thierry, who cared for the graveyard, and Delsaire, the local plumber, and Arnaud, the village handyman.

They liked a good gathering, Rocco remembered. Anything for a bit of excitement.

The men turned when they heard the vehicles and stepped away from the door. Rocco told Desmoulins to stop and jumped out. Leaving Godard and his men to take a look round, he walked into the café, nodding at the men, and found two uniformed officers with a dejected-looking Calloway slumped in a chair, his wrists handcuffed.

'Where is he?' Rocco felt dirty and tired and damp and didn't want to waste his time talking to this man, but to get on with tracking down Tasker. But he needed to get something from Calloway while he still could. His attitude clearly conveyed itself to the Englishman, because he drew his feet together and sat up straight, eyes wary.

'I dropped him off near the church,' he said quickly, without being asked. 'He said he was going to kill you.'

'Is that all?'

'Isn't that enough?'

'I mean, does he intend hurting anyone else?'

'I doubt it. He doesn't know anyone else. He's pretty much a mental mess right now; too much to think about and he'd explode.'

'What do you mean?'

'He's over the edge. It's as if he's lost all reason. Rambling, playing with his guns and threatening anyone who disagrees. He kicked Biggs out of the car because he said something he didn't like and he needed a decoy, and he only got me to bring him here by sticking his gun in my ribs. I think he's nuts – and he wasn't exactly the most stable of men, anyway. Then he met you.' When Rocco didn't say anything, he continued, 'Tasker's been pretty much top dog in his own world for years now. There are men above him on the human ladder of pond life, but far more below. He enjoys throwing his weight around but hasn't got the brains to run his own show, so he's been playing second fiddle to someone who does.'

'Ketch, you mean.'

'Yes. And I think Ketch knew how he felt. Which is probably why he sent him on this suicide mission. Tasker's problem was, he was too thick to turn it down.'

'You came, too,' Rocco pointed out.

Calloway smiled grimly. 'Yes. What does that say about me? Thing is, none of us knew what we were signing up to, not really. I suspect that in the long run, neither did Tasker.'

'The bank robbery.'

'Yes. It was supposed to be the real thing: in, out and away to the ferries, easy money. But it was no such thing. There was no cash drop, Tasker said, and another bunch of gunmen was already inside. I don't think we were meant to come out of that one.'

Calloway was no fool, Rocco recognised. He'd come along knowingly on an illicit venture, but had clearly put two and two together since it had gone wrong. 'What do you think it was really about?'

'We were a giant decoy squad, weren't we? You remember Fletcher – the big lug? He drove the Renault truck when we did this the first time round. But this trip he was off doing it solo, on direct orders from Ketch himself. The rest of us were assigned to the bank job. On the surface, all a bit disconnected, but we were being paid, so why question it?'

'You had no idea what Fletcher was doing?'

'No. He was given specific instructions about to-day, I know that – and told to keep his mouth shut. He could barely keep it in he was so made up, like a bloody kid in a toyshop. What was he doing?'

'He tried to kill President de Gaulle.'

'*What?*' Calloway shook his head. 'Fletcher? That's crazy. He wouldn't...' He stopped, eyes

330

going wide. 'The idiot.'

'What?'

'I should have guessed,' Calloway said bitterly. 'It didn't take Einstein to figure out something big was going on ... the black DS, the ramming and the Molotovs and pistols. I thought it was all a test run for someone else. But *Fletcher?*' He stared at Rocco. 'I mean, he wasn't political – he wasn't anything. He was a thug and a haulage driver, but that was it. Are you sure it was him?'

'I saw him.' Rocco wondered about it. Calloway sounded too shocked to be play-acting. Maybe Fletcher hadn't known what he was doing either; maybe he thought the target was someone low-grade – a business rival. But they'd never know now. 'If you thought it was something big, why did you go along with it?'

Calloway gave a wry smile. 'I needed the money, didn't I? I have gambling debts with people who break legs and things if they're kept waiting.'

'Nice friends you have.'

'Yeah, I know. It wasn't just us, though, running this thing. A French group was involved – some big man in Paris, according to Tasker.'

'Name?'

'He never said. The French provided the plans to the bank, too. Tasker pretended he was in the know all along, but all he really knew was that Ketch had been paid by this French crew to stage a "scenario", and we were the players.'

'A scenario?'

'That's what he called it. It was all part of some weird plan to tie up and confuse the cops in the area. Now we know why, right?' He squinted up at Rocco. 'Did it work?'

Rocco refused to answer. He wondered how Godard was getting on out in the village. He responded instead with another question of his own. 'What about the body of the tramp?'

Calloway's face paled and he clamped his lips shut. But he was beyond denying anything. 'Was that what he was? Poor bugger. That was Tasker's idea. He found the body under the truck ... I reckon he'd been sitting on the verge or had collapsed, and the truck ran over him. None of us saw him until we found him underneath the wheels. Anyway, Tasker reckoned you'd never find him in the burnt-out truck as long as we piled in some wood and lots of petrol.'

'But burning the truck was still part of the scenario?'

'Yes.'

Rocco wondered whether Calloway had been truly in the dark as much as he said, or was simply a very good actor. He was inclined to think a bit of both. 'What about the first DS?'

'What about it?'

'We found it at the scrapyard. Before it was broken up.'

'Now that wasn't part of the plan. It was supposed to disappear completely. I reckon it was hot from a previous job and we were using it for the last time. The scrap merchant – Bellin? – had orders to torch it and cut it up immediately.'

'Did he supply the car?'

'No. Both vehicles were supplied by someone else; we just collected them from a prearranged spot. They came fitted with the harnesses and the timber. We just had to drive them according to instructions.' He gave another dry smile. 'A rare case of hands across the sea, wouldn't you agree?'

Rocco said nothing. A babble of voices came from outside the café door, and Claude appeared with Desmoulins close behind. Godard was in the background, shaking his head.

'They can't see him anywhere,' said Claude. He shuffled his feet. 'I called home, but Alix isn't there. Thierry said he saw her walking down the lane towards your place less than twenty minutes ago.'

Then came the sound of a gunshot.

CHAPTER FIFTY-FOUR

Commissaire François Massin was suffering a mix of emotions.

A part of him was still recoiling at the earlier idea that Rocco, whom he'd found himself believing capable of many things, could be guilty of taking a bribe from a known criminal. For any commanding officer, discovering an officer under his command guilty of corruption was almost inevitably a stain on his own record, ignorance being rarely forgiven among the higher ranks of the Ministry. But now he was facing incontrovertible evidence that Rocco had been set up, and the possibility that he himself had been too easily led into believing the worst of a subordinate.

He walked around his office, trying to make

sense of the thoughts swirling around in his head. How had this happened? One moment everything was proceeding smoothly, the next an unwelcome focus of attention was on him, evidenced by the extended volley of telephone calls from the Ministry demanding reports and updates on the events leading up to the attack on de Gaulle's car, closely followed by the press requesting comments about the bank robbery at Béthune and rumours of an attack on an unnamed VIP at an unknown location.

Massin's only meagre consolation was that sorting out the flow of paperwork and briefings over the next few days would probably be the only way of extending his stay here. After that...

He stopped suddenly. The station was down to a skeleton staff, all other available officers taking part in securing the scene of the attack, helping with the Béthune bank investigation or joining the hunt for the Englishmen. The building had been left as quiet as the morgue it did not yet possess.

Yet he'd heard a noise from along the corridor. It had come from the empty office; at least, the office which had been empty until Colonel Saint-Cloud had commandeered it for his temporary base. He'd thought the security man was long gone, hard on the heels of his master now that the visit and the drama were over, no doubt sharing the president's relief at being back in the relative safety and comfort of Paris.

He walked along the corridor. If it was Saint-Cloud, he wanted to impress on him that Rocco was innocent; that no stain could therefore attach to his own position as *commissaire*. He felt almost ashamed at this instinct for self-interest, but it was too ingrained to change.

He stopped outside the office door and hesitated before entering. The security chief hadn't heard him coming, and was unlocking a steel cabinet and taking out some papers Massin had seen him placing inside when he had first arrived. On the top were four buff folders tied with ribbon. He knew these contained details of groups and individuals opposing the president. Next came a small sheaf of papers he recognised as official travel expense sheets; he'd used them himself when attending conferences or training classes. Then a thick folder he had seen going into the drawer of Saint-Cloud the first day, when he had requested the full use of the office along with the only set of keys to the drawer. The folder, he had explained, was his personal operations manual which went everywhere with him; a personal quirk, he'd explained with unaccustomed reserve, which detailed everything to be done in the event of something catastrophic happening to the president. Massin even recalled Saint-Cloud saying that he rarely if ever looked at it, the contents committed to memory, but always close by just in case. Massin had read it at the time as a not-so-subtle reminder of the importance of Saint-Cloud's office and a need for detailed procedure to be followed if necessary.

Saint-Cloud finally sensed his presence. He turned and looked at Massin with no degree of warmth.

'I trust you have that man of yours in custody,' he said curtly.

'Actually, no.' Massin stepped into the office and

walked across to the window, trying to formulate his words in as confident a manner as he could without sounding deferential. Anything he said now could find its way back to the Ministry through this man's lips, and he couldn't afford any misunderstanding. He had enough to deal with as it was. He finally decided on directness. 'You were wrong about Rocco,' he said, face to the glass. 'We were all wrong. He was set up. We – I – should have taken more time to investigate the circumstances before suspending him.'

'Really?' Saint-Cloud sounded supremely unconcerned, intent on his packing. 'Well, if you choose to believe that, it's up to you. I think the man is incompetent and a loose canon. You should have had him on a tighter rein.'

Massin felt his temper rise at the rebuke, and turned to face Saint-Cloud. 'But how could I? You had him assigned to you by orders of the Ministry. Now you are saying I wasn't controlling him?'

Saint-Cloud stopped what he was doing. Dropping a sheaf of papers into a box, he fastened his eyes on Massin. 'Yes. If you'd had more balls, you could have refused to let him go. But you didn't.'

'What?'

'Unfortunately, you've always been something of a paper officer, haven't you, Massin? Governed by rules and regulations like the St Cyr Academy swot that you always wanted to be.' His mouth twisted with contempt. 'You were a joke back then, did you know that? A little bootlicker who wanted to join the big boys. I hear you actually had the brass to apply midterm for a senior command post in Paris.'

Massin, as shocked by the insulting tone of Saint-Cloud's voice as the poisonous words, said, 'How do you know that?' He'd been assured that all such applications for transfers were in the strictest confidence and never revealed until a decision was made. He'd applied during a rush of dislike for this job and this place, anxious to get somewhere – anywhere – else. Since then, he'd had cause to rethink his application.

'How do you think I know? I have the ear of certain people in the Ministry, that's how. It comes with position and influence – but that's something I doubt you'll ever realise. Or maybe it's because I have no stains on my record ... unlike some.'

'What ... what do you mean?' Massin's voice sounded strangled, even to him. Saint-Cloud was touching on something buried deep, something shameful that should've been beyond the reaches of men like him. For a horrible moment he wondered about Rocco. Had the former army sergeant said something, finally breaking his silence? The risk had always been there, ever since he'd first set eyes on him at the cemetery outside Poissons, on his first morning in the job. It'd been an unwelcome jolt to the gut but one he'd had to face up to, hoping Rocco would never speak of what he knew.

'That business in Indochina; at Mong Khoua, wasn't it? It's common knowledge, of course, in certain quarters.' His eyes flashed with spite and he added, 'Little François Massin, the Academy *poltron*, shitting his pants in the middle of a battle. Hardly officer behaviour, was it?'

'That's outrageous!' Massin's face was white

with fury and shame, his stomach gripped by the realisation that the past was no longer the forgotten secret he'd imagined. 'Retract that immediately!'

'I will do no such thing.' Saint-Cloud stabbed a finger in the air before Massin's face. 'That is why you will never rise higher than *commissaire* of a backwater region based in a mud puddle like this one, Massin.' He managed somehow to imbue the title of *commissaire* with all the *gravitas* of a minor public *fonctionnaire* or town hall paper shuffler.

For one awful second, Massin contemplated walking back to his office and picking up his service weapon. A single shot should do it, wiping the sneering ugliness from Saint-Cloud's face for ever.

Then a sense of calm overcame him. Saint-Cloud didn't know everything after all. Massin had never been to the fortified base of Mong Khoua, another senseless loss of men and position in a brutal war of attrition. Saint-Cloud was simply feeding on rumour to mount a vile attack. And if Rocco had talked, he would at least have got the detail correct.

He reined himself in. Suddenly he saw the way forward. He'd made a mistake. He'd been so distracted ... no, not that ... in awe of Saint-Cloud's position and his mission here, so blinded by the opportunity of what the president's visit might mean for himself, that he'd been ready to doubt one of his own officers at the first accusation.

He took a deep breath. An apology to Rocco could never be enough. He still resented being dragged off that distant battlefield – even Rocco would be able to understand that indignity, no matter what the reason – but he was forced to recognise that he had been weak at the wrong moment when he should have been strong. For Rocco's sake and his own.

He turned to leave, walking past the cabinet Saint-Cloud had been emptying. As he did so, he noticed a folded map in the very bottom of the drawer. It was of a stretch of open countryside, the detail too small to be certain of its location, but clearly a rural area. A red mark had been made on the map, drawing his eye. Next to it was a heavy dark line beneath two words he had come to recognise all too well … but only in the last twenty-four hours.

Pont Noir.

CHAPTER FIFTY-FIVE

'In the name of God, he's got to be down there somewhere. And where's Alix?'

Rocco said nothing. Claude was talking to himself and breathing heavily. But it wasn't from the climb; his concerns for his daughter, Alix, were growing by the minute, and so far they had seen no sign of her or Tasker.

After hearing the shot earlier, Rocco, Claude, Desmoulins and Godard's men had spread out through the village, trying to determine where it had come from. But sound behaved oddly among the cluster of houses, and nobody could venture a definite origin without some element of doubt.

It was enough for Rocco to order everyone to stay back. The last thing he wanted was to give Tasker any easy targets.

Working on the basis that Tasker knew where he lived, Rocco and Claude had made their way up to the grotto to St Paul, which stood on a hill overlooking the village. A man-made cave attended by a statue of the Virgin Mary and three angels, the grotto was rarely used now but gave an ideal vantage point of the area around Rocco's house.

If Tasker had made his way down the lane, there were few places of concealment and it should be easy enough to spot him from here.

But so far there was nothing. Nothing, that is, Rocco realised with a feeling of dread, other than the body of a man lying in the middle of the lane. Dressed in workman's blues and a heavy canvas trench coat, he was fifty metres away from Rocco's house. A bicycle lay nearby, one wheel spinning slowly. He must have been riding down the lane and had been unlucky enough to bump into Tasker. That had been the origin of the gunshot.

Rocco scanned the body through a pair of binoculars. There was no way of telling from here whether he was alive or dead. What he actually wanted to do was charge down there with the Walther in his hand and make Tasker break cover. But apart from the danger to Alix and probably Mme Denis, that would be a short form of suicide. Instead, he clamped down on his impatience and worked on figuring out how to winkle the Englishman from wherever he was hiding.

He saw movement. At first he thought it was a trick of the light caused by the haze of smoke from chimney fires drifting across the village. But it was the man in the lane stirring. He looked around, then rolled quickly away to the cover of a farm building, where he sat shaking his head.

'It's old Antoine,' said Claude, seeing the man's face. 'He lives in Danvillers. He comes here once a week for supplies.'

'It's his lucky day, then,' Rocco observed.

'Really? How do you make that out?'

'Because he's still alive.'

The old man was studying his canvas coat with obvious consternation. The front looked torn, but the heavy fabric must have resisted the worst of Tasker's gunshot. Rocco glanced towards the village square, where his Traction stood across the road, blocking any exit. Godard's men were visible, ferrying people out of the way, gradually drawing them out of their houses to reduce the chances of Tasker latching onto potential hostages.

'Lucas – there!' Claude grabbed his shoulder and pointed. There was movement at the rear of Rocco's house. Two figures appeared, one slight, the other tall and bulky, imposing, even at this distance.

It was Tasker. And Alix. The Englishman towered over her with one big hand clamped on her shoulder.

Then he brought his other hand into view, and Rocco's gut went cold. In his free hand he was holding the stubby shape of a sawn-off shotgun or *lupara* as it was known among Sicilian gangsters. It was a frightening weapon up close and indiscriminate in the wide spread of the shot from its barrels. And he was now holding the gun

341

pointed at Alix's head.

'*Putain!*' Claude swore, and made to stand up. But Rocco reached out and held him down. A frontal assault was impossible. Tasker had the upper hand. For now.

Tasker looked up the slope, his eyes seeming to drill right into Rocco's as if he knew the effect the gun was having on him. He shouted something, the sound carrying up the hill, but not clear enough to distinguish the words.

But Rocco didn't need to hear them to know what the man was after. Tasker wanted him down there. Nothing else mattered. He'd been cut loose by his bosses and his twisted vision of what had happened saw only one ending: revenge. And that revenge was centred solely on Rocco.

He debated the wisdom of going down empty-handed. Whatever course he took, the chances were that Alix was in the greater danger – especially if Claude couldn't get close enough. If he could appear powerless, however, while having even a slight edge available to him, he might just get away with it.

'Give me your knife.'

Claude reached back and took out a bone-handled clasp knife he used for everything from skinning rabbits to peeling an apple, and passed it across.

Rocco quickly stripped out one of his shoelaces and cut it in two. He tied the end of one half through the trigger guard of the Walther, and looped the other end around his middle finger. Then he fed the gun down the right-hand sleeve of his coat. It was a close fit, but with enough play to move quite freely. He used the other half of the lace to secure his shoe, then stood up and brushed the layer of damp from the front of his coat.

Claude was staring up at him and hissed. 'What the hell are you doing? This isn't the OK Corral!'

'I know. But I don't see that we have much choice. He's right on the edge. If I don't go down there, he'll kill Alix.' He flicked a glance towards the square where Godard and his men were hustling people away. They seemed unaware of Tasker's appearance and there was no way Rocco could get word to Godard's sniper without warning the gunman. He would have to do this himself with Claude as a diversion. 'Can you follow me down and cover me? You'll have to get close.'

Claude nodded. 'You won't even hear me coming.' He patted the stock of his shotgun. 'Just give me one chance, that's all I need.'

Rocco nodded and stepped over the edge of the overlook, and began skidding down the slope so that Tasker could see him coming all the way. It was steep and uneven, with few handholds. If he fell, he wouldn't stop rolling until he hit the track below, which would be of no use to Alix. That would still put him above Tasker, with another hundred metres to go, but still too far away to do anything useful.

As he reached the track leading down to the square, Tasker's voice drifted up to him.

'Stick your hands out and show me they're empty, Rocco, or I'll shoot the bitch!'

Rocco did as he was told. As he started across the track, he looked towards the square and

343

caught a glimpse of Godard standing in the open. The *sous-brigadier* glanced his way and did a double take. But seeing Rocco's hands out, he caught on immediately that something was wrong. Rocco pretended to lose his balance momentarily and made a flattening gesture with his left hand, hoping Godard got the message to keep back. Having a bunch of *gardes mobiles* charging down the lane to the house would be disastrous.

He reached the other side of the track and checked for a way down that would bring him out onto the lane across from the house. The slope was less steep here, and littered with trees and bushes. But the absence of foliage meant Tasker would be able to see him coming all the way. If he tried to drop out of sight even for a second, he figured the Englishman was mad enough to take it out on Alix. Yet coming within gunshot range – even the shorter range of the sawn-off weapon – would be crazy and wouldn't help her at all.

He just hoped Claude was close by. If an opportunity presented itself, it would be brief, then gone.

As he walked down the slope, his senses seemed to come alive with greater clarity. The crunch of still-frozen grass stems beneath his shoes; the cold reaching through to the soles of his feet; rabbit droppings littered everywhere like sultanas sprinkled on icing sugar; the smell of a wood fire from Mme Denis' chimney and the sharper tang of cows in the farm building along the lane, with its steaming manure heap in the middle of the yard picked over by chickens. A cockerel crowed, blissfully unmindful of the drama unfolding out here, and Rocco tried to recall if this was how suddenly acute the various sounds and smells had become each time he'd faced danger and death in the jungles of Indochina.

Right now all he could remember from then was the sticky feel of camouflage paint on his face, the reek of unwashed clothing and the absolute stunning silence all around.

He brushed those thoughts aside. He had to focus on the here and now. Nothing else mattered.

CHAPTER FIFTY-SIX

Commissaire Massin walked back down the corridor to his office with an itchy sensation in the middle of his back. He tried not to hurry, but to preserve a sense of calm in spite of feeling that he had just stumbled on something truly grotesque.

Back in his office, he closed the door and went straight to his desk. Sliding open a side drawer, he took out his service revolver and checked the cylinder. Then he sat and waited. And listened.

He switched on the police channel loudspeaker fixed to the wall just behind him. He liked to keep an ear on daily events out in the field, but few days had held as much importance as this one. A subdued babble was coming in as officers came on the line seeking information and instructions, or giving out reports on their location and activities.

'...*farm worker saw a car heading north at speed. Am investigating*...'

345

'*Two-One, swing round and head towards Poissons. Reports of gunshots...*'

Poissons. Massin's ears pricked up. That was where Rocco lived.

'*...just heard the news... One Englishman dead! He got him ... the inspector got him!*'

Massin felt a jolt in his chest. The manhunt was closing in, and a man had been shot dead. 'The inspector' could only mean one person.

Rocco.

He desperately wanted more information, to get on the line and demand progress reports. But the channels needed to be kept clear so that the men could get on with the business in hand. He turned instead to the problem he had just discovered and thought about what to do. He was on the edge of feeling powerless, like some junior *gardien* on his first week in the job.

Should he ring the Ministry? If he did, how the hell could he even begin to explain what he suspected? They'd laugh him out of office and consign him to a mental ward down south, where he could be forgotten, the crackpot *commissaire* who had finally found the job too much to handle.

What he needed was something concrete ... some corroboration that wouldn't be ignored. But how to get it?

'*...gunshots in Poissons... We're getting everyone out. He's in the village somewhere ... armed with a shotgun. A civilian down but not seriously hurt. Rocco's gone after the Englishman.*'

Santer. Rocco's former captain in Clichy. He would know. Massin was well aware that Rocco had regular contact with him, and that the two shared a close friendship.

'*...more shots. Can't tell where, though. Bloody place is throwing echoes everywhere.*'

'*Christ, I hope he leaves some for the rest of us.*'

Massin turned down the radio, picked up the phone and asked the switchboard operator to put him through to Clichy. Keeping one ear on the corridor outside, he slid his revolver closer and waited while the phone rang.

'Santer.'

'Captain Santer,' Massin said quietly, and introduced himself. 'I want to advise you that I have ordered the suspension of Inspector Rocco to be lifted, following new evidence in his favour.'

'That's good news, sir,' Santer replied. 'Very good. I never doubted him. But ... if you'll excuse me asking, why are you telling me? Sir.'

Massin smiled at the caution in Santer's voice, edged with just a hint of old-cop indifference to higher authority. Maybe Santer really was the right man to talk to.

'Because I need your help, Captain. As does Inspector Rocco. And the very security of France could well hinge on anything you can tell me.'

Rocco weaved his way through the bushes, making sure he kept Tasker in his line of sight. The closer he got to the lane, he noted, the more twitchy Tasker seemed to become, pulling Alix closer to him, screwing the twin barrels of the sawn-off into the side of her neck and edging back to the corner of the house for protection.

'That's far enough!' Tasker shouted. 'I want to see your gun, Rocco.'

347

Rocco flicked his left hand. 'It's in my pocket.'

'Take it out and show it to me. Slowly.'

Rocco did so, taking out the revolver belonging to Biggs. He held it aloft by the barrel. At this distance, he doubted Tasker would recognise it. A gun was a gun.

'Now throw it away from you.' Tasker was grinning now, his movements edgy, clearly in a heightened state of excitement. His face was bristly and his clothes crumpled, and Rocco wondered whether he'd taken drink or drugs, but guessed the man was high on the sudden application of power.

High but not incapable. If anything it made him all the more dangerous.

He tossed the revolver into the nearest bush.

'Now your ankle gun.'

Rocco said, 'What do you think this is – Hollywood? We're not permitted to carry secondary weapons.'

Tasker gave it some thought, then nodded grudgingly. 'Okay. Open your fingers and flex them so I can see they're empty.'

Rocco did so. And felt the shoelace around his finger begin to slip. The knot was coming undone. He kept his face blank and focused on Alix. She looked unhurt but stressed, wincing where the shotgun barrels were grinding into her neck. He hoped she had the presence of mind to know what to do if anything happened. When anything happened.

'Get down on the road,' said Tasker. 'I want to see you up close.'

He waited until Rocco had made his way down onto the lane, then pushed Alix forward, almost

348

lifting her off the ground and making her cry out. They arrived at the gate crushed together and Tasker stopped, pressing Alix against the metal bars.

Rocco tensed. If Tasker opened fire now, he'd got nowhere to go.

'You can let her go,' said Rocco. 'She does not have to get hurt.'

'I said, get down.' Tasker lifted the butt of the gun, but kept the barrels against Alix's neck. 'I won't tell you again.'

Rocco dropped his hands halfway and lowered himself carefully to the ground in the press-up position. As he did so, he felt the Walther slip inside his sleeve. The shoelace was almost undone now. If he had to get up again and lift his arms, he wouldn't be able to stop it sliding about and out of his reach.

'You think this is going to be a confession, right?' Tasker grinned, and pushed his face alongside Alix's, grinding his hips against her buttocks in an obscene simulation. 'That I'm going to beg for freedom so I can go home?' The grin vanished and his voice hit a higher pitch. 'Home to what? Nothing. They've dumped me in it, you know that? Like I'm a fucking *nobody*.' A flare of anger turned his face red and he looked around as if suddenly aware that someone might be creeping up on him. 'Tell your men to stay back, Rocco, or I'll blow her brains all over this shitty village. And Jesus – what is that *stink?*'

A breeze had sprung up, carrying farmyard smells along the lane.

'It's called cow shit,' said Rocco. 'Look, why don't we talk? This doesn't have to end badly.'

'Badly? *Badly?*' Tasker's face twisted and a volley of spit came through the bars of the gate. 'What kind of word is that? This isn't just *bad*, you crappy, fucking, French copper. This is far worse than that. Because we're all going to end up the same way – don't you get it?'

Rocco tensed as he saw Tasker's grip tighten around the trigger guard of the shotgun. He readied himself to move, all the while knowing that in the time it would take this madman to press the trigger of the *lupara*, he'd be lucky if he got one foot beneath him. He felt sick and wondered how else he could have played this.

Then he heard a car engine approaching. He turned his head towards the village. Surely Godard or Desmoulins weren't coming down here. Then he realised the noise was coming from the other way – from the open countryside towards Danvillers.

It was a grey 2CV van, with a bale of straw strapped to the roof. A small crate full of chickens was fastened alongside, and the entire load was bobbing about furiously as the little car hit a series of undulations in the surface.

'It's a farmer,' Rocco called out, and wondered if the driver could see him lying in the middle of the road. Christ, after all this, he was going to end up as a road casualty statistic…

But Tasker wasn't listening. He was reacting instinctively, turning towards the noise and bringing the shotgun round. Poking it through the gate as the car appeared, he screamed, *'This is on you, Rocco!'* and pulled the trigger.

The roar of the gun drowned out the car engine

noise, blending with the following rattle as the windscreen and tinny bodywork of the car were peppered by lead shot. Luckily for the driver, the angle and distance were just enough to deflect the worst of the charge, and the glass cracked, but held fast. The driver ducked automatically, the car charging on as his foot jammed down hard in a reflex action on the accelerator.

Rocco began rolling, desperately kicking against the ground for impetus. There was no time to stand up; he'd just have to trust that he could stay out of the way of the wheels. As it was, the vehicle missed him by a whisker, showering him in a layer of sooty exhaust smoke and bits of straw and feathers from the load on the car roof. He continued moving, grabbing for the Walther in his sleeve. He felt the gun touch his palm and slide away, then held it, spun it round and began to stand up, finger curling around the trigger.

He found Tasker waiting for him.

The Englishman laughed like a maniac, an expression of near delight in his eyes, and raised the sawn-off. 'No fucking chance!' he shouted in triumph, spit dribbling from his mouth. His finger tightened around the trigger. 'You think I came over on the last banana boat? Too slow, Rocco. Say goodbye, copper!'

'Alix, Lucas – *down!*' Claude shouted from up on the slope above Rocco's shoulder.

Alix dropped instinctively as if her legs had been chopped beneath her. Slipping from Tasker's grip, she slumped to the ground like a rag doll. Her movement was so complete, so sudden, Tasker's face changed to one of shock, and he glanced down in dismay, his hostage momentarily gone.

It was enough.

The roar of Claude's gun was louder and sharper than the sawn-off, piercing the air with its energy like a runaway train. Rocco, half standing, felt a tug at the shoulder of his coat, and something stung his cheek. A rush of displaced air fanned his face.

The double charge hit Tasker in the centre of his chest, and he was punched backwards before he had time to register the pain, his weapon falling away to the side.

Rocco released his pressure on the trigger. He didn't need to shoot.

It was over.

CHAPTER FIFTY-SEVEN

'In the name of God, what were you doing?' Claude muttered, scooping up Alix in his arms and pulling her out of the gate away from Tasker's body. His voice was gruff with emotion and his face red. 'Am I going to have to keep doing this, getting you out of trouble? Only I should warn you, my girl, my heart is not what it was.' He pulled back and touched her neck where it had been rubbed raw by the pressure of the shotgun barrels. 'And look at you – you've got yourself hurt by that monster!'

'Father, stop it,' Alix replied, shaking with a mix of relief and laughter and dragging him close in a hug. 'I came down for some butter from the farm and he ... God, I never thought I'd say it, but you're my hero, do you know that?' She glanced over his shoulder at Rocco, mouthing a silent thank you, the tears finally coursing down her cheeks as reality began to hit home.

Rocco walked over to check the body. Not that he had any fears that Tasker was alive; no man could have withstood that volley of shot. He flicked back the dead man's jacket with the barrel of the Walther and checked for more weapons. Nothing. If Tasker had carried anything besides the sawn-off, he'd discarded it along the way.

He looked across the lane where the 2CV had ploughed into the verge, spilling the straw bale and its cargo of chickens in a heap across the bonnet. The driver was already out of the car, clearly unhurt, but staring back at Rocco, Claude and Tasker's body with open disbelief.

A powerful car engine sounded, approaching at speed. Godard and his men, most likely. They would have had a distant, if grandstand view of what had happened from along the lane, and would be coming to secure the scene. And no doubt the villagers would be here soon, eager to see what the cop in their midst had dragged into their serene rural world.

Mme Denis was the first. She came out of her gate and walked up to him, and checked him over, fastening an eye on the shoulder of his coat, where a stray shotgun pellet had opened up the fabric.

'You should learn to look after your clothes more,' she said pragmatically, pointedly ignoring the body on the ground. 'I can repair that, if you like.' She brushed at some pieces of straw on his sleeve. 'And it's your new one.'

'You don't have to–' he began. But she shushed him and tugged at the lapel.

'Yes, I do. Can't have you walking around looking like a tramp, can we?'

Rocco nodded and eased it off. If he didn't give in gracefully now, he'd only have to do it later. She took the garment and put it over her arm, smoothing down the fabric.

'Nasty business,' she commented. 'Is that it, then?'

'Almost,' he said, and thought about what he had to do next. 'Just some tidying up to do.'

Mme Denis walked over to Alix and took her hand, and led her away towards her house.

Claude watched them go, then broke the shotgun and took out the two spent shells. 'I only meant to fire one,' he said shakily. 'But I was so scared for her...' He gestured at the trigger and coughed, blinking hard. 'Do you want me for anything else, Lucas?'

Rocco thought about it. He needed someone. But Claude should stay here. There were plenty of others he could call on. 'No. This is your turf. They'll need to see you in charge. And you should be around for Alix. She's been through a lot.'

Claude nodded. 'Of course. Thank you. And ... thank you.' He lifted a hand, then marched along the lane to turn away a group of villagers coming towards them.

Godard's vehicle appeared, and Desmoulins was the first out, followed by Captain Canet, who began issuing instructions.

'You've done it again,' Desmoulins complained, glancing at Tasker's body. 'All the fun and I was miles away – Jesus, what the hell happened to him?'

'He got what he wanted.'

Canet came over and nodded. 'Good work.'

'Officer Lamotte ended it,' said Rocco. 'Is Massin coming?' He needed to speak to the *commissaire* urgently.

'No. He's fielding calls from the Ministry, the security agencies and every minister with a telephone, wanting to know what happened and where exactly *is* Pont Noir and Poissons-les-Marais. Sooner him than me, is all I can say.'

'It was hardly his fault any of this happened.'

'I know. But they'll still want to know why the area wasn't secured for the visit. You know what they're like: a bunch of self-interested pen-pushers looking for someone to blame.'

'It was unscheduled. Nobody knew about it until the last minute.' *Only someone who shouldn't have,* he thought; *someone who had slipped under the net.*

Canet tilted his head. 'Well, somebody clearly did; the man driving the truck for one.' He lifted his eyebrows. 'I'd wear a thick collar for a few days, if I were you. I know I will.' He turned and walked away to continue organising his men.

Rocco looked at Desmoulins. There was nothing more he could do here. 'How do you feel like taking a chance with your career and pension?'

Desmoulins grinned. 'Hellfire, you're going to close this down, aren't you? What do you want me to do?'

Rocco wasn't sure how things would go in the

next hour or so, but he needed someone close to corroborate what he was about to do. 'Stick close and listen. It could be interesting.' He glanced at Godard's vehicle. 'I need a lift to my car near the café, then a fast drive to Amiens.'

Desmoulins was already moving. 'Fast it is,' he said. 'Can we radio ahead?'

Rocco had thought of that. 'No,' he said. 'What I want to do, we don't want to broadcast.'

CHAPTER FIFTY-EIGHT

In Amiens, *Commissaire* Massin put down the phone from talking to Captain Santer and drew a deep breath. He had a sudden urge to be sick.

The story Santer had just told him had confirmed his wildest fears, and put him in the worst kind of dilemma. He was now in possession of numerous anecdotes, suppositions and allegations, all pointing towards a conspiracy inside the presidential security apparatus. A conspiracy to assassinate France's head of state.

He could barely believe it. Yet it was all so simple. And most of what he had heard would be sufficient for any ordinary man to find impossible to explain away, such was the collection of facts.

But Colonel Jean-Philippe Saint-Cloud was about as far from being an ordinary man as a person could get. He had the ear of the president and his colleagues, he was in the confidence of the highest men in the Ministry of the Interior,

356

he worked hand in glove with the most influential members of the country's security apparatus. His word carried weight and authority that was almost unrivalled anywhere.

In a word, he was untouchable.

Or was he?

Massin weighed up the risk of doing nothing; of sitting here and accepting that he had insufficient hard evidence to take action; that Saint-Cloud's word and position and background trumped anything and everything he had heard so far. Sitting here would be easy. Forgetting what he'd heard would soon go away, brushed beneath the carpet of quiet convenience protecting the state apparatus.

But he knew that he wouldn't forget, and neither would Rocco. And instinct told him that everything he'd heard was true and that his conclusions could not be faulted: Colonel Saint-Cloud, the president's chief security officer, had conspired out of a sense of fury and resentment to kill de Gaulle, using a disparate chain of disenchanted ex-soldiers, OAS killers, English gangsters and men hired by the Paris gang lord, Patrice Delarue.

It sounded crazy, even now. Yet impossible to ignore. But there was something else driving Massin; something almost intangible that would never find its way into any court of law, because it would be viewed with ridicule and derision. Except by him.

He would never be able to forget the insults Saint-Cloud had thrown at him as long as the man walked free.

The telephone rang, the harsh jangle unsettling

his nerves. He ignored it. Most likely the Ministry or one of any number of people with a drum to beat.

Massin stood up and straightened his uniform. Picked up his revolver and went to the door. Pulled it open.

Colonel Saint-Cloud was standing outside.

CHAPTER FIFTY-NINE

'What are you going to do with that?' Saint-Cloud murmured. 'Shoot someone?'

'I haven't decided yet,' Massin replied. 'Do you have any candidates?'

His response seemed to take Saint-Cloud by surprise, and almost without realising it, he stepped up close to the security officer, forcing him to move backwards. It was a tiny, maybe symbolic victory of wills, and he wasn't sure he could trust himself not to follow it up by simply pulling the trigger and having done with it. It would be an inglorious end to his own career, but at least he would gain a momentary satisfaction from it.

Saint-Cloud didn't reply, so Massin said, 'How long has the Pont Noir visit been known about?'

'It hasn't. I told you.'

'Really? But the British office in Arras knew. They were waiting for a date.'

'That's rubbish. It was probably wishful thinking on their part.' Saint-Cloud looked unsettled, as if caught off guard. 'Why are you asking?'

358

'Because I want to know how de Gaulle ends up on a near-deserted stretch of road in the middle of open country with no support team and no notification from you to this office.' He breathed heavily with a rush of certainty. 'The Ministry is also puzzled because they didn't know about it, either.'

The security man's face flushed with irritation. 'For God's sake, man, the president is not a slave to the Ministry or anyone else. He often moves without prior notice.'

'So you're saying he chose, on the spur of the moment, to come down here and all without telling you – his head of security? I find that surprising.'

'Do you?' Saint-Cloud took a deep breath. 'Maybe if you had worked with him for as long as I have, you would not be ... surprised.' He flapped a vague hand, twin spots of red appearing on his cheeks.

'So Pont Noir meant nothing to you before you came here?'

'How could it? Until that idiot Rocco came to me with his ridiculous supposition, I'd never heard of the place.'

'Yet he was correct, wasn't he? In every detail. It wasn't so ridiculous after all.'

'Clearly because he knew something I did not.' Saint-Cloud's voice snapped, and he glanced down at the gun in Massin's hand. 'I cannot stay here arguing all day. I have to get back to Paris.'

Massin watched him turn away, feeling his control of the situation beginning to fade. Maybe he'd made a horrendous mistake after all. Maybe

Saint-Cloud hadn't known, left out of the loop by his boss and principal. But that didn't make sense. He forced himself to try one last thing.

'You have a map in your office. It's in the drawer of the cabinet and Pont Noir is clearly marked. I saw it just now.'

Saint-Cloud shrugged without turning back. 'Rocco must have put it there in an effort to place any suspicions elsewhere.'

'Really. So if I contact Paul Comiti, who I'm sure was in the president's car today, he will tell me that this visit was completely unknown ... even to you?'

The mention of the chief of the bodyguard quartet that accompanied de Gaulle every step he took seemed to have a paralysing effect on Saint-Cloud. He stopped dead, shoulders stiffening. His head dropped, and he turned round to face Massin and walked back.

He was now holding a gun.

'You loathsome little cretin!' he shouted. 'How dare you question me!' His eyes flickered as if the light inside was faulty, and his mouth trembled, his lips curling with hatred and rage. 'Why could you not leave well alone? *Imbecile!* Do you not see that this country is on the road to hell ... that we once had an army which is now being emasculated?' He threw his head back. 'Of course, with men like you in charge, what can good people expect?'

Massin nodded, suddenly seeing with great clarity what this had all been about. What was driving Saint-Cloud and others like him. 'The army? Do you mean the army generally ... or the

1st Foreign Parachute Regiment in particular? Is that what this is about – revenge for a disbanded regiment?'

There was a moment when Massin thought he'd gone too far. Saint-Cloud's finger went white around the trigger and his face appeared to swell with indignation. He tensed, waiting for the arrival of oblivion, and wished he'd taken more decisive action instead of pushing the man like this. After all, who was there here to listen?

But Saint-Cloud hadn't finished. His voice came out softly. 'That wasn't enough? A once proud regiment reduced to ignominy ... a regiment that had shed the blood of its officers and men for this country – and for what? To be overrun by foreigners and weaklings and ... governed by vainglorious fools. Yes, that's what this is about, Massin. I would see that vile man dead for what he has done to us!' He sneered. 'But how would you know? You're a failed soldier and a failed country policeman. What would you know of tradition or honour?'

'Evidently more than you. What about Captain Lamy – was he part of this, too? Another parachute regiment sympathiser?'

'Lamy?' Saint-Cloud looked puzzled, then waved a hand. 'Lamy was an opportunist who blew with the wind. He even thought he could take my job. He knew about my affiliations with past members of the regiment and threatened to tell the authorities. I had to get him out of the way.'

Massin recalled what Santer had told him about the attack at Guignes, and why Lamy had been involved. 'You set him up. You used his brother and Delarue to get him on board, then fed the group false information about the car. They thought the president was on board because you told them he was. Just to get rid of Lamy.'

'Prove it.'

'Put down the gun, Colonel,' Massin said softly, and raised his own weapon. His hand was shaking, but even he couldn't miss from here.

Saint-Cloud moved even quicker, stepping right up to Massin and raising his own gun. He placed it against Massin's forehead, between his eyes.

As the cold, hard tip of the gun barrel ground into his skin, Massin felt his every nerve screaming at him to move away from what was surely coming. But he couldn't. He was rooted to the spot. He wondered, was this what real terror was like? Bringing you to a point where you accepted death because you couldn't do anything else?

Instead, he found his voice and said, 'Put it down, or I will shoot you.' And took up the slack in his trigger.

Saint-Cloud laughed out loud, a fine spray of saliva touching Massin's face. Up close, his eyes looked distanced, somehow, as if seeing things from a long way away, and Massin realised the man had lost his mind. 'You haven't got the courage, Massin. You're a sheep. You won't shoot me.'

'*He might not, but I will.*'

It was Rocco, standing at the end of the corridor, tall, dark and resolute, his eyes as cold as death. Behind him stood Desmoulins and Dr Rizzotti, their expressions deep in shock at what they had heard.

'You're no longer the presidential security chief, are you?' said Rocco. 'You haven't been for a while. Put the gun down.'

'He's what?' Massin blinked hard.

Saint-Cloud turned his head, his concentration broken. He frowned as if unsure of what had just happened, then looked back at Massin.

But the *commissaire* had stepped sideways and was now pointing his gun at Saint-Cloud's head, his face set.

The former security officer was stranded and knew it. He must have also known that his last words had been perfectly audible to the three men at the end of the corridor, and he had no way out.

Slowly, he lowered his pistol. 'So be it, gentlemen.' He looked at them one by one and said contemptuously, 'The game is played, it seems. Forgive me if I do not stay to sing "La Marseillaise"; I wish you well in your rotten Utopia.'

He gave a final withering look at Massin, then turned and walked away down the corridor, back rigid, his gun held down by his side. When he reached the office he'd been using, he stepped inside and closed the door.

Rocco started along the corridor after him, but Massin stopped him.

'Wait,' he said. 'I will do this–'

The gunshot was shockingly loud, sending a tremor through the glass panels in the office doors. A pigeon clattered away from the window sill in Massin's office, and someone shouted in the distance. Booted feet began pounding up the stairs towards them.

Rocco breathed deeply and looked at Massin.

363

'So he gets away with it. What'll it be – a military funeral with full honours?'

Massin shook his head and waved back two officers who appeared at the far end of the corridor with drawn weapons. 'He gets away with nothing,' he said quietly. 'Nor will any of the others involved in this business, including the criminal, Delarue. I will personally see to that.'

There was something in Massin's tone that Rocco hadn't heard before, and he wondered what had taken place here between the two officers before he, Desmoulins and Rizzotti had arrived.

He would probably never know. He watched as Rizzotti, accompanied by Desmoulins, walked past and opened the door to Saint-Cloud's office. After a few seconds, Desmoulins came out again and shook his head.

Rocco decided to make his escape for a while. He said to Massin, 'Do you need me for anything? Only I could really do with a strong coffee and cognac.'

'Of course. You deserve it.' Massin gestured at the radio loudspeaker chattering away quietly in his office and said, 'I understand the man Calloway is talking.'

'Yes. I think he knows a lot more than he's saying. He'll try to barter his way out of trouble.'

'That might prove useful. At least you managed to bring one of them back alive,' Massin ghosted a smile, 'which is somehow reassuring.' He turned to go, then said, 'When you come back, perhaps you could step in to my office and collect your badge and gun. You'll be needing them.'

ACKNOWLEDGEMENTS

With grateful thanks to Maggie Needham of Brackley photographic, for proving old technology did work; to Susie and everyone at Allison & Busby, for their continued belief in Rocco; and to David Headley, for his ongoing advice and support. Another team effort.

The publishers hope that this book has given you enjoyable reading. Large Print Books are especially designed to be as easy to see and hold as possible. If you wish a complete list of our books please ask at your local library or write directly to:

Magna Large Print Books
Magna House, Long Preston,
Skipton, North Yorkshire.
BD23 4ND

This Large Print Book for the partially sighted, who cannot read normal print, is published under the auspices of

THE ULVERSCROFT FOUNDATION